Ouida

In a Winter City

A sketch

Ouida

In a Winter City
A sketch

ISBN/EAN: 9783337097448

Printed in Europe, USA, Canada, Australia, Japan

Cover: Foto ©Andreas Hilbeck / pixelio.de

More available books at **www.hansebooks.com**

IN A WINTER CITY

A SKETCH

By OUIDA

AUTHOR OF

'PUCK' 'SIGNA' 'TRICOTRIN' 'TWO LITTLE WOODEN SHOES' ETC.

A NEW EDITION

LONDON

CHATTO & WINDUS

1899

PRINTED BY
SPOTTISWOODE AND CO., NEW-STREET SQUARE
LONDON

IN A WINTER CITY.

𝔄 Sketch.

CHAPTER I.

FLORALIA was once a city of great fame. It stands upon an historical river. It is adorned with all that the Arts can assemble of beauty, of grace, and of majesty. Its chronicles blaze with heroical deeds and with the achievements of genius. Great men have been bred within its walls; men so great that the world has never seen their like again.

Floralia, in her liberties, in her citizens, in her poets and painters and sculptors, once upon a

B

time had few rivals, perhaps, indeed, no equals, upon earth.

By what strange irony of fate, by what singular cynical caprice of accident, has this fairest of cities, with her time-honoured towers lifted to her radiant skies, become the universal hostelry of cosmopolitan fashion and of fashionable idleness? Sad vicissitudes of fallen fortunes! —to such base uses do the greatest come.

It is Belisarius turned croupier to a gaming-table; it is Cæsar selling cigars and newspapers; it is Apelles drawing for the "Albums pour Rire;" it is Pindar rhyming the couplets for "Fleur de Thé;" it is Praxiteles designing costumes for a Calico-ball; it is Phidias forming the poses of a ballet!

Perhaps the mighty ghosts of mediæval Floralia do walk, sadly and ashamed, by midnight under the shadow of its exquisite piles of marble and of stone. If they do, nobody sees them: the cigarette smoke is too thick.

As for the modern rulers of Floralia, they have risen elastic and elated to the height of the situation, and have done their best and uttermost to degrade their city into due accordance with her present circumstances, and have destroyed as much as they dared of her noble picturesqueness and ancient ways. They have tacked on to her venerable palaces and graceful towers, stucco mansions and straight hideous streets, and staring walls covered with advertisements, and barren boulevards studded with toy trees that are cropped as soon as they presume to grow a leaf, and have striven all they know to fit her for her fortunes, as her inn-keepers, when they take an antique palace, hasten to fit up a smoking-room, and, making a paradise of gas jets and liqueurs, write over it "Il Bar Americano."

It is considered very clever to adapt oneself to one's fortunes; and if so, the rulers of Floralia are very clever indeed; only the stucco and the straight streets and the frightful boulevards cost money, and Floralia has no money and a very heavy and terrible debt; and whether it be really worth while to deface a most beautiful and artistic city, and ruin your nobles and gentry, and grind down your artizans and peasants, and make your whole province impoverished and ill-content for the mere sake of pleasing some strangers by the stucco and the hoardings that their eyes are used to at home;—well, that perhaps may be an open question.

The Lady Hilda Vorarlberg had written thus far when she got tired, left off, and looked out of the window on to the mountain-born and poet-hymned river of Floralia. She had an idea that she would write a novel; she was always going to do things that she never did do.

After all they were not her own ideas that she had written; but only those of a Floralian, the Duca della Rocca, whom she had met the night before. But then the ideas of everybody have been somebody else's beforehand,—Plato's, or Bion's, or Theophrastus's; or your favourite newspaper's;—and the Lady Hilda, although she had been but two days in the Winter City, had already in her first drive shuddered at the stucco and the hoardings, and shivered at the boulevards and the little shaven trees. For she was a person of very refined and fastidious taste, and did really know something about the arts, and such persons suffer very acutely from what the peculiar mind of your modern municipalities calls, in its innocence, "improvements."

The Lady Hilda had been to a reception too the night before, and had gone with the preconceived conviction that a certain illustrious Sovereign had not been far wrong when she had called Floralia the Botany Bay of modern society; but then the Lady Hilda was easily bored, and not easily pleased, and liked very few things, almost none;—she liked her horses, she liked M. Worth, she liked bric-à-brac, she liked her brother, Lord Clairvaux, and when she came to think of it,—well, that was really all.

The Lady Hilda was a beautiful woman, and knew it; she was dressed in the height of fashion, *i. e.*, like a mediæval saint out of a picture; her velvet robe clung close to her, and her gold belt, with its chains and pouch and fittings, would not have disgraced Cellini's own working; her hair was in a cloud in front and in a club behind; her figure was perfect: M.

Worth, who is accustomed to furnish figures as well as clothes, had a great reverence for her; in her, Nature, of whom generally speaking he is disposed to think very poorly, did not need his assistance; he thought it extraordinary, but as he could not improve her in that respect, he had to be content with draping Perfection, which he did to perfection of course.

Her face also was left to nature, in a very blamable degree for a woman of fashion. Her friends argued to her that any woman, however fair a skin she might have, must look washed out without enamel or rouge at the least. But the Lady Hilda, conscious of her own delicate bloom, was obdurate on the point.

"I would rather look washed out than caked over," she would reply: which was cruel but conclusive. So she went into the world without painting, and made them all look beside her as if they had come out of a comic opera.

In everything else she was, however, as artificial as became her sex, her station, and her century.

She was a very fortunate woman; at least

society always said so. The Clairvaux people were very terribly poor, though very noble and mighty. She had been married at sixteen, immediately on her presentation, to a great European capitalist of nondescript nationality, who had made an enormous fortune upon the Stock Exchanges in ways that were never enquired into, and this gentleman, whose wealth was as solid as it sounded fabulous, had had the good taste to die in the first months of their wedded life, leaving her fifty thousand a year, and bequeathing the rest of his money to the Prince Imperial. Besides her large income she had the biggest jewels, the choicest horses, the handsomest house in London, the prettiest hôtel in Paris, &c., &c., &c.; and she could very well afford to have a fresh toilette a-day from her friend Worth if she chose. Very often she did choose. "What a lucky creature," said every other woman: and so she was. But she would have been still more so had she not been quite so much bored. Boredom is the ill-natured pebble that always *will* get in the golden slipper of the pilgrim of pleasure.

The Lady Hilda looked out of the window and found it raining heavily. When the sky of Floralia does rain, it does it thoroughly, and gets the disagreeable duty over, which is much more merciful to mankind than the perpetual drizzle and dripping of Scotland, Ireland, Wales, or Middlesex. It was the rain that had made her almost inclined to think she would write a novel; she was so tired of reading them.

She countermanded her carriage; had some more wood thrown on the fire; and felt disposed to regret that she had decided to winter here. She missed all her *bibelots*, and all the wonderful shades and graces of colour with which her own houses were made as rich, yet as subdued in tone as any old cloisonné enamel. She had the finest rooms, here, in an hôtel which had been the old palace of Murat; and she had sent for flowers to fill every nook and corner of them, an order which Floralia will execute for as many francs as any other city would ask in napoleons.

But there is always a nakedness and a gaudiness in the finest suites of any hôtel; and the Lady Hilda, though she had educated

little else, had so educated her eyes and her
taste that a *criant* bit of furniture hurt her as
the grating of a false quantity hurts a scholar.
She knew the value of greys and creams and
lavenders and olive greens and pale sea blues
and dead gold and oriental blendings. She
had to seat herself now in an arm-chair that was of
a brightness and newness in magenta brocade
that made her close her eyelids involuntarily to
avoid the horror of it, as she took up some letters
from female friends and wondered why they wrote
them, and took up a tale of Zola's and threw
it aside in disgust, and began to think that
she would go to Algeria, since her doctors had
agreed that her lungs would not bear the cold
of Paris this winter.

Only there was no art in Algeria and there
was plenty in Floralia, present and traditional,
and so far as a woman of fashion can demean
herself to think seriously of anything beyond
dress and rivalry, she had in a way studied art
of all kinds, languidly indeed and perhaps super-
ficially, but still with some true understanding
of it; for, although she had done her best, as

became a *femme comme il faut*, to stifle the intelligence she had been created with, she yet had moments in which M. Worth did not seem Jehovah, and in which Society scarcely appeared the Alpha and Omega of human existence, as of course they did to her when she was in her right frame of mind.

"I shall go to Algeria or Rome," she said to herself: it rained pitilessly, hiding even the bridges on the opposite side of the river; she had a dreadful magenta-coloured chair, and the window curtains were scarlet; the letters were on thin foreign paper and crossed; the book was unreadable; at luncheon they had given her horrible soup and a vol-au-vent that for all flavour it possessed might have been made of acorns, ship-biscuit and shalots; and she had just heard that her cousin the Countess de Caviare, whom she never approved of, and who always borrowed money of her, was coming also to the Hotel Murat. It was not wonderful that she settled in her own mind to leave Floralia as soon as she had come to it.

It was four o'clock.

She thought she would send round to the bric-à-brac dealers, and tell them to bring her what china and enamels and things they had in their shops for her to look at; little that is worth having ever comes into the market in these days, save when private collections are publicly sold; she knew the Hôtel Drouot and Christie and Manson's too well not to know that; still it would be something to do.

Her hand was on the bell when one of her servants entered. He had a card on a salver.

"Does Madame receive?" he asked, in some trepidation, for do what her servants might they generally did wrong; when they obeyed her she had almost invariably changed her mind before her command could be executed, and when they did not obey her, then the Clairvaux blood, which was crossed with French and Russian, and had been Norman to begin with, made itself felt in her usually tranquil veins.

She glanced at the card. It might be a bric-à-brac dealer's.

On it was written "Duca della Rocca." She paused doubtfully some moments

"It is raining very hard," she thought; then gave a sign of assent.

Everybody wearied her after ten minutes; still when it was raining so hard——

CHAPTER II.

"THEY SAY," the great assassin who slays as many thousands as ever did plague or cholera, drink or warfare; "they say," the thief of reputation, who steals, with stealthy step and coward's mask, to filch good names away in the dead dark of irresponsible calumny; "they say," a giant murderer, iron-gloved to slay you, a fleet, elusive, vaporous will-o'-the-wisp, when you would seize and choke it; "they say," mighty Thug though it be which strangles from behind the purest victim, had not been ever known to touch the Lady Hilda.

She seemed very passionless and cold; and no one ever whispered that she was not what she seemed. Possibly she enjoyed so unusual an immunity, first, because she was so very rich; secondly, because she had many male relations; thirdly, because women, whilst they envied, were afraid of her. Anyway, her name was altogether without reproach; the only defect to be found in her in the estimate of many of her adorers.

Married without any wish of her own being consulted, and left so soon afterwards mistress of herself and of very large wealth, she had remained altogether indifferent and insensible to all forms of love. Other women fell in love in all sorts of ways, feebly or forcibly, according to their natures, but she never.

The passions she excited broke against her serene contempt, like surf on a rocky shore. She was the despair of all the " tueurs de femmes " of Europe.

"Le mieux est l'ennemi du bien," she said to her brother once, when she had refused the hereditary Prince of Deutschland; "I can do exactly as I like; I have everything I want; I can follow all my own whims; I am perfectly happy; why ever should I alter all this?

What could any man ever offer me that would
be better?"

Lord Clairvaux was obliged to grumble that
he did not know what any man could.

"Unless you were to care for the man," he
muttered shamefacedly.

"Oh!—h!—h!" said the Lady Hilda, with
the most prolonged delicate and eloquent inter-
jection of amazed scorn.

Lord Clairvaux felt that he had been as silly
and rustic as if he were a ploughboy. He was an
affectionate creature himself, in character very
like a Newfoundland dog, and had none of his
sister's talent and temperament; he loved her
dearly, but he was always a little afraid of her.

"Hilda don't say much to you, but she just
gives you a look; and don't you sink into your
shoes!" he said once to a friend.

He stood six feet three without the shoes, to
whose level her single glance could so pathetically reduce him.

But except before herself, Lord Clairvaux,
in his shoes or out of them, was the bravest
and frankest gentleman that ever walked the

earth; and the universal recollection of him
and of his unhesitating habit of " setting things
straight," probably kept so in awe the calumny-
makers, that he produced the miracle of a woman
who actually was blameless getting the credit of
being so.   Usually snow is deemed black, and coal
is called swans-down, with that refreshing habit
of contrariety which alone saves society from
stagnation.

It never occurred to her what a tower of
strength for her honour was that good-looking,
good-tempered, stupid, big brother of her's, who
could not spell a trisyllable were it ever so, and
was only learned in racing stock and greyhound
pedigrees; but she was fond of him in a cool
and careless way, as she might have been of a
big dog, and was prodigal in gifts to him of
great winners and brood mares.

She never went to stay with him at Broomsdon;
she disliked his wife, her sister-in-law, and she was
always bored to death in English country houses,
where the men were out shooting all day, and
half asleep all the evening.   The country people,
the salt of the earth in their own eyes, were in-

finitesimal as ants in hers. She detested drives in pony-carriages, humdrum chit chat, and afternoon tea in the library; she did not care in the least who had bagged how many brace; the details of fast runs with hounds were as horribly tiresome to her as the boys home from Eton; and she would rather have gone a pilgrimage to Lourdes than have descended to the ball, where all sorts of nondescripts had to be asked, and the dresses positively haunted her like ghosts.

Five years before, at Broomsden, she had taken up her candlestick after three nights of unutterable boredom between her sister-in-law and a fat duchess, and had mentally vowed never to return there. The vow she had kept, and she had always seen Clairvaux in Paris, in London, in Baden—anywhere rather than in the home of their childhood, towards which she had no tenderness of sentiment, but merely recollections of the fierce tyrannies of many German governesses.

She would often buy him a colt out of the Lagrange or Lafitte stables; and always send half Boissier's and Siraudin's shops to his children

c

at Christmas time. That done, she considered
nothing more could be expected of her : it was
certainly not necessary that she should bore herself.

To spend money was an easy undemonstrative
manner of acknowledging the ties of nature,
which pleased and suited her. Perhaps she
would have been capable of showing her affection in nobler and more self-sacrificing ways; but
then there was nothing in her circumstances to
call for that kind of thing; no trouble ever came
nigh her; and the chariot of her life rolled as
smoothly as her own victoria *à huit ressorts.*

For the ten years of her womanhood the Lady
Hilda had had the command of immense wealth.
Anything short of that seemed to her abject
poverty. She could theorise about making herself into Greuze or Gainsboro' pictures in serge
or dimity; but, in fact, she could not imagine
herself without all the black sables and silver
fox, the velvets and silks, the diamonds and
emeralds, the embroideries and laces that made
her a thing which Titian would have worshipped.

She could not imagine herself for an instant

without power of limitless command, limitless caprice, ceaseless indulgence, boundless patronage, and all the gratifications of whim and will which go with the possession of a great fortune and the enjoyment of an entire irresponsibility.

She was bored and annoyed very often indeed because Pleasure is not as inventive a god as he ought to be, and his catalogue is very soon run through; but it never by any chance occurred to her that it might be her money which bored her.

When, on a very dreary day early in November, Lady Hilda, known by repute all over Europe as the proudest, handsomest, coldest woman in the world, and famous as an *élégante* in every fashionable city, arrived at the Hôtel Murat, in the town of Floralia, and it was known that she had come to establish herself there for the winter (unless, indeed, she changed her mind, which was probable), the stir in the city was extraordinary. She brought with her several servants, several carriage horses, immense jewel cases, and a pug dog. She was the great arrival of the season.

There was a Grand Duchess of Dresden, in-

deed, who came at the same time, but she brought
no horses; she hired her *coupé* from a livery-
stable, and her star, notwithstanding its royalty,
paled in proportion. Besides, the Grand Duchess
was a very little, shabby, insignificant person, who
wore black stuff dresses, and a wig without any
art in it. She was music-mad, and Wagner was
her prophet. The Club took no account of her.

There is a club in Floralia, nay, it is the
Club;—all other clubs being for purposes gymnas-
tic, patriotic, theatric, or political, and out of
society altogether.

The Club is very fond of black-balling, and
gives very odd reasons for doing so, instead of
the simple and true one, that it wants to keep
itself to itself. It has been known to object
to one man because his hair curled, and to another because he was the son of a king, and to
another because his boots were not made in Paris.
Be its reasons, however, good, bad, or indifferent,
it pleases itself; by its fiat newly-arrived women
are exalted to the empyrean, or perish in obscurity, and its members are the cream of masculine
Floralia, and spend all fine afternoons on the

steps and the pavement, blocking up the passage
way in the chief street, and criticising all equi-
pages and their occupants.

When the Lady Hilda's victoria, with the two
blacks, and the white and black liveries, swept
past the Club, there was a great stir in these
philosophers of the stones. Most knew her by
sight very well; two or three knew her personally,
and these fortunate few, who had the privilege to
raise their hats as that carriage went by, rose immediately in the esteem of their fellows.

"Je n'ai jamais rien connu de si épâtant," said
the French Duc de St. Louis, who belongs to a
past generation, but is much more charming and
witty than anything to be found in the present
one.

"Twelve hundred and fifty thousand francs
a-year," murmured the Marchese Sampierdareno,
with a sigh. He was married himself.

"Here is your 'affaire,' Paolo," said Don
Carlo Maremma to a man next him.

The Duca della Rocca, to whom he spoke,
stroked his moustache, and smiled a little.

" She is a very beautiful person," he answered;

"I have seen her before at the Tuileries and at
·Trouville, but I do not know her at all. I was
never presented."

"That will arrange itself easily," said the Duc
de St. Louis, who was one of those who had
raised their hats; "Maremma is perfectly right;
it is in every way the very thing for you. Moi,
je m'en charge."

The Duca della Rocca shrugged his shoulders
a very little, and lighted a fresh cigar. But his
face grew grave, and he looked thoughtfully
after the black horses, and the white and black
liveries.

At the English reception that night, which
the Lady Hilda disdainfully likened in her own
mind to a penal settlement, M. de St. Louis,
whom she knew very well, begged to be permitted
to present to her his friend the Duca della
Rocca.

She was dressed like a mediæval saint of a
morning; at night she was a mediæval princess.

She had feuille morte velvet slashed with the
palest of ambers; a high fraise; sleeves of the
renaissance; pointed shoes, and a great many

jewels. Della Rocca thought she might have stepped down out of a Giorgione canvas, and ventured to tell her so. He gave her the carte du pays of the penal settlement around her, and talked to her more seriously for some considerable time. Himself and the Duc de St. Louis were the only people she deigned to take any notice of; and she went away in an hour, or rather less, leaving a kind of flame from her many jewels behind her, and a frozen sense of despair in the hearts of the women, who had watched her, appalled yet fascinated.

"Mais quelle femme impossible!" said Della Rocca, as he went out into the night air.

"Impossible! mais comment donc?" said the Duc de St. Louis, with vivacity and some anger.

The Duc de St. Louis worshipped her, as every year of his life he worshipped three hundred and sixty-five ladies.   .

"Impossible!" echoed Della Rocca, with a cigar in his mouth.

Nevertheless, the next day, when the rain was falling in such torrents that no female creature was likely to be anywhere but before her fire, he called at the Hôtel Murat, and inquired if Miladi were visible, and being admitted, as better than nothing, as she would have admitted the bric-à-brac man, followed the servant upstairs, and walked into an atmosphere scented with some three hundred pots of tea roses, lilies of the valley, and hothouse heliotrope.

"Ah, ah! you have been to see her. Quite right," said the Duc de St. Louis, meeting him as he came down the steps of the hotel in the rain, when it was half-past five by the clock. "I am going also so soon as I have seen Salvareo at the Club about the theatricals; it will not take me a moment; get into my cab, you are going there too? How is Miladi? You found her charming?"

"She was in a very bad humour," replied Della Rocca, closing the cab door on himself.

"The more interesting for you to put her in a good one."

"Would either good or bad last ten minutes? —you know her: I do not, but I should doubt it."

The Duc arranged the fur collar of his coat.

"She is a woman, and rich; too rich, if one can say so. Of course she has her caprices——"

Della Rocca shrugged his shoulders.

"She is very handsome. But she does not interest me."

The Duc smiled, and glanced at him.

"Then you probably interested her. It is much better you should not be interested. Men who are interested may blunder."

"She is vain—she is selfish—she is arrogant," said Della Rocca, with great decision.

"Oh ho !—all that you find out already? You did not amuse her long ?——"

"C'est une femme exagérée en tout," pursued Della Rocca, disregarding.

"No! Exaggeration is vulgar—is bad taste. Her taste is excellent—unexceptionable——"

"Exagérée en tout!" repeated Della Rocca, with much emphasis. "Dress—jewels—habits —temper—everything. She had three hundred pots of flowers in her room!"

"Flower-pots, pooh !——that is English. It is very odd," pursued the Duc pensively, "but they really do like the smell of flowers."

" Only because they cost so much to rear in their fogs. If they were common as with us, they would throw them out of the window as we do."

" Nevertheless, send her three hundred pots more.   Il faut commencer la cour, mon cher."

Della Rocca looked out into the rain.

" I have no inclination—I dislike a woman of the world."

The Duc chuckled a little.

" Ah, ah ! since when, caro mio ? "

" There is no simplicity—there is no inno-cence—there is no sincerity——"

"Bah ! " said the Duc, with much disdain; " I do not know where you have got those new ideas, nor do I think they are your own at all. Have you fallen in love with a ' jeune Mees ' with apple-red cheeks and sweatmeats in her pocket ? Simplicity—innocence—sincerity.   Very pretty. Our old friend of a million vaudevilles, L'Ingénue. We all know her.   What is she in real truth ?— A swaddled bundle of Ignorance.   Cut the swad-dling band —ugh ! and Ignorance flies to Know-ledge as Eve did, only Ignorance does not want to know good and evil: the evil contents her:

she stops short at that.   Yes—yes, L'Ingénue will marry you that she may read Zola and Belot; that she may go to La Biche au Bois; that she may smoke cigars with young men; that she may have her dresses cut half-way down her spine ; that she may romp like a half drunk harlot in all the cotillons of the year ! Whereas your woman of the world, if well chosen——"

" Will have done all these things beforehand at some one else's expense, and will have tired of them,—or not have tired——; of the display of spine and of the cotillon she will certainly never have tired unless she be fifty——"

" That is not precisely what I mean," said the Duc, caressing his small white moustache. " No ; I said well chosen—well chosen. What it can matter to you whether your wife smokes with young men, or reads bad novels, or romps till breakfast, I do not see myself. There is a natural destiny for husbands. The unwise fret over it—the wise profit by it. But considering that you dislike these things in your own wife, however much you like and admire them in the

wives of other persons, I would still say, avoid
our friend of a million vaudevilles—la petite Mees
de seize ans. Ignorance is not innocence, it is
a great mistake to suppose that it even secures
it. Your Mees would seize Belot and Zola à la
reveille des noces——. Miladi yonder, for instance, when they come to her from her book-
seller's, throws them aside, unread——"

"There was a book of Zola's on her table to-
day——"

"I would bet ten thousand francs that she
had not gone beyond the title-page," interrupted
the Duc, with petulance. "TASTE, mon cher
Della Rocca, is the only sure guarantee in these
matters. Women, believe me, never have any
principle. Principle is a backbone, and no woman—except bodily—ever possesses any backbone. Their priests and their teachers and their
mothers fill them with doctrines and convention-
alities—all things of mere word and wind. No
woman has any settled principles ; if she have any
vague ones, it is the uttermost she ever reaches,
and those can always be overturned by any man
who has any influence over her. But Taste is

another matter altogether. A woman whose taste is excellent is preserved from all eccentricities and most follies. You never see a woman of good sense *afficher* her improprieties or advertise her liaisons as women of vulgarity do. Nay, if her taste be perfect, though she have weaknesses, I doubt if she will ever have vices. Vice will seem to her like a gaudy colour, or too much gold braid, or very large plaids, or buttons as big as saucers, or anything else such as vulgar women like. Fastidiousness, at any rate, is very good *postiche* for modesty: it is always decent, it can never be coarse. Good taste, inherent and ingrained, natural and cultivated, cannot alter. Principles—ouf!—they go on and off like a slipper; but good taste is indestructible; it is a compass that never errs. If your wife have it—well, it is possible she may be false to you; she is human, she is feminine; but she will never make you ridiculous, she will never compromise you, and she will not romp in a cotillon till the morning sun shows the paint on her face washed away in the rain of her perspiration. Virtue is, after all, as Mme. de Montes-

pan said, une chose tout purement géographique.
It varies with the hemisphere like the human
skin and the human hair; what is vile in one
latitude is harmless in another.   No philosophic
person can put any trust in a thing which
merely depends upon climate; but, Good
Taste——"

The cab stopped at the club, and the Duc in
his disquisition.

"Va faire la cour," he said, paternally, to his
companion as they went through the doors of
their Cercle.   "I can assure you, mon cher, that
the taste of Miladi is perfect."

" In dress, perhaps," assented Della Rocca.

" In everything.   Va faire la cour."

Paolo, Duca della Rocca, was a very handsome
man, of the finest and the most delicate type of
beauty; he was very tall, and he carried himself
with stateliness and grace; his face was grave,
pensive, and poetic; in the largest assembly people
who were strangers to him always looked at him,
and asked, " Who is that ?"

He was the head of a family, very ancient and
distinguished, but very impoverished; in wars and

civil war all their possessions had drifted away from them piece by piece, hence, he was a great noble on a slender pittance. It had always been said to him, and of him, as a matter of course, that he would mend his position by espousing a large fortune, and he had been brought up to regard such a transaction in the light of a painful but inevitable destiny.

But although he was now thirty-eight years of age, he had never seen, amongst the many young persons pointed out to him as possessing millions, anyone to whom he could prevail upon himself to sell his old name and title.

The Great Republic inspires, as it is well known, a passion for social and titular distinctions in its enterprising sons and daughters, which is, to the original flunkeyism of the mother country, as a Gloire de Dijon to a dog-rose, as a Reine Claude to a common blue plum. Nor are the pretty virgins whom the Atlantic wafts across, in any way afflicted with delicacy or hesitation if they can but see their way to getting what they want; and they strike the bargain, or their mothers do so for them, with a cynical candour as to their object which would almost stagger the manager of a Bureau de Mariage.

Many and various were the gold-laden damsels of the West, who were offered, or offered themselves, to him. But he could not induce himself; —his pride, or his taste, or his hereditary instincts, were too strong for him to be able to ally himself with rag and bone merchants from New York, or oil-strikers from Pennsylvania, or speculators from Wall Street.

No doubt it was very weak of him; a dozen men of the great old races of Europe married thus every year, but Paolo della Rocca loved his name, as a soldier does his flag, and he could not brave the idea of possibly transmitting to his children traits and taints of untraceable or ignoble inherited influences.

Over and over again he allowed himself to be the subject of discussion amongst those ladies whose especial pleasure it is to arrange this sort of matters; but when from discussion it had been ready to pass into action, he had always murmured to his match-making friend—

" A little more time !—next year."

"Bah! ce n'est qu'une affaire de notaire," said his special protectress in these matters, a still charming Russian ex-ambassadress, who constantly wintered in Floralia, and who, having had him as a lover when he was twenty and she was thirty, felt quite a maternal interest in him still as to his marriage and prospects.

Della Rocca was too much a man of the world and of his country not to be well aware that she spoke the truth; it was only an affair for the notaries, like any other barter; still he put it off; it would have to be done one day, but there was no haste,—there would always be heiresses willing and eager to become the Duchess della Rocca, Princess of Palmarola, and Marchioness of Tavignano, as his roll of old titles ran.

And so year by year had gone by, and he vaguely imagined that he would in time meet what he wanted without any drawbacks: a delusion common to everyone, and realised by no one.

Meanwhile, the life he led, if somewhat purposeless, was not disagreeable; being an Italian, he could live like a gentleman, with simplicity, and no effort to conceal his lack of riches;

D

nor did he think his dignity imperilled because he did not get into debt for the sake of display; he would dine frugally without thinking himself dishonoured; refuse to join in play without feeling degraded; and look the finest gentleman in Europe without owing his tailor a bill.

For other matters he was somewhat *désœuvré*. He had fought, like most other young men of that time, in the campaign of '59, but the result disappointed him; and he was at heart too honest and too disdainful to find any place for himself in that struggle between cunning and corruption, of which the political life of our regenerated Italy is at present composed. Besides, he was also too indolent. So for his amusement he went to the world, and chiefly to the world of great ladies; and for his duties made sufficient for himself out of the various interests of the neglected old estates which he had inherited; for the rest he was a man of the world; that he had a perfect manner, all society knew; whether he had character as well, nobody cared; that he had a heart at all, was only known to himself, his peasantry, and a few women.

CHAPTER III.

The next morning the sun shone brilliantly; the sky was blue; the wind was a very gentle breeze from the sea; Lady Hilda's breakfast chocolate was well made; the tea-roses and the heliotrope almost hid the magenta furniture and the gilded plaster consoles, and the staring mirrors. They had sent her in a new story of Octave Feuillet: M. de St. Louis had forwarded her a new volume of charming verse by Sully Prudhomme, only sold on the Boulevards two days before, with a note of such grace and wit that it ought to have been addressed to Elysium for Mme. de Sévigné; the post brought her only one letter, which announced that her brother, Lord Clairvaux, would come thither to please her, after the

● 2

Newmarket Spring Meeting, or perhaps before, since he had to see "Major Fridolin" in Paris.

On the whole, the next morning Lady Hilda, looking out of the hotel window, decided to stay in Floralia.

She ordered her carriage out early, and drove hither and thither to enjoy tranquilly the innumerable treasures of all the arts in which the city of Floralia is so rich.

A Monsignore whom she knew well, learned, without pedantry, and who united the more vivacious accomplishments of the virtuoso to the polished softness of the churchman, accompanied her. The Clairvaux people from time immemorial had been good Catholics.

Lady Hilda for her part never troubled her head about those things, but she thought unbelief was very bad form, and that to throw over your family religion was an impertinence to your ancestors. Some things in the ceremonials of her church grated on her æsthetic and artistic ideas, but then these things she attributed to the general decadence of the whole age in taste.

Her Monsignore went home to luncheon with her, and made himself as agreeable as a courtly churchman always is to every one ; and afterwards she studied the Penal Settlement more closely by calling on those leaders of it whose cards lay in a heap in her anteroom, and amused herself with its mind and manners, its attributes and antecedents.

"After all, the only people in any country that one can trust oneself to know are the natives of it," she said to herself, as she went to the weekly " day " of the infinitely charming Marchesa del Trasimene, *nata* Da Bolsena, where she met Della Rocca and M. de St. Louis, as everybody meets everybody else, morning, afternoon, and evening, fifty times in the twenty-four hours in Floralia, the results being antipathy or sympathy in a fatal degree.

In her girations she herself excited extreme attention and endless envy, especially in the breasts of those unhappy outsiders whom she termed the Penal Settlement.

There was something about her ! — Worth Pingât and La Ferrière dressed the Penal Settlement, or it said they did. Carlo Maremma always swore that there was a little dressmaker who lived opposite his stable who could have told sad truths about many of these Paris-born toilettes; but no doubt Maremma was wrong, because men know nothing about these things, and are not aware that a practised eye can tell the sweep of Worth's scissors under the shoulder-blades as surely as a connoisseur recognises the hand of Boule or Vernis Martin on a cabinet or an *étui*. At any rate, the Penal Settlement swore it was adorned by Worth, Pingât and La Ferrière in all the glories and eccentricities imaginable of confections, *unies* and *mélangées*, Directoire and Premier Empire, Juive and Louis Quinze; and if talking about a theory could prove it, certainly they proved that they bore all Paris on their persons.

But there was something about *her*—it was difficult to say what; perhaps it was in the tip of her Pompadour boot, or perhaps it hid in the back widths of her skirt, or perhaps it lurked in the black sable fur of her dolman, but a something that made them feel there was a gulf never to be passed between them and this world-famed *élégante*.

Lady Hilda would have said her secret lay in her always being just a quarter of an hour in advance of the fashion. She was always the first person to be seen, in what six weeks afterwards was the rage: and when the rage came, then Lady Hilda had dropped the fashion. Hence she was the perpetual despair of all her sex — a distinction which she was quite human enough to enjoy in a contemptuous sort of way; as contemptuous of herself as of others; for she had a certain vague generosity and largeness of mind which lifted her above mean and small emotions in general.

She had been steeped in the world, as people call that combination of ennui, excitement, selfishness, fatigue, and glitter, which forms the various delights of modern existence, till it had penetrated her through and through, as a petrifying stream does the supple bough put in it. But there were little corners in her mind which the petrifaction had not reached.

This morning—it was half-past five o'clock in

a November afternoon, and pitch dark, but of course it was morning still as nobody had dined, the advent of soup and sherry bringing the only meridian recognised in society—the Lady Hilda refreshed with a cup of tea from the samovar of her friend the Princess Olga Schouvaloff, who came yearly to her palace in the historical river-street of historical Floralia, and having been assured by Princess Olga, that if they kept quite amongst themselves, and never knew anybody else but the Floralian Russian and German nobility, and steadfastly refused to allow anybody else to be presented to them, Floralia was bearable—nay, even really agreeable,—she got into her coupé, and was driven through the gloom to her hotel.

Her head servant made her two announcements :—Madame de Caviare had arrived that morning, and hoped to see her before dinner.

Lady Hilda's brows frowned a little.

The Duca della Rocca had sent these flowers.

Lady Hilda's eyes smiled a little.

They were only some cyclamens fresh from the country, in moss. She had regretted to him the day before that those lovely simple wood flowers could not be found at florists' shops nor in flower women's baskets.

After all, she said to herself, it did not matter that Mila had come; she was silly and not very proper, and a nuisance altogether; but Mila was responsible for her own sins, and sometimes could be amusing. So the Lady Hilda, in a good-humoured and serene frame of mind, crossed the corridor to the apartments her cousin had taken just opposite to her own.

"He is certainly very striking looking—like a Vandyke picture," she thought to herself irrelevantly, as she tapped at her cousin's door; those cyclamens had pleased her; yet she had let thousands of the loveliest and costliest bouquets wither in her anteroom every year of her life, without deigning to ask or heed who were even the senders of them.

"Come in, if it's you, dear," said Madame Mila, ungrammatically and vaguely, in answer to the tap.

The Countess de Caviare was an English-woman, and a cousin, one of the great West country Trehillyons whom everybody knows, her mother having been a Clairvaux. She had been grandly married in her first season to a very high and mighty and almost imperial Russian, himself a most good-humoured and popular person, who killed all his horses with fast driving, gambled very heavily, and never amused himself anywhere so well as in the little low dancing places round Paris.

Madame Mila, as her friends always called her, was as pretty a little woman as could be imagined, who enamelled herself to such perfection that she had a face of fifteen, on the most fashionable and wonderfully costumed of bodies; she was very fond of her cousin Hilda, because she could borrow so much money of her, and she had come to Floralia this winter because in Paris there was a rumour that she had cheated at cards—false, of course, but still odious.

If she had made a little pencil mark on some of the aces, where was the harm in that?

She almost always played with the same people, and they had won heaps of money of her.

Whilst those horrid creatures in the city and on the bourse were allowed to " rig the market," and nobody thought the worse of them for spreading false news to send their shares up or down, why should not one poor little woman try to help on Chance a little bit at play ?

She was always in debt, though she admitted that her husband allowed her liberally. She had eighty thousand francs a year by her settle-ments to spend on herself, and he gave her another fifty thousand to do as she pleased with : on the whole about one half what he allowed to Blanche Souris, of the Château Gaillard theatre.

She had had six children, three were living and three were dead; she thought herself a good mother, because she gave her wet-nurses ever so many silk gowns, and when she wanted the children for a fancy ball or a drive, always saw that they were faultlessly dressed, and besides she always took them to Trouville.

She had never had any grief in her life, except the loss of the Second Empire, and even that she got over when she found that flying the Red

Cross flag had saved her hotel, without so much as a teacup being broken in it, that MM. Worth and Offenbach were safe from all bullets, and that society, under the Septennate, promised to be every bit as *leste* as under the Empire.

In a word, Madame Mila was a type of the women of her time.

The women who go semi-nude in an age which has begun to discover that the nude in sculpture is very immoral; who discuss ' Tue-la' in a generation which decrees Molière to be coarse, and Beaumont and Fletcher indecent; who have the Journal pour Rire on their tables in a day when no one who respects himself would name the Harlot's Progress; who read Beaudelaire and patronise Térésa and Schneider in an era which finds 'Don Juan' gross, and Shakespeare far too plain; who strain all their energies to rival Mlles. Rose Thé and La Petite Boulotte in everything; who go shrimping or oyster-hunting on fashionable sea-shores, with their legs bare to the knee; who go to the mountains with confections, high heels, and gold-tipped canes, shriek over their gambling

as the dawn reddens over the Alps, and know no
more of the glories of earth and sky, of sunrise
and sunset, than do the porcelain pots that hold
their paint, or the silver dressing-box that carries
their hair-dye.

Women who are in convulsions one day, and
on the top of a drag the next; who are in
hysterics for their lovers at noon-day, and in ecsta-
cies over baccarat at midnight; who laugh in little
nooks together over each other's immoralities,
and have a moral code so elastic that it will pardon
anything except innocence; who gossip over each
other's dresses, and each other's passions, in the
self-same, self-satisfied chirp of contentment, and
who never resent anything on earth, except any
eccentric suggestion that life could be anything
except a perpetual fête à la Watteau in a perpetual blaze of lime-light.

Pain ?—Are there not chloral and a flattering
doctor? Sorrow ?—Are there not a course at the
Baths, play at Monte Carlo, and new cases from
Worth ? Shame ?—Is it not a famine fever which
never comes near a well laden table ? Old Age ?
—Is there not white and red paint, and heads of

dead hair, and even false bosoms? Death?—
Well, no doubt there is death, but they do not
realise it; they hardly believe in it, they think
about it so little.

There is something unknown somewhere to
fall on them some day that they dread vaguely,
for they are terrible cowards. But they worry
as little about it as possible. They give the
millionth part of what they possess away in its
name to whatever church they belong to, and they
think they have arranged quite comfortably for all
possible contingencies hereafter.

If it make things safe, they will head bazaars
for the poor, or wear black in holy week, turn
lottery-wheels for charity, or put on fancy
dresses in the name of benevolence, or do any
little amiable trifle of that sort. But as for
changing their lives,—*pas si bête !*

A bird in the hand they hold worth two in the
bush; and though your birds may be winged on
strong desire, and your bush the burning parterre
of Moses, they will have none of them.

These women are not all bad; oh, no! they are
like sheep, that is all.. If it were fashionable to

be virtuous, very likely they would be so. If it
were *chic* to be devout, no doubt they would pass
their life on their knees. But, as it is, they
know that a flavour of vice is as necessary to their
reputation as great ladies, as sorrel-leaves to soup
à la bonne femme. They affect a license if they
take it not.

They are like the barber, who said, with much
pride, to Voltaire, "Je ne suis qu'un pauvre
diable de perruquier, mais je ne crois pas en Dieu
plus que les autres."

They may be worth very little, but they are
desperately afraid that you should make such a
mistake as to think them worth anything at all.
You are not likely, if you know them. Still,
they are apprehensive.

Though one were to arise from the dead to
preach to them, they would only make of him a
nine days' wonder, and then laugh a little, and
yawn a little, and go on in their own paths.

Out of the eater came forth meat, and from
evil there may be begotten good; but out of
nullity there can only come nullity. They
have wadded their ears, and though Jeremiah

wailed of desolation, or Isaiah thundered the wrath of heaven, they would not hear, — they would go on looking at each other's dresses.

What could Paul himself say that would change them ?

You cannot make saw-dust into marble; you cannot make sea-sand into gold. "Let us alone," is all they ask; and it is all that you could do, though the force and flame of Horeb were in you.

Mila, Countess de Caviare having arrived early in the morning and remained invisible all day, had awakened at five to a cup of tea, an exquisite dressing-gown, and her choicest enamel; she now gave many bird-like kisses to her cousin, heaped innumerable endearments upon her, and hearing there was nothing to do, sent out for a box at the French Theatre.

"It is wretched acting," said the Lady Hilda; "I went the other night but I did not stay half-an-hour."

"That of course, ma chère," said Madame Mila; "but we shall be sure to see people we know,—heaps of people."

"Such as they are," said the Lady Hilda.

"At any rate it is better than spending an evening alone. I never spent an evening alone in my life," said Mme. de Caviare, who could no more live without a crowd about her than she could sleep without chlorodyne, or put on a petticoat without two or three maids' assistance.

The French company in Floralia is usually about the average of the weakly patchwork troops of poor actors that pass on third rate little stages in the French departments; but Floralia, feminine and fashionable, flocks to the French company because it can rely on something *tant soit peu hazardé,* and is quite sure not to be bored with decency, and if by any oversight or bad taste the management should put any serious sort of piece on the stage, it can always turn its back to the stage and whisper to its lovers, or chatter shrilly to its allies.

They went into their box as the second act ended of *Mme. de Scabreuse;* a play of the period, written by a celebrated author; in which the lady married her nephew, and finding out that he was enamoured of her daughter, the offspring

E

of a first marriage, bought poison for them both,
and then suddenly changing her mind, with
magnificent magnanimity drank it herself, and
blessed the lovers as she died in great agonies.

It had been brought out in Paris with enormous success, and as Lady Hilda and the
Countess had both seen it half-a-dozen times
they could take no interest in it.

" You *would* come ! " said the former, raising
her eyebrows and seating herself so as to see
nothing whatever of the stage and as little as
possible of the house.

" Of course," replied Madame Mila, whose
lorgnon was ranging hither and thither, like a
general's spy-glass before a battle. " There was
nothing else to do—at least you said there was nothing. Look ! some of those women have actually
got the œuf de Pâques corsage—good heaven !—
those went out last year, utterly, utterly ! Ah,
there is Lucia San Luca—what big emeralds—
and there is Maria Castelfidardo, how old she is
looking. That is Lady Featherleigh—you remember that horrid scandal ?—Yes, I hear
they do visit her here. How handsome Luisa

Ottoseccoli looks; powder becomes her so;
her son is a pretty boy—oh, you never stoop
to boys; you are wrong; nothing amuses you
like a boy; *how* they believe in one! There
is that Canadian woman who tried to get
into notice in Paris two seasons ago—you
remember?—they make her quite Crême in
this place — the idea! She is dressed very
well, I dare say if she were always dumb she
might pass. She never would have been heard
of even here, only Attavante pushed her right
and left, bribed the best people to her parties,
and induced all his other *tendresses* to send her
cards. In love! of course not! Who is in love
with a face like a Mohican squaw's, and a
squeak like a goose's? But they are immensely
rich; at least they have mountains of ready
money; he must have suffered dreadfully before
he made her dress well. Teach her grammar, in any language, he never will. There is
the old Duchess—why, she was a centenarian
when we were babies—but they say she plays
every atom as keenly as ever—nobody can beat
her for lace either—look at that Spanish point.

There are a few decent people here this winter;
not many though; I think it would have been
wiser to have stopped at Nice. Ah mon cher,
comment ça va ?—tell me, Maurice, who is that
woman in black with good diamonds, there, with
Sampierdareno and San Marco ?"

'Maurice,' pressing her pretty hand, sank down
on to the hard bench behind her armchair, and
insinuated gracefully that the woman in black
with good diamonds was not "d'une vertu assez
forte," to be noticed by or described to such
ladies as Mila, Countess de Caviare; but since
identification of her was insisted on, proceeded
to confess that she was no less a person than
the wild Duke of Stirling's Gloria.

"Ah! is *that* Gloria !" said Madame, with
the keenest interest, bringing her lorgnon to
bear instantly. "How curious! I never chanced
to see her before. How quiet she looks, and
how plainly she is dréssed."

"I am afraid we have left Gloria and her
class no other way of being singular !" said the
Lady Hilda, who had muttered her welcome
somewhat coldly to Maurice.

Maurice, Vicomte des Gommeux, was a young Parisian, famous for leading cotillons and driving piebalds; he followed Mme. de Caviare with the regularity of her afternoon shadow; was as much an institution with her as her anodynes; and much more useful than her courier. To avoid all appearances that might set a wicked world talking, he generally arrived in a city about twenty-four hours after her, and, as she was a woman of good-breeding who insisted on *les mœurs,* always went to another hotel. He had held his present post actually so long as three years, and there were as yet no signs of his being dismissed and replaced, for he was very devoted, very obedient, very weak, saw nothing that he was intended not to see, and was very adroit at rolling cigarettes.

"Il est si bon enfant!" said the Count de Caviare, to everybody; he really was grateful to the young man, some of whose predecessors had much disturbed his wife's temper and his own personal peace.

"Bon soir, Mesdames," said the Duc de St Louis, entering the box. "Comtesse, charmé de

vous voir—Miladi à vos pieds. What a wretched
creature that is playing Julie de Scabreuse. I
blush for my country. When I was a young man,
the smallest theatre in France would not have endured that woman. There was a public then
with proper feeling for the histrionic as for every
other art; a bad gesture or a false intonation was
hissed by every audience, were that audience
only composed of workmen and work girls; but
now——"

"May one enter, Mesdames?" asked his
friend, Della Rocca.

"One may—if you will only shut the door.
Thanks for the cyclamens," said the Lady Hilda,
with a little of the weariness going off her delicate, proud face.

Della Rocca took the seat behind her, as the
slave Maurice surrendered his to M. de St. Louis.

"Happy flowers! I found them in my own
woods this morning," he said, as he took his seat.
"You do not seem much amused, Madame."

"Amused! The play is odious. Even poor
Desclée's genius could only give it a horrible fascination."

"It has the worst fault of all, it is unnatural."

"Yes; it is very curious, but the French will have so much vice in the drama, and the English must have so much virtue, that a natural or possible play is an impossibility now upon either stage."

"You looked more interested in the Majolica this morning——"

"How, did you see me?"

"I was passing through the tower of the Podestà on business. Is it not wonderful our old pottery? It is intensely to be regretted that Ginori and Carocci imitate it so closely; it vulgarises a thing whose chief beauty after all is association and age."

"Yes; what charm there is in a marriage plate of Maestro Giorgio's, or a sweetmeat dish of your Orazio Fontana's! But there is very scanty pleasure in reproductions of them, however clever these may be, such as Pietro Gay sends out to Paris and Vienna Exhibitions."

"You mean, there can be no mind in an imitation?"

"Of course; I would rather have the crudest

original thing than the mere galvanism of the corpse of a dead genius. I would give a thousand paintings by Froment, Damousse, or any of the finest living artists of Sèvres, for one piece by old Van der Meer of Delft; but I would prefer a painting on Sèvres done yesterday by Froment or Damousse, or even any much less famous worker, provided only it had originality in it, to the best reproduction of a Van der Meer that modern manufacturers could produce."

"I think you are right; but I fear our old pottery painters were not very original. They copied from the pictures and engravings of Mantegna, Raffaelle, Marcantonio, Marco di Ravenna, Beatricius, and a score of others."

"The application was original, and the sentiment they brought to it. Those old artists put so much heart into their work."

"Because when they painted a *stemma* on the glaze they had still feudal faith in nobility, and when they painted a Madonna or Ecce Homo they had still child-like belief in divinity. What does the pottery painter of to-day care for the coat of arms or the religious subject he may be commissioned to execute for a dinner service or a chapel ? It may be admirable painting—if you give a very high price—but it will still be only manufacture."

" Then what pleasant lives those pottery painters of the early days must have led ! They were never long stationary. They wandered about decorating at their fancy, now here and now there; now a vase for a pharmacy, and now a stove for a king. You find German names on Italian ware, and Italian names on Flemish grès ; the Nuremberger would work in Venice, the Dutchman would work in Rouen."

"Sometimes however they were accused of sorcery ; the great potter, Hans Kraut, you remember, was feared by his townsmen as possessed by the devil, and was buried ignominiously outside the gates, in his nook of the Black Forest. But on the whole they were happy, no doubt : men of simple habits and of worthy lives."

" You care for art yourself, M. Della Rocca ? "

There came a gleam of interest in her handsome, languid hazel eyes, as she turned them upon him.

" Every Italian does," he answered her.   " I do not think we are ever, or I think, if ever, very seldom connoisseurs in the way that your Englishman and Frenchman is so.   We are never very learned as to styles and dates; we cannot boast the huckster's eye of the northern bric-à-brac hunter; it is quite another thing with us; we love art as children their nurses' tales and cradle songs; it is a familiar affection with us, and affection is never very analytical; the Robbia over the chapel-door, the apostle-pot that the men in the stables drink out of; the Sodoma or the Beato Angelico that hangs before our eyes daily as we dine ; the old bronze *secchia* that we wash our hands in as boys in the Loggia—these are all so homely and dear to us that we grow up with a love for them all as natural as our love for our mothers.   You will say the children of all rich people see beautiful and ancient things from their birth; so they do, but not *as* we see them—here they are too often degraded to the basest household uses, and made no more account of than the dust which gathers on them; but that very neglect of them makes them the more kindred to us. Art elsewhere is the guest of the salon—with us she is the play-mate of the infant and the serving-maid of the peasant : the mules may drink from an Etruscan sarcophagus, and the pigeons be fed from a *patina* of the twelfth century."

Lady Hilda listened with the look of awakened interest still in her large eyes ; he spoke in his own tongue, and with feeling and grace ; it was new to her to find a man with whom art was an emotion instead of an opinion.

The art world she had met with was one that was very positive, very eclectic, very hypercritical, very highly cultured ; it had many theories and elegant phrases ; it laid down endless doctrines, and found pleasure in endless disputations. Whenever she had tired of the world of fashion, this was the world she had turned to ; it had imbued her with knowledge of art, and immeasurable contempt for those to whom art was a dead letter ; but art had remained with her rather an intellectual dissipation than a tenderness of sentiment.

" As you care for these things, Madame," con-

tinued Della Rocca, with hesitation, "might I
one day hope that you would honour my poor
villa? It has little else left in it; but there are
still a few rare pieces of Gubbio and Urbino and
Faenza, and I have a Calvary which, if not by
Lucca himself, is certainly by Andrea della
Robbia.'

"I shall be glad to see them. Your villa is
near?"

" About ten miles' distance, up in the hills.
It was once a great stronghold as well as palace.
Now it can boast no interest save such as may
go with fallen fortunes. For more than a century
we have been too poor to be able to do any more
than keep wind and water out of it; and it had
been cleared before my time of almost everything
of value. Happily, however, the chestnut woods
outside it have not been touched. They shroud
its nakedness."

"Your villa, Della Rocca?" cried Madame de
Caviare, who had known him for several years.
"I have never seen it; we will drive out there
some day when the cold winds are gone——"

"Vous me comblez de bontés," he answered,

with a low bow. " Alas, Madame, there is very little that will repay you : it is hardly more than a ruin. But if you and Miladi will indeed honour it——"

" It is a very fine place still," said the Duc de St. Louis, a little impatiently. " It has suffered in sieges; and is by so much the more interesting. For myself, I endure very much pain from having a whole house, and one built no later than 1730. My great grandfather pulled down the noble old castle, built at the same time as Château Gaillard —imagine the barbarism !—and employed the ponderous *rocaille* of Oppenord to replace it. It is very curious, but loss of taste in the nobles has always been followed by a revolution of the mob. The *décadence* always ushers in the democracy."

" We may well be threatened then in this day with universal equality ! " said the Lady Hilda, hiding a very small yawn behind her fan.

" Nay, Madame," said Della Rocca. " In this day the nobles do not even do so much as to lead a wrong taste ; they accept and adopt every form of it, as imposed on them by their tailors, their architects, their clubs, and their municipalities, as *rocaille* was imposed by the cabinet-makers."

"How fearfully serious you all are!" said Madame de Caviare. "There is that dreadful Canadian woman standing up—what rubies! how fond vulgar women always are of rubies. That *passe-partout* of hers is rather pretty; gold thread on *blondine* satin, is it not, Hilda? My glass is not very strong——"

Lady Hilda looked through her glass, and decided the important point in the affirmative.

"How she is rouged!" pursued the Countess. "I am sure Altavante did not lay *that* on; he is much too artistic. Maurice, have you a cigarette?"

"It is not allowed, ma chère," said the Lady Hilda.

"Pooh!" said Madame de Caviare, accepting a little delicate paper roll. "It was very kind of you, Hilda, to remind me of that; you wished me to enjoy it. Won't you have one too?"

Lady Hilda said "No" with her fan.

"If the Rocaille brought the Revolution,

Duc," she asked, "what will our smoking bring?
—the end of the world?"

"It will bring animosity of the sexes, aboli-
tion of the marriage laws, and large increase of
paralysis," replied M. de St. Louis with great
decision.

"You have answered me without a compliment
—what flattery to my intelligence."

"Miladi, I never flatter you. I am not in the
habit of imitating all the world."

"You look severe, Della Rocca," said Madame
Mila. "Do you disapprove of women smoking?"

"Madame, a woman of grace lends grace to all
she does, no doubt."

"That is to say, you don't approve it?"

"Madame, I merely doubt whether Lionardo
would have painted Mona Lisa had she smoked."

"What a good idea you give me!—I will be
painted by Millais or Cabanel, smoking. It will
be novel. The cigar shall be in my mouth.
I will send you the first photograph. Ah!
there is Nordlingen; he will come over here,
and he is the greatest bore in Europe. You
know what your King here said, when Nord-

'ingen had bored him at three audiences about
heaven knows what.—'I never knew the use of
sentinels before ; let that man be shot if he ask
audience again ! ' We cannot shoot him ; let us
go to supper. Duc, you will follow us, with M.
des Gommeux ?—and you, too, Della Rocca ?
There is that odious Canadian woman going ;
let us make haste ; I should like to see that blondine cloak close ; I shall know whether it looks
like Worth or Pingât."

She passed out on the Duc's arm, and the Lady
Hilda accepted Della Rocca's, while the well-
trained Maurice, who knew his duties, rushed to
find the footmen in the vestibule, and to arrest
another gilded youth and kindred spirit, a M. des
Poisseux, whom Madame Mila had espied in the
crowd, and charged him to bring with him to
supper. Madame Mila preferred, to all the world,
the young men of her world of five and twenty or
less ; they had no mind whatever, they had not
character enough to be jealous, and they were as
full of the last new scandals as any dowager of
sixty.

" They talk of the progress of this age : con-

trast M. de St. Louis with M. des Gommeux and
M. des Poisseux ! " said the Lady Hilda, with her
little contemptuous smile

Della Rocca laughed.

" You make me for the first time, Madame,
well content to belong to what the Gommeux and
the Poisseux would call a past generation. But
there are not many like our friend the Duc; he
has stepped down to us from the terraces of
Marly; I am certain he went to sleep one night
after a gavotte with Montespan, and has only just
awakened."

The supper was gay and bright; Lady Hilda,
rejecting chicken and champagne, and accepting
only ice-water and cigarettes, deigned to be
amusing, though sarcastic, and Madame Mila was
always in one of the two extremes—either syn-
cope, sal volatile, and hysterics, or laughter,
frolic, smoke and *risqué* stories.

She and her sisterhood spend their lives in this
see-saw; the first state is for the mornings, when
they remember their losses at play, their lovers'
looks at other women, the compromising notes
they have written, and how much—too much to be

F

safe—their maids knew of them ; the second state
is for the evenings, when they have their war-paint
on, have taken a little nip of some stimulant at
afternoon tea, are going to half-a-dozen houses
between midnight and dawn, and are quite sure
their lovers never even see that any other women
exist.

" He could not have a better illustration of the
difference between a woman with taste and a
woman without it," thought the Duc de St. Louis,
surveying the two ; the Countess had a million
or two of false curls in a tower above her pretty
tiny face, was almost as *décolletée* as a Greuze picture, chirped the fashionable slang of the boulevards and salons in the shrillest and swiftest of
voices, and poured forth slanders that were more
diverting than decorous.

Lady Hilda was dressed like a picture of Marie
Antoinette, in 1780 ; her rich hair was lifted from
her low fair forehead in due keeping with her
costume, she swept aside her cousin's naughty
stories with as much tact as contempt, and spoke
a French which Marie Antoinette could have
recognised as the language in which Voltaire once

scoffed, and André Chénier sighed. To be sure, she did smoke a little, but then even the most perfect taste cannot quite escape the *cachet* of its era.

"It was not necessary, my friend, to say that your place was so poor," said M. de St. Louis, as they went out of the hôtel together; he had known his companion from boyhood.

"I am not ashamed of my poverty," said Della Rocca, somewhat coldly. "Besides," he added, with a laugh which had not much mirth in it, "our poverty is as well known as that of the city. I think the most dishonest Della Rocca could not conceal it by any adroitness, any more than Floralia could conceal her public debt."

"That may be, but neither you nor the town need proclaim the state of your affairs," said the Duc, who never gave up an opinion. "You should let her be interested in you before you make it so evident; such silence is quite permissible. You need say nothing; you need hide nothing; you need only let things alone."

"My dear Duc," said Della Rocca, with a

laugh that had melancholy in it and some
irritation, " think for one moment of that
woman's position, and say could anything ever
induce her to change it—except one thing .
Riches could add nothing to her; the highest
rank could scarcely be any charm to her; she
has everything she can want or wish for;—if she
had the power of wishing left, which I doubt. The
only spell that might enchain her would be love, if
she have any capacity to feel it, which I doubt also.
Well—granted love aroused,—what would poverty or riches in her lover matter to one who
has secured for ever a golden pedestal of her own
from which to survey the woes of the world?
She refused the Prince of Deutchsland ; that I
know, since he told me himself; and men do
not boast of rejections ;—what position, pray,
would ever tempt her since she refused Deutchsland ? and he has all personal attractions, too, as
well as his future crown."

" Still, granting all that, to make your lack
of fortune so very conspicuous is to render your
purpose conspicuous also, and to draw her attention to it unwisely," said the Duc, who viewed

all these matters calmly, as a kind of mixture of diplomacy and business.

"Caro mio!" said Della Rocca lightly, as he descended the last step. "Be very sure that if I ever have such a purpose, your Lady Hilda has too much wit not to perceive it in a day. But I have not such a purpose. I do not like a woman who smokes."

And with a good night he walked away to his own house, which was a street or two distant. The Duc chuckled, no wise discomfited.

"An Italian always swears he will never do the thing he means to do in an hour," the Duc reflected as he got in his cab.

The Della Rocca Palace was let to many tenants and in various divisions; he himself retained only a few chambers looking upon the old quiet green garden, high walled, dark with ilex, and musical with fountains.

He crossed the silent courts, mounted the vast black stairways, and entered his solitary rooms. There was a lamp burning; and his dog got up and welcomed him. He slipped on an old velvet smoking coat, lighted a cigar, and sat down : the councils and projects of M. de St. Louis were not so entirely rejected by him as he had wished the Duc to suppose.

He admired her; he did not approve her; he was not even sure that he liked her in any way; but he could not but see that here at last was the marriage which would bring the resurrection of all his fortunes.

Neither did he feel any of the humility which he had expressed to M. de St. Louis. Though she might be as cold as people all said she was, he had little fear, if he once endeavoured, that he would fail in making his way into her graces. With an Italian, love is too perfect a science for him to be uncertain of its results.

Besides, he believed that he detected a different character in her to what the world thought, and she also thought was her own. He thought men had all failed with her because they had not gone the right way to work. After all, to make a woman in love with you was easy enough. At least he had always found it so.

She was a woman, too, of unusual beauty, and of supreme grace, and a great alliance; her

money would restore him to the lost power of his
ancestors, and save a mighty and stainless name
from falling into that paralysis of poverty and
that dust of obscurity, which are, sooner or later,
its utter extinction. She seemed cast across his
path by a caress of Fortune, from which it would
be madness to turn aside. True, he had a wholly
different ideal for his wife; he disliked those
world-famous *élégantes ;* he disliked women who
smoked, and knew their Paris as thoroughly as
Houssaye or Dumas; he disliked the extrava-
gant, artificial, empty, frivolous life they led;
their endless chase after new excitements, and
their insatiable appetite for *frissons nouveaux ;*
he disliked their literature, their habits, their
cynicism, their ennui, their sensuality, and their
dissipations; he knew them well, and disliked
them in all things; what he desired in his
wife were natural emotions, unworn innocence,
serenity, simplicity, and freshness of enjoyment;
though he was of the world, he did not care
very much for it; he had a meditative, imagina-
tive temperament, and the whirl of modern
society was soon wearisome to him; on the other

hand, he knew the world too well to want a woman beside him who knew it equally well.

On the whole, the project of M. de St. Louis repelled as much as it attracted him. Yet his wisdom told him that it was the marriage beyond all others which would best fulfil his destiny in the way which from his earliest years he had been accustomed to regard as in- . evitable; and, moreover, there was something about her which charmed his senses, though his judgment feared and in some things his taste disapproved her.

Besides, to make so self-engrossed a woman love;—he smiled as he sat and smoked in the solitude of his great dim vaulted room, and then he sighed impatiently.

After all, it was not a *beau rôle* to woo a woman for the sheer sake of her fortune; and he was too true a gentleman not to know it. And what would money do for him if it were hers and not his ?—it would only humiliate him, —he felt no taste for the position of a prince consort,—it would pass to his children certainly after him, and so raise up the old name to its olden dignity; but for himself——

He got up and walked to the window; the clear winter stars, large before morning, were shining through the iron bars and lozenged panes of the ancient casement; the fountain in the cortile was shining in the moonlight; the ducal coronet, carved in stone above the gateway, stood out whitely from the shadows.

"After all, she would despise me, and I should despise myself," he thought; the old coronet had been sadly battered in war, but it had never been chaffered and bought.

CHAPTER IV.

" WHAT do you think of Della Rocca, Hilda,"
asked Madame Mila at the same hour that night,
toasting her pink satin slipper before her dressing-room fire.

Lady Hilda yawned, unclasping her *rivière* of
sapphires.

" He has a very good manner. There is some
truth in what Olga Schouvaloff always maintains,
that after an Italian all other men seem boors."

"I am sure Maurice is not a boor!" said the
Countess, pettishly.

" Oh no, my dear; he parts his hair in the
middle, talks the last new, unintelligible, aristocratic *argot*, and has the charms of every
actress and dancer in Paris catalogued clearly in

a brain otherwise duly clouded, as fashion re-
quires, by brandy in the morning and absinthe
before dinner! Boors don't do those things, nor
yet get half as learned as to Mlle. Rose Thé and
la Petite Boulotte."

Madame Mila reddened angrily.

" What spiteful things to say; he never looked
at that hideous little Boulotte, or any of the
horrible creatures, and he never drinks; he is a
perfect gentleman."

"Not quite that, ma chère; if he had been,
he would never have let himself be called *bon
enfant* by *your* husband!"

Madame Mila raged in passionate wrath for
five minutes, and then began to cry a little,
whimperingly.

Lady Hilda gathered up her *rivière*, took her
candlestick, and bade her good night.

"It is no use making that noise, Mila," she
said coolly. " You have always known what I
think, but you prefer to be in the fashion; of
course you must go on as you like; only please
to remember,—don't let *me* see too much of
Des Gommeux."

Madame Mila, left alone to the contemplation of her pink slippers, fumed and sulked and felt very angry indeed; but she had borrowed a thousand pounds some six or eight times from the Lady Hilda to pay her debts at play; and of course it was such a trifle that she had always forgotten to pay it again, because if ever she had any ready money there was always some jeweller, or man dressmaker, or creditor of some kind who would not wait; and then, though it was not her fault, because she played as high as she could any night she got a chance to do so, somehow or other she generally lost, and never had a single sou to spare; —so she muttered her rage to the pink slippers alone, and decided that it was never worth while to be put out about the Lady Hilda's "ways."

"She is a bit of ice herself," she said to her slippers, and wondered how Lady Hilda or anybody else could object to what she did, or see any harm in it. Maurice always went to another hôtel.

Mme. Mila lived her life in a manner very

closely resembling that of the horrible creatures
Mlles. Rose Thé and Boulotte; really, when
compared by a cynic there was very little difference to be found between those persons and
pretty Madame Mila. But Rose Thé and Boulotte of course were creatures, and she was a
very great little lady, and went to all the courts
and embassies in Europe, and was sought and
courted by the very best and stiffest people,
being very *chic* and very rich, and very lofty in
every way, and very careful to make Maurice go
to a different hôtel.

She had had twenty Maurices in her time
indeed, but then the Count de Caviare never
complained, and was careful to drive with her
in the Bois, and pass at least three months
of each year under the same roof with her,
so that nobody could say anything; it being
an accepted axiom with Society that when
the husband does not object to his own dishonour, there is no dishonour at all in the matter
for any one. If he be sensitive to it then
indeed you must cut his wife, and there will be
nothing too bad to be said of her; but if he

only do but connive at his own shame himself, then all is quite right, and everything is as it should be.

When the Prince of Cracow, with half Little Russia in his possession, entertains the beautiful Lady Lightwood at a banquet at his villa at Frascati, Richmond, or Auteuil, a score of gilded lackeys shout "La voiture de Madame la Comtesse!" the assembled guests receive her sweet good night, the Prince of Cracow bows low, and thanks her for the honour she has done to him; she goes out at the hall door, and the carriage bowls away with loud crash and fiery steeds, and rolls on its way out of the park-gates. Society is quite satisfied. Society knows very well that a million roubles find their yearly way into the empty pockets of Lord Lightwood, and that a little later the carriage will sweep round again to a side-door hidden under the laurels wide open, and receive the beautiful Lady Lightwood: but what is that to Society? It has seen her drive away; that is quite sufficient, everybody is satisfied with that.

If you give Society very good dinners, Society

will never be so ill-bred as to see that side-door under your laurels.

Do drive out at the hall-door;—do;—for sake of les Bienséances—that is all Society asks of you; there are some things Society feels it owes to Itself, and this is one of them.

Of course, whether you come back again or not, can be nobody's business.

Society can swear to the fact of the hall-door.

Madame Mila was attentive to the matter of the hall-door; indeed, abhorred a scandal; it always made everything uncomfortable. She was always careful of appearances. Even if you called on her unexpectedly, Des Gommeux was always in an inner room, unseen, and you could declare with a clear conscience that you never found him alone with her, were the oath ever required in any draw-ing-room in defence of her character. Of course, you have no sort of business with who or what may be in inner rooms; Society does not require you to search a house as if you were a detective.

If you can say airily, " Oh, there's nothing in

it; I never see him there," Society believes you, and is quite satisfied: that is, if it wish to believe you; if it do not wish, nothing would ever satisfy it. No, not though there rose one from the dead to bear witness.

Madame Mila would not have done anything to jeopardise her going to Courts, and having all the Embassies to show her jewels in, for any thing that any man in the whole world could have offered her.

Madame Mila thought a woman who left her husband and made a scandal, a horrid creature; nay, she was worse, she was a Blunder, and by her blunder made a great deal of unpleasantness for other and wiser women. After a stupid, open thing of that kind, Society always gets so dreadfully prudish for about three months, that it is disagreeable for everybody. To run off with a man, and lose your settlements, and very likely have to end in a boarding-house in Boulogne ?— could anything be more idiotic ?

Madame Mila thought that a woman so forgetting herself deserved even a worse fate than the boarding-house. Madame Mila, who was quite content that her husband should make a fool of himself about Blanche Souris, or anybody else, so long as he walked arm-in-arm now and then with Des Gommeux, and called him "mon cher,"—was indeed in every iota the true Femme Galante of the 19th century.

The Femme Galante has passed through many various changes, in many countries. The dames of the Decamerone were unlike the fair athlete-seekers of the days of Horace; and the powdered coquettes of the years of Molière, were sisters only by the kinship of a common vice to the frivolous and fragile faggot of impulses, that is called Frou-frou.

The Femme Galante has always been a feature in every age; poets from Juvenal to Musset, have railed at her; artists, from Titian to Winterhalter, have painted her; dramatists, from Aristophanes to Congreve and Dumas Fils, have pointed their arrows at her; satirists, from Archilochus and Simonides to Hogarth and Gavarni, have poured out their aqua-fortis for her. But the real Femme Galante of to-day has been missed hitherto.

G

Frou-frou, who stands for her, is not in the least the true type. Frou-frou is a creature that can love, can suffer, can repent, can die. She is false in sentiment and in art, but she is tender after all; poor, feverish, wistful, changeful morsel of humanity. A slender, helpless, breathless, and frail thing, who, under one sad, short sin, sinks down to death.

But Frou-frou is in no sense the true Femme Galante of her day. Frou-frou is much more a fancy than a fact. It is not Frou-frou that Molière would have handed down to other generations in enduring ridicule, had he been living now. To her he would have doffed his hat with dim eyes; what he would have fastened for all time in his pillory would have been a very different, and far more conspicuous, offender.

The Femme Galante, who has neither the scruples nor the follies of poor Frou-frou, who neither forfeits her place nor leaves her lord; who has studied adultery as one of the fine arts and made it one of the domestic virtues; who takes her wearied lover to her friends' houses as she

takes her muff or her dog, and teaches her sons
and daughters to call him by familiar names; who
writes to the victim of her passions with the
same pen that calls her boy home from school;
and who smooths her child's curls with the same
fingers that stray over her lover's lips; who
challenges the world to find a flaw in her, and
who smiles serene at her husband's table on a
society she is careful to conciliate; who has woven
the most sacred ties and most unholy pleasures
into so deft a braid, that none can say where one
commences or the other ends; who uses the sanctity of her maternity to cover the lawlessness of
her license; and who, incapable alike of the self-
abandonment of love or of the self-sacrifice of
duty, has not even such poor, cheap honour as,
in the creatures of the streets, may make guilt
loyal to its dupe and partner.

This is the Femme Galante of the passing
century, who, with her hand on her husband's
arm, babbles of her virtue in complacent boast;
and ignoring such a vulgar word as Sin, talks
with a smile of Friendship. Beside her Frou-frou
were innocence itself, Marion de l'Orme were

a 2

honesty, Manon Lescaut were purity, Cleopatra were chaste, and Faustine were faithful.

She is the female Tartuffe of seduction, the Précieuse Ridicule of passion, the parody of Love, the standing gibe of Womanhood.

CHAPTER V.

THE next day the Duca della Rocca left cards on Lady Hilda and the Comtesse de Caviare; and then for a fortnight never went near either of them except to exchange a few words with them in other people's houses. M. de St. Louis, who was vastly enamoured of his project, because it was his project (what better reason has anybody?) was irritated and in despair.

" You fly in the face of Fate ! " he said, with much impatience.

Della Rocca laughed.

" There is no such person as Fate—she perished with all the rest of the Pagan world when we put up our first gas-lamp. The two I regret most of them all are Faunus and Picus; nowadays we make Faunus into a railway contractor, and shoot Picus for the market-stall."

"You are very romantic," said the Duc, with serene contempt. "It is an unfortunate quality; and I confess," he added, with a sigh, as if confessing a blemish in a favourite horse, "that, perhaps, she is a little deficient in the other extreme, a little too cold, a little too unimpressionable; there is absolutely no shadow of cause to suppose she ever felt the slightest emotion for anyone. That gives, perhaps, a certain hardness. It is not natural. ' Une petite faiblesse donne tant de charme.' "

"In a wife, one might dispense with the 'petite faiblesse' for anyone else," said Della Rocca, with a smile; the blemish did not seem much of a fault in his eyes.

"That is a romantic notion," said the Duc, with a little touch of disdain. "In real truth a woman is easier to manage who has had—a past. She knows what to expect. It is flattering to be the first object of passion to a woman.   But it is troublesome : she exacts so much ! "

" If I were not that, I have seldom cared to be anything," said Della Rocca.

" That is an Italian amorous fancy.   Romeo and Othello are the typical Italian lovers.   I never can tell how a northerner like Shakspeare could draw either.   You are often very unfaithful; but *while* you are faithful you are ardent, and you are absorbed in the woman.   That is one of the reasons why an Italian succeeds in love as no other man does.   'L'art de brûler silencieusement le cœur d'une femme " is a supreme art with you.   Compared with you, all other men are children.   You have been the supreme masters of the great passion since the days of Ovid."

" Because it is much more the supreme pursuit of our lives than it is with other men.   How can Love be of much power where it is inferior to fox-hunting, and a mere interlude when there is no other sport to be had, as it is with Englishmen ?"

" And with a Frenchman it is always inferior to himself ! " confessed the French Duc, with a

smile. " At least they say so. But every human being loves his vanity first. ' Only wounded
my vanity? ' poor Lord Strangford used to say.
' Pray what dearer and more integral part of myself could you wound ? ' He was very right. If
we are not on good terms with ourselves we can
never prevail with others."

" Yet a vain man seldom succeeds with
women ? "

" A man who lets them see that he is vain
does not: that is another matter. Vanity—ah !
there is Miladi, she has plenty of vanity ; yet it
is of a grandiose kind, and it would only take a
little more time and the first grey hair to turn
it into dissatisfaction. All kinds of discontent are
only superb vanities. Byron's, Musset's, Boling-
broke's ——"

A horse nearly knocked the Duc down in the
midst of his philosophies as he picked his way
delicately amongst the standing and moving carriages to the place where the white great-coats
with the black velvet collars of the Lady Hilda's
servants were visible.

The Lady Hilda's victoria stood in that open

square where it is the pleasure of fashionable
Floralia to stop its carriages in the course of the
drive before dinner.

The piazza is the most unlovely part of the
park : it has a gaunt red café and a desert of
hard-beaten sand, and in the middle there are
some few plants, and a vast quantity of iron
bordering laid out in geometrical patterns, with
more hard-beaten sand between them, this
being the modern Floralian idea of a garden ; to
which fatal idea are sacrificed the noble ilex
shades, the bird-filled cedar groves, the deep delicious dreamful avenues, the moss-grown ways,
and the leaf-covered fountains, worthy to shelter
Narcissus and to bathe Nausicaa, which their
wiser forefathers knew were alike the blessing
and the glory of this land of the sun.

Nevertheless—perhaps because it is the last
place in the world where anybody would be supposed ever voluntarily to stop a carriage—here
motley modern society delights to group its fusing
nationalities; and the same people who bored each
other in the morning's calls, and will bore each
other in the evening's receptions, bore each other

sedulously in the open air, and would not omit
the sacred ceremonial for anything — unless,
indeed, it rained.

Perhaps after all Floralia reads aright the
generation that visits it. The ilex shadows and
the cedar-groves need Virgil and Horace, Tasso
and Petrarca, Milton and Shelley.

The Lady Hilda, who never by any chance
paused in the piazzone, had stopped a moment
there to please Madame Mila, who, in the loveliest
Incroyable bonnet, was seated beside her.

The men of their acquaintance flocked up to
the victoria. Lady Hilda paid them scanty
attention, and occupied herself buying flowers
of the poor women who lifted their fragrant
basket-loads to the carriage. Madame Mila
chattered like the brightest of parrakeets, and
was clamorous for news.

"Quid novi?" is the cry in Floralia from morning till night, as in Athens. The most popular
people are those who, when the article is not to
be had of original growth, can manufacture it
Political news nobody attends to in Floralia;
financial news interests society a little more, be-

cause everybody has stocks or shares in something somewhere ; but *the* news is Gossip,—dear delicious perennial ever-blessed gossip, that reports a beloved friend in difficulties, a rival *in extremis*, a neighbour no better than she should be, and some exalted personage or another caught hiding a king in his sleeve at cards, or kissing his wife's lady-of-the-bedchamber.

Gossip goes the round of the city in winter as the lemonade stands do in summer.

If you wish to be *choyé* and asked out every night, learn to manufacture it ; it is very easy : take equal parts of flower of malice and essence of impudence, with several pepper-corns of improbability to spice it, some candied lemon-peel of moral reflections, and a few drops of the ammonia of indecency that will make it light of digestion, and the toothsome morsel will procure you welcome everywhere. If you can also chop up any real Paschal lamb of innocence in very fine pieces, so that it is minced and hashed and unrecognisable for ever, serve the mince with the vinegar of malignity, and the fresh mint of novelty, and you will he the very Carême

of gossip henceforward. Run about society
with your concoctions in and out of the best
houses, as fast as you can go, and there will
be no end to your popularity. You will be
as refreshing to the thirst of the dwellers in
them as are the lemonade-sellers to the throats
of the populace.

Perhaps Fate still lurked and worked in the
Latin land, and had hidden herself under the
delicate marabouts of the chapeau Incroyable;
at any rate, Madame Mila welcomed the Duc
and his companion with eagerness, and engaged
them both to dinner with her on the morrow in
a way which there was no refusing.

Madame Mila was discontented with the news
of the day. All her young men could only tell her
of one person's ruin—poor Victor de Salaris',
which she had always predicted and contributed to
cause, and which was therefore certainly the more
agreeable—and two scenes between married people
whom she knew: one because the brute of a husband would not allow his wife to have her tallest
footman in silk stockings; the other because the
no less a brute of a husband would not let *his*

vife have—a friendship. Madame Mila scarcely knew which refusal to condemn as the most heartless and the most vulgar.

The Lady Hilda dined with **her on the** morrow; and the little Comtesse, with the fine instinct at discovering future sympathies of a woman "qui a vécu," took care that Della Rocca took her cousin in to dinner.

"I would give all I possess to see Hilda *attendrie*," she said to herself: as what she possessed just then was chiefly an enormous quantity of unpaid bills, perhaps she would not have lost so very much. But the Lady Hilda was not *attendrie :* she thought he talked better than most men—at least, differently,—and he succeeded 'n interesting her, probably because he had been so indifferent in calling upon her. That was all. Besides, his manner was perfect; it was as *vieille cour* as M. de St. Louis's, and to the Italian noble alone is given the union of stateliest dignity with easiest grace.

Lady Hilda, who should have been born under Louis Quatorze, had often suffered much in her taste from an age when manner, except in the south, is only a tradition, smothered under cigar-ash, and buried in a gun-case.

As for him, he mused, while he talked to her, on the words of the Duc, who had known her all her life. Was it true that she had never felt even a passing "weakness?" Was it certain that she had always been as cold as she looked?

He wished that he could be sure.

After all, she was a woman of wonderful charm, though she did go about with Madame Mila, smoke cigarettes after dinner, and correct you as to the last *mot* made on the boulevards. He began to think that this was only the mere cachet of the world she lived in ; only the mere accident of contact and habit.

All women born under the Second Empire have it more or less; and, after all, she had but little of it; she was very serene, very contemptuous, very high-bred ; and her brilliant languid hazel eyes looked so untroubled that it would have moved any man into a wish to trouble their still and luminous depths.

She seemed to him very objectless and somewhat cynical. It was a pity. Nature had made

her perfect in face and form, and gifted her with
intelligence, and Fashion had made her useless,
tired, and vaguely cynical about everything, as
everybody else was in her world ; except that yet
larger number who resembled Madame Mila—a
worse type still, according to his view.

It was a pity that the coldness and corruption
of the great world had entered thus deeply into
her; so he thought, watching the droop of her
long eyelashes, the curve of her beautiful mouth,
the even coming and going of her breath under
her shining necklace of opals and emeralds.

He began to believe that the Duc was right.
There was no " past " in that calmest of indolent
glances.

"You smoke, Madame?" he said, a little
abruptly to her, after dinner.

She looked at her slender roll of paper.

"It is a habit—like all the rest of the things
one does. I do not care about it."

"Why do it then? Are you not too proud to
follow a habit, and imitate a folly ? "

She smiled a little, and let the cigarette pale
its ineffectual fires and die out.

"'They have not known how to deal with her," he thought to himself; and he sat down and played *écarté*, and allowed her to win, though he was one of the best players in Europe.

Fate had certainly been under the Incroyable bonnet of Madame Mila. For during the evening she suddenly recalled his villa, and announced her intention of coming to see it. In her little busy brain there was a clever notion that if she only could get her cousin once drawn into what the Duc would call a " petite faiblesse," she herself would hear no more lectures about Maurice ; and lectures are always tiresome, especially when the lecturer has lent you several thousands, that it would be the height of inconvenience ever to be reminded to repay.

A woman who has " petites faiblesses " is usually impatient with one who has none; the one who has none is a kind of standing insolence. Women corrupt more women than men do. Lovelace does not hate chastity in women; but Lady Bellaston does with all her might.

Pretty Madame Mila was too good-natured and also too shallow to hate anything; but if she could have seen her cousin "compromised" she would have derived an exquisite satisfaction and entertainment from the sight. She would also have felt that Lady Hilda would have become thereby more natural, and more comfortable company.

"Dear me, she might have done anything she had liked all these years," thought Madame Mila; "nobody would have known anything—and nothing would hurt her if it were known, whilst she has all that money."

For Madame Mila herself, perched on one of the very topmost rungs of the ladder of the world's greatness, and able therefore to take a bird's-eye view therefrom of everything, was very shrewd in her way, and knew that society never was known yet to quarrel with the owner of fifty thousand a-year.

So she carried her airy little person, laden this night with gold embroideries on dull Venetian red, until she looked like a little figure made in Lac, over to the *écarté* table when the *écarté* was finished, and arranged a morning at Palestrina for the day after to-morrow. He

H

could only express his happiness and honour,
and his regrets that Palestrina was little more
than an empty shell for their inspection.

The day after the morrow was clear and cloud-
less, balmy and delicious; such days as the
Floralian climate casts here and there generously
amidst the winter cold as a foretaste of its paradise of summer. The snow was on the more
distant mountains of course, but only made the
landscape more lovely, changing to the softest
blush colour and rose under the brightness of
the noonday sun. The fields were green with
the springing cereals; the pine-woods were filling
with violets; the water-courses were brimming
and boisterously joyous.

It was winter still; but the sort of winter
that one would expect in Fairyland or in the
planet Venus.

Madame Mila, clad in the strictest *directoire*
costume, with a wonderful hat on her head that
carried feathers, grasses, oleander flowers, and a
bird of Dutch Guiana, and was twisted up on one
side in a miraculous manner, descended with
her Maurice to the Lady Hilda's victoria, lent

her for the day. To drive into the country at all was an act abominable and appalling to all her ideas.

In Paris, except on race days, she never went further than the lake, and never showed her toilettes in the Assembly at Versailles, because of the endless drive necessary as a means to get there.

In country houses she carefully kept her own room till about five o'clock; and, when forced for her health to go to Vichy or St. Moritz, or any such place, she played cards in the mornings, and when she was obliged to go out, looked at the other invalids' dresses. Mountains were only unpleasant things to be tunnelled; forests were tolerable, because one could wear such pretty Louis Quinze hunting-habits and the *curée* by torchlight was nice; the sea again was made endurable by bathing costumes, and it was fun to go and tuck up your things and hunt for prawns or pearls in the rock-pools and shallows— it gave rise to many very pretty situations. But merely to drive into the country!—it was only fit occupation for a maniac. Though she had proposed it herself, the patient Maurice had a very *mauvais quart-d'heure* as they drove.

The Lady Hilda, who was too truly great an *élégante* ever to condescend in the open air to the eccentricities and *bizarreries* of Madame Mila—mountebankisms worthy a travelling show, she considered them to be—was clad in her black sables, which contrasted so well with the fairness of her skin, and drove out with the Princess Olga ; Carlo Maremma and M. de St. Louis fronting them in the Schouvaloff barouche. She did not hate the cold, and shiver from the fresh sea-wind, and worry about the badness of the steep roads as Madame Mila did ; on the contrary, she liked the drive, long though it was, and felt a vague interest in the first sight of Palestrina, its towers and belfries shining white on the mountain side, with the little villages clustered under its broad dark ring of forest.

"What a pity that Paolo is so poor !" said Carlo Maremma, looking upward at it.

" He carries his poverty with infinite grace," said the Princess Olga.

" He is worthy of riches," said the Duc.

Lady Hilda said nothing.

Palestrina was twelve miles and more from the city, and stood on the high hills facing the south-west; it was half fortress, half palace; in early times its lords had ruled from its height all the country round; and later on, in the latter half of the fifteenth century, a great Cardinal of the Della Rocca had made it into as sumptuous a dwelling-place as Caprarola or Poggio a Cajano.

Subsequently the family had ranged itself against the ruling faction of the province, and had suffered from war and confiscation; still later, Palestrina had been plundered by the French troops of Napoleon; yet, despoiled and impoverished as it was, it was majestic still, and even beautiful; for, unlike most such places, it had kept its girdle of oak and ilex woods; and its gardens, though wild and neglected, were unshorn of their fair proportions; and the fountains fell into their marble basins, and splashed the maiden-hair ferns that hung over them as they had done in another age for the delight of the great Cardinal and his favourites.

Della Rocca received them in the southern

loggia, a beautiful vaulted and frescoed open gal-
lery, designed by Bramante, and warm in the
noonday sun, as though January were June.

A king could not have had more grace of
welcome and dignity of courtesy than this ruined
gentleman—he had a very perfect manner, certainly, thought Lady Hilda once again. She was
one of those women (they are many) upon whom
manner makes more impression than mind or
morals. Why should it not? It is the charm
of life and the touchstone of breeding.

There was only one friend with him, a great
minister, who had retired from the world and
given himself up to the culture of roses and
strawberries. There was a simple repast, from
the produce of his own lands, ready in what had
been once the banqueting hall. It was made
graceful by the old Venetian glass, the old
Urbino plates, the old Cellini salt-cellars; and
by grapes, regina and salamana, saved from the
autumn, and bouquets of Parma violets and
Bengal roses, in old blue Savona vases. It
was a frugal meal, but fit for the Tale-tellers of
the Decameron.

They rambled over the great building first, with its vast windows showing the wide land-scape of mountain and plain, and far away the golden domes and airy spires of the city shining through a soft mist of olive trees. The glory of this house was gone, but it was beautiful still with the sweet clear sunlight streaming through its innumerable chambers, and touching the soft hues of frescoed walls that had grown faded with age, but had been painted by Spinello, by Francia, by the great Frate, and by a host whose names were lost, of earnest workers, and men with whom art had been religion.

It was all dim and worn and grey with the passage of time; but it was harmonious, ma-jestic, tranquil. It was like the close of a great life withdrawn from the world into a cloistered solitude and content to be alone with its God.

"Do not wish for riches," said the Lady Hilda to him, as he said something to her of it. "If you had riches you would desecrate this; you would 'restore' it, you would 'embellish' it, you would ruin it."

He smiled a little sadly.

"As it is, I can only keep the rains from entering and the rats from destroying it. Poverty, Madame, is only poetical to those who do not suffer it. Look!" he added, with a laugh, "you will not find a single chair, I fear, that is not in tatters."

She glanced at the great old ebony chair she was resting in, with its rich frayed tapestry seat, and its carved armorial bearings.

" I have suffered much more from the staring, gilded, and satin abominations in a millionaire's drawing-room. You are ungrateful——"

" And you, Madame, judge of pains that have never touched, and cannot touch you. However, I can be but too glad that Palestrina pleases you in any way. It has the sunshine of heaven, though not of fortune."

"And I am sure you would not give it up for all the wealth of the Rothschilds."

" No."

" How lovely this place would look," Madame Mila was saying at the same moment, out of his hearing, to the Princess Olga, "if Owen Jones could renovate it and Huby furnish it. Fancy

it with all the gilding re-gilded, and the pictures
restored, and Aubusson and Persian carpets
everywhere, and all those horrid old tapestries,
that must be full of spiders, pulled down and
burnt. What a heavenly place it would be—and
what balls one might give in it! Why, it would
hold ten thousand people!"

"Poor Paolo will never be able to do it," said
the Princess Schouvaloff, "unless——"

She glanced at the Lady Hilda where she sat,
at the further end of the chamber, whilst Della
Rocca leaned against the embrasure of the
window.

"I think she has a fancy for him," said
Madam Mila. "But as for marrying, you know,
—that, of course, is out of the question."

"I don't see why," said the Princess.

"Oh, out of the question;" said Madame Mila,
hastily. "But if she should take a liking to him,
it would be great fun. She's been so awfully
exaltée about all that sort of thing. Dear me,
what a pity all those nasty, old, dull frescoes
can't be scraped off and something nice and
bright, like what they paint now, be put there;

but I suppose it would take so much money. I should hang silk over them; all these clouds of pale angels would make me melancholy mad. There is no style I care a bit for but Louis Quinze. I am having new wall hangings for my *salon* done by the Ste. Marie Réparatrice girls; a lovely green satin—apple-green—embroidered with wreaths of roses and broom, after flower-groups by Fantin. Louis Quinze is so cheerful, and lets you have such lots of gilding, and the tables have such nice straight legs, and you always feel with it as if you were in a theatre and expecting the *Jeune Prémier* to enter. Here one feels as if one were in a church."

" A monastery," suggested Princess Olga.

Thereon they went and had their luncheon, and Madame Mila studying the Capo da Monte dessert-service, appraised its value—for she was a shrewd little woman—and wondered, if Paolo della Rocca were so poor as they said, why did he not send up all these old porcelains and lovely potteries to the Hôtel Drouot: Capo da Monte, she reflected, sells for more than its weight in gold, now that it is the rage of the fashion. She felt inclined to suggest this to him, only she was not quite sure how he might take it. Italians, she had heard, were so absurdly proud and susceptible.

After luncheon, they went into the green old gardens; green with ilex and arbutus and laurel and cypress avenues, although it was mid-winter; and the great minister discoursed on the charms of the country and the beauty of solitude in a way that should almost have awakened the envy of Horace in his grave; and the Duc de St. Louis disagreed with him in witty arguments that might have made the shades of Rochefoucauld and Rivarol jealous.

And they rambled and idled and talked and sauntered in those charming hours which an Italian villa alone can create; and then the Ave Maria chimed from the belfries of a convent up above on the hill, and the winds grew chill, and the carriages were called round to the steps of the southern terrace, and the old steward brought to each lady the parting gift of a great cluster of the sweet Parma violets.

" Well, it's been pleasanter than I thought

for," said Madame Mila, rolling homeward.
" But oh, this wretched, odious road ! I shall
catch my death of cold, and I daresay we shall
all be killed on these horrible hills in the dark !"

Lady Hilda was very silent as they drove
downward, and left Palestrina alone to grow grey
in the shades of the twilight.

CHAPTER VI.

" I THINK Italians are like Russian tea; they
spoil you for any other——" wrote Lady Hilda
to her brother Clairvaux.   It was not a very clear
phrase, nor very grammatical; but she knew
what she meant herself, which is more than all
writers can say they do.

Russian tea, or rather tea imported through
Russia, is so much softer and of so much sweeter
and subtler a flavour, that once drinking it you
will find all other tea after it seem flat or coarse.
When she had written this sentiment, however,
she tore up the sheet of note paper which
contained it, and tossed it in the fire; after all,
Clairvaux would not understand—he never un-

derstood anything, dear old fellow—and he would
be very likely to say all sorts of foolish things
while there was not the slightest reason for any
one's supposing.

"Do come out here as soon as you can," she
wrote instead. "Of course it will all depend on
your racing engagements; but if you do go to
Paris to see Charles Lafitte, as you say, pray
come on here. Not that you will care for
Floralia at all; you never do care for these art
cities, and it is its art, and its past, and its people
that make its irresistible charm. Floralia is
so graceful and so beautiful and so full of noble
memories, that one cannot but feel the motley
society of our own present day as a sort of desecration to it; the cocottes and cocodettes, the
wheel-skaters and poker-players, the smokers and
the baigneuses, the viveurs and the viveuses of
our time suit it sadly ill; it wants the scholars
of Academe, the story-tellers of Boccaccio; it
wants Sordello and Stradella, Desdemona and
Giulietta.

"One feels oneself not one half good enough
for the stones one treads upon; life here

should be a perpetual Kyrie Eleison ; instead of
which it is only a chorus of Offenbach's. Not
that society anywhere, now, ever does rise higher
than that; only here it jars on one more than
elsewhere, and seems as profane as if one 'played
ball with Homer's skull.'

"Floralia is a golden Ostensoir filled with
great men's bones, and we choke it up with cigar
ashes and champagne dregs. It cannot be
helped, I suppose. The destiny of the age
seems to be to profane all that have preceded it.
It creates nothing — it desecrates everything.
Society does not escape from the general influence; its kings are all kings of Brentford.

"Mila—who is here and happy as a bird—
thinks Jack Cade and the Offenbach chorus the
perfection of delight at all times.

"For myself, I confess, neither entertain me;
I fail to see the charm of a drawing-room democracy *décolleté* and *décousu ;* and I never did
appreciate ladies who pass their lives in balanc-
ing themselves awkwardly on the bar of Dumas's
famous Triangle ; but that may be a prejudice—
Mila says that it is.

" By-the-by, that odious young Des Gommeux
has followed her here—I make myself disagreeable to him.   I cannot do more.   Spiridion
has never interfered, and ' on ne peut pas être
plus royaliste que le roi.'   But you will skip
all this, or give it to your wife.   I know I
never read letters myself, so why should I
expect you to do so ?   I am so sorry to
hear of Vieille Garde's sprain ; it is too vex-
ing for you, just as he was so high in
the betting.   I hope Sister to Simonides turns
out worth all we gave for her.   There will be
racing here in April, but it would only make you
laugh—which would be rude ; or swear—which
would be worse.   So please come long before it."

She folded up her letter, wrote " Pray try and
come soon " across the top of it, and directed the
envelope to the Earl of Clairvaux, Broomsden,
Northampton, and then was provoked to think
that she did not want good, clumsy, honest
Clairvaux to come at all—not in her heart of
hearts, because Clairvaux was always asking questions, and going straight to the bottom of things
in his own simple, sturdy fashion, and never

understood anything that was in the very least complex.

And then again she was more irritated still with herself, for admitting even to her own thoughts that there was anything complex, or that she did not want to examine too closely— just yet. And then she sat and looked into the fire, and thought of Palestrina, with its sweet faint scent of Parma violets, and its dim noble frescoes, and its mountain solitudes, under the clear winter moon.

She sat dreaming about it a long time—for her, because she was not a person that dreamed at all usually. Her life was too brilliant, and too much occupied, and too artificial. She was thinking, with a great deal of money, without desecrating it by "restoration;" but by bringing all the art knowledge in the world to its enrichment, it would be possible to make it as great as it had been in the days of its cardinal. What a pastime it would be, what an interest, what an occupation almost for a lifetime to render that grand old palace once more the world's wonder it had been in the sixteenth century!

I

Then she rose suddenly with an impatient sigh, and went into her bedroom, and found fault with her maids : they had put Valenciennes on her petticoats, and she hated Valenciennes—no other lace had been so cheapened by imitation ; they had put out her marron velvet with the ostrich feathers for that day's wearing, when they should have laid out the silver-grey cloth with the Genoa buttons ; they were giving her glacé gloves instead of peau de Suède ; they had got out Pompadour boots, and she required Paysanne shoes ; it was a fine dry day. In point of fact, everything was wrong, and they were idiots, and she told them so as strongly as a high-bred lady can demean herself to speak. Each costume was put all together—dress, bonnet, boots, gloves—everything ; what business had they to go and mix them all up and make everything wrong ?

Her maids were used to her displeasure ; but she was very generous, and if they were ill or in sorrow she was kind, so that they bore it meekly, and contented themselves with complaining of her in all directions to their allies.

" If she would only have her petites affaires like other ladies she would be much easier to content," said her head maid, who had served the aristocracy ever since the earliest days of the Second Empire.

When there were no lovers, there were much fewer douceurs and perquisites; however, they endured that deprivation because Miladi was so very rich, and so easily plundered.

Miladi, now, arrayed in the silver-grey cloth with the Genoa buttons and the marabout feather trimming, went out to her victoria, en route to the galleries, of which she never tired, and the visits which immeasurably bored her. She had been in the great world for ten years, and the great world is too small to divert one for very long, unless one be as Madame Mila.

Nevertheless, the Lady Hilda found that Floralia interested her more than she would have believed that anything would do.

After all, Floralia was charming by the present, not only by the past.

If it had its kings of Brentford, with its Offenbach choruses, so had every other place; if it had a pot pourri of nationalties, it had some of the most agreeable persons of every nation; if trying to be very naughty it generally only became very dull—that was the doom of mcdern society everywhere.

There were charming houses in it, where there were real wit, real music, and real welcome. If people saw each other too often, strong friend-chips could come out of such frequency as well as animosities; and there was a great charm in the familiar, easy, pleasant intimacies which so naturally grew out of the artistic idling under these sombre and noble walls, and in the palaces where all the arts once reigned.

She had begun to take the fair city into her heart, as everyone who has a heart must needs do, having once dwelt within the olive girdle of its pure pale hills, and seen its green waters wash the banks erst peopled with the gorgeous splen-dours of the Renaissance.

She even began to like her daily life in it; the mornings dreamed away before some favourite Giorgione or Veronese, or spent in dim old shops full of the oddest mingling of rubbish and of

treasure; the twilights spent in picture-like old
chambers, where dames of high degree had made
their winter-quarters, fragrant with flowers and
quaint with old tapestries and porcelains; the
evenings passed in a society which, too motley to
be intimate, yet too personal to dare be witty,
was gradually made more than endurable to her,
by the sound of one voice for which she listened
more often than she knew, by the sight of one
face which grew more necessary to her than she
was aware.

" If one could be only quite alone here it would
be too charming," she thought, driving this morning, while the sun shone on the golden reaches
of the river, and the softly-coloured marbles
caught the light, and the picturesque old shops
gleamed many-hued as harlequin under the beet-
ling brows of projecting roofs, and the carved stone
of dark archways.

But if she had looked close into her own heart
she would have seen that the solitude of her
ideal would have been one like the French poet's
—solitude *à deux.*

She did not go, after all, to her visits; she went

instead, in and out of the studios whose artists adored her, though she was terribly hard to please, and had much more acquaintance with art than is desirable in a purchaser.

In one of the studios she chanced to meet the master of Palestrina; and he went with her to another atelier, and another and another.

She had her Paysanne shoes on, and her gold-headed cane, and let her victoria stand still while she walked from one to the other of those sculptors' and painters' dens, which lie so close together, like beavers' work in the old grey quarters of the city.

Up and down the dark staircases, and in and out the gloomy vaulted passages, her silver-grey cloth with the marabout ruches gleamed and glistened, and to many of the artists proved as beneficent as a silvery cloud to the thirsty fields in summer.

She was surprised to find how much she liked it. There was not much genius, and there was a great deal of bad drawing, and worse modelling, and she had educated herself in the very strictest and coldest canons of art, and really cared for nothing later than Luca Signorelli, and abhorred Canova and everything that has come after him.

But there were some little figures in marble of young children that she could conscientiously buy; and the little Meissonier and Fortuny-like pictures were clever, if they were mere trick-work and told no story; and the modern oak carvings were really good; and on the whole she enjoyed her morning unusually; and her companion looked pleased, because she found things to praise.

As she walked, with Della Rocca beside her, in and out the dusky passage ways, with the obnoxious Valenciennes under her skirts sweeping the stones, and her silvery marabouts glancing like hoar-frost in the shadows of the looming walls, the Lady Hilda felt very happy, and on good terms with herself and the world. No doubt, she thought, it was the fresh west wind blowing up the river from the sea which had done her so much good.

The golden Ostensoir, to which she had likened Floralia, no longer seemed filled with cigar-ash and absinthe dregs; but full of the fragrant rose-leaves of an imperishable Past, and the shining sands of a sweet unspent Time.

She made a poor sculptor happy for a year ; she freed a young and promising painter from a heavy debt ; she was often impatient with their productions, but she was most patient with their troubles.

She was only a woman of the world, touched for a day into warmer sympathies, but the blessings she drew down on her sank somehow into her heart, and made her haif ashamed, half glad.

What was the use of writing fine contemptuous things of society unless one tried to drop oneself some little holy relic into the golden Ostensoir ? She went home contented, and was so gentle with her maids that they thought she must be going to be unwell.

Her friend the Princess Olga came to chat with her, and they had their tea cosily in her dressing-room ; and at eight o'clock she went to dine with Mrs. Washington, an American Paris ienne or Parisian American, known wherever the world of fashion extended, and was taken into dinner by the Duca della Rocca.

After dinner there was a new tenor, who was less of a delusion than most new tenors are; and there was a great deal of very æsthetic and abstruse talk about music; she said little herself, but sat and listened to Della Rocca, who spoke often and eloquently, with infinite grace and accurate culture. To a woman who has cared for no one all her life, there is the strangest and sweetest pleasure in finding at last one voice whose mere sound is melody to her.

On the whole she went to bed still with that dreamful content which had come on her in the day —no doubt with the fresh sea wind. She knew that she had looked at her best in a dress of pale dead gold, with old black Spanish lace; and she had only one regret—that in too soft a mood she had allowed an English person, a Lady Featherleigh, of whom she did not approve, to be presented to her.

She was habitually the one desire and the one despair of all her countrywomen.

Except so far as her physical courage, her skill in riding, and her beautiful complexion, which no cold could redden, and no heat could change,

might be counted as national characteristics, the
Lady Hilda was a very un-English Englishwoman
in everything.

Indeed your true *élégante* is raised high above
all such small things as nationalities; she floats
serenely in an atmosphere far too elevated to be
coloured by country; a neutral ground on which
the leaders of every civilized land meet far away
from all ordinary mortality.

In Floralia she found a few such choice spirits
accustomed to breathe the same æther as herself, and with those she lived, carefully avoiding
the Penal Settlement as she continued to call the
cosmopolitan society which was outside the zone
of her own supreme fashion.

She saw it, indeed, in ball-rooms and morning
receptions; it sighed humbly after her, pined for
her notice, and would have been happy if she
would but even have recompensed it by an insolence, but she merely ignored its existence, and
always looked over its head innocently and cruelly
with that divine serenity of indifference and disdain with which Nature had so liberally endowed
her.

" Why should I know them ? They wouldn't please me," she would say to those who ventured to remonstrate, and the answer was unanswerable.

"I can't think how you manage, Hilda, to keep so clear of people," said Madame Mila, enviously. " Now, *I* get inundated with hosts of the horridest——"

" Because you cheapen yourself," said Lady Hilda, very coolly.

" I never could keep people off me," pursued the Comtesse. " When Spiridion had the Embassy in London, it was just the same ; I was inundated ! It's good nature, I suppose. Certainly, you haven't got too much of *that*."

Lady Hilda smiled ; she thought of those six or eight thousands which had gone for Madame Mila's losses at play.

" Good nature is a very indifferent sort of quality," she answered. " It is compounded of weakness, laziness, and vulgarity. Generally speaking, it is only a desire for popularity, and there is nothing more vulgar than *that*."

" I don't see that it is vulgar at all," said

Madame Mila, with some sharpness. "I like
to think I am popular; to see a mob look after
me; to have the shop-boys rush out to get a
glimpse of me; to hear the crowd on a race-day
call out ' ain't she a rare 'un ! my eye, ain't she
fit ! ' just as if I were one of the mares. I
often give a crossing-sweeper a shilling in London, just to make him ' bless my pretty eyes.'
Why, even when I go to that beastly place of
Spiridion's in Russia, I make the hideous serfs in
love with me ; it puts one on good terms with
oneself. I often think when the people in the
streets don't turn after me as I go—then I *shall*
know that I'm old ! "

Lady Hilda's eyebrows expressed unutterable
contempt ; these were sentiments to her entirely
incomprehensible.

" How very agreeable—to make the streets the
barometer of one's looks—' fair or foul.' So you
live in apprehension of a railway porter's indifference, and only approve of yourself if a racing
tout smiles ! My dear Mila, I never did believe
you would have gone lower in the scale of human
adorers than your Gommeux and Poisseux."

"At all events I am not so vain as you are,
Hilda," retorted the Comtesse. "*You* approve of
yourself eternally, whether all the world hates
you or not. I remember Charlie Barrington saying of you once—'I wonder why that woman
keeps straight—why should she? She don't care
a hang what anybody says of her.'"

' How discerning of Lord Barrington! If
people only 'keep straight' for the sake of what
other people say of them, I think they may just
as well 'go off the rails' in any manner they like.
Certainly, what I chose to do, I should do, without reference to the approbation of the mob—
either of the streets or of the drawing-rooms."

"Exactly what Barrington said," returned
Madame Mila; "but then why do you—I mean,
why don't you—amuse yourself?"

The Lady Hilda laughed.

"My dear! the Gommeux and the Poisseux
would not amuse me. I am not so happily constituted as you are."

Madame Mila coloured.

"That's all very fine talk, but you know it
isn't natural——"

" To live decently ?—no, I suppose it is not now-a-days. Perhaps it never was. But, my dear Mila, you needn't be too disquieted about me. If it make you any more comfortable as to my sanity, I can assure you it is not virtue ; no one knows such a word ; it is only indifference."

" You are very queer, Hilda," said Madame Mila, impatiently ; " all I know is, I should like to see you in love, and see what you'd say *then.*"

The Lady Hilda, who was never more moved by her feather-headed cousin's words than a rock by a butterfly, felt a sudden warmth on her face —perhaps of anger.

" In love ! " she echoed, with less languor and more of impetuosity than she had ever displayed, " are you ever in love, any of you, ever ? You have senses and vanity and an inordinate fear of not being in the fashion—and so you take your lovers as you drink your stimulants and wear your wigs and tie your skirts back—because everybody else does it, and not to do it is to be odd, or prudish, or something you would hate to be called. Love ! it is an unknown thing to you all.

You have a sort of miserable hectic passion, perhaps, that is a drug you take as you take chlorodyne—just to excite you and make your jaded
nerves a little alive again, and yet you are such
cowards that you have not even the courage of
passion, but label your drug Friendship, and beg
Society to observe that you only keep it for
family uses like arnica or like glycerine. You want
notoriety; you want to indulge your fancies, and
yet keep your place in the world. You like to
drag a young man about by a chain, as if he were
the dancing monkey that you depended upon for
subsistence. You like other women to see that you
are not too *passée* to be every whit as improper
as if you were twenty. You like to advertise
your successes as it were with drum and trumpet,
because if you did not, people might begin to
doubt that you had any. You like all that, and
you like to feel there is nothing you do not know
and no length you have not gone, and so you
ring all the changes on all the varieties of
intrigue and sensuality, and go over the gamut
of sickly sentiment and nauseous license as an
orchestra tunes its strings up every night! That

is what all you people call love; I am content enough to have no knowledge of it——"

"Good gracious, Hilda!" said Madame Mila, with wide-open eyes of absolute amazement; "you talk as if you were one of the angry husbands in a comedy of Feuillet or Dumas. I don't think you know anything about it at all; how should you? You only admire yourself, and like art and all that kind of thing, and are as cold as ice to everybody. 'À la place du cœur, vous n'avez qu'un caillou;' I've read that somewhere."

"'Elle n'a qu'un écusson,'" corrected Lady Hilda, her serenity returning. "If Hugo had known much about women he would have said— 'qu'un chiffon;' but perhaps a dissyllable wouldn't have scanned——"

"You never will convince me," continued Madame de Caviare, "that you would not be a happier woman if you had what you call senses and the rest of it. One can't live without sensations and emotions of some sort. You never feel any except before a bit of Kronenthal china or a triptych of some old fogey of a painter. You do care awfully about your horses to be sure. but then as

you don't bet on anything, I don't see what excitement you can get out of them. You won't
play—which is the best thing to take to of all,
because it will last; the older they grow, the
wilder women get about it; look at Spiridion's
aunt Seraphine—over eighty—as keen as a
ferret over her winnings, and as fierce as a
tom-cat over her losses. Now, that is a thing
that can't hurt any one, let you say what you
like; everybody plays, why won't you? If you
lost half your income in one night, it wouldn't
ruin you, and you have no idea how delicious it
is to get dizzy over the cards; you know one bets
even at poker to any amount——"

"Thanks; it won't tempt me," answered Lady
Hilda. "I have played at Baden, to see if it
would amuse me, and it didn't amuse me in the
least; no more than M. des Gommeux does!
My dearest Mila, I am sure that you people who
do excite yourselves over baccarat and poker, and
can feel really flattered at having a Maurice always
in attendance, and can divert yourselves with
oyster suppers and masked balls and cotillon
riots, are the happy women of this world, that I

K

quite grant you : oysters and Maurices and cotillon and poker are so very easy to be got——"

"And men like women who like them!"

"That I grant too; poker and cotillons
don't exact any very fine manners, and men
nowadays always like to be, metaphorically, in
their smoking-coats.   Only you see we are not
always all constituted of the same fortunate disposition ; poker and cotillons only bore me.
You should think it my misfortune not my fault.
I am sure it must be charming to drink a quantity of champagne, and whirl round like a South-
sea islander, and play pranks that pass in a
palace though the police would interfere in a
dancing garden, and be found by the sun drinking soup at a supper-table : I am sure it must be
quite delightful.   Only you see it doesn't amuse
me ;—no more than scrambling amongst a pack
of cards flung on their faces, which you say is
delightful too; or keeping a Maurice in your
pocket, like your cigar-case and your handker-
chief, which you say is most delightful of all.
But good bye, my dear, we shall quarrel if we
talk much longer like this; and we must not

quarrel till to-morrow morning, because your Dissimulée dress will look nothing without my Austraisienne one. What time shall I call for you? Make it as late as you can. I shall only just show myself."

"Three o'clock, then—that is quite early enough," muttered Madame Mila, somewhat sulkily; but she had teazed and prayed her cousin into accompanying her in Louis Seize costumes, most carefully compiled by Worth from engravings and pictures of the period, to the Trasimene costume ball, and would not fall out with her just on the eve of it, because she knew their entrance would be *the* effect of the night, accompanied as they would be by the Duc de St. Louis and M. des Gommeux as Grand Ecuyer de France, and as Petit Maître en chenille, of the same century.

"Say half-past," answered the Lady Hilda, as she closed the door and went into her own rooms on the opposite side of the staircase.

"I really begin to think she is jealous of Maurice and in love with him!" thought Madame Mila, in whose eyes Maurice was irresistible,

though with the peculiar optimism of ladies in
her position she was perfectly certain that he
was adamant also to all save herself. And the
idea of her fastidious cousin's hopeless passion
so tickled her fancy that she laughed herself into
a good humour as her maids disrobed her; and
she curled herself up in her bed to get a good
night's sleep out before donning the Dissimulée
costume for the Trasimene ball, so that she
should go at half-past three " as fresh as paint,"
in the most literal sense of the word, to all the
joyous rioting of the cotillon which Maurice was
to lead.

"You shine upon us late, Madame," said
Della Rocca, advancing to meet the Lady Hilda,
when they reached, at four o'clock in the morning, the vast and lofty rooms glittering with fancy
dresses.

"I only came at all to please Mila, and she
only comes for the cotillon," she answered him,
and she thought how well he looked as she
glanced at him. He wore a white Louis Treize
Mousquetaire dress, and he had the collar of the
Golden Fleece about his throat, for, amongst his

many useless titles, and barren dignities, he was, like many an Italian noble, also a grandee of Spain.

"You do not dance, Madame?" he asked.

"Very seldom," she answered, as she accepted his arm to move through the rooms. "When mediæval dresses came in, dancing should have been banished. Who could dance well in a long close clinging robe tightly tied back, and heavy with gold thread and bullion fringes; they should revive the minuet; we might go through that without being ridiculous. But if they *will* have the cotillon instead, they should dress like the girls in Offenbach's pieces, as many of them happen to be to-night. I do not object to a mixture of epochs in furniture, but romping in a rénaissance skirt!—that is really almost blasphemy enough to raise the ghost of Titian!"

"I am afraid Madama Pampinet and the Fiammina must have romped sometimes," said Della Rocca with a smile. "But then you will say the Decadence had already cast its shadow before it."

" Yes ; but there never was an age so vulgar as
our own," said the Lady Hilda. " That I am
positive of ;—look, even peasants are vulgar now :
they wear tall hats and tawdry bonnets on
Sundays ; and, as for our society, it is ' rowdy :'
there is no other word for it, if you understand
what that means."

" Canaille ? "

" Yes, Canaille. M. de St. Louis says, the
' femme comme il faut ' of his youth is extinct
as the dodo : language is slang, society is a
mob, dress is display, amusement is riot, people
are let into society who have no other claim to
be there but money and impudence, and are as
ignorant as our maids and our grooms, and more
so. It is all as bad as it can be, and I suppose
it will only go on getting worse. You Italians
are the only people with whom manner is not a
lost art."

" You do us much honour. Perhaps we too
shall be infected before long. We are sending our
lads to public schools in your country : they will
probably come back unable to bow, ashamed of
natural grace, and ambitious to emulate the

groom model in everything. This is thought an advanced education."

Lady Hilda laughed.

"The rich Egyptians go to English universities, and take back to the Nile a passion for rat-hunting and brandy, and the most hideous hats and coats in the universe; and then think they have improved on the age of the Pharaohs. I hope Italy will never be infected, but I am afraid; you have gasworks, tramways, and mixed marriages, and your populace has almost entirely abandoned costume."

"And in the cities we have lost the instinct of good taste in the most fatal manner. Perhaps it has died out with the old costumes. Who knows? Dress is after all the thermometer of taste. Modern male attire is of all others the most frightful, the most grotesque, the most gloomy, and, to our climate, the most unsuitable."

"Yes. Tall hats and tail coats appear to me to be like the locusts, wherever they spread they bear barrenness in their train. But the temper of your people will always procure to you some natural grace, some natural elegance."

" Let us hope so; but in all public works our
taste already is gone. One may say, without
vanity, that in full sense of beauty and of proportion, Italy surpassed of old all the world:
how is it, I often ask myself, that we have lost
so much of this ? Here in Floralia, if we
require gas-works we erect their chimneys
on the very bank of our river, ruining one
of the loveliest views in the world, and one
that has been a tradition of beauty for ages.
If it be deemed necessary to break down and
widen our picturesque old bridges, we render
them hideous as any railway road, by hedging
them with frightful monotonous parapets of cast-
iron, the heaviest, most soulless, most hateful
thing that is manufactured. Do we make a fine
hill-drive, costing us enormously, when we have
no money to pay for it, we make one, indeed, as
fine as any in Europe ; and having made it, then
we ruin it by planting at every step cafés, and
guinguettes, and guard houses, and every artificial
abomination and vulgarity in stucco and brick-
work that can render its noble scenery ridiculous.
Do we deem it advisable, for sanitary or other

purposes, to turn the people out of the ancient
market where they keep their stalls under the
old palace walls happily enough, summer and
winter, like so many Dutch pictures, we build
a cage of iron and glass like an enormous cu-
cumber frame, inexpressibly hideous, and equally
incommodious, and only adapted to grill the
people in June and turn them to ice in January.
What is the reason? We have liberal givers
such as your countryman Sloane, such as my countryman Galliera, yet what single modern thing
worth producing can we show? We have destroyed
much that will be as irreparable a loss to future
generations as the art destroyed in the great
siege is to us. But we have produced nothing
save deformity. Perhaps, indeed, we might not
have any second Michael Angelo to answer if we
called on him; but it is certain that we must
have architects capable of devising something in
carven stone to edge a bridge ; we must have
artists who, were they consulted, would say, ' do
not insult a sublime panorama of the most poetic
and celebrated valley in the world by putting into
the foreground a square guards' box, a stucco

drinking-house, and the gilded lamps of a dancing-garden.' We must have men capable of so much as that—yet they are either never employed or never listened to; the truth I fear is that a public work now-a-days with us is like a plant being carried to be planted in a city square, of which every one who passes it plucks off a leaf: by the time it reaches its destination the plant is leafless. The public work is the plant, and the money to be got from it is the foliage; provided each one plucks as much foliage as he can, no one cares in what state the plant reaches the piazza."

Lady Hilda looked at him as he spoke with an eloquence and earnestness which absorbed him for the moment, so that he forgot that he was talking to a woman, and a woman whose whole life was one of trifling, of languor, and of extravagance.

"All that is very true," she said, with some hesitation; "but why then do you hold yourself aloof—why do you do nothing to change this state of public things? You see the evil, but you prescribe no remedy."

" The only remedy will be Time," he answered
her. " Corruption has eaten too deeply into the
heart of this nation to be easily eradicated. The
knife of war has not cut it out; we can only
hope for what the medicines of education and of
open discussion may do; the greatest danger lies
in the inertia of the people; they are angry often,
but they do not move——"

" Neither do you move, though you are angry."

He smiled a little sadly.

" If I were a rich man I would do so. Poor as
I am I could not embrace public life without seeming to seek my own private ends from office. A
man without wealth has no influence, and his
motives will always be suspected—at least here."

" But one should be above suspicion——"

" Were one certain to do good—yes."

" But why should you despair? You have a
country of boundless resources, a people affectionate, impressionable, infinitely engaging, and
much more intelligent naturally than any other
populace, a soil that scarce needs touching
to yield the richest abundance, and in nearly
every small town or obscure city some legacy

of art or architecture, such as no other land can show——"

"Despair! God forbid that I should despair. I think there is infinite hope, but I cannot disguise from myself that there are infinite dangers also. An uneducated peasantry has had its religion torn away from it, and has no other moral landmark set to cling to; old ways and old venerations are kicked aside and nothing substituted; public business means almost universally public pillage; the new text placed before the regenerated nation is, 'make money, honestly if you can—but make money!' haste, avarice, accumulation, cunning, neglect of all loveliness, desecration of all ancientness—these, the modern curses which accompany 'progress'—are set before a scarcely awakened people as the proper objects and idols of their efforts. We, who are chiefly to be moved by our affections and our imaginations, are only bidden to be henceforth inspired by a joyless prosperity and a loveless materialism. We, the heirs of the godhead of the Arts, are only counselled to emulate the mechanical inventions and the unscrupulous commerce of the American

genius, and are ordered to learn to blush with
shame because our ancient cities, sacred with the
ashes of heroes, are not spurious brand-new lath
and plaster human ant-hills of the growth of yesterday! —— Forgive me, Madame," he said, inter-
rupting himself, with a little laugh, " I forget that
I am tedious to you.   With the taxes at fifty-two
per cent., a poor landowner like myself may incline
to think that all is not as well as it should be."

" You interest me," said the Lady Hilda, and
her eyes dwelt on him with a grave, musing
regard that they had given to no man, "and on
your own lands, with your own people—how is it
there ? "

His face brightened.

" My people love me," he said, softly. " As
for the lands—when one is poor, one cannot
do much ; but every one is content on them—
that is something."

" Is it not everything ? " said the Lady Hilda,
with a little sigh ; for she herself, who could
gratify her every wish, had never yet quite known
what content could mean.   " Let us go and look
at the ball-room ; Mila will be coming to know

if we have heard of MacMahon's death, that we talk so seriously."

She walked, on his arm, to the scene of tumult, where being hemmed in by lookers-on till the pressure left them scarcely any space to perform upon, the dancers were going through a quadrille with exceeding vivacity, and with strong reminiscences in it of some steps of the cancan ; Madame Mila and Lady Featherleigh particularly distinguishing themselves by their imitations of the Chimpanzee dance, as performed in the last winter's operetta of Ching-aring-aring-ching.

They were of course being watched and applauded very loudly by the ring of spectators as if they were really the actors in the Ching-aring-aring-ching, which afforded them the liveliest pleasure possible, great ladies being never so happy now-a-days as when they are quite sure that they might really be taken for comedians or courtezans.

It was hard upon Madame Mila that just as she had jumped so high that La Petite Boulotte herself could scarcely have jumped higher, the lookers-on turned their heads to see the Lady

Hilda in the doorway on the arm of her white Mousquetaire. Lady Hilda was beyond all dispute the most beautiful woman of the rooms, she threw them all into the shade as a rose diamond throws stars of strass ; and many of the men were so dazzled by her appearance there, that they actually lost the sight of Madame Mila's rose-coloured stockings twinkling in the air.

"Paolo fait bonne fortune," they said to one another, and began to make wagers that she would marry him, or, on the other hand, that she was only playing with him : opinion varied, and bets ran high.

Society bets on everything—peace and love, and honour and happiness, are only "staying" horses or "non-stayers," on whose running the money is piled. It is fortunate indeed and rare when the betting is "honest," and if the drinking waters of peace be not poisoned on purpose, or the smooth turf of a favourite's career be not sprinkled with glass, by those who have laid the odds heavily against it. So that they land their bets, what do they care whether or no the subject of their speculations be lamed for life and destined to drag out its weary days between the cab-shafts till the end comes in the knacker's yard ?

As for the Lady Hilda, she was so used to be the observed of all observers wherever she went, that she never heeded who looked at her, and never troubled herself what anybody might say.

She walked about with Della Rocca, talked with him, and let him sit by her in little sheltered camellia-filled velvet-hung nooks, because it pleased her, and because he looked like an old Velasquez picture in that white Louis Treize dress. Of what anybody might think she was absolutely indifferent ; she was not mistress of herself and of fifty thousand a year to care for the tittle-tattle of a small winter city.

It was very pleasant to be mistress of herself— to do absolutely as she chose—to have no earthly creature to consult—to go to bed in Paris and wake up in St. Petersburg if the fancy took her —to buy big diamonds till she could outblaze Lady Dudley- -to buy thoroughbred horses and old pictures and costly porcelains and all sorts of biblots, ancient and curious, that might please her taste—to obey every caprice of the moment and to have no one to be responsible to for its indulgence—to write a cheque for a large amount if she saw any great distress that was painful to look upon—to adorn her various houses with all that elegance of whim and culture of mind could gather together from the treasures of centuries—to do just as she pleased, in a word, without any one else to ask, or any necessity to ponder whether the expense were wise. It was very agreeable to be mistress of herself, and yet——

There is a capitalist in Europe who is very unhappy because all his wealth cannot purchase the world-famous Key of the Strozzi Princes.

Lady Hilda was never unhappy, but she was not quite content.

Out of the very abundance of her life she was weary, and there was a certain coldness in it all; it was too like one of her own diamonds.

She sighed a little to-night when her white Mousquetaire had led her to her carriage, and she was rolling across the bridge homeward, whilst Madame Mila's gossamer skirts were still twirling, and her rosy stockings still twinkling in

L

all the intricacies and diversions with which the Vicomte Maurice would keep the cotillon going until nine o'clock in the morning.

In the darkness of her carriage, as it went over the stones through the winding ill-lit streets, she saw soft amorous eyes looking at her under their dreamy lids ; she could not forget their look ; she was haunted by it—it had said so much.

The tale it had told was one she had heard indeed twenty times a year for ten long years, and it had never moved her ; it had bored her—nothing more.

But now—a sudden warmth, a strange emotion, thrilled in her, driving through the dark with the pressure of his hand still seeming to linger upon hers.

It was such an old old tale that his eyes had told, and yet for once it had touched her somehow and made her heart quicken, her colour rise.

" It is too ridiculous ! " she said to herself. " I am dreaming.   Fancy *my* caring ! "

And she was angry with herself, and when she reached her own rooms looked a moment at her full reflection in the long mirrors, diamonds and all, before she rang for her maid to come to her.

It was a brilliant and beautiful figure that she saw there in the gorgeous colours copied from a picture by Watteau le Jeune, and with the great stones shining above her head and on her breast like so many little dazzling suns.

She had loved herself very dearly all her life, lived for herself, and in a refined and lofty way had been as absolutely self-engrossed and amorous of her own pleasure and her own vanities as the greediest and cruellest of ordinary egotists.

"Am I a fool?" she said, angrily, to her own image. "It is too absurd! Why should he move me more than anyone of all the others?"

And yet suddenly all the life which had so well satisfied her seemed empty—seemed cold and hard as one of her many diamonds.

She rang with haste and impatience for her maid; and all they did, from the hot soup they brought to the way they untwisted her hair, was wrong; and when she lay down in her bed she could not sleep, and when the bright forenoon came full of the sound of pealing bells and gay

street songs and hurrying feet, she fell into
feverish dreams, and, waking later, did not know
what ailed her.

From that time Della Rocca ceased to avoid
the Hotel Murat ; he was received there oftener
than on her " day ;" he went about with her on
various pilgrimages to quaint old out-of-the-way
nooks of forgotten art which he could tell her of,
knowing every nook and corner of his native city ;
she almost always invited him when she had other
people to dine with her; her cousin did the same,
and he was usually included in all those mani-
fold schemes for diversions which women like
Madame Mila are always setting on foot, thinking
with Diderot's vagabond that it is something at
any rate to have got rid of Time.

Sometimes he availed himself of these opportunities of Fortune, sometimes he did not.   His
conduct had a variableness about it which did
more than anything else would have done to
arrest the attention of a woman sated with
homage as the Lady Hilda had been all her
days.   She missed him when he was absent;
she was influenced by him when he was present.

Beneath the softness of his manner there was a certain seriousness which had its weight with her. He made her feel ashamed of many things.

Something in his way of life also attracted her. There are a freedom and simplicity in all the habits of an Italian noble that are in strong contrast with the formal conventionalism of the ways of other men; there is a feudal affectionateness of relation between him and his dependants which is not like anything else; when he knows anything of agriculture, and interests himself personally in his people, the result is an existence which makes the life of the Paris flâneurs and the London idlers look very poor indeed.

Palestrina often saw its lord drive thither by six in the morning, walk over his fields, hear grievances and redress them, mark out new vine-walks with his bailiff, watch his white oxen turn the sods of the steep slopes, and plan trench-cuttings to arrest the winter-swollen brooks, long before the men of his degree in Paris or in London opened their heavy eyes to call for their morning taste of brandy, and awoke to the recollection of their night's gaming losses, or their wagers on coming races.

The finest of fine gentlemen, the grandest of grand seigneurs, in court or drawing-room or diplomatic circle, Paolo della Rocca, amongst his own grey olive orchards and the fragrance of his great wooden storehouses, was as simple as Cincinnatus, laughed like a boy with his old steward, caressed like a woman the broad heads of his beasts at the plough, and sat under a great mulberry to break his bread at noonday, hearkening to the talk of his peasants as though he were one of them.

The old Etrurian gentleness and love of the rural life are still alive in this land; may they never perish, for they are to the nation, as the timely rains to the vine, as the sweet strong sun to the harvest.

This simplicity, this naturalness, which in the Italian will often underlie the highest polish of culture and of ceremony, had a curious fascination for a woman in whose own life there had been no place for simplicity and no thought for nature.

She had been in the bonds of the world always,

as a child in its swaddling bands ; none the less so
because she had been one of its leaders in those
matters of supreme fashion wherein she had
reigned as a goddess. Her life had been altogether artificial; she had always been a great
garden lily in a hothouse, she had never known
what it was to be blown by a fresh breeze on a
sun-swept mocrland like a heather flower. The
hothouse shelters from all chills and is full of
perfume, but you can see no horizon from it;
that alone is the joy of the moorland. Now and
then, garden lily in a stove-heated palace though
she was, some vague want, some dim unful-
filled wish, had stirred in her; she began to
think now that it had been for that unknown
horizon.

" Men live too much in herds, in crowded
rooms, amongst stoves and gas jets," he said to
her once. " There are only two atmospheres
that do one morally any good—the open air and
the air of the cloister."

" You mean that there are only two things that
are good—activity and meditation ? "

" I think so. The fault of society is that it

substitutes for those, stimulants and stagnation."

He made her think—he influenced her more than she knew. Under the caressing subserviency to her as of a courtier, she felt the power of a man who discerned life more clearly and more wisely than herself.

The chief evil of society lies in the enormous importance which it gives to trifles. She began to feel that with all her splendour she had been only occupied with trifles. Nature had been a sealed book to her, and she began to doubt that she had even understood Art.

"If you can be pleased with this," says a great art-critic, 'this' being a little fres:o of St. Anne, "you can see Floralia. But if not,— by all means amuse yourself there, if you find it amusing, as long as you like; you can never see it."

The test may be a little exaggerated, but the general meaning of his words is correct.

Cosmopolitan and Anglo-American Floralia, for the main part, do not see the city they come to winter in; see nothing of its glories, of its sanctities, of its almost divinities; see only their own friends, their own faces, their own fans, flirtations, and fallals, reflected as in mirrors all around them, and filling up their horizon.

A Dutchman can be just as solemnly and entirely contemplative of a lemon-pip and a cheese-paring as an Italian of the Virgin in glory."

Cosmopolitan and Anglo-American Floralia is in love with its lemon-pips, and has no eyes for the Glory. When it has an eye, indeed, it is almost worse, because it is bent then on buying the Glory for its drawing-room staircase, or worse yet, on selling it again at a profit.

The Lady Hilda, who did not love lemon-pips, but who yet had never seen the Glory with that simplicity, as of a child's worship, which alone constitutes the true sight, began to unlearn many of her theories, and to learn very much in emotion and vision, as she carried her delicate disdainful head into the little dusky chapels and the quiet prayer-worn chauntries of Floralia.

Her love of Art had after all been a cold, she began to think a poor, passion. She had studied the philosophy of Art, had been learned in the contemplative and the dramatic schools, had known the signs manual of this epoch and the other, had discoursed learnedly of Lombard and Byzantine, of objective and subjective, of archaic and naturalistic; but all the while it had been not very much more than a scholarly jargon, a graceful pedantry, which had served to make her doubly scornful of those more ignorant. Art is a fashion in some circles, as religion is in some, and license is in others; and Art had been scarcely deeper than a fashion with her, or cared for more deeply than as a superior kind of furniture.

But here, in this, the sweetest, noblest, most hallowed city of the world, which has been so full of genius in other times, that the fragrance thereof remains, as it were, upon the very stones, like that Persian attar, to make one ounce of which a hundred thousand roses die, here something much deeper yet much simpler came upon her.

Her theories melted away into pure reverence, her philosophies faded into tenderness new revelations of human life came to her

before those spiritual imaginings of men to
whom the blue sky had seemed full of angels,
and the watches of the night been stirred by the
voice of God : before those old panels and old
frescoes, often so simple, often so pathetic, always
so sincere in faith and in work, she grew herself
simpler and of more humility, and learned that
art is a religion for whose right understanding
one must needs become " even as a little
child."

She had been in great art cities before ; in
the home of Tintoretto and the Veronese, in the
asylum of the Madonna de San Sisto, in the
stone wilderness of Ludwig where the Faun sleeps
in exile, in mighty Rome itself; but she had not
felt as she felt now.   She had been full of appre-
ciation of their art, but they had left her as they
had found her, cold, vain, self-engrossed, entirely
shut in a Holy of Holies of culture and of criticism ; she had covered her Cavalcaselle with
pencil notes, and had glanced from a predella or
a pietà to the pages of her Ruskin with a serene
smile of doubt.

But here and now Art ceased to be science,

and became emotion in her.   Why was it?—she
did not care to ask herself.

Only all her old philosophies seemed falling
about her like shed leaves, and her old self
seemed to her but a purposeless frivolous chilly
creature. The real reason she would not face, and
indeed as yet was not conscious of; the reason
that love had entered into her, and that love,
if it be worth the name, has always two hand-
maidens: swift sympathy, and sad humility,
keeping step together.

CHAPTER VII.

FOREIGN Floralia, *i.e.*, that portion of Floralia which is not indigenous to the soil, but has only flown south with the swallows, is remarkable for a really god-like consciousness—it knows everything about every body, and all things, past, present, and to come, that ever did, could, would, should, cannot, will not, or never shall happen; and is aware of all things that have ever taken place, and of a great many things that never have done so. It is much better informed about you than you are yourself; knows your morals better than your confessor, your constitution better than your doctor, your income better than your banker, and the day you were born on, better than your mother.

It is omniscient and omnipresent, microscopic
and telescopic; it is a court-edition of Scotland
Yard, and a pocket-edition of the Cabinet Noir;
it speeds as many interrogations as a telegraph-
wire, and has as many mysteries as the agony
column of a newspaper—only it always answers
its own questions, and has all the keys to its own
mysteries, and what is still more comforting,
always knows everything for " certain."

It knows that you starve your servants because
you are poor and like to save on the butcher and
baker; it knows that you overpay them because
you are rich and want them to keep your secrets,
it knows that your great grandmother's second
cousin was hanged for forgery at Tyburn; it
knows that your silk stockings have cotton tops
to them; it knows that your heirloom-guipure
is imitation, made the other day at Rapallo; it
knows that your Embassy only receives you because—hush—a great personage—ah, so very
shocking; it knows that you had green peas six
weeks before anybody else; it knows that you have
had four dinner parties this week and are living on
your capital; it knows that when you were in

Rome you only went to the Quirinal Wednesdays, because (*whisper, whisper, whisper*)—oh, indeed it is perfectly true—had it on the best authority—dreadful, incredible, but perfectly true !

In point of fact there is nothing it doesn't know.

Except, to be sure, it never knows that Mrs. Potiphar is not virtuous, or that Lady Messalina is not everything she should be; this it never knows and never admits, because if it did it could not very well drink the Potiphar champagne, and might lose for its daughters the Messalina balls. Indeed its perpetual loquacity, which is " as the waters come down at Lodore," has most solemn and impressive interludes of refreshing dumbness and deafness when any incautious speaker, not trained to its ways, hints that Mrs. Potiphar lives in a queer manner, or that Lady Messalina would be out of society anywhere else; then indeed does Anglo-Saxon Floralia draw itself up with an injured dignity, and rebuke you with the murmur of—Christian charity.

In other respects however it has the soul of Samuel Pepys multiplied by five thousand.

It watched the progress of intimacy between
Lady Hilda and the ruined lord of Palestrina,
and knew "all about it,"—knew a vast deal
more than the persons concerned, of course;
it always does, or what would be the use of
talking?

Gossiping over its bonbons and tea in
the many pleasant houses in which the south
wintering northern swallows nestle, it knew
that he and she had been in love years and
years before; the family would not let her marry
him because he was so poor; it was the discovery
of his letters to her that had killed poor old rich
Vorarlberg; he and her brother had fought in the
Bois—indeed!—oh yes, it was hushed up at the
time, but it was quite true, and he had shot her
brother in the shoulder; the surgeon who had
attended the wounded man had told the physician
who had attended the sister-in-law of the cousin of
the most intimate friend of the lady who had
vouched for this. There could not be better authority. But there never was anything against her?—
oh dear me, no, never anything—everybody said
this very warmly, because everybody had been,

hoped to be, or at least would not despair of being, introduced to her and asked to dinner. It was very romantic, really most interesting; they had not met for nine years, and now!—ah, that explained all her coldness then, and that extraordinary rejection of the Crown Prince of Deutschland, which nobody ever had been able to understand. But was it not strange that he had never tried to resume his old influence before? No, he was as proud as he was poor, and besides they had quarrelled after the duel with her brother; they had parted one night very bitterly, after one of the Empress's balls at St. Cloud, out on the terrace there; but he had always refused to give up her portrait; somebody had seen it upon his chest when he had been stripped in the hospital after Custozza; oh yes, they remembered that perfectly.

Altogether they made such a very pretty story that it was quite a pity that it was not true, and that the subjects of it had never met until the Duc de St. Louis had brought them face to face that winter. The one real truth which did begin to embitter the life of the Lady Hilda and lie

M

heavy on her thoughts, waking and sleeping, was
one that the garrulous gossiping Pepys-like
northern swallows, chirping so busily, did not
guess at all. Indeed, this is the sad fate which
generally befalls Gossip.

It is like the poor devil in the legend of
Fugger's Teuffelpalast at Trent ; it toils till cock-
crow picking up the widely-scattered grains of
corn by millions till the bushel measure is piled
high, and lo !—the five grains that are *the* grains
always escape its sight and roll away and hide
themselves. The poor devil, being a primitive
creature, shrieked and flew away in despair at his
failure. Gossip hugs its false measure and says
loftily that the five real grains are of no conse-
quence whatever.

The Duc de St. Louis, who had not got the five
grains any more than they had, yet who could
have told them their bushelful was all wrong,
like a wise man, seeing the project of his affections in a fair way towards realization—at least,
so he thought—prudently abstained from saying
one word about it to any one.

" Trop de zèle " spoiled everything, he knew,

from politics to omelettes, from the making of
proselytes to the frying of artichokes. A breath
too much has before now toppled down the most
carefully built house of cards. When to let
things alone is perhaps the subtlest, rarest, and
most useful of all knowledge.

A man here and there has it; it may be said
that no woman has, has had, or ever will have it.
If Napoleon had had it he might have died at
eighty at St. Cloud instead of St. Helena. But
genius, like woman, never has been known to
have it. For genius and caution are as far apart
as the poles.

"Tout va bien," the Duc said to himself,
taking off his hat to her when he saw Della
Rocca by her carriage; meeting them in discussion before some painting or statue that she was
about to buy; or watching them *tête-à-tête* on
some couch of a ballroom, or in some nook of a
gas-lit grove of camellias.

"Tout va bien," said the Duc, smiling to himself, and speeding on his way to his various mis-
sions, reconciling angry ladies, making the prettiest
flatteries to pretty ones, seeking some unobtain-

able enamel, ivory, or elzevir, penning sparkling
proverbs in verse, arranging costume quadrilles, preventing duels, and smiling on débutantes, adjusting old quarrels, and hearing new
tenors; always in a whirl of engagements, always
courted and courteous, always the busiest, the
wittiest, the happiest, the most urbane, the most
charming, the most serene person in all Floralia.
"Tout va bien," said the Duc, and the town
with him: the two persons concerned were
neither of them quite so sure.

Meanwhile, for a little space the name and fame
and ways and wonders of the Lady Hilda which
filled Floralia with a blaze as of electric lights,
quelling all lesser luminaries, was almost dis-
regarded in a colossal sentiment, a gigantic discussion, a debate which, for endless eloquence
and breathless conflict, would require the dithy-
rambs of Pindar meetly to record:—the grave
question of who would, and who would not, go to
the Postiche ball.

"Number One goes to dine with Number Two,
only that he may say he did so to Number Three,"
some cynic has declared; but Floralia improves

even on this ; before it goes to dine or dance,
it spends the whole week in trying to find
out who all the Number Fours will be, or in
declaring that if such and such a Number
Four goes it does not think it can go itself—
out of principle—all which diversions wile its
time away and serve to amuse it as a box of
toys a child. Not that it ever fails to go and
dine or dance,—only it likes to discuss it
dubiously in this way.

The Postiche ball was really a thing to move
society to its depths.

The wintering-swallows had never been so
fluttered about anything since the mighty and
immortal question of the previous season, when
a Prince of the H. R. Empire, a United Nether-
lands Minister, and a Duc et Pair of France, had
all been asked to dinner together with their
respective wives at an American house, and the
hostess and all the swallows with her had lived in
agonies for ten days previously, torn to pieces by
the terrible doubts of Precedence ; beseeching
and receiving countless counsels and councillors,
and consulting authorities and quoting precedents

with the research of Max Müller and the zeal of
Dr. Kenealy.

But the Postiche ball was a much wider, indeed almost an international matter; because the
Anglo-Saxon races had staked their lives that it
should be a success; and the Latin and Musco-
vite had declared that it would be a failure; and
everybody was dying to go, and yet everybody
was ashamed to go, a state of mind which constitutes the highest sort of social ecstacy in this
age of composite emotions.

Mr. and Mrs. Joshua R. Postiche, some said,
were Jews, and some said were Dutch, and some
said were half-castes from Cuba, and some said
were Americans from Arkansas, and some said had
been usurers, and some gin-spinners, and some
opium dealers, and some things even yet worse;
at any rate they had amassed, somehow or other,
a great deal of money, and had therefore got into
society by dint of a very large expenditure and
the meekest endurance of insults; and had
made an ancient palace as gaudy and garish as
any brand-new hotel at Nice or Scarboro', and
gathered in it all the cosmopolitan crowd of

Floralia; some of the Italian planets and Mus-
covite stars alone hanging aloof in a loftier
atmosphere, to the very great anguish of the
Joshua R. Postiches.

The ball was to be a wonderful ball, and the cotillon presents were whispered to have cost thirty
thousand francs, and there were various rumours
of a "surprise" there would be at it, as poor
Louis Napoleon used to promise the Parisians
one for the New Year. Louis Napoleon's pro-
mises always ended in smoke, but the surprise
of the Joshua R. Postiches was always to be
reckoned on as something excellent:—salmon
come straight from the Scotch rivers; lobsters
stewed in tokay du krone; French comic actors
fetched from Paris; some great singer, paid
heaven knew what for merely opening her
mouth; some dove flying about with jewels in
his beak for everybody, or something of that
sort, which showed that the Joshua R. Postiches,
wherever they had been "raised," or even if they
had kept a drinking-bar and eating-shop in
Havannah, as some people said, were at all events
persons who knew the requirements of their own

generation and the way to mount into "La Haute."

Why they wanted to get there no mortal coula tell; they had no children, and were both middle-aged; but no doubt, if you have not been used to them, the cards of countesses are as balm in Gilead, and to see a fashionable throng come up your staircase is to have attained the height of human desire.

At any rate, the Joshua R. Postiches had set their souls on this sort of social success, and they achieved it; receiving at their parties many distinguished and infinitely bored personages who had nothing to do in Floralia, and would have cut them in Paris, Vienna, or London, with the blandest and blankest stare of unconsciousness.

Madame Mila was on the point of adding herself to those personages.

" I *must* go to the ball," she said. " Oh, it will be the best thing of the season except Nina Trasimene's—I must go to the ball—but then I can't endure to know the woman."

" Can't you go without knowing her?" said the Lady Hilda. " That has been done——"

Madame Mila did not feel the satire.

"Yes; one could do it in Paris or London but not in a little place like this," she answered, innocently. " I must let them present her to me—and I must leave a card. That is what's so horrid. The woman is dreadful; she murders all the languages, and the man's always looking about for a spittoon, and calls you my lady. They are too dreadful! But I must go to the ball. Besides, our own people want Maurice to lead the cotillon. Now Guido Salvareo is ill, there's nobody that can come near Maurice——"

" But I suppose he would not dare to go if you were not there ?"

" Of course he would not go; the idea ! But I mean to go—I must go. I'm only thinking how I can get out of knowing the woman afterwards. It's so difficult in a small place, and I am always so good-natured in those things. I suppose it's no use asking you to come, Hilda ? else, if you would, *you* could cut them afterwards most deliciously, and I should do as you did. Left to myself, I'm always too good-natured."

" I would do most things to please you, my dear Mila," answered her cousin, " but I don't think I can do that. You know it's my rule never to visit people that I won't let visit me—and I don't like murdered languages, and being called ' my lady.' "

" Oh, the people are horrid—I say so," an-swered the Comtesse. " I shall have nothing to do with them, of course—after their ball."

" But surely, it's very low, Mila, that sort of thing. I know people do it nowadays. But really, to be a guest of a person you intend to cut next day——"

" What does it matter ? She wants my name on her list; she gets it ; I'm not bound to give her anything more. There is nothing unfair about it. She has what she wants, and more than she could expect. Of course, all that kind of persons must know perfectly well that we only go to them as we go to the opera, and have no more to do with them than we have with the opera door-keepers. Of course they know we don't visit them as we visit our own people. But if snobbish creatures like those find pleasure in en-

tertaining us, though they know quite well what
we think of them, and how we esteem them, and
why we go to them—well, I don't see that they
deserve anything better."

" Nor I," said the Lady Hilda. " Only I
shouldn't go to them—that's all. And it *is* very
funny, my love, that you, who have lived in all
the great courts of Europe, and have had your own
Embassy in London, should care one straw for a
ball at the Joshua R. Postiche's. Good gracious !
You must have seen about seventy thousand balls
in your time ! "

"I am only six years older than you, Hilda,"
said she, tartly. "I suppose you've been telling
Della Rocca not to go to the Postiche's—Olga
and the Baroness and Madame Valkyria, and
scores of them have been trying to persuade him
all the week, because if he stay away so many of
the other men will; and none of us can stir him
an inch about it. ' On peut être de très-braves
gens—mais je n'y vais pas,' that is all he says;
as if their being ' braves gens ' or not had anything to do with it; and yet I saw him the other
day with his hand on a contadino's shoulder in

the market-place, and he was calling him 'carissimo mio.'"

"One of his own peasants, most likely," said the Lady Hilda, coldly. "I have never heard these Postiches even mentioned by M. Della Rocca, and I certainly have nothing whatever to do with where he goes or doesn't go."

"He is always with you, at any rate," said Madame Mila; "and if you would make him go, it would only be kind of you. You see we want *everybody* we know, so that we may be sure to make the square dances only of our own people, and not to see anything of anybody the Postiches may have asked themselves. Little Dickie Dorrian, who's managing it all, said to the woman Postiche, 'I'll bring the English division if you'll spend enough on the cotillon toys; but I won't undertake the Italians.' Now if Della Rocca——"

"Would you want a new dress, Mila?" said the Lady Hilda; "I am sure you must if you're going to a woman you can't know the next day."

"I should like one, of course," said the Comtesse, "but I've had thirty new ones this season already—and what I owe Worth!—not to talk of the Maison Roger——"

"Let me give you one," said the Lady Hilda. "Worth will do anything at short notice for either of us ; and I must think this poor Postiche woman ought to see you in a new dress, as she's never to see you again."

"You are a darling, Hilda!" said Madame Mila, with ardent effusion, rising to kiss her cousin.

Lady Hilda turned to let the caress fall on the old guipure lace fichu round her throat, and drew her writing-things to her to pen a telegram to M. Worth.

"I suppose you don't care to say what colour?" she asked as she wrote.

"Oh no," answered the Comtesse. "He remembers all the combinations I've had much better than I do. You dictate to him a little too much ; I've heard him say so——"

"He never said so to me," said the Lady Hilda, with a laugh. "Of course I dictate to him. Whatever taste your dress-maker, man or woman, may have—and he has genius—there are little touches which should always come from oneself, and which can alone give originality. That is why all that herd of women, who really do go to Worth but yet are nobodies, look hardly the better for him; he thinks about us, and we think about ourselves; but he doesn't think about them, and as they have no thought themselves the result is that they all look as conventional and similar as if they were dolls dressed for a bazaar. Women ought to be educated to more sense of colour and form. Even an ugly woman ought to be taught that it is her duty to make her ugliness as little disagreeable as possible. If the eyes and the taste of women were cultivated by artistic study, an ill-dressed woman would become an impossibility. If I were ever so poor," continued the Lady Hilda impressively, " if I were ever so poor, and had to sew my own gowns, and make them of serge or of dimity, I would cut them so that Giorgione or Gainsborough, if they were living, would be able to look at me with complaisancy—or at all events without a shudder. It is not half so much a question of material as it is of taste. But nowadays the people who cannot afford material have no taste; so that after us, and the women whom Worth manages to make look decently in spite of themselves, there is nothing but a multitude of hideously-attired persons, who make the very streets appalling either by dreariness or gaudiness:—they never have any medium. Now a peasant girl of the Marche, or of the Agro Romana, or of the Pays de Vaud, is charming, because her garments have beauty of hue in them, and that other beauty which comes from perfect suitability and—— Ah! come sta Duca?"

She interrupted herself, and turned to Della Rocca, who was standing behind her, the servant's announcement of him having been unheard: it was her day to receive.

"Oh, that the rest of your sex, Madame," he said, after his salutations were made, "could sit at your feet and take in those words of wisdom! Yes, I heard most that you said; I can understand your tongue a little; you are so right; it is the duty of every woman to make herself as full of grace as she can; all cannot be lovely, but none need be unlovely."

" Exactly; women are reproached with thinking too much about dress, but the real truth is, they do not think enough about it—in the right way. They talk about it dreadfully, in the vulgarest fashion, but bring any thought to it they don't. Most women will wear anything if it be only *de rigueur.* I believe if I, and Princess Metternich, and Madame de Gallifet, and Madame Aguado, and a few like us wore that pea-green silk coat and waistcoat which the Advanced Thought Ladies of America are advocating as the best new kind of dress for women, that you would see ten thousand pea-green coats and waistcoats blazing in the streets the week afterwards——"

" Not a bad idea for the Cotton Costume ball," said Madame Mila. " I will have a pea-green coat and waistcoat, a tall hat, and hessians ; and call myself ' Advanced Thought.' "

" To be completely in character, Mila, you must have blue spectacles, a penny whistle, a phial full of nostrums, a magpie for your emblem, and a calico banner, inscribed ' Everything is Nothing ! '——"

" Charming ! It shall be the best thing there.

Draw it for me, Della Rocca, and I will send the sketch to Paris, so that it can all come in a box together, magpie and all."

He drew a sheet of paper to him, and sketched the figure in ink, with spirit.

" You have all the talents—so many thanks," said Madame Mila, looking over his shoulder.

Della Rocca sighed.

" If I have them I have buried them, Madame —but, indeed, I can make no such claim."

" So many thanks," echoed the Comtesse. " Pray, don't say a word about it, or we shall have a dozen 'Advanced Thoughts' in calico. Hilda, I am just going to Nina's to see about the *Muscadins.* I have resolved we shall play that piece or no other. I shall be back in ten minutes, ask Olga to wait ; " and Madame Mila wafted herself out of the room, and downstairs to the courtyard, where the coupé and the exemplary Maurice were waiting.

" How she does amuse herself ! " said Lady Hilda, a little enviously. " I wish I could do it. What *can* it matter whether they play the *Muscadins* or anything else ! "

x

"Plus on est fou, plus on rit," said Della
Rocca, sketching arabesques with his pen. "Nay,
that is too impolite in me to charming Madame
Mila.   But, like all old proverbs, it is more true
than elegant."

"Do you know, Madame," he continued, with
a little hesitation, " I have often ventured to think
that, despite your brilliancy, and your position,
and all your enviable fate, you are not altogether— quite happy?   Am I right?   Or have I
committed too great an impertinence to be
answered?"

"No impertinence whatever," said the Lady
Hilda, a little wearily. "You may be right; I
don't know; I am not unhappy certainly; I have
nothing to be unhappy about; but— most things
seem very stupid to me.   I confess Mila's endless
diversions and excitements are quite beyond me.
There is such a terrible sameness in everything."

"Because you have no deeper interests," he
answered her.   He still sat near her at her
writing-table beside the fire, and was playing with
the little jewelled boy who held her pen-wiper.

She did not answer him; and he continued

"I think you have said yourself, Madame, the cause why everything seems more or less wearisome to you—you have ' nothing to be unhappy about'; that is—you have no one for whom you care."

He thought that her proud delicate face coloured a little; or it might be the warmth from the fire of oak-logs and pine-cones.

"No; I don't care about people," she answered him indifferently. " When you have seen a person a few times—it is enough. It is like a book you have read through ; the interest is gone ; you know the *mot d'énigme.*"

" You speak of society; I spoke of affections."

The Lady Hilda laughed a little.

"I can't follow you. I do not feel them. I like Clairvaux, my brother, certainly, but we go years without seeing each other quite contentedly."

"I spoke of affections, other affections," replied Della Rocca, with a little impatience. "There is nothing else that gives warmth or colour to life. Without them there is no glow

N 2

in its pictures, they are all painted *en grisaille.*
Pleasure alone cannot content any one whose
character has any force, or mind any high intelligence. Society is, as you say, a book we soon
read through, and know by heart till it loses all
interest. Art alone cannot fill more than a certain part of our emotions ; and culture, however perfect, leaves us unsatisfied. There is
only one thing that can give to life what your
poet called the light that never was on sea or
land—and that is human love."

His eyes rested on her; and for once in her
life her own eyes fell; a troubled softness came
for a moment on her face, dispersing all its
languor and its coldness. In another moment
she recovered herself, and smiled a little.

"Ah! you are *appassionato,* as becomes your
country."

Della Rocca looked at her with something
of disappointment and something of distaste ;
he rose and approached the grand piano.

"You allow me ?" he said, and touched a
few of the chords. He sang very low, and almost
as it were to himself, a canzone of the people—

" Si tu mi lasci, lasciar non ti voglio,
Se m' abbandoni, ti vo seguitare
Se passi il mare, il mar passare io voglio,
Se giri il mondo, il mondo vo' girare," &c.

The words were very simple, but the melody was passionate and beautiful; his voice, so low at first, rose louder, with all the yearning tenderness in it with which the song is laden; and the soft sounds echoed through the silent room, as they had echoed ten thousand times in moonlit nights of midsummer, over the land where Romeo and Stradella and Ariosto loved.

His voice sank softly into silence; and Lady Hilda did not move.

There was a mist that was almost like tears in her proud eyes; she gazed into the fire, with her cheek leaning on her hand; she did not speak to him; there was no sound but the falling of some burning wood upon the hearth.

" The simplest contadina in the land would understand that," he said as he rose; " and you, great lady though you are, cannot? Madame, there are things, after all, that you have missed."

"Go back and sing again," she said to him, taking no notice of his words; "I did not know you ever sang——"

"Every Italian does;—or well or ill," he answered her. "We are born with music in us, like the birds."

"But in society who hears you?"

"No one. An atmosphere of gas, candles, ennui, perfume, heat, and inane flatteries! ah no, Madame—music is meant for silence, moonlight, vinepaths, summer nights——"

"This is winter and firelight, a few armchairs and a great deal of street noise; all the same, go back and sing me more."

She spoke indifferently and lightly, leaning her hand back on her chair, and hiding a little yawn with her hand; she would not have him see that he had touched her to any foolish, momentary weakness. But he had seen. He smiled a little.

"As you command," he answered, and he went back and made her music as she wished; short love lyrics of the populace, sonnets set to noble airs, wild mournful boat-songs, and

snatches of soft melodies, such as echo all the
harvest-time through the firefly-lighted corn:
things all familiar to him from his infancy, but
to her unknown, and full of the force and
the yearning of the passion which was unknown to her also, and in a certain way derided
by her.

He broke off abruptly, and came and leaned
on the chimney-piece near her, with his arm
amongst the little pug-dogs in Saxe, and figures
and fountains in Capo di Monte, which she
had collected in a few weeks from the bric-à-brac
people. He did not speak; he only looked at
her where she sat, with the firelight and the
dying daylight on the silver fox-furs fringing
her dress, on the repoussé gold and silver work
of her loose girdle, on the ends of the old
Spanish lace about her throat; on the great
rings that sparkled on her white fingers, which
were lying so idly clasped together on her
lap.

"You sing very beautifully," she said, calmly,
at length, with her eyes half closed and her
head lying back on the chair-cushions. "It

is very strange you should be so mute in
society."

"I never sang to a crowd in my life, and
never would. Music is an impulse, or it is
nothing. I could never sing save to some
woman who——"

He paused a moment.

"Who was music in herself," he added witn
a smile; it was not what had been upon his
lips.

"Then you should not have sung to me," she
said, still with half-closed eyes and a careless
coldness in her voice. "I am all discord; have
you not found that out?—every woman is, now-
a-days; we have lost the secret of harmony;
we are always wanting to be excited, and never
succeeding in being anything but bored."

"These are mere words, Madame," he answered her, "I hope they are not true. By
discord I think you only mean inconsistency.
Pardon me—but I think you are all so wearied
because of the monotony of your lives. I dare
say that sounds very strangely to you, because
you pursue all the pleasures and all the ex-

travagances that are obtainable. But then all these are no novelties, they are merely habits. Habit is nothing better than a harness; even when it is one silvered and belled. You have exhausted everything too early; how can it have flavour? You pursue an unvarying routine of amusement: how can it amuse? The life of the great world is, after all, when we once know it well, as tiresome as the life of the peasant— perhaps more so. I know both."

"All that may be right enough," said the Lady Hilda, "but there is no help for it that I see. If the world is not amusing, that is not our fault. In the Beau Siècle, perhaps, or in Augustan Rome—"

"Be very sure it was the same thing. An artificial life must grow tiresome to any one with a mind above that of a parrot or a monkey. If we can be content with it, we deserve nothing better. What you call your discord is nothing but your dissatisfaction—the highest part of you. If it were not treason to say so, treason against this exquisite apparel, I would say that you would be more likely to know happiness were you condemned to the serge and the dimity you spoke of to Madame Mila an hour ago."

He had sunk on a stool at her feet as he spoke, and caressed the silver fox and the gold girdle lightly; his hand touched hers in passing, and her face grew warm. She put a feather screen between her and the fire.

"That is the old argument of content in the cottage &c.," she said, with a slight laugh. "I do not believe in it in the least. If it be 'best repenting in a coach and six' it must be best to be bored in an arm-chair——"

"Perhaps ! It is not I, certainly, who should praise poverty !" he said, with some bitterness, and more sadness; "and, indeed, poverty or riches has little to do with the question of happiness; happiness can come but from one thing——."

"A good conscience ? How terribly moral you are."

"No :—from our emotions, from our passions, from our sympathies ; in fine, from Love."

His hand still played with the gold gypsire of the girdle as he sat at her feet; his eyes were

lifted to her face; his voice was very low; in all
his attitude and action and regard there were an
unuttered solicitation, an eloquence of unspoken
meaning; she was silent :—then the door opened;
he dropped the girdle, and rose to his feet; there
came a patter of high heels, and a chime of swift
aristocratic voices ; and into the room there
entered the Princess Olga, attended by her con-
stant shadow, Don Carlo Maremma, with Lady
Featherleigh behind her, accompanied by *her*
attendant, Prince Nicolas Doggondorf.

"Ma chère, there is a regular riot going on at
Nina's," said the Princess Olga, advancing with
both hands outstretched. "All about those
Muscadins. Mila has seceded in full form, and,
of course, M. des Gommeux with her. Blanche
will only play if they have '*Il faut qu'une
porte*,' &c., which is as old as the hills, and Mila
won't play at all if Blanche be allowed to play
anything. They have quarrelled for life, so
have Mila and Nina. They are slanging each
other like two street boys. Alberto Rimini
is on his knees between them, and the Duc
is declaring for the five thousandth time that it is

the last he will ever have to do with theatricals. I left while I could escape with life. What a pity it is that playing for charity always developes such fierce hostilities. Well, Paolo,—have you thought better of the Postiche ball? No? How stiff-necked you are! I do believe Carlo will be the only Italian there!"

"It will be a distinction to inscribe on his tombstone, Madame," said Della Rocca. "But then he goes under command——."

"And under protest," murmured Don Carlo.

"Which does not count. When one is no longer a free agent——."

Princess Olga hit him a little blow with her muff.

"But why should you not go to the Postiches? Just as you go to the Veglione; it is nothing more."

"Madame,—I am very old-fashioned in my ideas, I dare say, but I confess I think that no one should accept as a host a person he would never accept as his guest. I may be wrong——'

"Of course you are wrong. That is not the question at all," said Princess Olga, who did

not like people to differ with her. "Joshua R.
Postiche will never dream of being asked to
shoot your wild ducks or your partridges. All he
wants is that you should just be seen going up
his staircase, and drinking his champagne.
Society is full of Postiches : low people, with a
craze for entertaining high people. They don't
care how we insult them, nor how we laugh at
them, provided our cards lie in the bowl in their
hall. We take them at their own valuation, and
treat them as we treat the waiters at Spillman's
or Doney's ; we have paid the bill with our cards."

"That is to say, we have paid with our names
—which should represent all the honour, dignity,
and self-respect that we have inherited, and are
bound to maintain, for our own sakes and for
those who may come after us."

"Oh, mon Dieu, quel grand sérieux ! " cried
the Princess, impatiently. "But, of course, if
you've been sitting with Hilda you have got more
stiff-necked than ever. What do you say,
Hilda ? Isn't it ill-natured of him ? He need
only walk in, bow once to the woman, and look
on at the edge of the ball-room for twenty

minutes. The other men will go if he will do
as much as that."

"I think M. della Rocca quite right not 'to do
as much as that,'" said the Lady Hilda. "Why
Society ever does as much as that, or half as
much, or anything at all, for Joshua R. Postiche,
I can never tell. As it does,—to be consistent
everybody should dine with the fruit woman from
the street corner, and play écarté with their own
chimney sweeps."

"Oh, we shall come to that, Madame," said
Nicolas Doggondorf. "At least, if chimney
sweeping ever make heaps of money; I don't
think it does; it only chokes little boys——."

"Ce bon Monsieur Postiche sold rum and
molasses," murmured Don Carlo.

"What's it to us what he sold?" said Lady
Featherleigh. "We've nothing to do with him;
we're only going to his ball. You talk as if we
asked the man to dinner."

"What does the Archduchess Anna always say:
'Où je m'amuse—j'y vais.' So we do all. I hear
he has been put up for the Club; is it true?"
added the Princess to Carlo Maremma.

"Yes, Krunensberg has put him up," he answered her, "but he shall never get into it, while there are any of us alive."

"Et s'il n'y a qu'un, moi je serai celui-là," quoted Della Rocca.

"But he has lent Krunensberg heaven knows what—-some say two million francs," said Lady Featherleigh.

Prince Krunensberg was a great personage, and, for a foreigner, of great influence in the Club.

"Chère dame," said Della Rocca, "if we elect all Krunensberg's creditors we shall have to cover three streets with our club-house!"

"Oh my dear! I am half dead!" cried Madame Mila, flashing into the room, gorgeous in the feathers of the golden pheasant, arranged on the most exquisite combination of violet satin, and bronze velvet, and throwing her muff on one side of her and her parasol on the other, while Maurice des Gommeux, who was the most admirable of upper servants, stooped for them and smoothed their ruffled elegance. "I am half dead! Such a scene I never went through in my life. I, who

hate scenes, and never have any hardly even with
Spiridion! Oh, has Olga told you? Yes; it is
horrible, infamous, intolerable!—after all I have
done for that odious Dumb Asylum—and my
costumes ordered for the *Muscadins*, and half
the part learnt! It is all Krunensberg's doing—
and the Duc didn't stand out one half as he
should have done ; and Blanche !—the idea—
the little wretch is made of wood, and can't
even open her mouth ! As for Krunensberg, he deserves to be shot! It is all his influence that has set Nina against the *Muscadins*
—just to spite me ! What I have gone through
about this wretched theatre—and then to have
that little chit of a Blanche set over my head, a
little creature, only married out of her convent
last year ;—it is unbearable; of course, neither I
nor des Gommeux shall play. Oh, here comes
the Duc ;—no, Duc, it is not the slightest use! If
you have that ridiculous musty old piece of
De Musset's, or if you have Blanche in it at all
you don't have Me in anything. A nice morning's work you have made of it ! Nina and I
shall never speak again."

The Duc laid his hat aside; his delicate fea-
tures were puckered, weary, and troubled.

"Mais, Madame, **pardon**!—mais vous avez
toutes dit les choses les plus affreuses !——"

"Women always do, Duc, when they are in a
passion," said Lady Hilda. "There is nothing
like a scene for discovering our real opinions of
one another. Why ! you look actually—worried !
I thought nothing ever ruffled you by any chance
whatever."

"Madame," said M. de St. Louis, stretching
himself, with a sigh, in a low chair beside her and
the fire, "I have always sedulously cultivated
serenity. I believe serenity to be the whole
secret of human health, happiness, longevity, good
taste, sound judgment, everything in point of fact
that is desirable in the life of a human being.
But, alas ! we are all mortal, and our best plans
are but finite. In an evil moment, when Pan-
dora's box was packed, there was put in with it
by the malice of Mercury a detonating powder,
called Amateur Rivalry. When all the other
discords were dispersed, this shot itself into the
loveliest forms and the gentlest bosoms; and

where it explodes—the wisest man stands helpless. He cannot reconcile the warring elements
nor retain any personal peace himself. I am the
slave of Madame Mila; I adore the dust of the
exquisite shoes of Madame Nina; I am penetrated
with the most absolute devotion to Madame
Blanche;—when these heavenly graces are ready
to rend each other's hair, what can I do? What
can I be except the most unhappy person upon
earth? To reconcile ladies who are infuriated is
a hopeless dream; it were easier to make whole
again a broken glass of Venice. It makes one
almost wish," added the Duc with a second sigh,
"almost wish that Molière had never been
created, or, being created, had never written. But
for Molière I doubt very much if the Drama, as an
Art, would have lingered on to the present
time."

"Console yourself, my dear Duc," said Lady
Hilda, "console yourself with a line from
Molière: 'Cinq ou six coups de bâton entre
gens qui s'aiment ne font que ragaillardir l'amitié.'
Mila, Nina, and Blanche will kiss each other
to-morrow; they must, or what becomes of the

great Contes de Mère d'Oie Quadrille to open the Roubleskoff ball next week?"

"I shall never speak to either of them as long as I live," said Madame Mila, still ruffling all her golden feathers in highest wrath. "As for the quadrille—the Roubleskoff must do as they can. I do think Krunensberg has made Nina perfectly odious; I never saw anybody so altered by a man in my life. Well, there's one thing, it won't last. His 'affairs' never do."

"It will last as long as her jewels do," said Carlo Maremma.

"Oh, no, he can't be quite so bad as that."

"Foi d'honneur!—since he left the Sant' Anselmo you have never seen her family diamonds except in the Paris paste *replica*, which she tells you she wears for safety, and because it is such a bore to have to employ policemen in plain clothes at the balls——"

"Talk of policemen!" said Madame Mila, "they say we're to have a caution sent us from the Prefecture about our playing baccarat the other night at the café—they say no gambling is allowed in the city—the idea!"

" While the State organises the lotteries !—
how very consistent," said the Lady Hilda.

" All your gaming is against the law, angels
of my soul," said Carlo Maremma.

" Then we'll all leave Floralia," said Madame
Mila. " The idea of not being able to do what
one chooses in one's own rooms !—there is one
thing, we can always go up to Roubleskoff's ;—
they will never dare to caution him. But what
is the use of all this fuss ?—everybody plays—
everybody always will play."

" The Prefect is much too wise a man ever to
imagine he can prevent ladies doing what they
like," said Maremma. " It is those tremendous
losses of young De Fabris the other night that
have made a stir, and the Prefect thinks it necessary to say something; he is afraid of a
scandal."

" Good gracious ! As if anything filled a city
half so well as a scandal ! Why don't Floralia
have a good gaming place like Monte Carlo ?
we shouldn't want to use our own rooms
then——"

" I confess," said the Duc, in his gentle, medi-

tative voice, " I confess that, like Miladi here, I
fail to altogether appreciate the moral horror of
a game at baccarat entertained by a municipality
which in its legislation legalises the lottery. All
gaming may be prejudicial to the moral health
of mankind; it is certainly so to their purses. I
am prepared to admit, even in face of Madame
Mila's direst wrath, that all forms of hazard are
exceedingly injurious to the character and to the
fortunes of every person tempted by them. It
may be impossible even to exaggerate their bane-
ful influences or their disastrous consequences.
But how can a government which publicly
patronizes, sustains, and enriches itself by
lotteries, have any logic in condemning the
pastime of hazard in a private drawing-room
or a private club-house? I confess I cannot see
how they reconcile both courses. A government, whatever it be, should never be an
anomaly."

" Lotteries are to us what bull-fighting is to
Spaniards, and revolutions are to the French,"
said Carlo Maremma. "Every nation has its
especial craze. The lottery is ours."

"But is it for a government to intensify and pander to, and profit by a national insanity?" said Della Rocca with much seriousness. "When Rome bent to the yell of Panem et Circences, the days of her greatness were numbered. Besides, the Duc is quite right—it is a ridiculous anomaly to condemn games while you allow lotteries. Great harm may result from private gambling—greater still from the public gaming-tables—but the evil after all is not a millionth part so terrible as the evil resulting from the system of public lotteries. The persons who are ruined by ordinary gaming, are, after all, persons who would certainly be ruined by some vice or another. The compound of avarice and excitement which makes the attraction of hazard does not allure the higher kinds of character; besides, the vice does not go to the player—the player goes to the vice. Now, on the contrary, the lottery attacks openly, and tries to allure in very despite of themselves the much wider multitude that is the very sap and support of a nation—it entices the people themselves. It lures the workman to throw away his wage—

the student to spend his time in feverish dreams
—the simple day-labourer to consume his content in senseless calculations that often bring his
poor empty brain, to madness. The lottery
assails them in the street, is carried to them in
their homes, drops them some poor prize at first
to chain them in torment for ever afterwards. It
changes honesty to cunning, peace to burning
desire, industry to a perpetual waiting upon
chance, manly effort to an imbecile abandonment
to the dictates of signs and portents, and the expectancy of a fortune which never comes. High-
born gamblers are only the topmost leaves of the
tree of the State ; they may rot away without
detriment to the tree, but the lottery lays the axe
to the very trunk and root of it, because it demo-
ralises the people."

Lady Hilda listened, and watched him as he
spoke with a grave and almost tender meditation
in her eyes ; which M. de St. Louis saw, and
seeing, smiled.

" Say all that in the Chamber, caro mio," muttered Carlo Maremma.

" I would go to the Chambers to say it, or to

worse places even, were there any chance it would
be attended to.   Madame Mila, have I been so
unhappy as to have offended you?"

"I am a top leaf that may rot! I was never
told anything so rude in my life—from you too!
the very soul of ceremonious courtesy."

Della Rocca made his peace with her in flowery
flattery.

"Well, I shall play baccarat to-night in this
hotel, just because the Prefect has been so odious
and done that," said Madame Mila.   "You will
all come home with me after the Roubleskoff's
dinner?   Promise!"

"Of course," said the Princess Olga.

"Of course," said Lady Featherleigh.

"Of course," said everybody else.

"And if the gendarmes come in?"

"We will shoot them!"

"No; we will give them champagne—surer
and more humane."

"I wish the Prefect would come himself—I
should like to tell him my mind," continued Madame Mila.   "So impudent of the man!—when
all the Royal Highnesses and Grand Dukes and

Duchesses in Europe only come to winter cities
for play. He *must* know that."

" My dear Mila, how you do put yourself out
about it," said the Lady Hilda. " Send ten
thousand francs to the public charities—you may
play all night long in the cafés then."

" Madame, j'ai l'honneur de vous saluer," murmured Della Rocca, bending low before her.

When the door had closed upon him and left
the others behind, a sudden blankness and dull-
ness seemed to fall on her : she had never felt
the same thing before. Bored she had often been,
but this was not *ennui*, it was a kind of loneliness—it was as if all about her grew grey and
cold and stupid.

More ladies came in, there were endless
laughter and chatter; Princess Olga wanted some
tea, and had it; the other women cracked bonbons with their little teeth like pretty squirrels
cracking fir-cones ; they made charming groups
in the firelight and lamplight; they made plans
for a hundred diversions; they were full of the
gayest of scandals ; they dissected in the most
merciless manner all their absent friends ; they

scolded their lovers and gave them a thousand contradictory orders ; they discussed all the news and all the topics of the day, and arranged for dinner parties, and driving parties, and costume quadrilles, and bazaar stalls, and boxes at the theatre, and suppers at the cafés; and agreed that everything was as dull as ditchwater, and yet that they never had a minute for anything ; and the Lady Hilda with the jubilant noise and the twittering laughter round her, thought how silly they all were, and what a nuisance it was having a day—only if one hadn't a day it was worse still, because then they were always trying to run in at all hours on every day, and one was never free for a moment.

" Thank goodness, they are gone ! " she said, half aloud, to the Saxe cups and the Capo di Monte children on the mantelpiece, when the last flutter of fur and velvet had vanished through the door, and the last of those dearest friends and born foes had kissed each other and separated.

Left alone, she stood thinking, by the fire, with all the lights burning behind her in that

big, empty room. What she thought was a very
humble and pensive thought for so disdainful a
lady. It was only——

" Is it myself ? or only the money ? "

She stood some time there, motionless, her
hand playing with the gold girdle as his hand had
done ; her face was pale, softened, troubled.

The clock amongst the Saxe dogs and the
Capo di Monte little figures chimed the half-
hour after six. She started as it struck, and
remembered that she was to dine at eight with
the Princess Roubleskoff; a big party for an
English royalty on his travels.

" Anyhow, it would be of no use," she said
to herself. " Even if I did wish it, it could
never be."

And she was angry with herself, as she had
been the night before; she was impatient of these
new weaknesses which haunted her. Nevertheless
she was more particular about her appearance
that night than her maids had ever known her
be ; she was very difficult to satisfy ; tried and
discarded four wholly new confections of her
friend Worth's, miracles of invention and of

costliness, and at length had herself dressed quite simply in black velvet, only relieved by all her diamonds.

" He said fair women should always wear black," she thought : it was not her Magister of Paris of whom she was thinking as the sayer of that wise phrase. And then again she was angry with herself for remembering such a thing, and attiring herself in obedience to it, and would have had herself undrest again only there was but one small quarter of an hour in which to reach the Roubleskoff villa ; a palace of the fairies four miles from the south-gate. So she went as she was ; casting a dubious impatient glance behind her at the mirrors.

" I look well," she thought with a smile, and her content returned.

She knew that he would be present at the dinner. There is no escaping destiny in Floralia : people meet too often.

The dinner disappointed her.

She thought it very long and very stupid. She sat between the Grand Duke of Rittersbähn and the Envoy of all the Russias, and Della

Rocca was not placed within her sight; and after the dinner the young English Prince would talk to no one but herself, delightedly recalling to her how often she had bowled his wickets down when they had been young children playing on the lawns at Osborne. She felt disloyally thankless for his preference. He monopolised her. And as the rooms filled with the crowd of the reception she merely saw the delicate dark head of Della Rocca afar off, bent down in eager and possibly tender conversation with his beautiful country-woman, the Duchess Medici-Malatesta. She felt angered and impatient.

If she had sat alone and neglected, as less lovely women often do, instead of being monopolised by a prince, with twenty other men sighing to take his place when etiquette should permit them, she could scarcely have been more ill-content.

Never in all her life had it befallen her to think angrily of another woman's beauty ; and now she caught herself irritatedly conning, across the width of the room, the classic profile and the immense

jewel-like eyes of the Malatesta Semiramis.
Never in all her life had it happened to her
to miss any one thing that she desired, and now
a strange sense of loneliness and emptiness came
upon her, unreasoned and unreasoning; and
she had such an impatience and contempt of
herself too all the while!—that was the most
bitter part of it.

After all it was too absurd,——

As soon as the departure of the royal guests
permitted anyone to leave, she went away, contemptuous, ill at ease, and out of temper with
herself and all the world; half ignorant of what
moved her, and half unwilling to probe her own
emotions further.

"Plus on est fou, plus on rit," she murmured
to her pillow two hours later with irritable
disdain, as she heard the voices of Mme. Mila
and her troop noisily passing her door as they
returned to their night-long baccarat, which was
to be doubly delightful because of the Prefect's
interdict.

"I wish I had been born an idiot!" thought
the Lady Hilda—as, indeed, any one must do

who finds himself burdened with aching brains
in this best of all possible worlds.

" Perhaps, after all, you were right," said the
Duc de St. Louis, driving back into the town
with Della Rocca that night. " Perhaps you were
right. Miladi is most lovely, most exquisite,
most perfect. But she has caprices—there is no
denying that she has caprices and extravagancies
which would ruin any one short of the despotic
sovereign of a very wealthy nation."

The Duc was a very wise man, and knew that
the escalier dérobé is the only way that leads in
conversation to any direct information. Their
demeanour had puzzled him, and he spoke accordingly with shrewd design.

Della Rocca heard him with a little annoy-
ance.

" She has not more caprices than other women that I know of," he answered. " Her faults
are the faults rather of her *monde* than of herself."

" But she has adopted them with much affection ! "

" They are habits—hardly more."

" And you were correct too in your diagnosis when you saw her first," continued the Duc, pitilessly. " To me she is most amiable always; but to the generality of people, it must be admitted that she is not so amiable."

" The amiability of most women," replied Della Rocca, " is nothing more than that insatiate passion for admiration which makes them show their persons almost nude at Trouville, and copy the ways and manners of *femmes entretenues* in the endeavour to rival such with us. If they wish to be decent, they do not dare to be ; they must be popular and *chic* before all."

" You are severe, but perhaps you are right. Miladi is certainly above all such vulgarities. Indeed, she is only a little too much above everything——"

" It is better than to be below everything— even below our respect—as most of our great ladies are."

" Certainly. Still she is a little — a little selfish." .

" How should she be otherwise ? She is quite alone—she has no one to care for——"

" Most women make something to care for;
she has many family ties, if she cared for them—
but she does not. No; she is beautiful, charming, *grande dame en tout*—but I begin to think
that it is well for the peace of mankind that
she remains so invulnerable. She would probably make any man who loved her very unhappy if she married him."

" If he were a weak man, not otherwise."

" Pouf! Do you think any man would ever
have control over *her* ? "

" I am quite sure that she would never care for
any man who had not."

" He would be a very bold person," murmured
the Duc. " However, I am very glad that you
think more highly of her. You know, mon cher,
what always was my opinion as to yourself——"

Della Rocca coloured, and saw too late that his
companion had forced his card from his hands
in the most adroit manner. He busied himself
with lighting a cigar.

" For myself," he said, coldly, " I can have no
object in what I say. My own poverty is barrier
sufficient. But I should be unjust not to admit

what I think of her, as a friend. I believe that
the habits of the world are not so strong with her
that they can satisfy her; and I believe that with
her affections touched, with tenderer ties than
she has ever known, with a home, with children,
with a woman's natural life, in fact, she would be
a much happier and very different person. Mais
tout cela ne me regarde pas."

The Duc glanced at him and laughed softly,
with much amusement.

"Ça vous regarde de bien près—bon succès et
bon soir!" he said, as he got out of the carriage
at his hôtel in the city. "I told him to marry
her," he thought; "but if he expect to convert
her too, he must be the boldest and most
sanguine man in Europe."

Lady Hilda made up her mind that she was
tired of Floralia, as she meditated over her chocolate the next morning, after a night which chloral
had made pretty passable, only the baccarat
people had screamed so loudly with laughter on
the other side of the corridor, that they had
awakened her once or twice. Yes, she certainly
was tired of it. The town was charming,—but

then one couldn't live on pictures, marbles, and recollections, and one got so sick of seeing the same people morning, noon, and night. The fogs were very bad. The drainage was dreadful. The thermometer was very nearly what it was in Normandy or Northamptonshire for what she could see. If one did take the trouble to go into society, one might as well do it all for a big world and not a little one. It was utter nonsense about her lungs in Paris. She would go back. She would telegraph her return to Hubert.

Hubert was her maître d'hôtel.

She did telegraph, and told herself that she would find immense interest in the fresco paintings which were being executed in the ball-room of that very exquisite hôtel "entre cour et jardin," which she had deserted in Paris, and in making nooks and corners in her already over-filled tables and cabinets for the tazze and bacini and ivories and goldsmith's work she had collected in the last two months ; and decided that the wall decorations of the drawing-rooms, which were of rose satin, with Louis Quinze panelling, were all very barbarous, utterly incorrect, and should never have been borne with so long, and should be altered at once; the palest amber satin was the only possible thing, with silver mirrors and silver cornices, and not a touch of gilding anywhere; the idea had occurred to her before a picture in the galleries, where a silver casket was painted against an amber curtain; she would have it done immediately, and she would go back to Paris and have her old Thursday evenings again.

After all, Paris was the only place worth living in, and doctors were always alarmists—old women—everything that was stupid, unless you were very very ill, when they did seem to dilate into demi-gods, because of course you were weakened with morphine and other stuff, and did not want to die; though you ought to want to die, being a Christian, if you were in the very least degree consistent; since if you were quite sure that the next world would be so very much better than this, it was utterly illogical to be afraid of going to it:—but then were you quite sure?

The Lady Hilda sighed. This dreadful age,

which has produced communists, pétroleuses, and liberal thinkers, had communicated its vague restlessness even to her; although she belonged to that higher region where nobody ever thinks at all, and everybody is more or less devout in seeming at any rate, because disbelief is vulgar, and religion is an ' affaire des mœurs,' like decency, still the subtle philosophies and sad negations which have always been afloat in the air since Voltaire set them flying, had affected her slightly.

She was a true believer, just as she was a well-dressed woman, and had her creeds just as she had her bath in the morning, as a matter of course.

Still, when she did come to think of it, she was not so very sure. There was another world, and saints and angels and eternity, yes, of course,—but how on earth would all those baccarat people ever fit into it? Who could, by any stretch of imagination, conceive Madame Mila and Maurice des Gommeux in a spiritual existence around the throne of Deity?

And as for punishment and torment and all that other side of futurity, who could even think of the mildest purgatory as suitable to those poor flippertygibbet inanities who broke the seventh commandment as gaily as a child breaks his indiarubber ball, and were as incapable of passion and crime as they were incapable of heroism and virtue ?

There might be paradise for virtue, and hell for crime, but what in the name of the universe was to be done with creatures that were only all Folly ? Perhaps they would be always flying about like the souls Virgil speaks of, " suspensæ ad ventos," to purify themselves ; as the sails of a ship spread out to dry. The Huron Indians pray to the souls of the fish they catch ; well, why should they not ? a fish has a soul if Modern Society has one ; one could conceive a fish going softly through shining waters forever and forever in the ecstacy of motion ; but who could conceive Modern Society in the spheres ?

Wandering thus from her drawing-room furniture to problems of eternity, and only succeeding in making herself unsettled and uncomfortable, the Lady Hilda, out of tune with everything, put off her cashmere dressing-gown, had herself wrapped in her sables, and thought she would go out ;—it was just twelve o'clock.

Looking out of the window she saw a lady all sables like herself, going also out of the hôtel to a coupé, the image of her own.

"Who is that ? " she asked of her favourite maid.

"That is Mdlle. Léa, Miladi," said the maid. "She came last night. She has the suite above."

"How dare you mention her ? " said the Lady Hilda.

The little accident filled up the measure of her disgust. Mdlle. Jenny Léa was a young lady who had seduced the affections of an Emperor, three archdukes, and an untold number of the nobility of all nations ; she was utterly uneducated, inconceivably coarse, and had first emerged from a small drinking shop in the dens of Whitechapel ; she was the rage of the moment, having got a needy literary hack to write her autobiography, which she published in her own name, as "Aventures d'une Anglaise ; " the book had no decency, and as little wit, but it professed to show up the scandals of a great Court, and it made some great men ridiculous and worse, so eighty thousand copies of it had been sold over Europe, and great ladies leaned from their carriages eager to see Mdlle. Jenny Léa pass by them.

Mdlle. Jenny Léa, indeed, having put the finishing stroke to her popularity by immense debts and a forced sale of her effects in Paris, was the sensation of the hour, only sharing public attention with the Père Hilarion, a young and passionately earnest Dominican, who was making a crusade against the world, in a noble and entirely vain fervour, from the pulpits of all the greatest churches on the Continent. It was "the thing" to go and hear Père Hilarion, weep with him and pray with him, and then coming out of the church doors to read Jenny Léa and talk of her. It is by these admirable mixtures that Society manages to keep itself alive.

The Père Hilarion was breaking his great heart over the vileness and the hopelessness of it all, as anyone who has any soul in him must be disposed to do. But to Society the Père Hilarion was only a sort of mental liqueur, as Jenny Léa

was an American " pick-me-up : "—that was all.
Society took them indifferently, one after the other
Of the two, of course it preferred Jenny Léa.

The Lady Hilda in supreme disgust went out
in her sables, as Mdlle. Jenny Léa in hers drove
from the door.

" What good things sumptuary laws must have
been," she thought. " If such creatures had to
dress all in yellow now, as I think they had once
(or was it Jews ?), who would talk of them, who
would look at them, who would lose money about
them ? Not a soul. And to think that there
have been eighty thousand people who have bought
her book ! "

" Has anything offended you, Madame ? Who
or what is so unhappy ? " said the voice of Della
Rocca, as she crossed the pavement of the court
between the lines of bowing hôtel functionaries,
who had bent their spines double in just the same
way to Mdlle. Léa three minutes previously.

" Nothing in especial," she answered him,
coldly. " Those baccarat people kept me awake
half the night ; I wish the gendarmes *had* interfered. What wretched weather it is ! "

"It is a little cold ; but it is very bright," said Della Rocca, in some surprise, for the day, indeed, was magnificent and seasonable. "I was coming in the hope that I might be admitted, though I know it is too early, and not your day, and everything that it ought not to be. But I was so unfortunate last night ; you were so mono-polised——"

She deigned to smile a little, but she continued to move to her brougham.

"Your climate is the very Harpagon of climates. I have not seen one warm day yet. I am thinking of returning to Paris."

He grew very pale.

"Is not that very sudden?" he asked her ; there was a great change in his voice.

"Oh, no ; I have my house there, as you know, and Monsieur Odissôt is painting the ball-room in frescoes. I have quite a new idea for my drawing-rooms, too ; after all, furnishing is one of the fine arts; do you like that young Odissôt's talent? His drawing is perfection ; he was a pupil of Hippolyte Flandrin. Good morning.'

She was in her coupé by this time, and he was obliged to close the door on her; but he kept his hand upon it.

" Since you are leaving us so soon and so cruelly, Madame, would you honour my own old chapel frescoes as you promised ?—they might give you some ideas for your ball-room."

Lady Hilda deigned to smile fairly and fully this time.

" Is that a satire or a profanity—or both together ? "

" It is jealousy of Camille Odissôt ! I will go to Paris and paint your frescoes, Madame, if you will let me ; I can paint in fresco and in tempera; I was a student in the Academy of San Luca in my time."

His words were light, and his manner also, but his eyes had a language that made the Lady Hilda colour a little and look out of the other window of her coupé.

" I must first call upon Olga; I have promised," she answered, irrelevantly. " But I will join you at your palace in an hour ; perhaps she will come with me ; I should not like to leave,

certainly, without having seen your chapel. **Au
revoir.**"

" If you do leave, Madame, I follow !—to paint
the ball-room."

He shut the carriage-door, and stood bareheaded in the wintry wind as the impatient horses
dashed away. When it had disappeared he put
his hat on, lighted a cigar, and strolled to his own
house.

" She will not go to Paris," he said to himself.
He knew women well.

In an hour and a half she arrived at his own
gates, bringing the Princess Olga with her.

She saw the grand old garden, the mighty
staircases, the courts that once held troops of
armed men; she saw his own rooms, with their
tapestries that Flemish John Rosts had had the
doing of so many centuries before; she saw the
exquisite dim silent chapel, whose walls, painted
by the Memmi in one portion and continued by
Masaccio, were amongst the famous things of the
city. She was moved and saddened; softened
too ; after all, the decay of a great race has an unutterable pathos; it will touch even a vulgar mind;

she, arrogant and fastidious as to birth, as though she had been born before the '89, was touched by it to the core.

She had heard, too, of how he lived; without debt, yet with dignity, with the utmost simplicity and without reproach; there was something in his fortunes which seemed to her worthier than all distinction and success, something that stirred that more poetic side of her nature, which the world had never allowed to awake, but which had been born with her nevertheless. She was serious and dreaming as she lingered in the beautiful old chapel, under whose mosaic pavement there lay the dust of so many generations of his race. He noticed her silence and thought to himself:

"Perhaps she is thinking how base it is in a man as poor as I to seek a woman so rich as herself;"—but she was not thinking that at all as she swept on in her sables, with her delicate cheeks, fair as the lovely Niphétos rose, against the darkness of the fur.

That immortality which she had been doubting in the morning, did not seem so absurdly

impossible here. There was religion in the place,
a different one to what she had known kneeling
at the *messe des paresseux* in the Madeleine; the
sort of religion that a woman only becomes
aware of when she loves.

She started and seemed to wake from a dream
when Princess Olga suggested that it was time
to go; Princess Olga was a person of innumerable engagements, who was always racing after
half an hour without ever catching it, like the
Minister-Duke of Newcastle, and like ninety-nine
people out of every hundred in the nineteenth
century. There was some bric-à-brac the Princess wanted somebody to cheapen for her;
she bade him come and do it; he complied will-
ingly enough. They went all three to that bric-
a-brac shop, and thence to another, and yet
another. Then Princess Olga, who was used
to a more brilliant part than that of the "terza
incommoda," left them to themselves over the
faïence and marqueterie.

Lady Hilda who, despite all her fashion, liked
walking like every healthy woman, dismissed her
horses and walked the length of the river-street,

he with her. People meeting them began to make conjectures, and bets, harder than ever ; and Italian ladies, looking out of their carriage windows, wondered for the five-millionth time at the reedom of English women—as indeed Italian ladies have good cause to do in far more reprehensible liberties.

They walked down to the piazzone and back again. It was growing dusk. She went home to her hôtel, and let him enter with her, and had some tea by the firelight ; all the while he made love to her with eyes and gesture and word, as only an Italian can, and she avoided explicit declaration of it, and direct need to reply to it, with all the consummate tact that ten years' practice in such positions had polished in her.

It was a charming pastime—were it nothing more. It was quite a pity when Madame Mila entered unsuspecting, and full of new wrongs in the matter of the *Muscadins* and fresh gossip concerning some forty people's marriages, divorces, debts, ignominies, and infamies. It is fortunate that there are so many wicked people in Society, for if there were not, what would the good people have to talk about? they would die of paralysis of the tongue.

"You will not leave us for Paris, yet?" he murmured as he rose, with a sigh, only heard by her ear.

She smiled, and balanced a Devoniensis tea-rose idly in her hands.

"Not just yet, if your weather prove better."

He drew the tea-rose away from her fingers unseen even by the quick marmoset eyes of little Madame Mila, who as it chanced was busied making herself a cup of tea. She let it go.

"You should have seen all the men looking after that horrible Léa," said Madame Mila, drinking her compound of cream and sugar, as the door closed on him. "They have eyes for nothing else, I do think; and only fancy her having the very suite above mine—it is atrocious! They say the things at her sale fetched fabulous sums. Little pomatum and rouge pots, five hundred francs each! They say she has fixed her mind on young Sant' Andrea here; I suppose she has heard he is enormously rich. Oh, did you know Gwendolen Doncaster has come? She has

lost all her money at Monte Carlo, and she has
dyed her hair a nice straw colour ; she looks fifteen years younger, I do assure you. Don is
shooting in Dalmatia—of course she abuses him
—poor old Don ! I wonder how we should have
got on if he had married me, as he wanted.
Gwen told me Lord Derbyshire has run off with
Mrs. Wheelskaitte—what he *can* see in her! And
those open scandals are so stupid, where is the
use of them ? Surely you can do what you like
without calling all the world in to see you doing
it. When a woman has an easy husband she *never*
need compromise herself, and Wheelskaitte certainly always was that. Oh, you never would know
them, I remember, because they were new people ;
she was an odious creature and very ugly, but
they gave very good parties in London, and their
cottage was as nice a one as you could go to for
Ascot. You used to like little Wroxeter, did not
you? he was such a pretty boy—he has just left
Eton, and he is wild to marry a girl out of a
music-hall, so Gwen says. Those creatures get
all the good marriages nowadays :—and two hundred débutantes waiting to be presented at the

Q

Drawing-room this month! Have you seen the
new book 'Confessions d'un Feu Follet'? Maurice has just brought it to me. It is rivalling
Jenny Léa, and they say it is worse—quite un-
mentionable—everybody is talking about it. It
was out last week, and they have sold five editions. The man called Bistrim in it is Bismarck.
No; I don't know that it is witty. I don't
think things are witty nowadays. It is horrible
and *infecte*—but you can't put it down till you've
done it. Old Lady Mauleverer is dying at the
Pace hôtel here—of undigested scandal, Featherleigh says, but I believe it's gastritis—what a
nasty old woman she has always been. I have
just left a card with inquiries and regrets; I do
hope she won't get better. I won ever so much
at play last night. I forgot to tell you so: I
bought that *rocaille* necklace on the Jewellers'
Bridge; it was only six thousand francs, and it
really did belong to the Comtesse d'Albany. It's
very pretty too——— '

So Madame Mila discoursed, greatly to her
own satisfaction. She loved so much to hear her
own tongue, that she always chose the stupidest

and silliest of her lovers for her chief favours—a clever man had always ideas of his own, and was sure to want to express them sometime or another. All she desired were listeners and echoes. Discussion may be the salt of life to a few, but listeners and echoes are the bonbons and cigarettes that no woman can do without.

The Lady Hilda sitting looking into the fire, with her eyes nearly closed, murmured yes, and no, and indeed, in the proper places, and let her run on, hearing not one word. Those fingers which had entangled themselves so softly with her own withdrawing the tea-rose, had left a magnetic thrill upon her—a dreamy, lulling pleasure.

That evening the good Hubert received a second telegram contradicting the first, which had announced his mistress's return, and putting off that return indefinitely. The good Hubert, who was driving her best horses, drinking her best wines, drawing large cheques for accounts never examined, and generally enjoying his winter, was much relieved, and hastened to communicate the happy change to Monsieur Camille Odissôt, whom the first telegram had also cast into great consternation; since that clever but idle young gentleman, having been pre-paid half the sum agreed on for the fresco-painting, had been spending it joyously after the tastes of young artists, assisted by a pretty brown actress of the Folies Marigny, and had not at that moment even begun to touch the walls and the ceiling of the ball-room confided to his genius.

"But you had better begin, though she is not coming back," said the good Hubert, surveying the blank waste of prepared plaster. "Miladi is not often out of temper, but when she is, ouf! I would as soon serve a Russian. Better begin; paint your best, because she knows — Miladi knows, and she is hard to please in those things. Not but what I dare say, as soon as you have done it all, she will take it into her head that it looks too cold, or looks too warm, or will not compose well, or something or other, and will cover it all up with silk and satin. But that will not matter to you."

"Not at all," said Monsieur Camille, who, though he had been a pupil of Flandrin, had learned nothing of that true master's conscientiousness in art, but was a clever young man of a new generation, who drew beautifully, as mechanically as a tailor stitches beautifully, and was of the very wise opinion that money was everything.

CHAPTER VIII.

THE Postiche ball came off, and was a brilliant success. Madame Mila announced the next morning when she got up that she had never enjoyed anything better—not even at the Tuileries.

"And the hostess?" said Lady Hilda.

"I didn't even see her, thank goodness," said Madame Mila, frankly. "I went late, you know, and she'd been standing at the door four hours, and had got tired, and had gone off duty into the crowd somewhere. Of course it wasn't my business to go and look for her."

"Of course not, but you brought off your *cotillon* things?"

"Yes. There they are," said Madame Mila, unconscious of any satire. "I never saw such *luxe* —no, not even in the dear old Emperor's time— the things everybody got must have cost hundreds of thousands of francs. Certainly little Dickie managed it beautifully. He ordered the whole affair, you know."

"Little Dickie, or anybody else, could float Medea herself in society if she would brew cotillon toys of a new sort in her cauldron," said the Lady Hilda.

"Medea?" said Madame Mila, who knew about her because she had seen Ristori so often. "Poor thing! it was that horrid Jason that deserved to be put out of society, only men never do get put out of it for anything they do ; I don't know how it is—we cut no end of women, but we never cut a man. Well, I assure you, my dear, the ball was charming—*charming*, though you do look so contemptuous. We had all our own people, and saw nobody else, all night. I don't think I need bow to the woman, do you ? I'm not supposed to have seen her, though I do know her by sight, a little podgy sunburnt-looking

fat creature with liveries for all the world like
what the sheriffs have in England at assize time.
No; I'm sure I needn't bow to her. I told
Dickie beforehand I shouldn't."

"No doubt Dickie was delighted to have you
on any terms."

"Of course; and I'll send a card to-day," said
Madame Mila, with the magnanimous air of one
who does a very noble thing.

From that time thenceforward she would forget
the Joshua R. Postiches and everything concerning them as absolutely as if she had never heard
anything about them; the woman's second ball,
if she gave one, would be nothing new, and no
sort of fun whatever.

"You're always at me about Maurice," she
said, pursuing her own ideas, "Look at Olga
with Carlo Maremma!—she did make him go last
night, and he was the only Italian there. You
talk of Maurice—Olga is twice as careless as I
am ——"

"Olga is my friend; don't discuss her, please."

"Oh, that's very fine!—when you are always
finding fault with me about Maurice!"

"I should not let any third person blame you."

"You are very strange, Hilda," said Madame Mila, eyeing her with a curious wonder, and ruffling herself up in her embroidered pink cashmere dressing-gown, as if she were a little bird in the heart of a big rose. " Why should you defend people behind their back? Nobody ever does. We all say horrible things of one another; but we don't mean half of them, so what does it matter? I don't blame Olga, not in the least; Schouvaloff is a brute, and, besides, he knows it very well, and he doesn't mind a bit; indeed, of course he's glad enough ——"

"I do blame Olga ; but I can't see how *you* can," said her cousin, coldly.

Madame Mila ruffled herself more, looking more and more like a little angry bird in the middle of a pink rose.

"I ? Pray what *can* anybody say of me ? Spiridion is always with me half the year at least. Spiridion is extremely fond of Maurice, so are all the children. He's at another bôtel, right at the other end of the place ; really I can't see why

I must rush out of a town because a friend happens to come into it also ——"

" My dear Mila, pray don't talk that nonsense to me," said her cousin, serenely. " I daresay ten years hence you will marry your little Lili to M. des Gommeux; people do do that sort of thing, though they find fault with the plots of the old Greek plays. I suppose it " saves society ; " at least, it saves appearances. Olga is imprudent, I know, and wrong; but, at least she has the courage of her opinions; she does not talk all that pusillanimous prurient absurdity about ' friendship.'"

" Nobody can understand you, Hilda; and I don't know what you mean about Greek plays," muttered Madame Mila. " Everybody lives in the same way : you talk as if it were only *me !* Spiridion never says a word to me; what business have you ? "

" None in the least, dear ; only you will bring up the subject—Qui s'excuse s'accuse. That is all. You are not coming out this morning ? Au revoir then ; I am going to see a newly-found San Cipriano il Mago outside the gates ;

they think it is by Il Moretto. The face and
dress are Venetian, they say ; but you care nothing about all that, do you ? "

" Nothing," said Madame Mila, with a yawn.
" I suppose if it take your fancy you'll be buying
the whole church with it in, if you can't get
it any other way. I wish I'd your money, I
wouldn't waste it on old pictures, that cnly make
a room dark ; and the kind of light *they* want is
horribly unbecoming to people."

" I promise you I shall not hang an altar-piece
in a room," said the Lady Hilda. " I leave that
for the heretics and the bourgeoisie. Good-bye,
my dear."

" Who's going with you ? " cried Madame
Mila, after her : Lady Hilda hesitated a moment.

" Nina is, and the French artist who has dis-
covered the Moretto, and——M. della Rocca."

Madame Mila laughed, and took up a little
mirror to see if all the colour on her face were
quite right. One horrible never-to-be-forgotten
day — one eyebrow had been higher than the
other.

Lady Hilda, descending the hôtel staircase,

met the faithful Maurice ascending. That slender and indefatigable leader of cotillons swept his hat to the ground, twisted the waxed ends of his small moustache, and murmured that he was about to inquire of the servants if Madame la Comtesse were "tout-à-fait remise après ses fatigues incroyables."

Lady Hilda, whom he feared very greatly, passed him with a chilly salutation, and he went on up the stairs, and in two minutes' time was assuring Madame Mila that she was "fraîche comme la rosée du matin," which did credit to his ready chivalry of compliments, since he was aware of all the mysteries of those bright cheeks and that small pomegranate-like mouth, and had even once or twice before great balls, given an artistic touch or two to their completion, having graduated with much skill and success in such accomplishments under the tuition of Mademoiselle Rose Thè, and La Petite Boulotte.

The San Cipriano was to be found in a church some five miles out of the city ; a lonely church set high on a fragrant hill-side, with sheep amongst the olive boughs, and the ox-plough under the vines that were all about it, and high hedges ot wild roses and thickets of arbutus rambling around its old walled graveyard.

The paths close round it were too steep for the horses, and the last half mile had to be climbed on foot.

It was one of those spring days which often fall in February ; the ground was blue with violets, and the grass golden with crocus and hepatica ; there were butterflies and bees on the air ; the mavis and blackbird were singing.

The San Cipriano hung over a side altar in the dark, desolate, grand old church, where no worshipper ever came except a tired peasant, or a shepherd sheltering from a storm.

Della Rocca pulled aside the moth-eaten curtains from the adjacent window, and let the sunshine in. Some little children were sitting on the altar-steps stringing daisies and berries ; the light made a halo about their heads ; the deep Venetian colours of the forgotten picture glanced like jewels through the film of the dust of ages. Its theme was the martyrdom of the Magician and of S. Justina ; beneath were the crowds of

Nicomedia and the guards of Diocletian, above
were the heavens opened and the hosts of waiting
angels.   It was a great theme greatly treated by
the great Brescian who, although the pupil of
Titian and the rival of Veronese is so little
known, save in the cities that lie betwixt the
Dolomites and the Apennines.

"It is one of the most beautiful legends that
we have, to my thinking," said Della Rocca, when
they had studied it minutely and in all lights.
"It has been very seldom selected by painters
for treatment; one wonders why; perhaps because there is too much human passion in it for
a sacred subject."

"Yes," said Lady Hilda, dreamily.   "One
can never divest oneself of the idea that S. Justina loved him with an earthly love."

"Oh, Hilda! how pagan of you," said the
Marchesa del Trasimene, a little aghast.

"Not at all.   Why should we doubt it?" said
Della Rocca, quickly.   "Why should we deny
that a pure love would have power against the
powers of the world?"

Lady Hilda looked at him, and a great softness

came into her face ; then she stooped to the little children playing with the berries on the altar-steps, and put some money in their little brown hands.

"It is a very fine picture," she said, after a moment's pause. "I do not think I have ever seen brown and gold and crimson so beautifully managed, and fused in so deep a glow of colour save in Palma Vecchio's S. Barbara—you remember—in S. Maria Formosa in Venice ?"

"The portrait of Violante Palma—yes. But this subject has a deeper and warmer interest. S. Barbara with her tower and her cannon is too strong to touch one very much. One cannot think that she ever suffered."

"Yet S. Barbara has a very wide popularity, if one may use the word to a saint."

"All symbols of strength have ; the people are weak ; they love what will help them. It is very singular what deep root and vast fame one saint has, and how obscure remains another ; yet both equal in holiness and life, and courage of death. Perhaps the old painters have done it by the frequency of their choice of certain themes."

"Oh, no," said Lady Hilda; "be sure the painters rather followed the public preference than directed it. Poets lead; painters only mirror. I like this San Cipriano very much. They did not say too much of it. It is left to dust and damp. Could I buy it do you think?"

"I dare say,— I will inquire for you to-morrow. We sell anything now. When the public debt is a little heavier, and the salt tax is protested against, we shall sell the Transfiguration—why not?—we have a copy at S. Peter's. Indeed, why keep the S. Cecilia doing nothing in a dark old city like Bologna, when its sale with a few others might make a minister or a senator well off for life?"

"Do not be so bitter, Paolo," said the Marchesa Nina, "you might have been a minister yourself."

"And rebuilt Palestrina out of my commission on the tax on cabbages! Yes, I have lost my opportunities."

The Lady Hilda was gazing at the clouds of angels in the picture, who bore aloft the martyred souls in their immortal union; and from them she glanced at the little fair wondering faces of the peasant children. She had never thought about children ever in any way, save as little figures that composed well in Stothard's drawings, in Sir Joshua's pictures, in Correggio's frescoes. Now, for a second, the thought glanced through her that women were happy who had those tender soft ties with the future of the world. What future had she?—You cannot make a future out of diamonds, china, and M. Worth.

"You really wish to buy the San Cipriano?" he asked her, as they passed over the worn, damp pavement towards the sunlight of the open door.

"Yes—you seem to think it sacrilege?"

"No; I think the moral decadence of feeling which makes it possible for my nation to sell such things is a sacrilege against our past, and a violation of the rights of our posterity;—but that is another matter, and no fault of yours. What will you do with it when you have it?"

"I will put it in my oratory in Paris."

The answer jarred on him; yet there was no other which he could have expected.

R

"How naturally you think of buying all you see!" he said, a little impatiently. "I suppose that power of acquisition—that wand of possession—is very dear to you."

"What do you mean? I do not know—it is a habit. Yes; I suppose one likes it."

"No doubt. Your riches are to you as his magic was to San Cipriano yonder: the willingest of slaves."

"What!—an evil spirit then?"

"Not necessarily. But——"

"But what?"

"A despot, though a slave. One who holds your soul; as the powers of darkness held his, until a great and spiritual love set him free."

They were passing out of the open doorway into the calm golden light of the passing day. Through the fine tracery of the olive-boughs the beautiful valley shone like a summer sea. Before them, above the southern mountains, the sun was going down. Her eyes grew dim for a moment as she looked. His hand had closed on hers; she let it lie within his clasp; it was the first gesture of tenderness she had ever allowed to him. Then at a sudden recollection she withdrew it, and she smiled with her old serene indifference.

" You *will* talk to me in unknown tongues! S. Justina was a holy woman; I am not. I am not sure that I ever did any unselfish thing in all my life. How many violets there are;—gather me some."

The others drew near; he left her and gathered the violets. They were countless; the old church was left alone to perish; no foot of priest or worshipper now ever trod upon their purple glories.

She leaned over the low wall of the grave-yard, and watched the setting sun. She felt that her eyes were full of tears.

" If I had met him earlier——" she thought.

They walked down through the olive thickets, along the grassy slopes of the hill, to the carriage, and drove home in the now waning light.

She was capricious, contemptuous, ironical, arrogant, in everything she said, lying back with the furs covering her from the chill evening winds.

" Does going to a church alway make you so caustic, cara mia ? " said the Marchesa Nina.

Della Rocca was very silent. The French artist kept up the ball of talk with her and the lovely Marchesa, and played the gay game well. The sun sank quite; the brief twilight came; then darkness; the horses took them down through the walled lanes and the rose hedges into the narrow streets, where here and there the lamps were twinkling, and the glow of the wood fires shone through the grated casements.

The carriage paused first at the Hôtel Murat.

"I shall see you to-night at Princess Fürstenberg's, Hilda, of course ? " said the Marchesa.

" Oh, yes," said the Lady Hilda as she descended, drawing her sables closer around her. " You will be there, I suppose?" she added, with a little change of her voice, to Della Rocca, as he held his arm for her to alight. He looked straight down into her eyes.

" I think not," he said, simply. "Good night, Madame."

He stood with his head uncovered, whilst she went up the steps of the hotel; then, as the door closed on her, he walked away to his own old house.

Lady Hilda went up to her own rooms; she had a knot of violets with her. Before she put them in water she touched them with her lips —as any girl of sixteen or any peasant Gretchen might have done.

That night at the Princess Fürstenberg's—one of the pleasantest houses of the winter city—men and women both said to one another that they had never seen her looking more beautiful, or more magnificent in the blaze of her jewels, but they found her colder, and more difficult to converse with than ever, and were more than ever hopelessly impressed with the sense of their own absolute nullity in her eyes.

He was not there.

She stayed but a brief time; long enough to chill every one there like ice, which was the effect she always produced in society, when it was so unhappy as not to please her; then, having frozen it, she left it,—the ladies who remained breathing freer when her delicate loveliness and her mighty emeralds had ceased to outshine them. She sank back in her carriage with a great sigh.

The homeward streets led past the palace of the Della Rocca. She let the window down, and looked outward as she passed it. She saw a single casement alone lighted in the great black mass of frowning stone, with its machicolated walls and iron stanchions. It was above the entrance ; she knew it was his favourite room ; where his books were, and his old bronzes, and his favourite weapons.

Her eyes filled with tears again as she looked up at the solitary light. She felt for the little cluster of violets that she had fastened under the great emeralds in her bosom,—his hand had gathered them.

" If anyone had told me I would care ! " she thought to herself.

The tears on her lashes stole slowly down, and dimmed the emeralds and refreshed the violets.

She was the most heartless creature in the world ; the coldest and most self-engrossed of women, her friends and acquaintances were saying after her departure, in the drawing-rooms of the Princess Fürstenberg ; not like her cousin; dear little Madame Mila was all good nature, all kindliness, all heart.

At the Fiera for the orphan children the week before had not dear little Madame Mila slaved herself to death ; bustling about in the most bewitching costume ; whirling like a little Japanese wind-mill; wearing the loveliest little muslin apron, with huge pockets, into which thousands of francs were poured ; turning the lottery-wheel indefatigably for three days, and selling cigars she had lighted, and lilies of the valley she had kissed, at the most fabulous prices for the good of the poor ? And had not Lady Hilda con· temptuously refused to have anything to do with the Fiera at all?

The almoner of the charities, indeed, had received a fifty-thousand franc note anonymously. But then, how could anybody divine that the Lady Hilda had sent it because a chance word of Della Rocca's had sunk into her mind ? Whereas everybody saw Madame Mila whirling, and saying so prettily, " Pour nos pauvres !—pour nos chers pauvres ! "

CHAPTER IX.

THE next morning they brought her a note; it said that he had inquired about the San Cipriano, but the matter had to be referred to some authority absent in Rome, and there could be no answer for a few days, perhaps weeks; the note was signed with the assurance of the highest consideration of the humblest of her servants,— Paolo della Rocca.

The note might have been read from the house-top: she had had letters from him of a different strain; charming little brief letters, about a flower, about an opera-box, about a piece of pottery, always about some trifle, but making the trifle the medium of a delicately-veiled homage, and a softly-hinted tenderness.

She tossed the note into the fire, and saw his name burn in the clear flame of a pine branch : why could he not have called instead of writing?

She was restless all day, and nothing pleased her :—not even M. de St. Louis, who did call and sat a long time, and was in his most delightful humour, and full of new anecdotes about everybody and everything :—but he did not mention Della Rocca.

The Duc found no topic that suited her. It was the Corso di Gala that afternoon, would she not go?

No : her horses hated masks, and she hated noise.

The Veglione on Sunday—would she not go to that?

No : those things were well enough in the days of Philippe d'Orléans, who invented them, but they were only now as stupid as they were vulgar; anybody was let in for five francs.

Did she like the new weekly journal, that was electrifying Paris?

No: she could see nothing in it: there was no wit now-a-days—only personalities, which grew more gross every year.

The Duc urged that personalities were as old as Cratinus and Archilochus, and that five hundred years before Christ the satires of Hipponax drove Bupalus to hang himself.

She answered that a bad thing was not the better for being old.

People were talking of a clever English novel translated everywhere, called "In a Hothouse," the hothouse being society—had she seen it?

No: what was the use of reading novels of society by people who never had been in it? The last English "society" novel she had read had described a cabinet minister in London as going to a Drawing-room in the crowd, with everybody else, instead of by the *petite entrée;* they were always full of such blunders.

Had she read the new French story "Le Bal de Mademoiselle Bibi?"

No: she had heard too much of it; it made you almost wish for a Censorship of the Press.

The Duc agreed that literature was terribly

but truly described as " un tas d'ordures soig-
neusement enveloppé."

She said that the " tas d'ordures " without the
envelope was sufficient for popularity, but that
the literature of any age was not to be blamed
—it was only a natural growth, like a mushroom;
if the soil were noxious, the fungus was bad.

The Duc wondered what a censorship would
let pass if there were one.

She said that when there was one it had let
pass Crebillon, the Chevalier Le Clos, and
the "Bijoux Indiscrets;" it had proscribed Mar-
montel, Helvetius, and Lanjuinais. She did
not know how one man could be expected to be
wiser than all his generation.

The Duc admired some majolica she had purchased.

She said she began to think that majolica was
a false taste; the metallic lustre was fine, but
how clumsy the forms; one might be led astray
by too great love of old work.

The Duc praised a magnificent Sèvres panel,
just painted by Riocreux and Goupil, and given
to her by Princess Olga on the New Year.

She said it was well done, but what charm was there in it? All their modern iron and zinc colours, and hydrate of aluminum, and oxide of chromium, and purple of Cassius, and all the rest of it, never gave one-tenth the charm of those old painters who had only green greys and dull blues and tawny yellows, and never could get any kind of red whatever; Olga had meant to please her, but she, for her part, would much sooner have had a little panel of Abruzzi, with all the holes and defects in the pottery, and a brown contadina for a Madonna; there was some interest in that,—there was no interest in that gorgeous landscape and those brilliant hunting figures.

The Duc bore all the contradictions with imperturbable serenity and urbanity, smiled to himself, and bowed himself out in perfect good humour.

"Tout va bien," he thought to himself; "Miladi must be very much in love to be so cross."

The Duc's personal experience amongst ladies had made him of opinion that love did not improve the temper.

"The carriage waits, Miladi," said her servant.

"I shall not drive to-day," said Lady Hilda.
"Tell them to saddle Saïd."

It was a brilliant day; all the bells were pealing; and the sunshine and the soft wind streaming in. She thought a ten-mile stretch across
the open country might do her good; at any
rate, it would be better than sitting at home, or
pacing slowly in the procession of the Corso di
Gala, which was only a shade less stupid than
the pelting Corso.

Saïd was a swift, nervous, impetuous horse;
the only sort of horse she cared to ride; and he
soon bore her beyond the gates, leaving the
carriages of her friends to crush each other in
the twisting streets, and vie in state liveries and
plumes and ribbons and powdered servants, and
amuse the good-natured, kindly, orderly crowds
of Floralia, clustered on the steps of churches
and under the walls of palaces.

She rode against the wind, as straight as
the state of the roads would permit her, as
wonderful a sight to the astonished country
people as though she had been S. Margarita on

her dragon. Saïd took a few stone walls and sunkened fences, which put him on good terms with himself. She was in no mood to spare him, or avoid any risks it might amuse him to run; and they had soon covered many more miles than she knew.

"Where are we?" she asked her groom, when Saïd slackened his pace at last.

The groom, who was a Scotchman, had no idea and no power of asking.

"It does not matter," said his mistress, and rode on again.

They were on a tolerably broad road, with a village above them, on a steep green vine-clad hill; there were the usual olive orchards everywhere, with great almond trees full of blossom and white as driven snow, and farther still all around the countless curves of the many mountain spurs that girdle the valley of Floralia. There was another stone wall in front of them; beyond it the turf looked fresh and pleasant; she put Saïd at it, but someone from a distance called out to her in Italian, "For God's sake stop the horse!"

On the other side of the wall the ground fell suddenly to a depth of twenty feet.

She caught up Saïd's head in time only by a moment; he stood erect on his hind legs a second, but she kept her seat unshaken; she thought he would lose his balance and fall back on her; but she stilled and controlled him with the coolest nerve. As he descended on his front feet, Della Rocca came through a high iron gate on the left, leapt a ditch, and sprang to the horse's head.

"How can you do such mad things?" he said, with a quiver in his voice. "That gate was locked; I could only shout to you. I thought I was too late——"

His face was pale as death; her colour had not even changed. She looked at him and smiled a little.

"So many thanks—it is a silly habit taking walls; I learned to like it when I was a child, and rode with my brother. Saïd is not frightened now; you may let him alone. Where are we?"

"On the ground of Palestrina."

" Palestrina ! I see nothing of your villa."

" We are eight miles from the villa. It lies beyond those other hills—but all the ground here is mine. I was visiting one of my farms. By heaven's mercy I saw you——"

His voice still faltered, and his face was pale with strong emotion; his hand had closed on hers, and rested on her knee.

" You were behind that tall gate then ? "

" Yes; I have the key of that gate, but the lock was rusted. Come and rest a moment, you are a long way from Floralia. There is an old farmhouse here ; they are all my own people."

She dismounted and threw the bridle to her groom.

" It terrifies you more than it did me," she said, with a little laugh.

He took both her hands and kissed them ; he did not answer, neither did she rebuke him.

He led her through the iron gate down a grassy path between the grey gnarled olive trees and the maples with their lithe red boughs ; there was a large old house with clouds of pigeons round it, and great mulberry trees near, and sculp-

tured shields and lions on the walls ; women ran
to him delightedly, men left their ploughs afar
off and came, eager and bareheaded, to see if there
was any chance to serve him; he was their
prince, their lord, their idol, their best friend ; as
their fathers had followed his to the death, so
would they have followed him. Half a dozen
flew to do each word of his bidding; brought in
the horse, brought out an oaken settle for her in
the sun, brought fresh water from the spring,
fresh lemons from the tree, fresh violets from the
hedges. At a sign from him one of the shepherd-
boys, who was famous for his singing, came and
stood before them, and sang to his guitar some of
the love-songs of the province in a sweet tenor
voice, liquid as the singing of nightingales. The
green and gracious country was around, the low
sun made the skies of the west radiant, the smell
of the woods and fields rose fresh from the
earth. She drank the draught he made for her,
and listened to the singing, and watched the
simple pastoral, old-world life around her, and
felt her heart thrill as she met the amorous
worship of his eyes.

S

She had never thought of natural beauty, or of
the lives of the poor, save now and then when
they had been recalled to her by some silvery
landscape of Corot, or some sad rural idyl of
Millet; as she sat here, she felt as if she had
passed all her life in some gorgeous heated
theatre, and had only now come out into the
open air, and under the arch of heaven.

There was a wonderful dreamy, lulling charm
in this olive-hidden solitude ; she did not care to
move, to think, to analyze.   He did not speak to
her of love ; they both avoided words, which,
spoken, might break the spell of their present
peace and part them; but every now and then his
eyes looked into hers, and were heavy with the
langour of silent passion, and stirred her heart to
strange sweet tumult.

When the boy sang the passionate, plaintive
love-songs, then her face grew warm, and her
eyelids fell—it was no longer an unknown tongue
to her.

She would not think of the future—she re-
signed herself to the charm of the hour.

So also did he.

The night before he had resolved to avoid her, to cease to see her, to forget her. She had wounded him, and he had told himself that it was best to let the world have her, body and soul. Now chance had overruled his resolve : he could not war with his fate—he let it come as it might. He had found his way to influence her ; he knew that he could move her as no other could ; yet he hesitated to say to her what must unite them or part them.

Besides, since this woman had grown dear to him with a passion born alike out of her physical beauty and his own sense of power on her, and his insight into the richer possibilities of her nature, the colder calculations which had occupied him at his first knowledge of her seemed to him base and unworthy : if he had not loved her he would have pursued her with no pang of conscience; having grown to love her, to love her loveliness, and her pride, and her variableness, and her infinite charm, and her arrogant faults, to love *her* in a word, and to desire indescribably to lead her from the rank miasma of the pleasures and pomps of the world into a clearer and higher

s 2

spiritual atmosphere, he recoiled more and more, day by day, from seeking her as the medium of his own fortune, he checked himself more and more in the utterance of a passion which could but seem to her mingled at the least with the lowest of motives.

He was her lover, he did not disguise it from himself or her ; but he paused before doing that which would make him win or lose it all; not because he feared his fate, but because he could not bring himself to the acceptance of it.

"Sing me something yourself," she said to him ; and he took the boy's mandolin and, leaning against the porch of the house, touched a chord of it now and then, and sang her every thing she would, while the sun shone in the silver of the olives and the afternoon shadows stole slowly down the side of the mountains. Then he sat down on the steps at her feet, and talked to her of his people, of his land, of his boyhood and his youth.

"I have lived very much in the great world," he said, after a time. "This world which you think is the only one. But I am never so well content as when I come back here under my olives. I suppose you cannot understand that?"

"I am not sure—yes, perhaps. One grows tired of everything," she answered with a little sigh.

"Everything that is artificial, you mean. People think Horace's love of the rural life an affectation. I believe it to be most sincere. After the strain of the conventionality and the adulation of the Augustan Court, the natural existence of the country must have been welcome to him. I know it is the fashion to say that a love of Nature belongs only to the Moderns, but I do not think so. Into Pindar, Theocritus, Meleager, the passion for Nature must have entered very strongly; what *is* modern is the more subjective, the more fanciful, feeling which makes Nature a sounding-board to echo all the cries of man."

"But that is always a northern feeling?"

"Inevitably. With us Nature is too *riante* for us to grow morbid about it. The sunshine that laughs around us nine months of every year, the fruits that grow almost without culture, the

flowers that we throw to the oxen to eat, the
very stones that are sweet with myrtle, the very
sea sand that is musical with bees in the rosemary,
everything we grow up amongst from infancy
makes our love of Nature only a kind of unconscious joy in it—but here even the peasant
has that, and the songs of the men that
cannot read or write are full of it.   If a field
labourer sing to his love he will sing of the
narcissus and the crocus, as Meleager sang to
Heliodora twenty centuries ago——"

"And your wild narcissus is the true narcissus; the Greek narcissus, with its many bells
to one stem?"

"Yes.   In March and April it will be out
everywhere in the fields and woods about
here.   I thought once that you loved flowers
as you loved art, merely as a decoration of
your salon.   But I was wrong.   They are
closer to your heart than that.   Why do you
deny your emotions?   Why do you mask
yourself under such cold phrases as those you
used to me yesterday?"

She smiled a little.

" How should I remember what I said so long back as yesterday ? "

" That is hard !—for those who hear may remember for a lifetime. Your words kept me from where you were last night."

" What I say at any time is worth but little thought. I fear you think too well of me always," she said, on a sudden vague impulse and the first pang of humility that she had ever allowed to smite the superb vanity that had always en-wrapped her.

With a soft grace of action he touched with his lips the hem of her riding skirt.

"No," he said simply, "you might indeed 'daze one to blindness like the noonday sun.' But I am not blind. I see in you many errors, more against yourself than others ; I see the discontent which always argues high unsatisfied desire, and the caprice which is merely the offshoot of too long indulgence of all passing fancies ; but what matter these ?—your nature and the nobility of it lie underneath them in a vein of gold unworked. You have had the language of flattery to nausea : I do not give it you ; I say but what I believe."

The tears sprang into her eyes, and the music of his voice thrilled through her.

She did not care to wait for the words that she knew would follow as his fingers stole and clasped hers close, and she felt on her the gaze she did not dare to meet. She rose, and glanced to the west.

"The sun is just gone behind the hills. I shall be late. Will you tell them to bring me Saïd?'

He rose, too, and did not oppose her departure.

"I rode here myself, fortunately," he said. "You must allow me to go with you into Floralia; the roads are bad and hard to find."

They brought Saïd out of the great wooden sweet-smelling outhouse, and he raised her in silence to her saddle. He gave her a little knot of the fragrant leafless calycanthus with a few sprays of myrtle; she put it in her bosom; it was already dusk, and he saw the softened dimness of her eyes.

They rode down together in the declining light through the winding ways of the outlying country into the town; it was quite dark when they reached the gates ; they had ridden fast and spoken scarcely at all.

As he lifted her from Saïd in the gloom within the scarcely lighted street, he pressed her softly for one second in his arms, so that she felt the beating of his heart.

" A rive derci ! " he murmured.

She left him in silence, and without rebuke.

"Is that you, Duca ? " said the voice of Madame Mila in the darkness, as a carriage, gorgeous with amber and gold liveries and with Carnival camellias at the horses' heads, pulled up with great noise and haste before the hotel door.

" Is that you, Duca ?   I am so glad ; I wanted to speak to you.   The Corso was horridly stupid. I don't care a bit except for the pelting days, do you.   I sprained my arm last year in Rome with the pelting, and I really blinded poor Salvareo for a week.   Why, dear me, that's Saïd !   Have you and Hilda been riding together ? "

" I met your cousin, Madame, by chance ; she had lost her way.   It is very easy to do so amongst our hills."

" How very fortunate that you met her ! " said
Madame Mila, with a little saucy laugh. " She
will kill herself riding that horrid Saïd some day
—perhaps she will listen to you if you tell her
not. What was it I wanted to say,—oh, I want a
very good box for the Veglione. You are one of
the directors of the opera, are you not ? "

" Yes."

" I thought so. Well, mind I have one; big
enough to hold the supper table comfortably;
and see Maurice about it, and dine with me to-
morrow, will you ? Nina and Olga and the
usual people. Dear me, how these horses do
fidget. How very nice that you should have
met dear Hilda just when she 'd lost her way !
Good bye; but, of course, you 'll be at the
Roubleskoffs' to-night ? I wish it wasn't costume. I'm England, and I'm embroidered all
over with Union Jacks; and I have a little
Khedive on a gold stick that keeps tumbling up
and down; and I carry a ship in full sail on the
top of my head. I assure you it's very trying to
be a Naval Power. How ever I shall be able to
waltz with that ship !——"

Della Rocca rode away in the darkness, as the skirts of Madame Mila vanished in the hotel doorway with the gleam of the golden-pheasant trimmings shining under the gas lamp.

He went home to his solitary dinner, and scarcely touched it, and barely even noticed his dog. He sat alone a long time, thinking, in the same room where, four months before, he had pondered on the Duc de St. Louis's counsels, and had decided to himself that this woman, beautiful, though she was, was arrogant, unimpressionable, extravagantly capricious, and in every way antagonistic to him.

Now, he was passionately in love with her himself; he knew that she was deeply moved by him; he believed that he had only to ask and have; and yet he hesitated.

It was the marriage of all other marriages for him; he had softened and subdued her in a manner which could not but intoxicate his vanity, though he had less vanity than most men; he did not distrust her character, because he believed that there was a vague lofty nobility in it, and a latent, though untouched, tenderness; of her

caprices, of her changefulness, of her moods of
contempt, and of impatience, he had no fear; he
would substitute other emotions for them.   And
yet he hesitated; he was unresolved; he was
doubtful whether to accept the empire he had
obtained.

He would have concluded a marriage of interest
as coldly and tranquilly as any other man with a
woman to whom he was indifferent.   But with
this woman whose mere touch thrilled him to the
heart, and whose imperious eyes had only grown
gentle for his sake!—never had he felt his
poverty so painfully as in this moment when
supreme Fortune seemed to have smiled upon
him.

Though he loved her with passion, he almost
wished that he had never seen her face.

After all, though generous, she was arrogant;—
sooner or later she might make him feel that the
golden sceptre was hers and not his.   To his
temper, which, although gentle, was deeply ingrained with the pride which had been transmitted
to him from many generations of a feudal nobility,
such a possibility seemed unendurable.   He sat

still lost in thought till his lamp grew low, and the wind rising loud, shook the leaded panes of the old high windows.

"I suppose when Fortune does smile at us, we always quarrel with her so," he thought, with some impatience of his own irresolution.

After all, what other man in Europe would not have been content?

He got up, caressed the dog, turned the lamp higher, and went into his bed-chamber.

"Get out the white mousquetaire dress," he said to his old servant. "I will go to the Roubles-koff ball."

All patrician Floralia was at the Roubleskoff ball, one of the last great entertainments of the expiring Carnival. In six more days there would come the Day of Ashes; and Floralia would repent her sins in sadness,—that is, with only musical parties, a dinner here and there, and no suppers at all; (perhaps a ball might be squeezed in once or twice by grace of the Russian Calendar, but, then, if you took advantage of that you were *brouillé* with all the *codini* at once).

He reached the Roubleskoff villa late, not so

late but what he was in time to see the arrival of
the woman who had sat with him at her feet, and
talked with him of Meleager and the white narcissus flowers.

Lady Hilda entered like a sovereign, and drew
all eyes on herself.

She was attired as Vittoria Colonna, and
carried her purples and cloth of gold with more
than royal grace; the colour on her cheek was
heightened, her eyes had a dewy brilliancy;
what they spoke to her she seemed hardly to
hear.

He was as her shadow all the evening.

They were both feverishly happy; both curiously troubled. Neither cared to look onward.

Society there assembled said that it was a
great thing for the Duca della Rocca; and wondered whether they would live most in Floralia
or Paris.

" C'est moi qui a inspiré cela," said the Duc de
St. Louis, with much self-complacency, sitting
down to the whist table; he was quite sure that
all was right; he had seen the look in the eye
of both of them.

"She will compromise herself at last. Oh, what a comfort it will be!" thought little Madame Mila, carrying her frigate in full sail airily through the mazes of the cotillon, with a sleeveless bodice on, cut so low that it was really as good—or as bad—as if she had had nothing at all. She did not wish any harm, of course, only, really, Hilda, with a lover like other people, would be so much more natural and agreeable.

"But they will marry, people say," suggested M. des Gommeux, to whom alone she confided these ideas.

"When do people ever say anything that is true?" said Madame Mila, with profound contempt, tossing her little head till the Naval Power of England was in jeopardy. She was irritated to hear Maurice even talk about marriage; it was an improper thing for him even to mention, considering his relation to herself. When he approached any young girl or marriageable woman of any sort, Madame Mila bristled like a little angry terrier that sees a cat; on the whole, she was still more exacting than Mlles.

Rose Thè and Boulotte, and whereas in society he could escape from them, he could in nowise escape from her.

If it had been a question of marriage for her cousin, indeed, Madame Mila would have opposed it tooth and nail; she had a feeling, a very accurate one, that Della Rocca did not approve of herself, and that he would certainly never allow his wife, if he had one, to be very intimate with her. But Madame Mila knew what other people did not; that there could be no question of such a marriage for her cousin; and so she smiled on Della Rocca, and was always engaging him to dinner; because Lady Hilda, with her lover about her, like any one else, would be so much more humanized and natural, and would sympathise so much better with other people.

That kind of virtue of Hilda's—if it were virtue—was such an odd, chilly, unpleasant thing, she thought; to live in that way, with hundreds of men seeking her, and cold alike to them all, was something so very unnatural; it was almost as bad as being one of those queer women who wouldn't tie their skirts back, or wear high heels, or dress their hair properly :—it was so strange, too, in a person who, in all other matters, was the very queen of fashion, the very head and front of the most perfect worldliness.

It was very late and daylight quite when Lady Hilda, contrary to her custom, left the ball; she had been happy with a warmth and feverishness of happiness altogether new to her; nothing more had passed between them, but they had been together all the night, although never alone.

She stood a moment in the doorway facing the daylight. Most women are ruined by such a test; she looked but the fairer for it, with the sunrise flush touching her cheeks, and the pearls and the diamonds in her hair.

"I may come to you early," he murmured, as she paused that instant on the step.

"Yes—no. No: I shall be tired. Wait till the evening. You are coming to Mila."

The words were a denial; but on her lips there was sweetness, and in her eyes a soft emotion as she moved onward and downward to the carriage.

He was not dissatisfied nor dismayed. As

T

he drew the furs over her gold-laden skirts, his head bore lower and lower, and his lips touched her hand and her arm.

" The sun is up. I never am so late as this," she said, as though she did not feel those kisses ; but, by the clear light of the day-dawn, he saw the blood mantle over her throat and bosom, and the tremulous shadow of a smile move her mouth.

The horses sprang forward ; he stood on the lower step, grave and lost in thought.

"Is it too early to offer felicitations, my friend?" said the Duc de St. Louis, passing to go homeward ; he had been playing whist all night.

" I do not understand you," he answered, with the tranquil falsehood of society.

The question annoyed him deeply. He loved this woman with all the tenderness and passion of his temperament, and loved her the more for the ascendency he had gained over her and the faults that he saw in her; he loved her generously, truly, and with purer desire than most men. Yet what would his love for her ever look to the world?—since he was poor.

Meanwhile she, with her fair hair tumbled

about her pillows, and her gorgeous cloth of
gold lying on a couch like a queen's robes
abandoned, slept restlessly, yet with a smile
on her face, some few hours : when she awoke
it was with a smile, and with that vague sweet
sense of awakening to some great joy, which
is one of the most precious gifts of happiness ;
dreamful misty sense of expectation and recollections blending in one, and making the light
of day beautiful.

She lay still some time, awake, and yet
dreaming, with half-closed eyelids and her thick
hair loosened and covering her shoulders, and
the sweet scent close at hand of a glassful of
myrtle and calycanthus, that she had been very
careful to tell them to set near her bed. Lazily,
after awhile, she rang a little bell, and bade her
maids open her shutters, the grand light of the
noonday poured into the chamber.

"Give me a mirror," she said to them.

When they gave her one, she looked at herself
and smiled again : she was one of those women
who are lovely when they wake : there are not
many.

T 2

They brought her her chocolate, and she sipped a little of it, and lay still, looking at the myrtle and hearing the ringing of church bells from across the water; she was happy; it seemed to her that all her life before had not been happiness after all;—only pleasure.

An hour later her maid brought her a telegram. She opened it with a little impatience. Why should anything break in on her day dream?

It merely said that her brother was in Paris, and would come onward; and be with her that night. She let the papers fall, as though she were stung by an adder.

It recalled to her what she had forgotten.

CHAPTER X.

Lord Clairvaux arrived in time for Madame Mila's dinner. He was an affectionate and sunny-tempered man; he did not notice that his sister did not once say she was glad to see him.

Della Rocca did notice it, with that delicate unerring Italian perception, which is as fine as a needle and as subtle as mercury.

He saw, too, that something had come over her; some cloud; some change; she had lost much of her proud serenity, and she looked at him now and then with what seemed to him almost like contrition; she avoided being alone with him; he was troubled at it, but not alarmed; he knew very well that she loved him. He let her be.

An Italian has infinite passion, but he has also infinite patience in matters of love. Nor was he, now that he was assured of his power over her, wholly content to use it; if he married her, the world would always say that it was for her wealth. That means of raising his own fortunes which had seemed to him so material and legitimate all his life, now seemed to him unworthy and unmanly since he had grown to care for her. He knew that such riches as she possessed were precisely those with which he had always intended to rebuild the fallen greatness of his race; but since he had loved her it looked very different.

The charm of their intercourse to him was the ascendency he had won over her, the power that he had gained to lift her nature to a higher level: where would his influence be when he had once stooped to enrich himself by its means?

These fancies saddened him and checked him, and made him not unwilling to linger on about her, in all that indistinct sweetness of half-recognised and half-unspoken love.

The position, uncertain as it was, had its

charm; he felt that this woman, with all her insolence and indifference and absorption by the world, was, in his hands, only a creature of emotions and of passions, who would flush at his touch, and grow unnerved under his gaze; he knew that he was very dear to her since, had he not been, for the audacity of his caresses he would have been driven out of her presence.

"Ama chi t'ama, e lascia dir la gente," he said to himself in the wise burden of the people's love-song; and he let destiny go as it would.

Meanwhile, she, dissatisfied, with a conscience ill at ease, and disinclined to look into the future, saw him morning, noon, and night, but avoided seeing him alone, and usually had her brother near.

Lord Clairvaux could only stay a week, and was utterly unconscious that his presence was unwelcome; he was taken to see the two Arab mares of Della Rocca; he was taken to Palestrina; he was taken to studios and chapels, which had no more interest for him than they would have had for a setter dog : but he was quite ignorant of why he was taken.

He did what Lady Hilda told him to do; he
always did when he and she were together;
he was a simple, kindly, honest gentleman,
who regarded England as the universe, and all
the rest of the world as a mere accident.
His sister's contempt for her country and his
politics, her philosophy of indifferentism, her
adoration of primitive art, her variable disdain,
and her intellectual pharisaism had always seemed
to him very wonderful, and not altogether comfortable; but he admired her in a hopeless kind
of way, and it was not in his temper to puzzle
over people's differences of opinion or character.

"Hilda thinks all the old dead fellows were
gods, and she thinks all of us asses," he would
say humbly. "I don't know, you know,—she's
awfully clever. I never was. It may be so,
only I never will believe that England is used
up, as she says; and I like the east wind myself;
and what she can see in those saints she's
just bought, painted on their tiptoes, or in those
old crooked pots;—but if she'd stayed in the
country, and hunted twice a week all winter, you
know she would not have been like that."

"It would have been a great pity had Miladi been anything save what she is," said Della Rocca, to whom he expressed himself in this manner, in such French as he could command, and who was amused and astonished by him, and who took him a day's wild fowl shooting in the marshes, and a day's wild boar hunting in the next province, and wondered constantly why so kindly and gallant a gentleman should have been made by the good God so very stupid.

"Oh, you think so; I don't," said Lord Clairvaux. "Hilda isn't my idea of a happy woman. I don't believe she is happy. She spends half her life thinking how she will dress herself; and why will they dress now like the ruffs and things of Queen Elizabeth, and the effigies on the tombstones? and the other half she spends buying things she never looks at, and ordering things she dislikes when they're done, and reading books that make her think her own countrymen are a mere lot of block-heads and barbarians. Not that I pretend to understand her; I never did; only I think if

she didn't think everybody else such a fool she'd
be more comfortable."

Della Rocca smiled.

"Pardon me,—you will disturb the birds."

Lord Clairvaux recollected that he ought not
to talk of his sister to a stranger, and, bringing
his gun to his shoulder, fired into a covey of wild
ducks.

"What a handsome fellow that is, like an old
picture," he thought to himself, as he looked at
Della Rocca, who sat in the prow of the boat;
but he did not connect him in his thoughts with
Lady Hilda in any way: for ten years he had
got so tired of vainly wondering why this man
and that did not please her, and had been made
so vexed and perplexed by her rejection of the
Prince of Deutschland, that he had ceased to
think of her as a woman who could possibly
ever care for anybody.

One night, however, when he had been there
five days, he was walked about in the crowd of
the Veglione by little Madame Mila, masked, and
draped as black as a little beetle; and Madame
Mila, who was getting tired of things standing

still, and could no more help putting her tiny
finger into all kinds of pasties, and making mis-
chief in a kittenish way, than she could help
going on enamelling since she had once begun it,
laughed at him, teazed him, and told him, what
startled him.

" But she isn't here, and he is ! " he gasped
feebly, in protest at what he had heard, gazing
over the motley crowd.

" What a goose you are ;—as if that showed
anything ! They can meet much better than in
this place," said Madame Mila, with a saucy
laugh.

He turned on her with a heavy frown.

" Hang it, Mila ! you don't dare to mean——"

Madame Mila was frightened in an instant.

" Oh, dear, no ; of course not ; only I do assure
you they've been always together ever since I've
been in Floralia. I thought you knew——"

" Damn it, no ! " he muttered. "I beg your
pardon, I never see anything ; I mean, I'm quite
sure there's nothing to see."

" Well, ask her," said Madame Mila : then she
added sweetly, "you know I'm so fond of dear

Hilda; and people do talk so horridly here for nothing at all; and Italians are not so scrupulous as *we* are."

He went home in haste, and was told that Miladi had retired to bed full two hours before. In the morning he sent to ask when he could see her. She sent back word that she should be happy to see him at breakfast at twelve. At ten he received a telegram from his wife asking him to return, because his eldest boy, Cheviot, was unwell, and they feared typhoid fever.

"Damn it all, what a worry!" said Lord Clairvaux to himself, and then went out and smoked on the bank of the river, and looked over the stone parapet moodily.

"Bon-jour, monsieur," a voice said, passing him.

Della Rocca was driving past with a fiery little horse on his way to Palestrina. Lord Clairvaux felt inclined to stop the horse; but what could he say if he did?

What a nuisance it was, he thought; but what could go right in a country where they shot their foxes, and called their brushes tails, and

hung them under the ears of cart-mules and
ponies ?—a country where they treated the foxes
as they did, to say nothing of the Holy Father,
must be a land of malediction.

He smoked through two great cigars, and
walked about the town unhappily, and when it
was noon went upstairs to his sister. He did
not dare to go a moment before the time.

"Dear Freddie, is it you ? " said the Lady
Hilda, listlessly; she looked very lovely and
very languid, in a white cashmere morning
gown, with a quantity of lace about it, and her
hair all thrown back loosely, and tied like the
Venere alla Spina's.

"I have to go away by the night train. Poor
little Cheviot's ill," he said disconsolately, as he
took her hand; he never ventured on kissing her;
years before she had taught him that such endearments were very ridiculous and disagreeable.

"Dear me, I am very sorry. Will you have
coffee, or tea, or wine?" she asked absently, as
she went to the table where the breakfast was.

"Chevy's ᵥery ill," said Lord Clairvaux,

who thought she showed small sympathy. "You used to like Chevy."

"He was a pretty little child. I hate boys."

"You wouldn't if you had them of your own," said Lord Clairvaux, and grumbled inaudibly as he took some cutlets.

Lady Hilda coloured a little.

"I have really not imagination enough to follow you:—will you have coffee? I hope it's nothing serious with Cheviot?"

"Fever, his mother thinks; any way I must go. I saw your friend the Duca della Rocca this morning: he was out early."

He thought this was approaching the subject in a masterly manner.

"Italians always rise early," said the Lady Hilda, giving him his cup.

"And he was at the Veglione last night—"

"All Italians go to the Veglione."

"You have seen a great deal of him, haven't you?" asked Lord Clairvaux, looking at her across the table, and thinking how pretty all that white was which she had on, and what a difficult person she was to begin anything with; he had never felt so nervous since the time when he had once been called on to move the Address when Parliament opened.

" One sees a great deal of everybody in a small society like this."

" Because you know people talk about you and him,—so they say at least."

" They are very good, whoever they are : who are they ? "

" Who ?—Oh, I don't know ; I heard so."

" How very nice of you to discuss me with other people ! "

Lord Clairvaux cast a glance at her and was very much frightened at the offence he saw in her contemptuous face : how pale she was looking too, now he thought of it, and she had shadows underneath her eyes quite new to her.

" What sort of a fellow is he ? " he muttered. He seemed a duffer to me about his fields—such ploughs, by heavens !—and such waste in the stackyards *I* never saw. But it isn't farming here at all; it's letting things go wild just anyhow— "

" It is not being wiser than Nature, and sacri-

ficing all loveliness to greed—if you mean *that*,"
said Lady Hilda, with coldest disdain. "The
life here has still the old Theocritan idyllic
beauty, thank heaven."

"Theocritus? Oh, I know; I never could
construe him; but I do know a straight furrow
and decently kept land when I see it. But I
say, you know, I don't want to be officious or
anything; but do you think it's wise to see so
very much of him? You know he's an Italian,
and I dare say hasn't a bit of principle, nor a
penny in his pocket."

The hazel eyes of the Lady Hilda flashed
golden beams of wrath.

"How very grateful of you!—when he has
entertained you to the best of his ability, and
went out of his way to find sport for you, very
little to his own pleasure, moreover, for I can
assure you *his* soul does not lie in his gun-
barrel!"

"I don't want to say anything against him,"
murmured Lord Clairvaux, who was the most
grateful and most just of mortals. "He was
very kind and courteous, and all that—and I

don't say he's a bad shot, though he's a bad
farmer—and he is an awfully good-looking fellow,
like an old picture, and all that. Only I must
go to-night, Hilda, and I do want to speak to
you."

"You are speaking all this time I believe,"
said Lady Hilda icily, looking across at him
with the coldest challenge in her darkening
eyes.

"I never could think why you didn't take
Deutschland," he muttered, reverting to an old
grievance.

"He didn't please me. Is that all you wanted
to say?"

"But I thought you'd have cared to be a
reigning sovereign?"

"Of a small State?" said the Lady Hilda,
with an eloquent lift of her eyebrows.

"Well, there was De Ribeaupierre; he was
everything anybody could want; Vienna, too; I
used to think an Ambassadress's life would just
suit you."

"Always calling on people and writing notes?
No life on earth more tiresome."

U

" I suppose you want to be an Empress ? "

" Oh dear no," answered his sister. " I have known two Empresses intimately ; and it is a career of great tedium : you can never do what you like."

"Then, I suppose, you are content as you are ? '

" I suppose so, if anybody ever is. I don't think anyone is. I never met anybody who was. They say pigs are ; but one sees so little of pigs hat one can't make much psychological study of them."

Lord Clairvaux grumbled, sighed, and took his courage *à deux mains.*

"Well, never mind the other men ; they are past and gone, poor wretches ; what do you mean to do about this one ? "

" This what ? " said Lady Hilda, looking languidly at him through the flowers on the breakfast table. She knew quite well what he meant.

" What do you mean to do with him ? " repeated Lord Clairvaux solemnly, pushing his plate away. " It's all very pretty, I daresay.

Romeo and moonlight and poetry and all that
sort of thing; Italians are the deuce and all
for that, only I shouldn't have thought you'd
have cared for it; and besides, you know it can't
go on:—the man's a gentleman, that I grant;
and, by heaven, that's a great deal now-a-days,
such blackguards as we're getting,—three card
scandals in the club already this very winter, and
George Orme's was regular sharping, just what
any cad might do, by Jove! But you know you
can't go on with it; you can't possibly mean it
seriously, now, do you?"

Lady Hilda laughed that little cold, contemptuous laughter which her brother always
shivered under, and which Della Rocca had
never heard.

"I don't seriously mean to cheat at cards! My
dear Frederic, you must say what you mean, if
you mean anything at all, a little more clearly,
please. Why will all Englishmen get their talk
into such odd confusion? I suppose it comes of
never learning grammar at Eton."

"Well, hang it then, I'll say it clearly," retorted Clairvaux, with some indignation. "Mila

tells me you and this Italian that's always after you, have taken a liking to one another: is it true?—and what do you mean to do with him? There!"

He was horribly frightened when he had said it, but what he thought was his duty, that he did: and he conceived it to be his duty to speak.

All the blood leapt into the fair face of the Lady Hilda, her nostrils dilated in a fine anger, her lips grew pale.

"Mila is a little wretch!" she said, with strong passion; then was still; she was too generous to quote her own generosity, or urge her past gifts as present claims. "She is a little fool!" she added, with bitter disdain; "and how can *you* cheapen my name by listening to her chattering folly? Besides, what have you to do with me— or what has she? I am not used to dictation— nor to interference!"

"Oh, I know," said her brother, humbly. 'And I beg your pardon, you are sure, and all that;—only, just tell me, how will it end?"

"How will what end?"

" This fancy of yours."

Lady Hilda grew very pale.

" My dear Clairvaux," she said, with chilliest contempt, " you are not my keeper, nor my husband, nor anything else, except one of my trustees. I do not know that being a trustee gives you a title to be impertinent. You really talk as you might to your gamekeeper's daughter, if you thought you saw the girl ' going wrong.' What M. Della Rocca feels for me is merely sympathy in ideas and tastes. But if it were anything else, whose business would it be ? "

Lord Clairvaux laughed.

" Yes!—you are a likely creature to inspire friendship ! As if there were ever a woman worth looking at who could keep a man at that !— don't let us fence about it, Hilda. Perhaps *I* haven't any right to say anything. You're your own mistress and all that, and answerable to nobody. Only, can you deny that I am your brother ? "

" I have always understood you were ! I confess you make me regret the circumstance."

" Now that's ill-natured, very ill-natured," he

murmured pathetically. " But you won't make
me quarrel. There must be two to quarrel, and
I won't be one. We have always been good
friends, more than good friends. I thought I
was the only person on earth you did like——"

" And, like everyone else, you consider that the
liking you inspire confers a privilege to be impertinent," said his sister, with all that disdainful anger flashing from her languid eyes, which
none of her family ever cared very much to meet.

She had risen from her chair, and was moving
to and fro with a restless, controlled impatience.
She remained very pale. Clairvaux kept his
position on the hearth-rug, with a dogged good
humour, and an uneasy confusion blended together which, at any other time, would have
diverted her.

"Perhaps I may be impertinent," he said,
humbly, "though, hang me, if I can see that
that's a natural sort of word to be used between
a brother and sister. I know you're a mighty
great lady, and 'a law to yourself,' as some poet
says; and never listen to anybody, and always
go your own ways, and all that,—but still, if you

never speak to me afterwards, I must say what
I want to say. This man is in love with you,
it's my belief you're in love with him — Mila
says so, and she knows. Now, granted that it is
so (if it isn't there's nothing to be angry about),
what I say is, how do you mean it to end?
Will you marry him?"

Her face changed, flushed, and then grew pale
again.

" Of course not! You know it is impossible!"

" Does he know why it is impossible?"

" No—why should he? Really you do not
know what you are talking about. You are
interfering, in the most uncalled-for manner,
where there is not the slightest necessity for any
interference."

" Then you are letting him fall in love with
you in the dark, and when you have had enough
of the sport will throw him over?"

" You grow very coarse, Clairvaux. Oblige
me by dropping the subject."

"I didn't know I was coarse. That is what
you are going to do. You accept all his court

row—and then you'll turn round on him some
fine morning..and say you've had enough of it.
At least, I can't see what else you will do—since
you cannot marry him.   You'll hardly lower
yourself to Mila's level and all the other women's
—by heavens, if I thought you would, if I
thought you had done, I'd soon see if this fellow
were as fine a swordsman as they say!"

Lady Hilda turned her face full on him.

"So my brother is the first person that ever
dared to insult me?" she said, with utmost
coldness, as she rose from the breakfast table
and swept his feet in passing with the lace
that fringed the hem of her cashmere robes.

She gave him one parting look, and left the
chamber.

He stood cowed by the golden fire of those
superb imperious hazel eyes.   He was nervous
at what he had done, and unhappy and perplexed.   He stood alone, pulling at his fair
beard, in troubled repentance.   He knew what
her wrath would be.   She was not a woman who
quickly forgave.

"I've blundered; I always do blunder," he

thought sadly to himself. "She must care awfully about him to be so angry."

He waited all alone many minutes; he was sincerely sorry; perhaps he had been coarse; he had not meant to be; only, the idea of *her* talked about, and with lovers!—just like all those other women whom their husbands or brothers ought to strangle—it was only fashion, they said, only the way of the world, all that immorality;—"Damn the world," he said to himself, ruffling his beard in sad bewilderment.

He scribbled a trite, rough, penitent note, and sent it to her by her maid. They brought him a closed envelope: when he opened it he found only his own note inside—sent back without any word.

Honest Clairvaux's eyes filled with tears.

"She'll never see me again before I go to-night," he thought to himself, tossing his poor little rejected morsel into the wood fire. "And I must go to-night, because of poor little Chevy. How horrid it is!—I couldn't be angry like that with her!"

He stood some moments more, knitting his

fair, frank forehead, and wishing that he were less stupid in managing things; he had never in his life before presumed to condemn and counsel his sister—and this was the result!

Suddenly an idea struck him, and he rose.

"I will tell him," he thought. "I will tell him himself. And then I shall see what sort of stuff he is made of;—I can fight him afterwards if he don't satisfy me;—I'll tell him as if I suspected nothing—I can make an excuse, but when he hears it he'll show what he's made of;— oh, Lord, if it were only an Englishman she'd taken a liking to!—and to think that she's treated half the best men in Europe as if they were only so many stones under her feet!"

With a groan, Lord Clairvaux took up his hat, and went forth towards the Palazzo Della Rocca.

At six o'clock that evening he had to take his departure without seeing his sister again. He went away with a heavy heart.

"How extraordinary she is!" he thought. "Never even to ask me if I told the man anything or not. And never to bid one good-bye!

Well, I've done for the best—I can't help it.
She'll be sorry if poor little Chevy should die."

But the boy did not die; so that his father
never learned whether that event would have
touched the heart of Lady Hilda or not.

All the following day she shut herself up in
her rooms. She said she was ill; and, in truth,
she felt so. Della Rocca called three times in
the day, but she did not see him; he sent up a
great bouquet of the pale yellow tea rose of
which she was so fond; he had fastened the
flowers together with an antique silver zone, on
which was the Greek Love in relief; the Love
of the early Hellenic poets, without wings and
with a mighty sword, the Love of Anacreon,
which forges the soul as a smith his iron, and
steeps it in icy waters after many blows.

She understood the message of the Love, but
she sent no message back.

It was a lovely day; underneath the windows
the carriages were rolling; there was the smile
of spring on the air as the fleecy clouds went
sailing past; she could see the golden reaches
of the river and the hyacinth-hued hills

where Palestrina lay; her heart was heavy; her pulse was quick; her conscience was ill at ease; her thoughts were restless and perturbed. Solitude and reflection were so new to her; they appalled her. When she had been unwell before, which had been but seldom, she had always beguiled herself by looking over the jewels in their cases, sorting rare old Marcantonios and Morghens, skimming French feuilletons, or planning new confections for her vast stores of old laces. But now none of these distractions were possible to her; she sat doing nothing, weary, feverish, and full of a passionate pain.

The fact which her brother had told to Della Rocca was that, if she married again, all her riches would pass away from her.

At the time of her marriage her father had been deeply involved in debt; gambling, racing, and debts of every other kind had been about him like spiders' webs; the great capitalist, Vorarlberg, had freed him on condition of receiving the hand of his young daughter in exchange. She was allowed to know nothing of these matters; but under such circumstances it

was impossible for the family to be exacting
as regarded sentiments: she was abandoned entirely to the old man's power. Fortunately for
herself, he was taken ill on the very day of the
nuptials, and, after a lingering period of suffering,
died, leaving her mistress of half of one of the
finest fortunes in Europe. By birth he was a
Wallachian Jew, brought up in London and Paris,
but he had been naturalised in England, when a
youth, for commercial objects, and the disposition of his property lay under his own control.
A year or two after his death a later will was
found by his lawyers, still leaving her the same
income, but decreeing that in the event of her
second marriage everything should pass away
from her to the public charities, save alone her
jewels, her horses, all things she might have
purchased, the house in Paris, which had been
a gift, and some eight hundred a year already
secured to her. The new will was proved, and she
was informed that she could enjoy her fortune
only by this tenure. She was indifferent. She
was quite sure that she would never wish to
marry any one. She loved her wealth and spent

it magnificently; and when men sought her whose own position would have made the loss of her own money of no moment, she still repulsed them, thinking always " le mieux est l'ennemi du bien."

The fact of this later will was scarcely known beyond the precincts of the law and the circle of their own family; but since she had met Della Rocca, the remembrance of it had kept her awake many a night, and broken roughly many a day-dream.

To surrender her fortune to become his wife never once occurred to her as possible; ten years' enjoyment of her every whim had made it seem so inalienably hers. She had entered so early into her great possessions, that they had grown to be a very part of her. The old man who had been her husband but in name was but a mere ghostly shadow to her. The freedom and the self-indulgence she had so long enjoyed had become necessary to her as the air she breathed. She could no more face the loss of her fortune than she could have done that of her beauty. It was not the mere vulgar vaunt

or ostentation of wealth that had attraction for
her; it was all the supremacy, the ease, the
patronage, the habits, that great wealth alone
makes possible; it was the reign which she had
held throughout Europe; it was the charm of
perfectly irresponsible power. To give up these
and hear the cackle of all the fools she had
eclipsed mocking at her weakness!—it would be
beyond all endurance.

What was she to do?

The lax moralities of the women of her time
were impossible to her proud and loftier character; and besides, she felt that a woman who preferred the world to him, would not find in Della
Rocca a forgiving or a submissive lover. When
he knew, what would he say?

She turned sick at the thought. After all, she
had played with him and deceived him; he would
have just cause of passionate reproach against
her. His love had no wings, but it had a sword.

"Will Miladi be able to dine?" her maid
asked her, vaguely alarmed at the strange stillness
and the great paleness of her face.

"Was I to dine anywhere?" she said wearily,

She was to dine at the Archduchess Anna's. The Archduchess Anna was passing through Floralia after three months at Palermo for health, and was staying in strict *incognita*, and infinite glee, as the Countess Von Feffers at the Hotel del Rè; enjoying herself endlessly, as the gay-hearted lady that she was, even indulging once in the supreme delight of driving in a cab, and with no other recognition of her great rank than consisted in the attendance upon her of the handsomest of the king's chamberlains.

"Dress me, then," said Lady Hilda, with a sigh. She could not excuse herself to the Archduchess, whom she had known intimately for years, and who was to leave Floralia in a week.

"What gown does Madame select?" asked her maid.

"Give me any you like," she answered.

She did not care how she would look; she would not meet him; she knew that he had no acquaintance with the imperial lady.

The maids, left to themselves, gave her the last new one from Worth; only six days arrived; a dress entirely white, with knots of purple

velvet, exactly copied from a picture of
Boucher, and with all the grace of dead
Versailles in its folds. She put a rococo necklace on, with a portrait of Maria Theresa in it,
and went listlessly to the dinner; she was not
thinking about her appearance that night, or she
would have said that she was too pale to wear all
that white.

"Goodness me, Hilda, how ill you do look,"
said Madame Mila, meeting her on the stairs,
and who was going also.

"No, thanks, I won't drive with you; two
women can't go in a carriage without one being
chiffonnée. That's an exquisite toilette; that
white brocade is delicious—stamped with the
lilies of France,—very pretty; only you're too
pale for it to-night, and it's a pity to wear it only
for the Archduchess. She never knows what
anybody's got on their backs. Is anything the
matter, dear?"

"Nothing in the world."

"Then you must have got a headache? You
certainly do look very ill. I do so hope we shall
get away in time for the Veglione. It's the very

x

last night, you know.   I had such fun last time.
I *intrigué'd* heaps of people, and Doggendorff I
drove wild ; I told him everything about his wife
and Lelio Castelpucci, and all against himself
that she'd ever told me.   It was such fun—he'd
not an idea who I was, for when we were at
supper, he came running in breathless to tell us
of a horrible little mask with a voice like a
macaw's ;—you know I'd put a pebble under my
tongue."

"Very dangerous pastime, and a very vulgar
one," said the Lady Hilda, descending the staircase.   "How can you go down into that horrible
screeching mob, Mila ?   It is so very low."

"My dear, I go anywhere to amuse myself,
and Maurice was always near me, you know, so if
I had been insulted——   There's eight o'clock
striking."

The Hotel del Rè was but ten minutes' drive
along the famous river-street, which has such an
Arabian Nights-like beauty when the lamps are
lighted, and gleam in long lines adown each
shore, and mirror themselves in the water, whilst
dome, and bell-tower. and palace-roof raise them-

selves darkly against the steel-blue sky of the night.

The Archduchess had been spending a long day in the galleries, studying art under the guidance of the handsome chamberlain; she was hungry, happy, and full of the heartiest spirits; she was a very merry and good-natured person, about five-and-forty years old, fat and fair, very badly dressed, and very agreeable, with a frank laugh, and a strong love of humour; she had had more escapades than any princess in Europe, and smoked more cigars than a French newspaper writer, and had married more daughters to German cousins than anybody else in the Almanac de Gotha.

Had she been any lesser being, Society would have turned its back on her; but, being who she was, her nod was elevation, and her cigar-ash honour,—and, to do her justice, she was one of the most amiable creatures in all creation.

"Ma chère, you are lovelier than ever!— and how do you like this place?—and is the dear little pug alive? I lost my sweet Zaliote of asthma in Palermo," said the Archduchess, welcoming the Lady Hilda, as she did everything with ardour.

Lady Hilda, answering, felt her colourless cheeks grow warm; in the circle standing round she recognised Della Rocca. The Archduchess had taken a fancy to the look of him in the street, and had bade the chamberlain present him, and then had told him to come to dinner: she liked to surround herself with handsome men. From Madame Mila he had learned in the morning that her cousin would dine there at night.

Madame Mila concluded in her own mind that Freddie had had a row with his sister upon the matter, but that Della Rocca had had nothing said to him about it by either of them. Madame Mila concluded also that Hilda had grown sensible, and was doing like other women, though why she looked so ill about it, Madame Mila could not imagine. Madame Mila did not comprehend scruples.

It was very painful, for instance, to be allied to any one of the Greek Church, and a great grief to the Holy Father; but still it was very nice to be married to a Schismatic, because it enabled you to go to balls a fortnight longer : if it was still your husband's carnival, you know, nobody could say anything.

Madame Mila thought you should always do your best to please everybody; but then you should take care that you pleased yourself first most of all. The world was easy enough to live in if you did not worry : there were always unpaid bills to be sure, and they were odious. But then Hilda never had any unpaid bills; so she never could have anything to annoy her.

Apropos of bills, she hoped Della Rocca would not use his influence with her cousin so as to prevent her paying other people's bills. Of course he wouldn't do this just at present; but when men had been lovers a little while, she reflected, they always turned the poetry into prose, and grew very nearly as bad as husbands.

Madame Mila watched them narrowly all through dinner.

" If I thought he'd make her stingy, I'd make her jealous of Giulia Malatesta to-morrow," she thought to herself. Madame Mila on occasion

had helped or hindered circumstance amongst
her friends and enemies with many ingenious
little devices and lucky little anonymous notes,
and other innocent shifts and stratagems. It
was no use being in the world at all unless you
interfered with the way it went; to be a mere
puppet in the hands of Fate, with the strings of
accident dangling to and fro, seemed to her
clever little brains quite unworthy the intelligence of woman.

She never meant to do any harm, oh, never;
only she liked things to go as she wished them.
Who does not? If a few men and women had
been made wretched for life, and people who
loved one another devotedly had been parted for
ever, and suspicion and hatred had crept into the
place of trust and tenderness in certain house-
holds, Madame Mila could not help that, any
more than one can help other people being
splashed with mud when one drives down a lane
in bad weather. And nobody ever thought
Madame Mila could do any harm; pretty, good-
natured, loquacious, little Madame Mila, running
about with her little rosebuds at fancy fairs, and

saying so sweetly, "Pour nos pauvres—pour nos chers pauvres!"

"The best little woman in the world," as everybody said, Madame Mila would kiss her female enemies on both cheeks wherever she met them; and when she had sent an anonymous letter (for fun), always sent an invitation to dinner just after it, to the same direction.

"I wish I knew how it is really between them," she thought at the Archduchess's dinner-table, divided between her natural desire to see her cousin let fall that "white flower of a blameless life," which stinks as garlic in the nostrils of those who have it not, and her equally natural apprehension that Paolo della Rocca as a lover would not let his mistress pay other persons' debts, and would also be sure to see all her letters.

"She'll tell him everything about everybody," thought Madame Mila, uncomfortably; for Della Rocca had a look in his eyes of assured happiness, which, to the astute experience of Madame Mila, suggested volumes.

Meantime she was also harassed by an appre-

hension that she would not be able to withdraw
in time for the Veglione, where Maurice, a baignoir, and a supper-table awaited her. If the Archduchess should sit down to play of any sort hope
was over, escape would be impossible till daydawn;
and Madame Mila hated playing with the Archduchess; with such personages she was afraid to
cheat, and was obliged to pay.

With all the ingenuity, therefore, of which she
was mistress, she introduced the idea of the
Veglione into the mind of her hostess, and so
contrived to fascinate her with the idea, that the
Archduchess, who had gone in her time to five
hundred public masked balls, was as hotly ani-
mated into a desire to go to this one as though
she had been just let out of a convent at eighteen
years old.

Madame Mila delightedly placed her baignoir
at the disposition of her imperial highness, and
her imperial highness invited all her guests to
accompany her; such invitations are not optional;
and Lady Hilda, who hated noise as her horses
hated masks, was borne off by the mirthful, chattering, and gay-hearted lady, who had no ob-

jection to noise, and loved fun and riot like a street boy.

Lady Hilda thought a Veglione, and a liking for it, both beneath contempt; yet she was not unwilling to avoid all chance of being alone with Della Rocca even for a moment. She knew what he would say :—his eyes had said it all the evening a thousand times.

The Archduchess Anna and Madame Mila were both in the very highest spirits; they had taken a good deal of champagne, as ladies will, and had smoked a good deal and got thirsty, and had more champagne with some seltzer water, and the result was the highest of high spirits. Nothing could be more appropriate to a Veglione; as no reasonable being could stay by choice in one for an hour, it is strongly advisable that reason should be a little dethroned by a very dry wine before entering the dingy paradise. Of course nobody ever sees great ladies ' the worse for wine'; they are only the better, as a Stilton cheese is.

Happy and hilarious, shrouded and masked beyond all possibility of identification, and ready for any adventure, the Archduchess Anna was no sooner in the box than she was out of it, and declared her intention of going down into the crowd. Madame Mila, only too glad, went with her, and some half-dozen men formed their escort. Lady Hilda excused herself on the plea of a headache, a plea not untrue, and alone with the Duc de St. Louis awaited the return of her hostess. She had only put on her mask for entry, and had now laid it beside her; she threw aside her domino, for the heat of the box was stifling, and the whiteness of her dress shone as lilies do at moonlight. She leaned her cheek on her hand, and looked down on to the romping, screaming, many-coloured throngs.

"You are not well to-night, Madame?" said the Duc, with the affectionate solicitude that he felt for all pretty women.

He was puzzled as to how her relations could stand with Della Rocca: the previous night he had thought everything settled, but now he did not feel quite so sure.

"The Archduchess is so noisy; it always gives me a headache to dine with her," said

Lady Hilda. "She is very good-natured; but her talking is—— !"

"She is an admirable heavy dragoon—*manqué*," said the Duc. "Most good-natured, as you say, but trying to the tympanum and the taste. So Clairvaux left last night?"

"Yes: Cheviot was taken ill."

"I should have thought it was a racer taken ill by the consternation he seemed to be in. I saw him for a moment only."

She was silent, watching the whirling of the pierrots, harlequins, scaramouches and dominoes, who were shrieking and yelling in the throng below.

"I think he liked his shooting with Paolo?" said the Duc, at a hazard.

"He likes shooting anywhere."

"Certainly there is something wrong," thought the Duc, stooping a little to look at her brocaded white lilies. "What an exquisite toilette!—is one permitted to say so?"

"Oh dear, no!" said the Lady Hilda petulantly. "The incessant talk about dress is so tiresome and so vulgar; the women who want their costumes praised are women who have only just begun to dress tolerably, and are still not quite sure of the effects!"

"You are right, as always," said the Duc, with a little bow and a little smile. "But now and then perfection surprises us into involuntary indiscretion. You must not be too severe."

"Somebody should be severe," she said, contemptuously. "Society is a Battle of the Frogs, for rivality in dress and debt."

The Duc laughed.

"What do you know about it, Madame? You who are as above rivals as above debts? By the way, you told me you wanted some old Pesaro vases. I found some yesterday at Biangini's shop that might please you; they come out of an old pharmacy in Verona; perhaps the very pharmacy of Romeo's apothecary; and there are some fine old pots too ——"

"I am tired of buying things."

"The weariness of empire!—nothing new. You must take to keeping hens and chickens, as the Emperor John Vatices did. How does

Camille Odissot succeed with your ball-room frescoes ? "

" I have no idea. Very ill, I dare say."

" Yes, it is a curious thing that we do not succeed in fresco. The grace is gone out of it; modern painters have not the lightness of touch necessary; they are used to masses of colour, and they use the palette knife as a mason the trowel. The art too, like the literature of our time, is all detail; the grand suggestive vagueness of the Greek drama and of the Umbrian frescoes are lost to us under a crowd of elaborated trivialities; perhaps it is because art has ceased to be spiritual or tragic, and is merely domestic or melodramatic ; the Greeks knew neither domesticity nor melodrama, and the early Italian painters were imbued with a faith which, if not so virile as the worship of the Phidian Zeus, yet absorbed them and elevated them in a degree impossible in the tawdry Sadduceeism of our own day. By the way, when the weather is milder you must go to Orvieto ; you have never been there, I think ; it is the Prosodion of Signorelli. What a fine Pagan he was at heart! He admired masculine beauty like a Greek; he must have been a sin-gularly happy man—few more happy ——"

The Duc paused as the handle of the door turned; he was only talking because he saw that she was too weary or too languid to talk herself; the door opened, and Della Rocca entered the box again, having escaped from the Arch-duchess.

"We were speaking of Orvieto; you know more of it than I do. I was telling Miladi that she must go there about Easter time," said the Duc, hunting for his crush hat beneath the chair. "Take my seat, mon cher, for a mo-ment; I see Salvareo in the crowd, and I must speak to him about her imperialissima's supper. I shall be back in an instant."

He departed, with no intention of returning, and was assailed in the corridor by a party of masks, who bore him off gaily between them down the staircase into the laughing, screaming, and capering multitude.

Della Rocca did not take his chair, but sank into the seat behind her, while his hand closed on hers.

"Will you not even look at me?" he murmured.

She drew her hand away, and put her mask on, slipping its elastic round her delicate ears.

"How the crowd yells!" she said, impatiently. "Will the Archduchess stay there long, do you think?"

With gentlest audacity and softest skill he had slipped off the mask and had laid it behind him before she had realised what he was doing; his hand had touched her as lightly as though a feather brushed a rose.

She rose in amazed anger, and turned on him coldly.

"M. Della Rocca! how dare you presume so far? Give me my mask at once—"

"No," he said, softly; and he took hold of her hands and drew her towards the back of the box where no eyes could reach them, and knelt down before her as she sat there in the dusky shadow of the dark red draperies.

"Oh, my love—my love!" he murmured; that was all; but his arms stole about her, and his head drooped till his forehead rested on her knees.

For the moment she did not repulse him she did not stir nor speak; she yielded herself to the embrace, mute and very pale, and moved to a strange tumult of emotion, whether of anger or of gladness she barely knew.

He lifted his head, and his eyes looked into hers till her own could look no longer.

"You love me?" he whispered to her, whilst his arms still held her imprisoned.

She was silent; under the purple knot of velvet at her breast, he saw her heart heave, her breath come and go; a hot colour flushed over all her face, then faded, and left her again pale as her white brocade.

"It were of no use if—if I did," she muttered. "You forget yourself;—leave me."

But he knelt there, looking at her till the look seemed to burn her like flame; yet she did not rise:—she, the very hem of whose garment no man before him had ever dared to touch.

"You love me!" he murmured, and said the same thing again and again and again. in all

the various eloquence of passion. She trembled
a little under his close caress ; the dusky red of
the box whirled around her; the shouting of
the multitude below beat like the sound of a
distant sea on her ears.

As he kneeled at her feet she touched his
forehead one moment with her hand in a gesture
of involuntary tenderness.

"It is of no use," she said, faintly again.
"You do not understand—you do not know."

"Yes: I do know," he answered her.

"You know!"——

"Yes: your brother told me."

"And yet?——"

"Since we love one another, is not that
enough?"

She breathed like a person suffocated; she
loosened herself from his arms, and drew away
from him, and rose.

"It makes no change in you, then!" she said,
wonderingly, and looked at him through a blind-
ing mist, and felt sick and weary and bewildered,
as she had never thought it possible to feel.

"Change in me? What change? save that

Y

I am freer to seek you—that is all. Oh, my empress, my angel !—is not love enough? Has your life without love contented you so well that you fear to face love alone?"

He still knelt at her feet and kissed her hands and her dress, as he spoke; he looked upward at the pale beauty of her face.

She shivered a little as with cold.

"That is folly," she muttered. "You must know it is of no use. I could not live—poor."

The word stung him: he rose to his feet; he was silent. After all, what had he to offer her? he loved her—that was all.

She loosened the loose chain about her throat, and looked away beyond him at the lights of the theatre. With an effort she recovered her old indifferent cold manner.

"You have forgotten yourself: it is all folly : you must know that : you surprised me into— weakness—for a moment. But it is over now. Give me my mask, and take me to the carriage."

"No !"—— He leaned against the door, and looked down on her: all the rapture of expectancy and of triumph had faded from his face; the pallor and suffering of a great passion were on it; he had known that she loved the things of the world; but **he had** believed that she loved him more.

He was undeceived. He looked at this beautiful woman with the gold chain loosed about her throat, and the white brocaded lilies gleaming in the gloom, and only by a supreme effort did he subdue the bitterness and brutality which lie underneath all strong passions.

"One moment!" he said, as she moved to reach the door. "Can you say you have no love for me?"

Her colour varied.

"What is the use? Give me my mask."

"Can you say you do not love me?"

She hesitated; she wished to lie and could not.

"I did not say that," she murmured. "Perhaps if things were different—— But, as it is— it is no use."

The half-confession sufficed, it loosened **his** lips to passionate appeal; with all the eloquence natural to him and to his language, he poured

out on her all the supplication, all the entreaty,
all the persuasion, that he was master of; he
lavished every amorous endearment that his language held; he painted the joys of great and
mutual passion with a fervour and a force that
shook her like a whirlwind; he upbraided her
with her caprices, with her coldness, with her
selfishness, till the words cut her like sharp
stripes : he besought her by the love with which
he loved her till the voluptuous sweetness of it
stole over all her senses, and held her silent
and enthralled.

He knelt at her feet, and held her hands in his.

" Does your life content you ? " he said at the
last. " Can greatness of any sort content a woman
without love ?   Can any eminence, or power, or
possession make her happiness without love ?
Say that I am poor; that coming to me you
would come to what in your sight were poverty;
is wealth so great a thing measured against the
measureless strength of passion ?   Are not the
real joys of our lives things unpurchaseable ?
Oh, my love, my love !   If you had no preference
for me I were the vainest fool to urge you;   but,

as it is—does the world that tires you, the
society that wearies you, the men and women
who fatigue you — the adulation that nauseates
you—the expenditure that after all is but a vulgarity in your sight—the acquisition that has
lost its charm for you with long habit, like the
toys of a child ; are all those things so supreme
with you that you can send me from you for
their sake? Is not one hour of mutual love
worth all the world can give?"

His arms held her close, he drew her down
to him nearer and nearer till his head rested on
her breast, and he felt the tumultuous throbbing
of her heart. For one moment of scarce conscious weakness she did not resist or repulse
him, but surrendered herself to the spell of his
power. He moved her as no mortal creature
had ever had strength to do ; a whole world
unknown opened to her with his touch and his
gaze; she loved him. For one moment she
forgot all else.

But all the while, even in the temporary
oblivion to which she had yielded, she never
dreamed of granting what he prayed.

The serenity and pride in her were shaken to their roots; she was humbled in her own sight; she was ashamed of the momentary delirium to which she had abandoned herself; she strove in vain to regain composure and indifference: come what would, he was near to her as no other man had ever been.

She drew her domino about her with a shudder, though the blood coursed like fever in her veins.

"You must hate me—or forget me," she murmured, as she tried to take her mask from his hand. "You *know* it is no use. I could not live— poor. Perhaps you are right; all those things are habits, follies, egotisms—oh, perhaps. But such as they are—such as I am—I could never live without them."

He stood erect, and his face grew cold.

"That is your last word, Madame?"

"Yes. What else should I say? No other —" her voice faltered a moment and grew very weak "No other man will ever be anything to me, if that content you. But more—is impossible."

He bowed low in silence, and gave her up her mask.

She felt afraid to look up at his face.

The door opened on them noisily; the Archduchess and Madame Mila were returning to refresh themselves with their supper ere descending again to fresh diversions. Behind them came the Duc de St. Louis and all the men of their party, and their servants with the tressels for the setting of the table in their box.

They were fuller than ever of laughter, mirth, high spirits, and riotous good humour; their white teeth shone under the lace of their loups, and their eyes sparkled through the slits. They had frightened some people, and teased more, and had been mistaken for two low actresses and jested with accordingly, and were as much flattered as the actresses would have been had they been taken for princesses.

The Lady Hilda prayed of the Archduchess's goodness to be excused from awaiting the supper; she had been ill all day, and her headache was very severe.

The Archduchess was in too high spirits to listen very much, or to care who went or who stayed.

"Take me to the carriage, Duc," said Lady Hilda, putting her hand on the arm of M. de St. Louis.

Della Rocca held the door open for her. He bowed very low, once more, as she passed him.

CHAPTER XI.

THE next day was Ash Wednesday.

Madame Mila awoke too late for mass, and with a feverish throbbing in her temples. She and the Archduchess had only left the Veglione as the morning sun came up bright and tranquil over the shining waters of the river from behind the eastern hills.

Madame Mila yawned and yawned again a score of times, drank a little green tea to waken herself, thought how horrid Lent was, and ran over in her mind how much she would confess at confession.

She determined to repent her sins very penitently. She would only go to musical parties, she would wear no low bodices, she would eat fish twice a-week—the red mullets were really very nice—and she would go for all holy week *en retraite*: if she did all that, the most severe monitor could not require her to give up Maurice.

Poor Maurice! she smiled to herself, in the middle of a yawn; how devoted he was!—he only lived on her breath, and if she dismissed him would kill himself with absinthe. She really believed it. She did not dream that Maurice, submissive slave though he was, had his consolations for slavery, and was at that moment looking into the eyes of the prettiest artist's model in Floralia.

It was the Day of Ashes, as all the bells of the city had tolled out far and wide; and Madame Mila, over her green tea, really felt penitent. For the post had brought her three terribly thick letters, and the letters were bills; and the sum total that was wanted immediately was some sixty thousand francs, and how could a poor dear little woman who had spent all her money send that or a tenth of it: and Spiridion wouldn't—he had too many bills of Blanche Souris' to pay; and poor Maurice couldn't—he invariably lost at play much more than he possessed, after the manner of his generation.

Madame Mila really cried about it, and felt ready to promise any amount of repentance if she could get those sixty thousand francs this Lent.

"And to think of me running myself off my feet in that muslin apron collecting for the poor!" she thought, with a sense that heaven behaved very ill to her in return for her charities. "I suppose I must ask Hilda," she reflected; "she always does give when you ask her—if that man don't prevent her now.'

For the champagne and the mask and the great joyousness of her soul had prevented Madame Mila from observing any difference between her cousin and Della Rocca, and as he had left the box immediately after her cousin, she had supposed that they had gone away together—why shouldn't they?

"I must ask Hilda to lend it me," she said to herself.

To say lend was agreeable to her feelings, not

of course that there was any serious necessity to repay between such near relatives; and she sent her maid across the corridor to enquire when she could come into her cousin's room.

The maid returned with a little unsealed note which the Lady Hilda had desired should be given to Madame Mila when she should awake. The note only said: "I am gone to Rome for some few weeks, dear; write to me at the Iles Britanniques if you want anything."

"Good gracious, what can have happened!" said Madame Mila, in utter amaze. "They must have quarrelled last night." And she proceeded to cross-examine all the hotel people.

Lady Hilda had left by the morning train, and had not taken her carriage horses with her, only the riding horses, and had kept on her rooms at the Murat: that was all they knew.

"She is very uncertain and uncomfortable to have to do with," thought Madame Mila, in vague irritation. "Anybody else would have asked me to go with her."

A sudden idea occurred to her, and she sent

her maid to find out if the Duca della Rocca were in Floralia.

At his palace they said that he was.

" Dear me, perhaps he'll go after her," thought Madame Mila. "But I don't know why she's so secret about it, and takes such precautions. Nobody'd cut her for anything she might do so long as she's all that money; and so long as she don't marry she can't lose it."

Madame Mila did not understand it at all. Her experience in the world assured her that her cousin might have Della Rocca, or anybody else, constantly beside her whenever she liked, and nobody would say anything—so long as she had all that money.

She felt that she was badly treated, that there was something not confided to her, and also she certainly ought to have been asked to go to Rome at her cousin's expense. She was sulky and irritated.

" Hilda is so queer and so selfish," she said to herself, and began a letter to the Iles Britanniques; with many tender endearments and much pathos, and the most gracefully-worded appeal possible for the loan of the sixty thousand francs.

She would have gone to Rome herself, being well aware that written demands are much more easily repulsed than spoken ones. But she had no money at all. She had lost a quarter's income at play since she had been in the town, and she could not pay the hotel people till her husband should send her more money, and he was hunting bears on the Pic du Midi, with Blanche Souris established at Pau, and when that creature was with him he was always very tardy in answering letters for money, bears or no bears, and of course he would make the bears his excuse now.

Fairly overwhelmed, poor little Madame Mila had a long fit of hysterics, and her maids had to send in great haste for ether and the Vicomte Maurice.

She rallied by dinner time enough to eat two dozen oysters, some lobster croquettes, an omelette *aux fines herbes,* and some prawn soup, with a nice little bottle of Veuve. Clicquot's sweetest wine, the most *maigre* repast in the world, and one that must have satisfied even S. Francis had he been there; but still things were very dreadful, and on the whole she was in the proper frame of mind for the Day of Ashes, and in the confessional next morning sobbed so much that her confessor was really touched, and was not too severe with her about her Maurices, past, present, or to come.

CHAPTER XII.

In three weeks' time Lady Hilda returned from Rome.

She had been affectionately received by the Holy Father; she had been the idol of the nobles of the Black; she had bought a quantity of pictures, and marbles, and bronzes, and Castellani jewellery; she had gone to early mass every day, and ridden hard every day; she had thought Totila would have been more bearable than Signor Rosa, and she had shuddered at the ruined flora of the Colosseum and the scrapings and bedaubings of the Palace of the Cæsars.

She returned contemptuous, disgusted, tired of the age she lived in, and regretful that she

had not spared herself the sight of so much
desecration. She conceived that Genseric or
the Constable de Bourbon must have been much
less painful than a syndicate and an army of
bricklayers. She refused to go out anywhere on the
score of its being Lent, and she meditated going
to London for the season to that very big house
in Eaton Square, which she honoured for about
three months in as many years. She hated
London, and its society was a mob, and its
atmosphere was thickened soda-water, and no
other place had such horrible endless dinner
parties. Still she was going;—when?—oh, to-
morrow or next week.

But to-morrow became yesterday, and next
week became last week, and her black and white
liveries were still airing themselves on the steps
of the Murat, and her black horses still were
trotting to and fro the stones of Floralia,
bearing little Madame Mila hither and
thither.

Their own mistress stirred out but little; it
was damp weather, and she coughed, and she
shut herself up with millions of hyacinths and

z

narcissi, and painted a St. Ursula on wood for her chapel in Paris.

She painted well, but the St. Ursula progressed but slowly.

When she was alone she would let her palette fall to her side and sit thinking; and the bells would ring across the waters till she hated them.

What was the use of painting a St. Ursula? St. Ursula did not want to be painted; and all art was nothing but repetition : nobody had found out anything in colour really, since Giotto, though to be sure he could not paint transparencies or reflections. And she would leave her St. Ursula impatiently, and read Cavalcaselle and Zugler and Winckelmann and Rumohr and Passavant, and when she did go out would go to some little remote, unvisited chapel and sit for hours before some dim disputed fresco.

She would be in London next week, in its blaze of gas, jewels, luxury, and political discussion; she said that she liked these calm, dusky, silent places, alone with S. Louis and S. Giles and S. Jerome.

Madame Mila puzzled over her conduct in vain. She did not dare to ask anything, because there were those sixty thousand francs, and her cousin had helped her about them, and you cannot say very intrusive or impertinent things to a person who is lending you money; but it was very odd, thought Madame Mila incessantly, because she evidently was unhappy about the man, and wanted him, and yet must have sent him away. Of course she couldn't have married him; but still there were ways of managing everything; and in Hilda's position she really could do as she liked, and nobody ever would even have said a word.

Of course she would not have married him; that Madame Mila knew; but Society would have made no objection to his being about her always like her courier and her pug and the rest of her following; and if Society doesn't object to a thing, why on earth should you not do it?

Il ne faut pas être plus royaliste que le roi: there cannot be the slightest necessity to be more scrupulous than the people that are round you; indeed, to attempt to be more so is to

z 2

be disagreeable and tacitly impertinent to others.

There is a certain latitude, which taken, makes you look much more amiable. Madame Mila was kissed on both cheeks really with sincerity by many ladies in many cities, merely because her nice management of her Maurice made their Maurices easier for them, and their pleasant consciousness of her frailty was the one touch which made them all akin. Polyandry made easy is a great charm in Society—there is no horrid scandal for any one, and no fuss at all: Monsieur is content and Madame enjoys herself, everybody goes everywhere, and everything is as it should be.

" If that old man had lived, Hilda would have been glad to be like everyone else," Madame Mila thought, with much impatience. " Of course, because she is quite free, she don't care a bit to use her freedom."

Madame Mila herself felt that although her passion for Maurice was the fifty-sixth passion of her soul, and the most ardent of all her existence, that even Maurice himself would have lost some

of his attraction if he had lost the pleasant
savour of incorrectness that attached to him, and
if she had not had to take all those precautions
about his going to another hotel, &c., &c., which
enabled her to hold her place in courts and embassies, and made her friends all able to say with
clear consciences, "Nothing in it, oh *dear!* nothing in it whatever!" Not that she cared about
anyone believing that there was nothing in it;
she did not even wish anybody to believe it;
she only wanted it said—that was all; because,
whilst it can be said, a woman " goes everywhere " still, and though Heloise or Francesca
may be willing to " lose the world for love," the
Femme Galante has no notion of doing anything
of the sort.

"She must have refused him?" the Duc de
St. Louis said to her more than once, harassed
by chagrin at the failure of his project, and by
a curiosity which his good breeding for-
bade him to seek to satisfy at the fountain
head.

"Oh, I daresay she did," said Madame Mila.
" Of course she did. But if she care for him,

why should she send him away?—il y a des
moyens pour tout. They are *brouillés* somehow,
that is certain. Oh, yes—certain! He was here
when Hilda came back, and we passed him one
day in the street, and he took off his hat and
bowed, and looked very cold and pale and went
onwards; and he has never called once. Now
you know he is gone to the Marshes, and after
that they say he is going into Sicily to see after
that brigand Pibro. It is not like an Italian
to be so soon repulsed."

"It is very like an Italian to be too proud to
ask twice," said the Duc, and added with a little
smile, "He never said anything to me. Only
once lately he said that he was sure that Miladi
would be a very different creature if she had home
interests and children!"

"Good gracious!" said Madame Mila, "she
was quite right to have nothing to do with him
if he have that kind of ideas. How little he
knows her too! Hilda is quite unnatural about
children; quite horrid; she never speaks to
them; and when she saw my dear little Lili
dressed as Madame l'Archiduc for the babies'

fancy ball at the Elysée, what do you think she said?—she told me that I polluted the child's brain before it could distinguish right from wrong, and that a mixture of Judic and Fashion at five years old was disgusting; and Lili looked lovely!—she was so prettily rouged, and Maurice had given her a necklace of pink pearls. But Hilda has no human feeling at all."

"Della Rocca did not think so," said the Duc.

" Della Rocca was in love," said Madame Mila, scornfully, "with the beaux yeaux de sa cassette too;—as well. They may only have quarrelled, you know. Hilda is very disagreeable and difficult. By the way, Deutschland went after her to Rome, and proposed to her again."

" Indeed! and she refused him again?"

" Oh, yes. She refuses them all. I did fancy she was touched by Della Rocca, but you see it came to nothing; she is as cold as a crystal. She likes to know that heaps of men are wretched about her, and she likes to study those dingy old paintings, and that is all she does

like, or ever will like. She will be very unhappy as she grows older, and I dare say she
will be quite capable of leaving all her money
away from her family to build a cathedral, or
found a School of Art."

And Madame Mila, impatient, nodded to the
Duc, and dashed away in the victoria behind
the white and black liveries. She was managing
to enjoy her Lent after all : her mind being at
rest about those sixty thousand francs, there was
no occasion to be so very rigid ; low bodices
she did not wear, because she was a woman of
her word; but then she had half a hundred
divine confections, cut square, or adorned with
ruffs, or open *en cœur* with loveliest lace and
big bouquets of roses, to make that form of
renunciation simpler ; there was plenty going
on, and little " sauteries," which nobody could
call balls, and pleasant gatherings, quite harmless, because only summoned for "music," and
altogether, what with the oasis of mi-Carême,
and the prolongation of the Carnival in Russian
houses, life was very endurable ; and there were
Neapolitan oysters to fast upon comfortably.

Heaven tempers the wind to the shorn lamb, and it would be hard if Society did not soften penitence to the Femme Galante.

The Lady Hilda did keep her Lent, and kept it strictly, and was never seen at the "sauteries," and rarely at the musical parties. But then everyone knew that she was *dévote* (when she was not slightly Voltairean), and it could not be expected that a woman going to reign in the vast world of London would put herself out to be amiable in Floralia. Yet, had they only known it, she loved Floralia in her own heart as she had never loved any other place upon earth. The beautiful small city set along its shining waters, with all the grace of its classic descent, its repose of contemplative art, its sanctity of imperishable greatness, had a hold upon her that no other spot under the sun could ever gain. If she thought others unworthy of it, she thought herself no less unworthy. It seemed to her that to be worthy to dwell in it, one needed to be wise and pure and half divine, even as St. Ursula herself.

And all the pride in her was shaken to the

roots: she was full of a restless, dissatisfied
humility; there were times when she hated herself,
and was weary of herself to utter impatience.
She shut herself up with her art studies and the
old frescoes, because they pained her less than
any other thing.   She was passionately unhappy : though to other people she only seemed
a trifle more cynical and more contemptuous
than before, no more.

The easy morality with which her cousin
would have solved all difficulty, was not possible
to her.   She would not have cheated the old
dead man from whom her riches came, by
evading him in the spirit of his will whilst
adhering to the letter.   Unless she gave up her
riches, her lover could be nothing to her: and
the thought of giving them up never even occurred
to her as possible.   She did not know it, because
she was so very tired of so many things; but the
great world she had always lived in was very
necessary to her, and had absolute dominion
over her; it became tiresome, as the trammels
of empire do to a monarch; but to lay down her
sceptre would have been an abdication, and an

abnegation, impossible to her. And she despised herself because they were impossible; despised herself because to his generosity she had only responded with what at best was but a vulgar egotism; despised herself because she had been so weak that she had permitted his familiarities and his caresses unrebuked; despised herself for everything with that self scorn of a proud woman, which is far more intense and bitter than any scorn that she has ever dealt out upon others.

She had lived all her life on a height of unconscious, but no less absorbing, self-admiration. She had looked down on all the aims and objects and attainments and possessions of all other persons with a bland and superb vanity; she had been accustomed to regard herself as perfect, as others all united to tell her that she was; and her immunity from mean frailties and puerile emotions had given her a belief that she was lifted high above the passions and the follies of humankind; now, all of a sudden, she had dropped to the lowest depths of weakness and of selfishness—passion had touched her, yet had left her without its courage.

In those long, lonely, studious days in Lent, studying her religious art with wandering thoughts, she grew to hate herself; yet, to resign her empire for another's sake never even distantly appeared to her as possible.

One day, in a little private chapel, where there were some fine dim works in tempera, only to be seen by earliest morning light, she was startled by seeing him near her; he was coming from the sacristy on business of the church; he looked at her quickly, and would have passed on with a silent salutation, but she approached him on an impulse which a moment later she regretted.

"Need you avoid me?" she said, hurriedly. "Surely—I go from here so soon—we might still be friends? People would talk less——"

He looked down on her with a cold severity which chilled her, like the passing of an icy wind.

"Madame," he answered her, with a fleeting smile, "your northern lovers, perhaps, may have been content to accept such a position. I am, I confess, thankless. I thought you too proud to

heed what 'people said'; but if that trouble
you—I go myself to Sicily to-morrow."

Then he bowed very low once more, and, with
nis salutation to the altar, went on his way
through the dusky shadows of the little chapel
out into the morning sunshine of the street.

Her eyes grew blind with tears, and she sank
down before a wooden bench upon her knees; yet
could not pray there for the bitterness and
tumult of her heart.

She found her master in him.

His passionless unpardoning gaze sank into
her very soul, and seemed like a ruthless light,
that showed her all the wretchedness of pride and
self-love and vainest ostentations, which she had
harboured there and set up as her gods.

She comprehended that she had wronged
him, and that he would not forgive. After
all—knowing what she knew, she had had
no right to deal with him as she had done.
She had allowed him to bask in the sun of a fool's
paradise; and then had awakened him rudely, and
had sent him adrift. She had been ungenerous:
she saw it, and hated her own fault with the

repentance of a generous temper. She had
gone through the world with but little heed
for the pain of others; but his pain smote
her conscience. After all, he had a title to up-
braid her passionately; that he refrained from
doing so made her own self-reproach the keener.
There had been so many moments when with
justice he might have felt certain that she loved
him: and how could he guess the rest? She
knew that she had wronged him; and she was
humbled in her own sight; she had lost her own
self-respect, and her own motives seemed to her
but poor, and almost base.

No amorous entreaty, no feverish pursuit of
her, had ever moved her so intensely as that
silent condemnation, as that contemptuous rejection, of her poor half-hearted overture of
peace.

When she left the chapel she loved him as she
had never done before; yet it never occurred to
her to abandon her riches for his sake. The
habits and the ways of the world were too close
about her; its artificial needs and imperious
demands were too entirely her second nature; its

admiration was too necessary to her, and her custom of deference to its conventional laws too much an instinct; she had been too long accustomed to regard the impulses of the heart as insane follies, and poverty of life as pain and madness.

The same evening he did leave the town for Sicily, where he had lands which, though beautiful, were utterly unproductive, and constantly harried by the system of brigandage, which paralysed the district. "He will get shot most likely. He has declared that he will not return without having captured Pibro," said an Italian in her hearing, at a musical gathering, dedicated to the music of Pergolese. Pibro was a notorious Sicilian robber. The sweet chords sounded very harsh and jangled in her ears; she left early, and went home and took a heavy dose of chloral, which only gave her dark and dreary dreams.

"What miserable creatures we are!" she thought, wearily. "We cannot even sleep naturally—poor people can sleep;—they lie on hard benches, and dream with smiles on their faces."

She got up and looked out at the moonlight

on the river, and walked to and fro her chamber;
a lofty, slender, white figure in the pale gleam
of the lamp-rays.

A passionate, feverish, disordered pain consumed her. It terrified her. Would it be thus
weeks, months, years—all her life?

"Perhaps it is the chloral that unnerves one,"
she thought; "I will not take it any more."

"Only fancy, ma chère," said Madame Mila to
her next morning, with the pretty cat-like cruelty
of the Mila species, "only fancy—that poor dear
Della Rocca is gone to his death in Sicily. So
they say. There is a horrid brigand who has
been hanging some of his farmers there to trees,
and burning their cottages, Della Rocca's
farmers, you know; and he is gone to see about
it, and to capture the wretched creature,—as if he
could when all the soldiers and all the police have
failed! He will be quite certain to be shot; isn't
it a pity? He is so handsome, and if he would
marry that little American Spiffler girl with all
her millions he might be very happy. That little
Spiffler is really not unpresentable, and her people
still give the largest dot ever heard of if they can

get one of the very old titles; and they will make
no difficulty about religion; they were Jumpers
or Shakers or something themselves; he might
send her to the Sacré Cœur for a year or two."

" If he be gone to be shot, what use would the
Spiffler dot be ? " said Lady Hilda, with coolest
calm, as on a subject not even of most remote
interest, and she went on glazing a corner of the
draperies of her St. Ursula with carmine.

" The marriage was proposed to him, I know,"
continued Madame Mila, unheeded.   " The
Featherleighs undertook it, but he refused point
blank. '*Je ne me vends pas,*' was all he said.   It
was very rude, and really that little Spiffler might
be made something of; those very tiny creatures
never look vulgar, and are so easy to dress ; as it
is, I dare say Furstenberg will take her, if Nina
will let him ; it is on the tapis, and Della Rocca
won't come back alive, I suppose—isn't it a hare-
brained thing to do ?—there are gendarmes to
look after the brigands, but it seems he has some
fancy because they were his own people that suffered—but no doubt he told you all about it, as
you and he are such friends."

A A

"He merely said he was going to Sicily," said the Lady Hilda, languidly, still glazing her St. Ursula.

Madame Mila eyed her curiously.

"You look very pale, dear; I think you paint too much, and read too much," she said, affectionately. "I wish you had tried to persuade him into this Spiffler affair; it would be just the marriage for him, and a girl of seventeen may be drilled into anything, especially when she has small bones and little colour and good teeth; if Furstenberg gets her he will soon train her into good form—only he will gamble away all her money, let them tie it up as they may; and they can't tie it up very much if they want to make a high marriage. Good men won't sacrifice themselves unless they get some control of the fortune. They wouldn't have tied it at all with Della Rocca. Wouldn't the little Spiffler have been better for him than Sicily?"

"It depends upon taste," said the Lady Hilda, changing her brushes.

"Very odd taste," said Madame Mila. "They say Pibro always cuts the heads off the men he

takes, and sends them into Palermo—the heads
you know—with lemons in their mouths like
boars; isn't it horrible? And Della Rocca intends
going up after the monster in his very fastnesses
upon the mountains! Fancy that beautiful head
of his!—— Really, dear, you do look very ill:
when will you go to London?"

"Oh, some time next week."——

She went to the window and opened it; the
room swam round her, the sounds of the streets
grew dull upon her ears.

"I wish you wouldn't go till after the races,"
said Madame Mila, placidly. "I mean to stay.
The place is really very nice, though one does
see the same people too often. Fancy poor
Paolo ending like John the Baptist—the head in
the charger, you know—I wonder you let him go,
for you had a great deal of influence over him,
and say what you like, the Spiffler girl would have
been better. How can you keep that window
open, with the tramontana blowing?—thanks so
much for lending me the horses—goodness! what
is the matter?"

Madame Mila paused frightened; for the first

time in all her life Lady Hilda, leaning against the strong north wind, had lost her consciousness and had fainted.

" How very strange people are," thought Madame Mila, when an hour later her cousin had recovered herself, and had attributed her weakness to the chloral at night and the scent of her oil paints. " If she cared for him like that, why didn't she keep him when she had got him ?—she might have hung him to her skirt like her châtelaine; nobody would ever have said anything; I do begin to think that with all her taste, and all her cleverness, she has, after all, not so very much savoir faire."

No one had much savoir faire to Madame Mila's mind who did not manage always to enjoy themselves without scruples and also without scenes.

The house in London was ordered to be kept ready night and day, but no one went to occupy it. M. Camille Odissot, stimulated by dread of his patroness's daily arrival in Paris, worked marvels of celerity upon the ballroom walls, and

drew with most exquisite precision bands of
Greek youths and maidens in the linked mazes
of the dance, but none went to admire his
efforts and execution.   No fashionable newspapers announced the Lady Hilda's arrival in
either city; she stayed on and on in Floralia.

"When I know that he is safe out of Sicily I
will go," she said to herself; and let the piles
of letters and invitation cards lie and accumulate
as they would.

She ceased to paint, and left the St. Ursula
unfinished; he had sketched it out for her on the
panel, and had first tinted it en grisaille.   She
had not the courage to go on with it; she changed
her mode of life, and rode or drove all the day
long in the sweet fresh spring weather.   When she
was not in the open air she felt suffocated.   The
danger which he ran was no mere exaggeration
of her cousin's malicious inventiveness, but was
a fact, true and ghastly enough; no one heard of
or from him, but his friends said that it was the
most fatal madness that had led him to risk his
life in the fastnesses of the Sicilian thieves.

"It is sheer suicide," they said around her.

"What had he to do there?—if the law cannot enforce itself, leave it alone in its impotency. But he had some idea that because his own villages were amongst those who suffered most, it was his place to go there and do what the law cannot do:—he was always Quixotic, poor Paolo. The last thing heard of him was that he had left Palermo with an escort of men whom he had chosen and paid himself, and had gone up towards the mountains. His dead body will be the first tidings that we have; the monster Pibro has spies in all directions, and holds that district in a perfect reign of terror."

She went out into society as Easter came, and heard all that they said, and gave no sign of what she suffered. Worth sent her new marvels of the spring, and she wore them, and was endlessly courted and envied, and quoted and wondered at. She was a little chillier and more cynical than ever, and women observed with pleasure that she was looking ill and growing too thin, which would spoil her beauty. That was all. But she had never thought such pain possible in life as she endured now.

"If he die it is I who will have killed him," she said in her own heart night and day.

Once she found herself in her long lonely rides near Palestrina, and met the old steward, and recognised him, and went into the sad, silent, deserted house; and listened to the old man's stories of his beloved lord's boyhood and manhood, and of the people's clinging feudal attachment to him, and of his devotion to them in the time of the cholera pestilence.

"There is not an old charcoal burner or a little goatherd on the estates that would not give his life for Prince Paolo," the steward said to her, crying like a child because there was no news from Sicily.

The same evening she went to a great Pasqua ball at the Trasimene villa. As they fastened the diamonds over her hair and in her bosom she felt to hate the shining, senseless, soulless stones; —they were the emblem of the things for which she had lost him; and at that very hour, for ought they knew, he might be lying dead on some solitary shore by the fair blue sea of Theocritus !

With a heart sick with terror and uncertainty she went to the brilliant crowds of the Trasimene house; to the talk that was so frivolous and tedious, to the dances she never joined in, to the homage she was so tired of, to the monotonies and personalities and trivialities that make up society.

M. de St. Louis hurried up to her:

" Madame, quelle chance !—our new Herakles has slain his Dragon. Maremma has just had telegrams from Palermo. Della Rocca has positively captured the scoundrel Pibro, and taken him into the city, much wounded, but alive, and in the king's gaol by this time. A fine thing to have done, is it not? Of course we shall all praise it, since it has succeeded; although, in truth, a madder exploit never was attempted. Paolo was ten days in the mountains living on a few beans and berries: he has received no hurt whatever; I should think they will give him the Grand Cordon of the Santissima Annunziata. It is really a superb thing to have done. The monster has been the terror of that district for ten years. Palermo went utterly mad with joy. It is quite a pity there is no Ariosto to celebrate such a feat. It is very Ariosto-like. Indeed, all the best Italians are so. Englishmen have long ceased to be in any manner Shakesperian; but Italians remain like their poets."

The Duc wandered away into the subtlest and most discursive analysis of the Ariostian school and of the national characteristics which it displayed and was nurtured on; but she had no ear to hear it.

Outwardly she sat indifferent and calm, but her brain and her heart were in tumult with the sweetest, loftiest, grandest pride that she had ever known — pride without egotism, without vanity, without a thought of self; true pride, exultant in heroism, not the arrogant pride of self-culture, of self-worship, of self-love, not the paltry pride of rank and acquisition and physical perfection, not the pride of which all the while she had been half contemptuous herself. And then—his life was safe !

Yet, had he stood before her then she must have given him the same answer—at least, she thought so.

"What a fine thing to have done!" said Madame Mila, pausing by her in the middle of a waltz, with her brocade train ablaze with gold. "And now he can come back and marry the Spiffler girl. What do you say, Duc?"

"He will never marry la petite Spiffler," said the Duc, "nor any one else," he added, with a glance of meaning at Lady Hilda.

All eyes turned upon her. She played idly with her fan—one painted long ago by Watteau.

"M. della Rocca has succeeded, so it is heroism," she said, calmly. "Had he failed, I suppose it would have been foolhardiness."

"Of course," said the Duc. "Surely, Madame, Failure cannot expect to use the same dictionary as Success?"

"He must have the Santissima Annunziata, and marry the big Spiffler dot," said Madame Mila.

"Nay, Comtesse, that were bathos indeed, to make la petite Spiffler *cousine du roi!* Anyhow, let us rejoice that he is living, and that the old Latin race is still productive of heroes. I suppose we shall have details the day after to-morrow."

" Whatever could he do it for ? " said Madame Mila, as she whirled away again in the encircling arm of her Maurice : to Madame Mila such trifles as duty, patriotism, or self-sacrifice could not possibly be any motive power amongst rational creatures. " Whatever could he do it for ?—I suppose to soften Hilda. But he must know very little about her; she hates anything romantic ; you heard she called it foolhardy. He *never* will be anything to her, not if he try for ten years. She cares about him after her fashion, but she cares much more about herself."

Lady Hilda did not sleep that night.

She did not even lie down; dry-eyed and with fever in her veins, she sat by the window watching the bright pale gold of the morning widen over the skies, and the sea-green depth of the river catch the first sun-rays and mirro them.

She was so proud of him — ah heaven, so proud ! The courage of her temper answered to the courage of his action. It was Heraklean— it was Homeric—that going forth single-handed

to do what the law could not or would not do,
and set free from tyranny of brute force those
poor tillers of the soil who could not help
themselves. The very folly and madness of that
utter disregard of peril moved her to reverence;
she who had all her life been environed with
the cool, calm, cautious, and circumspect customs of the world.

For one moment it seemed to her possible to
renounce everything for his sake. For one moment her own passion for the mere gauds and
pomps and possessions of the world looked to
her beside the simplicity and self-sacrifice of his
own life so poor and mean that she shrank from
it in disgust. For one moment she said to
herself—" Love was enough."

He had been ready to give up his life for
a few poor labourers, who had no other claim
on him than that they lived upon the soil
he owned; and she who loved him had not
the courage to renounce mere worldly riches
for his sake. She hated herself, and yet she
could not change herself. She cared for power,
for supremacy, for indulgence, for extravagance;

she dreaded to hear the tittering mockery of the women she had eclipsed so long at all her present weakness; it was all so poor, so base, so unworthy, yet it enchained her: the world had been her religion; no one casts off a creed long held without hard and cruel strife.

"Oh, my love, how far beneath you I am!" she thought, she whose pride had been a bye-word, and whose superb vanity had been an invulnerable armour.

She could have kneeled down and kissed his hands for very humility; yet she could not resolve to yield.

"I might see him once more, before I go," she thought, and so coward-like she put the hour of decision from her. They must part, but she might see him once more first.

She would go away of course, and her life in the Winter City would be with the things of the past, and she would grow used to the pain of dead passion, and feel it less with time—other women did, and why not she?

So she said to herself; and yet at moments a sort

of despair appalled her: what would her future
be ?   Only one long empty void, in whose hollow‑
ness the " pleasures " of the world would rattle
like dead bones.   She began to understand that
for a great love there is no death possible.   It is
like Ahasuerus the Jew : it must live on in tor‑
ment for ever.

And how she had smiled at all these things
when others had spoken of them !

The days passed slowly one by one; the
beautiful city was in its spring glory, and ran
over with the blossoms of flowers, as though it
were the basket that Persephone let fall.   The
news-sheets were full of this deed which he had
done in Sicily; she bought them all, down to the
tawdriest little sheet that held his name, and read
the well-known story again and again a hundred
and ten hundred times ; his friends expected him
to arrive in the town each day, but no one heard
anything direct from himself.

" It is strange he writes to none of us," said
Maremma ; " can anything have happened ? "

" Oh, no; the papers would know it," said the
Duc de St. Louis.

She overheard them, and listened with dry lips and a beating heart.

Why did he write to no one? The news-sheets had announced that he had left Palermo for Floralia.

"He may be coming back by the marshes," someone else suggested; "he is reclaiming land there."

Perhaps he stayed away, she thought, because he had heard that she still remained in his native city.

It was mid-April. Madame Mila was organising picnics under old Etruscan walls, and alfresco dinners in villa gardens, and she and her kind were driving out on the tops of drags, and playing baccarat upon anemone-studded lawns by moonlight, and driving in again, at or after midnight, singing Offenbach choruses, and going to the big Café in the town for supper and champagnes; be it in winter or summer, spring or autumn, town or country, youth or middle-age, Madame Mila and her kind, contrive to make no difference in their manner of life whatever; they would sing Schneider's songs in the Tombs of the

Prophets, they would eat lobster salad on Mount Olivet, and they would scatter their cigar ash over Vaucluse, Marathon, the Campo Santo, or the grave at Ravenna with equal indifference; they are always amused, and defy alike the seasons and the sanctities to stop them in their amusement.

It was mid-April, and with the beginning of May would come the races, and with the races the Winter City would become the Summer City, and the winter-fashion always fled with one bound to fresh fields and pastures new, and left the town to silence, sunshine, roses, fruits, its own populace with their summer songs and summer skies, and perhaps here and there an artist or a poet, or some such foolish person, who loved it best so in its solitude.

"Do come with us, Hilda," said Madame Mila one mid-April morning.

Madame Mila was attired in the simplest morning costume of cream-hued Sicilienne covered with écru lace, and she had a simple country Dorothy hat of cream-coloured velvet, lined *bleu-de-ciel*, with wreaths of delicate nemophilæ and convolvuli and floating feathers, set on one side of her head; Lancret might have painted her on a fan, or Fragonard on a cabinet; she was just going to drive out with five carriages full of her friends to a picnic at Guido Salvareo's villa; they were to dine there, play lansquenet there, and come back in the small hours; they had all postillions, silk-jacketted, powdered, and with ribboned straw hats; the horses were belled, and the bells were jingling in the street; Madame Mila was in the most radiant spirits; she had won five hundred napoleons the night before, and had them all to adventure over again to-night.

"Do come with us, Hilda," she urged. "You do nothing but go those stupid long drives by yourself; it is very bad for you; and it will be charming to-day; Salvareo has such taste; it is really quite romantic to sit upon those anemones, and have the goats come and stare at you; and he always does things so well, and his cook is so good. Do come with us; I am sure it would do you good."

Lady Hilda looked up from the S. Ursula, which she was finishing:

" My dear Mila !—you know perfectly well how I detest that kind of thing. Teresa's songs, drag seats, and eager efforts to imitate the worst kind of women !—go to it, if it amuse you; but, with all gratitude, allow me to decline."

" How disagreeable you are ! " said Madame Mila, pettishly. " One must do something with oneself all these long days : if it were Palestrina, I suppose you would go."

Lady Hilda deigned to give no reply. She touched in the gold background of her Saint. Madame Mila looked at her with irritation ; no one likes to be despised, and she knew that her cousin did very nearly despise her, and all the ways and means of enjoyment in which her heart delighted.

Lady Hilda, tranquilly painting there, annoyed her inexpressibly. Why should any woman be above the box-seats of drags and all their con comitant attractions ?

She took her revenge.

. " Do as you like of course, but you always *do* do that," she said carelessly. " There are two seats vacant. St. Louis and Carlo Maremma were to have gone with us, but they went to Della

Rocca instead. Oh, didn't you know it?—he
reached Palestrina two days ago very ill with
marsh fever. It is fever and cholera and ague
and all sorts of dreadful things all together.
Isn't it odd?—to have escaped all that danger
in Sicily, and then get this in the swamps
coming back? Nobody knew it till late last
night, when his steward got frightened, and
sent in for the physicians. He is very bad, I
believe—not likely to live. You know they go
down under that—sometimes in twenty-four
hours."

Lady Hilda seemed to reach her at a single
step, though the distance of the room was
between them.

" Is that true ?—or is it some jest ?"

Madame Mila, appalled, looked up into her face.

" It is true, quite true. Oh, Hilda, take your
hand off; you hurt me. How could I tell you
would care about it like that."

" Is it true ?" muttered her cousin again.

"Indeed, indeed it is," she whimpered
trembling. "Oh let me go, you spoil my lace.
If you cared for the man like that, why didn't

B B 2

you keep him when you had got him? I know you could not have married him, but nobody would have said anything."

Lady Hilda put her out into the corridor, and closed the door and locked it within.

Madame Mila, frightened, astonished, and out-raged, went down to her Maurice, and the drag, and the ribboned and powdered postillions, and the horses with their jingling bells and plaited tails; the gay calvacade rattled off along the river-street towards the city gates as the clocks tolled three.

Lady Hilda and S. Ursula were left alone.

Within less than half-an-hour the black horses were harnessed and bore their mistress towards Palestrina. Never before moved by impulse, impulse alone governed her now; the impulse of despair and remorse. She cared nothing who saw her or who knew; for once she had forgotten herself.

The long drive seemed eternity; she thought the steep winding mountain roads would never end; when Palestrina came in sight, pale and stately against its dark background of forest trees, she felt as if her heart would break. He had gone through all those perils afar off, only to be dying there !

It was five o'clock by the convent chimes when they reached the crest of the hill on which the old place stood. The lovely hillside was covered with the blue and white of the wild hyacinths and gold of the wild daffodils. The lofty stone pines spread their dark green roofs above her head. Flocks of birds were singing, in the myrtle thickets, their sweet shrill evensong. The shining valley lay below like a cloud of amber light. The surpassing loveliness, the intense stillness of it all, made the anguish within her unbearable. What she had missed all her life long !——

There was a chapel not far from the house set in the midst of the pines, with the cross on it summit touching the branches, and its doorway still hung round with the evergreens and flowers of its passed Easter feasts. There were men and women and children standing about on the turf in front of it ; they were most of them crying bitterly.

She stopped her horses there, and called a woman to her, but her lips would not frame the question. The woman guessed it:—

"Yes, my beautiful lady," she said, with many tears. "We have been praying for Prince Paolo. He is very ill, up yonder. The marsh sickness has got him. May the dear Mother of God save him to us. But he is dying, they say——"

"We would die in his stead, if the good God would let us," said one of the men, drawing near: the others sobbed aloud.

She put out her hand to the man—the slender proud hand that she had refused to princes. Wondering, he fell on his knee and would have kissed her hand. She drew back in horror.

"Do not kneel to me! I have killed him!" she muttered; and she urged her panting horses forward to the house.

She bade them tell the Duc de St. Louis to come to her upon the terrace. She leaned there tearless, white as death, still as marble; the beautiful, tranquil spring time all around, and the valley shining like gold in the light of the descending sun. It seemed to her that ages passed before the soft step of her old friend sounded near her: he was surprised and startled, but he did not show it.

"There is still hope," he hastened to say, ere she could speak. "Within the last hour he is slightly better; they give him quinine constantly. If the chills and shivering do not return, it is just possible that he may live. But——"

His voice faltered in its serenity, and he turned his head away.

"It is not likely?"

Her own voice had scarcely any sound of its natural tone left in it, yet long habit was so strong with her that she spoke calmly.

"It is not likely. This deadly marsh-poison is short and fierce. After the fatigue and fasting in Sicily it has taken fearful hold on him. But in an hour or two they will know—one way or the other."

"I will stay here. Come and tell me—often. And if—if the worst come—let me see him. Leave me now."

He looked at her, hesitated, then left her as she asked. He guessed all that passed in her thoughts; all that had gone before: and he knew that she was not a woman who would bear pity, and that she was best left thus in solitude.

Like a caged animal she paced to and fro the long length of the stone terrace.

She was all alone.

The flower-like radiance of the declining day shone everywhere around, the birds sang, the dreamy bells rang in the Ave Maria from hill to hill, all was so still, so peaceful, so beautiful; yet with the setting of the sun, his life might go out in darkness.

In her great misery, her soul was purified. The fire that consumed her burned away the dross of the world, the alloy of selfishness and habit and vain passions. "Oh, God! give me his life, and I will give him mine!" she cried in her heart all through those terrible hours; and yet recoiled in terror from the uselessness and daring of her prayer. What had she ever done that she could merit its fulfilment?

He might have been hers, all hers; and she had loved the base things of a worldly greatness better than himself. And now he lay dying there, as the sun dropped westward and night came.

She felt no chill of evening. She felt neither hunger nor thirst. Crowds of weeping people hung about in the gardens below. She heard nothing that passed round her, save the few words of her old friend, when from time to time he came and told her that there was no change.

The moon rose, and its light fell on the stone of the terrace, and through the vast deserted chambers opening from it; on the grey worn marbles of the statues, and on the pale angels of the frescoes.

It was ten o'clock: the chimes of the convent above on the mountains told every hour. Unceasingly she paced to and fro, to and fro, like some mad, or wounded creature. The silence and serenity of the night, the balmy fragrance of it, and the silvery light, were so much mockery of her wretchedness. She had never thought that there could be agony like this——and yet from heaven no sign!

Nearly another hour had passed before her friend approached her again. She caught the

sound of his step in the darkness; her heart
stood still; her blood was changed to ice, frozen
with the deadliness of the most deadly fear on
earth; she could only look at him with wide-
opened, strained, blind eyes.

For the first time he smiled:—

"Take comfort," he said, softly. "He has
fallen asleep, he is less exhausted, they say that
he may live. How cold you are!—this night will
kill you!"

She dropped down upon her knees on the
stone pavement, and all her bowed frame was
shakened by convulsive weeping.

He drew aside in reverence and left her alone
in the light of the moon.

When midnight came hope was certain.

The sleep still lasted; the fever had abated,
the cold chills had not returned.

She called her old friend to her out into the
terrace.

"I will go now. Send to me at daybreak and
keep my secret."

"May I tell him nothing?"

"Tell him to come to me—when he is able."

" Nothing more ? "

" No; nothing. He will know——"

" But——"

She turned her face to him in the full moonlight, with the tears of her joy coursing down
her cheeks, and he started at the change in her
that this one night of suffering had wrought.

" No, say nothing more. But—but—you
shall see what my atonement shall be, and my
thankfulness."

Then she went away from him softly in the
darkness and the fragrance of the April night.
The Duc looked after the lights of her carriage
with a mist over his own eyes, but he shrugged
his shoulders with a sigh.

" Who can ever say that he knows a woman!
Who can ever predcit what she will not say,
or will not do, or will not be ! " he murmured,
as he turned and went within to watch beside
the bed of his friend, as the stars grew clearer
and the dawn approached.

CHAPTER XIII.

A MONTH later Paolo della Rocca led his wife through what had once been his mother's chambers at Palestrina, and which were now prepared for her, with all their wide windows unclosed and looking out to the rose and golden afternoon glories of the bright south-west.

In the little oratory, which opened out of the bed-chamber, there was hung an altar picture; it was the picture of San Cipriano il Mago.

"Take it as my marriage gift," he murmured to her. "You threw away your magic wand and renounced the world for me,—oh, my love, my love! God grant you the Saints' reward!"

She laid her hands upon his heart, and leant her cheek upon them.

" My reward is here."

" And you will never repent ? "

" Did Cyprian repent when he broke his earthly bonds and gained eternal life ? Once I was blind, but now I see. The world is nothing :—Love is enough ! "

CHAPTER XIV.

"C'EST étonnant!" murmured the Duc de St.
Louis the same evening softly to himself, standing on the steps of the Hôtel Murat, after
assisting in the morning at those various civil
ceremonies and impediments with which our
beloved Italy, in her new character as a nation
of Free Thought, does her best to impede and
deter all such as cling to so old-world and
pedantic a prejudice as marriage.

The dènoûment of the drama which he
himself had first set in action had fallen upon
him like a thunder-bolt. He had had no con-
ception of what would happen. He had thought
to enrich his friend by one of the finest fortunes

in Europe, and lo!—the Duc remained in an amazement and a sense of humiliation from which he could not recover.

"C'est étonnant!" he murmured again and again. "Who would ever have believed that Miladi was a woman to beggar herself and play the romance of the 'world lost for love?' If I had only imagined—if I had only dreamed! I will never propose a marriage to any living being again; never."

"You have nothing to be so remorseful about, Duc," said Lord Clairvaux, with a sigh, himself utterly exhausted by all the law work that he had been obliged to go through. "It is very funny certainly—she of all women in the world! But they are happy enough, and he really is the only living,creature that ever could manage her. If anybody had ever told me that any man would change Hilda like that!"

"Happy!" echoed M. de St. Louis, with his delicate and incredulous smile. He was a man who had no delusions; he was perfectly aware that there were no marriages that were happy; some were calm, this was the uttermost, and to remain calm required an immense income; money alone was harmony.

Lord Clairvaux lighted a very big cigar, and grumbled that it had been horrible to have to leave England in the Epsom month, but that he thanked goodness that it was the last of her caprices that he would be worried with; and he hoped that this Italian would like them when he had had a year or two of them.

"I don't know, though, but what it is the only sensible caprice she ever did have in her life; eh?" he added; "except buying Escargot and giving him to me after the races—you remember?—Hang it, I've never seen such a Chantilly before or since as that was!"

"We never do see such a race as the one that we happen to win," murmured M. de St. Louis.

"Of course it's an awful cropper to take, and all that; but I'm not sure but what she's done a wise thing, though all the women are howling at her like mad," continued Lord Clairvaux; "a woman can't live for ever on *chiffons*, you see."

" Most women can—admirably. They buy at eighty as much white hair, the coiffeurs tell me, as they buy blonde or black at twenty."

" Ah, but they can't, if they have a bit of heart or mind in them. Hilda has both."

" The case is so rare I could not prescribe for it—let us hope Miladi's own prescription will suit her," said the Duc, whose serene good-humour was still slightly ruffled.

" Well, she always was all extremes and con-traries," said Lord Clairvaux. " You never could say one minute what she wouldn't do the next. By George! you know there is nothing too odd for her to go in for; I should not wonder an atom if when we come here two or three years hence, we find her worshipping a curly Paolino, seeing to the silkworms, and studying wine-making: she's really tried ever-thing else, you know."

" Everything except happiness? Well, very few of us get any chance of trying that, or would appreciate it if we did get it. Happi-ness," pursued the Duc pensively, " must, after

q q

all, be almost as monotonous as discontent—
when one is used to it. It is comforting to
think so; for there is very little of it. I cannot
realize Miladi amongst the babies and the wine-
presses; but you may be right."

"Well, you know she's tried everything else,"
repeated Lord Clairvaux. "It will be like
Julius Cæsar and his cabbage-garden."

"You mean Diocletian," said the Duc. "Do
you leave to-night? We may as well go as far as
Paris together.'

And he turned back into the hotel to bid
farewell to Madame Mila.

Madame Mila,—who had made the religious
and civil ceremonies gorgeous in the last new
anomalous anachronisms, with a classic and clinging dress, quite Greek in its cut, covered all
over with the eyes out of peacocks' feathers,
and a cotte de maille boddice, stiff as paste-
board, with gold and silver embroideries,—was
now on the point of departure from the Winter
City across the Mont Cenis, and was covered up
in the most wonderful of hooded cloaks trimmed
with the feathers of the Russian diver and the

grebe; about one hundred and fifty birds, happy, peaceful, and innocent under their native skies, had died to trim the wrap, and it would probably be worn about half-a-dozen times; for feathers are so very soon tumbled, as everybody knows.

"They are quite mad, both of them!" said the little lady, giving her small fingers in adieu, and turning to see that Maurice had all the things she wanted, and was duly hooking them on to her ceinture of oxydised silver.

She travelled with her two maids, a courier, and a footman, but none of them did as much hard work as the indefatigable Maurice.

"Perhaps, Madame," said the Duc, who indeed thought so himself; but was not going to admit it too strongly of two persons who, despite their lamentable weakness, remained his favourites. "But if a few people were not mad occasionally there would be no chance for the sanity of the world."

"Well, they will repent horribly, that is one comfort; she most of all," said Madame Mila, with asperity. "She ought to have been prevented; treated for lunacy, you know; in France they

would have managed it at once with a conseil
de famille. Maurice, you are screwing the
top of that flacon on all wrong—do take more
care! She will repent horribly, but she don't
see it now. Of course if she had had to lose
the jewels *they* would have brought her to reason.
As it is she don't in the least realise the horrible
thing that she's done ;—not in the least, not in
the least! And the *idea* of going to his villa
to-day! So unusual you know ;—so positively
improper! So utterly contrary to all custom!
When I said to her, too, that she wouldn't
be able even to afford Worth, she laughed,
and answered, that she would have one dress
from him every year for old friendship's sake
for the Palestrina vintage balls, and that he
would be sure to embroider her the loveliest
Bacchic symbolisms and put the cone of the
thyrsus for buttons !—only fancy! She could
actually jest about *that!* How miserable she
will be in three months when she has come back
to her senses; and how miserable she will make
him! "

"Chère comtesse," said the Duc, taking up

his hat and cane, " everybody repents everything. It is a law of Fate. The only difference is that some people repent pleasantly, and some unpleasantly. Let us hope that our beautiful Duchesse will repent pleasantly. Madame, j'ai l'honneur de vous saluer — Bon voyage ; au revoir."

THE END.

PRINTED BY
SPOTTISWOODE AND CO., NEW-STREET SQUARE
LONDON

CHATTO & WINDUS'S
LIST OF CHEAP POPULAR NOVELS
BY THE BEST AUTHORS.
Picture Covers, TWO SHILLINGS each.

BY EDMOND ABOUT.
The Fellah.

BY HAMILTON AÏDÉ.
Carr of Carrlyon.
Confidences.

BY MRS. ALEXANDER.
Maid, Wife, or Widow?
Valerie's Fate. | Blind Fate.
A Life Interest.
Mona's Choice.
By Woman's Wit.

BY GRANT ALLEN.
Strange Stories.
Philistia. | Babylon.
The Beckoning Hand.
In All Shades.
For Maimie's Sake.
The Devil's Die.
This Mortal Coil.
The Tents of Shem.
The Great Taboo.
Dumaresq's Daughter.
The Duchess of Powysland.
Blood-Royal.
Ivan Greet's Masterpiece.
The Scallywag.
At Market Value.
Under Sealed Orders.

BY EDWIN LESTER ARNOLD.
Pura the Phœnician.

BY FRANK BARRETT.
A Recoiling Vengeance.
For Love and Honour.
John Ford; & His Helpmate.
Honest Davie.
A Prodigal's Progress.
Folly Morrison.
Lieutenant Barnabas.
Found Guilty.
Fettered for Life.
Between Life and Death.
The Sin of Olga Zassoulich.
Little Lady Linton.
Woman of the Iron Bracelets.
The Harding Scandal.

BY SHELSLEY BEAUCHAMP.
Grantley Grange.

BY BESANT AND RICE.
Ready-Money Mortiboy.
With Harp and Crown.
This Son of Vulcan.
My Little Girl.
The Case of Mr. Lucraft.
The Golden Butterfly.
By Celia's Arbour.
The Monks of Thelema.
'Twas in Trafalgar's Bay.
The Seamy Side.
The Ten Years' Tenant.
The Chaplain of the Fleet.

BY WALTER BESANT.
All Sorts & Conditions of Men.
The Captains' Room.
All in a Garden Fair.
Dorothy Forster.
Uncle Jack.
Children of Gibeon.
World went very well then.
Herr Paulus.
For Faith and Freedom.
To Call her Mine.
The Bell of St. Paul's.
The Holy Rose.
Armorel of Lyonesse.
St. Katherine's by the Tower.
The Ivory Gate.
Verbena Camellia Stephanotis.
The Rebel Queen.
Beyond the Dreams of Avarice.
The Revolt of Man.
In Deacon's Orders.

BY AMBROSE BIERCE.
In the Midst of Life.

BY FREDERICK BOYLE.
Camp Notes.
Savage Life.
Chronicles of No-Man's Land.

BY HAROLD BRYDGES.
Uncle Sam at Home.

BY ROBERT BUCHANAN.
The Shadow of the Sword.
A Child of Nature.
God and the Man.
Annan Water.
The New Abelard.
The Martyrdom of Madeline.
Love Me for Ever.
Matt: a Story of a Caravan.
Foxglove Manor.
The Master of the Mine.
The Heir of Linne.
Woman and the Man.
Rachel Dene.
Lady Kilpatrick.

BY BUCHANAN & MURRAY.
The Charlatan.

BY HALL CAINE.
The Shadow of a Crime.
A Son of Hagar.
The Deemster.

BY COMMANDER CAMERON.
Cruise of the 'Black Prince.'

CHIEF INSPECTOR CAVANAGH.
Scotland Yard, Past & Present

BY AUSTIN CLARE.
For the Love of a Lass.

BY MRS. ARCHER CLIVE.
Paul Ferroll.
Why Paul Ferroll Killed Wife.

BY MACLAREN COBBAN.
The Cure of Souls.
The Red Sultan.

BY C. ALLSTON COLLINS.
The Bar Sinister.

BY WILKIE COLLINS.
Armadale.
After Dark. | No Name.
A Rogue's Life. | Antonina.
Hide and Seek. | Basil.
The Dead Secret.
Queen of Hearts.
My Miscellanies.
The Woman in White.
The Moonstone.
Man and Wife.
Poor Miss Finch.
Miss or Mrs.?
The New Magdalen.
The Frozen Deep.
The Law and the Lady.
The Two Destinies.
The Haunted Hotel.
The Fallen Leaves.
Jezebel's Daughter.
The Black Robe.
Heart and Science.
'I say No.' | Blind Love.
The Evil Genius.
Little Novels.
The Legacy of Cain.

BY MORTIMER COLLINS.
Sweet Anne Page.
Transmigration.
From Midnight to Midnight.
A Fight with Fortune.

MORT. AND FRANCES COLLINS.
Sweet and Twenty. | Frances.
The Village Comedy.
You Play Me False.
Blacksmith and Scholar.

BY M. J. COLQUHOUN.
Every Inch a Soldier.

BY DUTTON COOK.
Leo. | Paul Foster's Daughter.

BY C. EGBERT CRADDOCK.
The Prophet of the Great
Smoky Mountains.

BY MATT CRIM.
Adventures of a Fair Rebel.

BY B. M. CROKER.
Pretty Miss Neville.
Proper Pride. | 'To Let.'
A Bird of Passage.
Diana Barrington.
A Family Likeness.
Village Tales and Jungle
Tragedies.
Two Masters. | Mr. Jervis
The Real Lady Hilda.
Married or Single?

London: CHATTO & WINDUS, 111 St. Martin's Lane, W.C.

BY WILLIAM CYPLES.
Hearts of Gold.

BY ALPHONSE DAUDET.
The Evangelist.

BY ERASMUS DAWSON.
The Fountain of Youth.

BY JAMES DE MILLE.
A Castle in Spain.

BY J. LEITH DERWENT.
Our Lady of Tears.
Circe's Lovers.

BY DICK DONOVAN.
The Man-hunter.
Caught at Last!
Tracked and Taken.
Who Poisoned Hetty Duncan?
The Man from Manchester.
A Detective's Triumphs.
In the Grip of the Law.
Wanted!
From Information Received.
Tracked to Doom.
Link by Link.
Suspicion Aroused.
Dark Deeds.
Riddles Read.
Mystery of Jamaica Terrace.
The Chronicles of Michael
    Danevitch.

BY MRS. ANNIE EDWARDES.
A Point of Honour.
Archie Lovell.

BY M. BETHAM-EDWARDS.
Felicia.
Kitty.

BY EDWARD EGGLESTON.
Roxy.

BY G. MANVILLE FENN.
The New Mistress.
Witness to the Deed.
The Tiger Lily.
The White Virgin.

BY PERCY FITZGERALD.
Bella Donna.
Polly.
The Second Mrs. Tillotson.
Seventy-five Brooke Street.
Never Forgotten.
The Lady of Brantome.
Fatal Zero.

BY PERCY FITZGERALD, &c.
Strange Secrets.

BY ALBANY DE FONBLANQUE.
Filthy Lucre.

BY R. E. FRANCILLON.
Olympia.
One by One.
Queen Cophetua.

BY R. E. FRANCILLON—*cont.*
A Real Queen.
King or Knave.
Romances of the Law.
Ropes of Sand.
A Dog and his Shadow.

BY HAROLD FREDERIC.
Seth's Brother's Wife.
The Lawton Girl.

PREFACED BY BARTLE FRERE.
Pandurang Hari.

BY EDWARD GARRETT.
The Capel Girls.

BY GILBERT GAUL.
A Strange Manuscript Found
    in a Copper Cylinder.

BY CHARLES GIBBON.
Robin Gray.
For Lack of Gold.
What will the World Say?
In Honour Bound.
In Love and War.
For the King.
Queen of the Meadow.
In Pastures Green.
The Flower of the Forest.
A Heart's Problem.
The Braes of Yarrow.
The Golden Shaft.
Of High Degree.
The Dead Heart.
By Mead and Stream.
Heart's Delight.
Fancy Free.
Loving a Dream.
A Hard Knot.
Blood-Money.

BY WILLIAM GILBERT.
James Duke.
Dr. Austin's Guests.
The Wizard of the Mountain.

BY ERNEST GLANVILLE.
The Lost Heiress.
The Fossicker.
A Fair Colonist.

BY REV. S. BARING GOULD.
Eve.
Red Spider.

BY HENRY GREVILLE.
A Noble Woman.
Nikanor.

BY CECIL GRIFFITH.
Corinthia Marazion.

BY SYDNEY GRUNDY.
The Days of his Vanity.

BY JOHN HABBERTON.
Brueton's Bayou.
Country Luck.

BY ANDREW HALLIDAY.
Every-Day Papers.

BY THOMAS HARDY.
Under the Greenwood Tree.

BY BRET HARTE.
An Heiress of Red Dog.
The Luck of Roaring Camp.
Californian Stories.
Gabriel Conroy.
Flip.
Maruja.
A Phyllis of the Sierras.
A Waif of the Plains.
A Ward of the Golden Gate.

BY JULIAN HAWTHORNE.
Garth.
Ellice Quentin.
Sebastian Strome.
Dust.
Fortune's Fool.
Beatrix Randolph.
Miss Cadogna.
Love—or a Name.
David   Poindexter's   Disap-
    pearance.
The Spectre of the Camera.

BY SIR ARTHUR HELPS.
Ivan de Biron.

BY G. A. HENTY.
Rujub the Juggler.

BY HENRY HERMAN.
A Leading Lady.

BY HEADON HILL.
Zambra the Detective.

BY JOHN HILL.
Treason-Felony.

BY MRS. CASHEL HOEY.
The Lover's Creed.

BY MRS. GEORGE HOOPER.
The House of Raby.

BY TIGHE HOPKINS.
'Twixt Love and Duty.

BY MRS. HUNGERFORD.
In Durance Vile.
A Maiden all Forlorn.
A Mental Struggle.
Marvel.
A Modern Circe.
Lady Verner's Flight.
The Red-House Mystery.
The Three Graces.
An Unsatisfactory Lover.
Lady Patty.
Nora Creina.
The Professor's Experiment.

BY MRS. ALFRED HUNT.
Thornicroft's Model.
The Leaden Casket.
Self-Condemned.
That Other Person.

BY WILLIAM JAMESON.
My Dead Self.

BY HARRIETT JAY.
The Dark Colleen.
The Queen of Connaught.

BY MARK KERSHAW.
Colonial Facts and Fictions.

London: CHATTO & WINDUS, 111 *St. Martin's Lane,* W.C.

BY R. ASHE KING.
A Drawn Game.
'The Wearing of the Green.'
Passion's Slave.
Bell Barry.

BY EDMOND LEPELLETIER.
Madame Sans-Gêne.

BY JOHN LEYS.
The Lindsays.

BY E. LYNN LINTON.
Patricia Kemball.
Atonement of Leam Dundas.
The World Well Lost.
Under which Lord ?
With a Silken Thread.
The Rebel of the Family.
'My Love!'
Ione.
Paston Carew.
Sowing the Wind.
The One Too Many.
Dulcie Everton.

BY HENRY W. LUCY.
Gideon Fleyce.

BY JUSTIN McCARTHY.
Dear Lady Disdain.
The Waterdale Neighbours.
My Enemy's Daughter.
A Fair Saxon.
Linley Rochford.
Miss Misanthrope.
Donna Quixote.
The Comet of a Season.
Maid of Athens.
Camiola: Girl with a Fortune.
The Dictator.
Red Diamonds.
The Riddle Ring.

BY HUGH MacCOLL.
Mr. Stranger's Sealed Packet.

BY GEORGE MACDONALD.
Heather and Snow.

BY MRS. MACDONELL.
Quaker Cousins.

BY KATHARINE S. MACQUOID.
The Evil Eye.
Lost Rose.

BY W. H. MALLOCK.
The New Republic.
Romance of the 19th Century.

BY J. MASTERMAN.
Half-a-dozen Daughters.

BY BRANDER MATTHEWS.
A Secret of the Sea.

BY L. T. MEADE.
A Soldier of Fortune.

BY LEONARD MERRICK.
The Man who was Good.

BY JEAN MIDDLEMASS.
Touch and Go.
Mr. Dorillion.

BY MRS. MOLESWORTH.
Hathercourt Rectory.

BY J. E. MUDDOCK.
Stories Weird and Wonderful.
The Dead Man's Secret.
From the Bosom of the Deep.

BY D. CHRISTIE MURRAY.
A Life's Atonement.
Joseph's Coat.
Val Strange.
A Model Father.
Coals of Fire.
Hearts.
By the Gate of the Sea.
The Way of the World.
A Bit of Human Nature.
First Person Singular.
Cynic Fortune.
Old Blazer's Hero.
Bob Martin's Little Girl.
Time's Revenges.
A Wasted Crime.
In Direst Peril.
Mount Despair.
A Capful o' Nails.

BY D. CHRISTIE MURRAY AND HENRY HERMAN.
One Traveller Returns.
Paul Jones's Alias.
The Bishops' Bible.

BY HENRY MURRAY.
A Game of Bluff.
A Song of Sixpence.

BY HUME NISBET.
'Bail Up!'
Dr. Bernard St. Vincent.

BY W. E. NORRIS.
Saint Ann's.

BY ALICE O'HANLON.
The Unforeseen.
Chance ? or Fate ?

BY GEORGES OHNET.
Doctor Rameau.
A Last Love.
A Weird Gift.

BY MRS. OLIPHANT.
Whiteladies.
The Primrose Path.
Greatest Heiress in England.

BY MRS. ROBERT O'REILLY.
Phœbe's Fortunes.

BY OUIDA.
Held in Bondage.
Strathmore.
Chandos.
Under Two Flags.
Idalia.
Cecil Castlemaine's Gage.
Tricotrin.
Puck.
Folle Farine.
A Dog of Flanders.
Pascarèl.
Signa.
In a Winter City.
Ariadnê.
Moths.
Friendship.

BY OUIDA—continued.
Pipistrello.
Bimbi.
In Maremma.
Wanda.
Frescoes.
Princess Napraxine.
Two Little Wooden Shoes.
A Village Commune.
Othmar.
Guilderoy.
Ruffino.
Syrlin.
Santa Barbara.
Two Offenders.
Wisdom, Wit, and Pathos.

BY MARGARET AGNES PAUL.
Gentle and Simple.

BY JAMES PAYN.
Lost Sir Massingberd.
A Perfect Treasure.
Bentinck's Tutor.
Murphy's Master.
A County Family.
At Her Mercy.
A Woman's Vengeance.
Cecil's Tryst.
The Clyffards of Clyffe.
The Family Scapegrace.
The Foster Brothers.
The Best of Husbands.
Found Dead.
Walter's Word.
Halves.
Fallen Fortunes.
What He Cost Her.
Humorous Stories.
Gwendoline's Harvest.
Like Father, Like Son.
A Marine Residence.
Married Beneath Him.
Mirk Abbey.
Not Wooed, but Won.
£200 Reward.
Less Black than Painted.
By Proxy.
High Spirits.
Under One Roof.
Carlyon's Year.
A Confidential Agent.
Some Private Views.
A Grape from a Thorn.
From Exile.
Kit : a Memory.
For Cash Only.
The Canon's Ward.
The Talk of the Town.
Holiday Tasks.
Glow-worm Tales.
The Mystery of Mirbridge.
The Burnt Million.
The Word and the Will.
A Prince of the Blood.
Sunny Stories.
A Trying Patient.

BY EDGAR A. POE.
The Mystery of Marie Roget.

London: CHATTO & WINDUS, 111 St. Martin's Lane, W.C

BY MRS. CAMPBELL PRAED.
The Romance of a Station.
The Soul of Countess Adrian.
Outlaw and Lawmaker.
Christina Chard.
Mrs. Tregaskiss.

BY E. C. PRICE.
Valentina.
Gerald.
Mrs. Lancaster's Rival.
The Foreigners.

BY RICHARD PRYCE.
Miss Maxwell's Affections.

BY CHARLES READE.
It is Never Too Late to Mend.
Hard Cash.
Peg Woffington.
Christie Johnstone.
Griffith Gaunt.
Put Yourself in His Place.
The Double Marriage.
Love Me Little, Love Me Long.
Foul Play.
The Cloister and the Hearth.
The Course of True Love.
The Autobiography of a Thief.
A Terrible Temptation.
The Wandering Heir.
A Simpleton.
A Woman-Hater.
Singleheart and Doubleface.
Good Stories of Man, &c.
The Jilt.
A Perilous Secret.
Readiana.

BY MRS. J. H. RIDDELL.
Her Mother's Darling.
The Uninhabited House.
Weird Stories.
Fairy Water.
Prince of Wales's Garden Party.
Mystery in Palace Gardens.
The Nun's Curse.
Idle Tales.

BY AMÉLIE RIVES.
Barbara Dering.

BY F. W. ROBINSON.
Women are Strange.
The Hands of Justice.
The Woman in the Dark.

BY JAMES RUNCIMAN.
Skippers and Shellbacks.
Grace Balmaign's Sweetheart.
Schools and Scholars.

BY DORA RUSSELL.
A Country Sweetheart.

BY W. CLARK RUSSELL.
Round the Galley Fire.
On the Fo'k'sle Head.
In the Middle Watch.
A Voyage to the Cape.
A Book for the Hammock.
Mystery of the 'Ocean Star.'
Romance of Jenny Harlowe.
An Ocean Tragedy.
My Shipmate Louise.
Alone on a Wide Wide Sea.

BY W. CLARK RUSSELL—*cont.*
The Phantom Death.
The Good Ship 'Mohock.'
Is he the Man?
Heart of Oak.
The Convict Ship.

BY ALAN ST. AUBYN.
A Fellow of Trinity.
The Junior Dean.
The Master of St. Benedict's.
To his Own Master.
Orchard Damerel.
In the Face of the World.
The Tremlett Diamonds.

BY GEORGE AUGUSTUS SALA.
Gaslight and Daylight.

BY GEORGE R. SIMS.
The Ring o' Bells.
Mary Jane's Memoirs.
Mary Jane Married.
Tales of To-day.
Dramas of Life.
Tinkletop's Crime.
Zeph: a Circus Story.
My Two Wives.
Memoirs of a Landlady.
Scenes from the Show.
The Ten Commandments.
Dagonet Abroad.
Rogues and Vagabonds.

BY ARTHUR SKETCHLEY.
A Match in the Dark.

BY HAWLEY SMART.
Without Love or Licence.
The Plunger.
Beatrice and Benedick.
Long Odds.
The Master of Rathkelly.

BY T. W. SPEIGHT.
The Mysteries of Heron Dyke.
The Golden Hoop.
By Devious Ways.
Hoodwinked.
Back to Life.
The Loudwater Tragedy.
Burgo's Romance.
Quittance in Full.
A Husband from the Sea.

BY R. A. STERNDALE.
The Afghan Knife.

BY R. LOUIS STEVENSON.
New Arabian Nights.

BY BERTHA THOMAS.
Proud Maisie.
The Violin-player.
Cressida.

BY WALTER THORNBURY.
Tales for the Marines.
Old Stories Re-told.

BY ANTHONY TROLLOPE.
The Way We Live Now.
Mr. Scarborough's Family.
The Golden Lion of Granpère.
The American Senator.
Frau Frohmann.
Marion Fay.
Kept in the Dark.
The Land-Leaguers.
John Caldigate.

BY FRANCES E. TROLLOPE.
Anne Furness.
Mabel's Progress.
Like Ships upon the Sea.

BY T. ADOLPHUS TROLLOPE.
Diamond Cut Diamond.

BY J. T. TROWBRIDGE.
Farnell's Folly.

BY IVAN TURGENIEFF, &c.
Stories from Foreign Novels.

BY MARK TWAIN.
Tom Sawyer.
A Tramp Abroad.
The Stolen White Elephant.
Pleasure Trip on Continent.
The Gilded Age.
Huckleberry Finn.
Life on the Mississippi.
The Prince and the Pauper.
Mark Twain's Sketches.
A Yankee at the Court of King Arthur.
The £1,000,000 Bank-note.

BY SARAH TYTLER.
Noblesse Oblige.
Citoyenne Jacqueline.
The Huguenot Family.
What She Came Through.
Beauty and the Beast.
The Bride's Pass.
Saint Mungo's City.
Disappeared.
Lady Bell.
Buried Diamonds.
The Blackhall Ghosts.

BY C. C. FRASER-TYTLER.
Mistress Judith.

BY ALLEN UPWARD.
The Queen against Owen.
The Prince of Balkistan.

BY ARTEMUS WARD.
Artemus Ward Complete.

BY AARON WATSON AND LILLIAS WASSERMANN.
The Marquis of Carabas.

BY WILLIAM WESTALL.
Trust-Money.

BY MRS. F. H. WILLIAMSON.
A Child Widow.

BY J. S. WINTER.
Cavalry Life.
Regimental Legends.

BY H. F. WOOD.
Passenger from Scotland Yard.
Englishman of the Rue Cain.

BY CELIA PARKER WOOLLEY.
Rachel Armstrong.

BY EDMUND YATES.
Castaway.
The Forlorn Hope.
Land at Last.

London: CHATTO & WINDUS, 111 St. Martin's Lane, W.C.

AN ALPHABETICAL CATALOGUE
OF BOOKS IN FICTION AND
GENERAL LITERATURE
PUBLISHED BY
CHATTO & WINDUS
III ST. MARTIN'S LANE
CHARING CROSS
LONDON, W.C.
[MAR. 1901.]

Adams (W. Davenport), Works by.
A Dictionary of the Drama: being a comprehensive Guide to the Plays, Playwrights, Players, and Playhouses of the United Kingdom and America, from the Earliest Times to the Present Day. Crown 8vo, half-bound, 12s. 6d. [*Preparing.*]
Quips and Quiddities. Selected by W. DAVENPORT ADAMS. Post 8vo, cloth limp, 2s. 6d.

Agony Column (The) of 'The Times,' from 1800 to 1870. Edited with an Introduction, by ALICE CLAY. Post 8vo, cloth limp, 2s. 6d.

Alexander (Mrs.), Novels by. Post 8vo, illustrated boards, 2s. each.
'Maid, Wife, or Widow? | Blind Fate.

Crown 8vo, cloth, 3s. 6d. each; post 8vo, picture boards, 2s each.
Valerie's Fate. | A Life Interest. | Mona's Choice. | By Woman's Wit.

Crown 8vo, cloth 3s. 6d. each.
The Cost of her Pride. | Barbara, Lady's Maid and Peeress. | A Fight with Fate.
A Golden Autumn. | Mrs. Crichton's Creditor. | The Step-mother.
A Missing Hero. Crown 8vo, cloth, gilt top, 6s.

Allen (F. M.).—Green as Grass. Crown 8vo, cloth, 3s. 6d.

Allen (Grant), Works by. Crown 8vo, cloth, 6s. each.
The Evolutionist at Large. | Moorland Idylls.
Post-Prandial Philosophy. Crown 8vo, art linen, 3s. 6d.

Crown 8vo, cloth extra, 3s. 6d. each; post 8vo, illustrated boards, 2s. each.
Babylon. 12 Illustrations. | The Devil's Die. | The Duchess of Powysland.
Strange Stories. Frontis. | This Mortal Coil. | Blood Royal.
The Beckoning Hand. | The Tents of Shem. Frontis. | Ivan Greet's Masterpiece.
For Maimie's Sake. | The Great Taboo. | The Scallywag. 24 Illusts.
Philistia. | Dumaresq's Daughter. | At Market Value.
In all Shades. | Under Sealed Orders.
Dr. Palliser's Patient. Fcap. 8vo, cloth boards, 1s. 6d.

Anderson (Mary).—Othello's Occupation. Crown 8vo, cloth, 3s. 6d.

Antrobus (C. L.).—Quality Corner: A Study of Remorse. Crown 8vo, cloth, gilt top, 6s.

Arnold (Edwin Lester), Stories by.
The Wonderful Adventures of Phra the Phœnician. Crown 8vo, cloth extra, with 12 Illustrations by H. M. PAGET, 3s. 6d.; post 8vo, illustrated boards, 2s.
The Constable of St. Nicholas. With Frontispiece by S. L. WOOD. Crown 8vo, cloth, 3s. 6d.

Artemus Ward's Works. With Portrait and Facsimile. Crown 8vo, cloth extra, 3s. 6d.—Also a POPULAR EDITION post 8vo, picture boards, 2s.

Ashton (John), Works by. Crown 8vo, cloth extra, 7s. 6d. each.
Humour, Wit, and Satire of the Seventeenth Century. With 82 Illustrations.
English Caricature and Satire on Napoleon the First. With 115 Illustrations.
Modern Street Ballads. With 57 Illustrations.
Social Life in the Reign of Queen Anne. With 85 Illustrations. Crown 8vo, cloth, 3s. 6d.

Crown 8vo, cloth, gilt top, 6s. each.
Social Life under the Regency. With 90 Illustrations,
Florizel's Folly: The Story of GEORGE IV. With Photogravure Frontispiece and 12 Illustrations.

Bacteria, Yeast Fungi, and Allied Species, A Synopsis of. By W. B. GROVE B.A. With 87 Illustrations. Crown 8vo, cloth extra, 3s. 6d.

Bardsley (Rev. C. Wareing, M.A.), Works by.

English Surnames : Their Sources and Significations. Crown 8vo, cloth, 7s. 6d.
Curiosities of Puritan Nomenclature. Crown 8vo, cloth, 3s. 6d.

Baring Gould (Sabine, Author of 'John Herring,' &c.), Novels by.

Crown 8vo, cloth extra, 3s. 6d. each ; post 8vo, illustrated boards, 2s. each.
Red Spider.　　　　　　　　　　| **Eve.**

Barr (Robert: Luke Sharp), Stories by.　Cr. 8vo, cl., 3s. 6d. each.

In a Steamer Chair. With Frontispiece and Vignette by DEMAIN HAMMOND.
From Whose Bourne, &c, With 47 Illustrations by HAL HURST and others.
Revenge! With 12 Illustrations by LANCELOT SPEED and others.
A Woman Intervenes. With 8 Illustrations by HAL HURST.
The Unchanging East : Notes on a Visit to the Farther Edge of the Mediterranean. With a
Frontispiece. Crown 8vo, cloth, gilt top, 6s.
The Adventures of a Merry Monarch. With numerous Illustrations. Crown 8vo, cloth, gilt
top, 6s.　　　　　　　　　　　　　　　　　　　　　　　　　　　　[Shortly

Barrett (Frank), Novels by.

Post 8vo, illustrated boards, 2s. each; cloth, 2s. 6d. each.
The Sin of Olga Zassoulich.	**John Ford;** and His Helpmate.
Between Life and Death.	**A Recoiling Vengeance.**
Folly Morrison. | **Honest Davie.**	**Lieut. Barnabas.** | Found Guilty.
Little Lady Linton.	**For Love and Honour.**
A Prodigal's Progress.	

Crown 8vo, cloth, 3s. 6d. each ; post 8vo, picture boards, 2s. each ; cloth limp, 2s. 6d. each.
Fettered for Life. | **The Woman of the Iron Bracelets.** | **The Harding Scandal.**
A Missing Witness. With 8 Illustrations by W. H. MARGETSON.

Crown 8vo, cloth, 3s. 6d. each.
Under a Strange Mask. With 19 Illusts. by E. F. BREWTNALL. | **Was She Justified?**

Barrett (Joan).—Monte Carlo Stories. Fcap. 8vo, cloth, 1s. 6d.

Besant (Sir Walter) and James Rice, Novels by.

Crown 8vo, cloth extra, 3s. 6d. each ; post 8vo, illustrated boards, 2s. each ; cloth limp, 2s. 6d. each.
Ready-Money Mortiboy.	**The Golden Butterfly.**	**The Seamy Side.**
My Little Girl.	**The Monks of Thelema.**	**The Case of Mr. Lucraft.**
With Harp and Crown.	**By Celia's Arbour.**	**'Twas in Trafalgar's Bay.**
This Son of Vulcan.	**The Chaplain of the Fleet.**	**The Ten Years' Tenant.**

*** There are also LIBRARY EDITIONS of all the above, excepting Ready-Money Mortiboy and
The Golden Butterfly, handsomely set in new type on a large crown 8vo page, and bound in cloth
extra, 6s. each ; and POPULAR EDITIONS of **The Golden Butterfly** and of **The Orange Girl,**
medium 8vo, 6d. each ; and of **All Sorts and Conditions of Men,** medium 8vo, 6d. : cloth, 1s.

Besant (Sir Walter), Novels by.

Crown 8vo, cloth extra, 3s. 6d. each ; post 8vo, illustrated boards, 2s. each ; cloth limp, 2s. 6d. each.
All Sorts and Conditions of Men. With 12 Illustrations by FRED. BARNARD.
The Captains' Room, &c. With Frontispiece by E. J. WHEELER.
All in a Garden Fair. With 6 Illustrations by HARRY FURNISS.
Dorothy Forster. With Frontispiece by CHARLES GREEN.
Uncle Jack, and other Stories. | **Children of Gibeon.**
The World Went Very Well Then. With 12 Illustrations by A. FORESTIER.
Herr Paulus: His Rise, his Greatness, and his Fall. | **The Bell of St. Paul's.**
For Faith and Freedom. With Illustrations by A. FORESTIER and F. WADDY.
To Call Her Mine, &c. With 9 Illustrations by A. FORESTIER.
The Holy Rose, &c. With Frontispiece by F. BARNARD.
Armorel of Lyonesse: A Romance of To-day. With 12 Illustrations by F. BARNARD.
St. Katherine's by the Tower. With 12 Illustrations by C. GREEN.
Verbena Camellia Stephanotis, &c. With a Frontispiece by GORDON BROWNE.
The Ivory Gate. | **The Rebel Queen.**
Beyond the Dreams of Avarice. With 12 Illustrations by W. H. HYDE.
In Deacon's Orders, &c. With Frontispiece by A. FORESTIER. | **The Revolt of Man.**
The Master Craftsman. | **The City of Refuge.**

Crown 8vo, cloth, 3s. 6d. each.
A Fountain Sealed. With a Frontispiece. | **The Changeling.**

Crown 8vo, cloth, gilt top, 6s. each.
The Orange Girl. With 8 Illustrations by F. PEGRAM. | **The Fourth Generation.**

The Charm, and other Drawing-room Plays. By Sir WALTER BESANT and WALTER H. POLLOCK.
With 50 Illustrations by CHRIS HAMMOND and JULE GOODMAN. Crown 8vo. cloth, gilt edges, 6s.
or blue cloth, to range with the Uniform Edition of Sir WALTER BESANT'S Novels, 3s. 6d.
Fifty Years Ago. With 144 Illustrations. Crown 8vo, cloth, 3s. 6d.
The Eulogy of Richard Jefferies. With Portrait. Crown 8vo, cloth, 6s.
London. With 125 Illustrations. Demy 8vo, cloth, 7s. 6d.
Westminster. With an Etched Frontispiece by F. S. WALKER, R.E., and 130 Illustrations by
WILLIAM PATTEN and others. LIBRARY EDITION, demy 8vo, cloth gilt and gilt top, 18s. ;
POPULAR EDITION. demy 8vo, cloth, 7s. 6d.
South London. With an Etched Frontispiece by F. S. WALKER, R.E., and 118 Illustrations.
Demy 8vo, cloth, gilt top, 18s.
East London. With an Etched Frontispiece by F. S. WALKER, and 55 Illustrations by PHIL
MAY, L. RAVEN HILL, and JOSEPH PENNELL. Demy 8vo, cloth, 18s.
Jerusalem : The City of Herod and Saladin. By WALTER BESANT and E. H. PALMER. Fourth
Edition. With a new Chapter, a Map, and 11 Illustrations. Small demy 8vo, cloth, 7s. 6d.
Sir Richard Whittington. With Frontispiece. Crown 8vo, art linen, 3s. 6d.
Gaspard de Coligny. With a Portrait. Crown 8vo, art linen, 3s. 6d.

Beaconsfield, Lord. By T. P. O'CONNOR, M.P. Cr. 8vo, cloth, 5s.

Bechstein (Ludwig).—As Pretty as Seven, and other German Stories. With Additional Tales by the Brothers GRIMM, and 98 Illustrations by RICHTER. Square 8vo, cloth extra, 6s. 6d.; gilt edges, 7s. 6d.

Bellew (Frank).—The Art of Amusing: A Collection of Graceful Arts, Games, Tricks, Puzzles, and Charades. With 300 Illustrations. Crown 8vo, cloth extra, 4s. 6d.

Bennett (W. C., LL.D.).—Songs for Sailors. Post 8vo, cl. limp, 2s.

Bewick (Thomas) and his Pupils. By AUSTIN DOBSON. With 95 Illustrations. Square 8vo, cloth extra, 3s. 6d.

Bierce (Ambrose).—In the Midst of Life: Tales of Soldiers and Civilians. Crown 8vo, cloth extra, 3s. 6d.; post 8vo, illustrated boards, 2s.

Bill Nye's Comic History of the United States. With 146 Illustrations by F. OPPER. Crown 8vo, cloth extra, 3s. 6d.

Bindloss (Harold).—Ainslie's Ju-Ju: A Romance of the Hinterland. Crown 8vo, cloth, 3s. 6d.

Blackburn's (Henry) Art Handbooks.

Academy Notes, 1901. [*May.*	**Grosvenor Notes,** Vol. III., **1888-90.** With 230 Illustrations. Demy 8vo cloth, 3s. 6d.
Academy Notes, 1875-79. Complete in One Vol., with 600 Illustrations. Cloth, 6s.	**The New Gallery, 1888-1892.** With 250 Illustrations. Demy 8vo, cloth, 6s.
Academy Notes, 1890-94. Complete in One Vol., with 800 Illustrations. Cloth, 7s. 6d.	**English Pictures at the National Gallery.** With 114 Illustrations. 1s.
Academy Notes, 1895-99. Complete in One Vol., with 800 Illustrations. Cloth, 6s.	**Old Masters at the National Gallery.** With 128 Illustrations. 1s. 6d.
Grosvenor Notes, Vol. I., **1877-82.** With 300 Illustrations. Demy 8vo, cloth 6s.	**Illustrated Catalogue to the National Gallery.** With 242 Illusts. Demy 8vo, cloth, 3s
Grosvenor Notes, Vol. II., **1883-87.** With 300 Illustrations. Demy 8vo, cloth, 6s.	

Illustrated Catalogue of the Paris Salon, 1901. With 400 Illusts. Demy 8vo, 3s. [*May.*

Bodkin (M. McD., Q.C.).—Dora Myrl, the Lady Detective. Crown 8vo, cloth, 3s. 6d.

Bourget (Paul).—A Living Lie. Translated by JOHN DE VILLIERS. With special Preface for the English Edition. Crown 8vo, cloth, 3s. 6d.

Bourne (H. R. Fox), Books by.
English Merchants: Memoirs in Illustration of the Progress of British Commerce. With 32 Illustrations. Crown 8vo, cloth, 3s. 6d.
English Newspapers: Chapters in the History of Journalism. Two Vols., demy 8vo, cloth, 25s.
The Other Side of the Emin Pasha Relief Expedition. Crown 8vo, cloth, 6s.

Boyle (Frederick), Works by. Post 8vo, illustrated bds., 2s. each.
Chronicles of No-Man's Land. | **Camp Notes.** | **Savage Life.**

Brand (John).—Observations on Popular Antiquities; chiefly illustrating the Origin of our Vulgar Customs, Ceremonies, and Superstitions. With the Additions of Sir HENRY ELLIS. Crown 8vo, cloth, 3s. 6d.

Brayshaw (J. Dodsworth).—Slum Silhouettes: Stories of London Life. Crown 8vo, cloth, 3s. 6d.

Brewer (Rev. Dr.), Works by.
The Reader's Handbook of Famous Names in Fiction, Allusions, References, Proverbs, Plots, Stories, and Poems. Together with an ENGLISH AND AMERICAN BIBLIOGRAPHY, and a LIST OF THE AUTHORS AND DATES OF DRAMAS AND OPERAS. A New Edition, Revised and Enlarged. Crown 8vo, cloth. 7s 6d.
A Dictionary of Miracles: Imitative, Realistic, and Dogmatic. Crown 8vo, cloth, 3s. 6d.

Brewster (Sir David), Works by. Post 8vo, cloth, 4s. 6d. each.
More Worlds than One: Creed of the Philosopher and Hope of the Christian. With Plates.
The Martyrs of Science: GALILEO, TYCHO BRAHE, and KEPLER. With Portraits.
Letters on Natural Magic. With numerous Illustrations.

Brillat-Savarin.—Gastronomy as a Fine Art. Translated by R. E. ANDERSON, M.A. Post 8vo, half-bound, 2s.

Bryden (H. A.).—An Exiled Scot: A Romance. With a Frontispiece, by J. S. CROMPTON, R.I. Crown 8vo, cloth, 6s.

Brydges (Harold).—Uncle Sam at Home. With 91 Illustrations. Post 8vo, illustrated boards, 2s.; cloth limp, 2s. 6d.

Buchanan (Robert), Novels, &c., by.

Crown 8vo, cloth extra, 3s. 6d. each; post 8vo, illustrated boards, 2s. each.

The Shadow of the Sword.
A Child of Nature. With Frontispiece.
God and the Man. With 11 Illustrations by Lady Kilpatrick. [FRED. BARNARD].
The Martyrdom of Madeline. With Frontispiece by A. W. COOPER.

Love Me for Ever. With Frontispiece.
Annan Water. | Foxglove Manor.
The New Abelard. | Rachel Dene.
Matt: A Story of a Caravan. With Frontispiece.
The Master of the Mine. With Frontispiece.
The Heir of Linne. | Woman and the Man.

Red and White Heather. Crown 8vo, cloth extra, 3s. 6d.

The Wandering Jew: a Christmas Carol. Crown 8vo, cloth, 6s.

The Charlatan. By ROBERT BUCHANAN and HENRY MURRAY. Crown 8vo, cloth, with a Frontispiece by T. H. ROBINSON, 3s. 6d.; post 8vo, picture boards, 2s.
Andromeda: An Idyll of the Great River. Crown 8vo, cloth, gilt top, 6s.

Burton (Robert).—The Anatomy of Melancholy. With Transla-

tions of the Quotations. Demy 8vo, cloth extra, 7s. 6d.
Melancholy Anatomised: An Abridgment of BURTON'S ANATOMY. Post 8vo, half-cl., 2s. 6d.

Caine (Hall), Novels by. Crown 8vo, cloth extra, 3s. 6d. each.; post

8vo, illustrated boards, 2s. each; cloth limp, 2s. 6d. each.
The Shadow of a Crime. | A Son of Hagar. | The Deemster.
Also LIBRARY EDITIONS of The Deemster and The Shadow of a Crime, set in new type, crown 8vo, and bound uniform with The Christian, 6s. each; and CHEAP POPULAR EDITIONS of The Deemster, The Shadow of a Crime, and A Son of Hagar, medium 8vo, portrait-cover, 6d. each.

Cameron (Commander V. Lovett).—The Cruise of the 'Black

Prince' Privateer. Post 8vo, picture boards, 2s.

Canada (Greater): The Past, Present, and Future of the Canadian

North-West. By E. B. OSBORN, B.A. With a Map. Crown 8vo, cloth, 3s. 6d.

Captain Coignet, Soldier of the Empire: An Autobiography.

Edited by LOREDAN LARCHEY. Translated by Mrs. CAREY. With 100 Illustrations. Crown 8vo, cloth, 3s. 6d.

Carlyle (Thomas).—On the Choice of Books. Post 8vo, cl., 1s. 6d.

Correspondence of Thomas Carlyle and R. W. Emerson, 1834-1872. Edited by C. E. NORTON. With Portraits. Two Vols., crown 8vo, cloth, 24s.

Carruth (Hayden).—The Adventures of Jones. With 17 Illustra-

tions. Fcap. 8vo, cloth, 2s.

Chambers (Robert W.), Stories of Paris Life by.

The King in Yellow. Crown 8vo, cloth, 3s. 6d.; fcap. 8vo, cloth limp, 2s. 6d.
In the Quarter. Fcap. 8vo, cloth, 2s. 6d.

Chapman's (George), Works. Vol. I., Plays Complete, including the

Doubtful Ones.—Vol. II., Poems and Minor Translations, with Essay by A. C. SWINBURNE.—Vol. III., Translations of the Iliad and Odyssey. Three Vols., crown 8vo, cloth, 3s. 6d. each.

Chapple (J. Mitchell).—The Minor Chord: The Story of a Prima

Donna. Crown 8vo, cloth, 3s. 6d.

Chaucer for Children: A Golden Key. By Mrs. H. R. HAWEIS. With

8 Coloured Plates and 30 Woodcuts. Crown 4to, cloth extra, 3s. 6d.
Chaucer for Schools. With the Story of his Times and his Work. By Mrs. H. R. HAWEIS. A New Edition, revised. With a Frontispiece. Demy 8vo, cloth, 2s. 6d.

Chess, The Laws and Practice of. With an Analysis of the Open-

ings. By HOWARD STAUNTON. Edited by R. B. WORMALD. Crown 8vo, cloth, 5s.
The Minor Tactics of Chess: A Treatise on the Deployment of the Forces in obedience to Strategic Principle. By F. K. YOUNG and E. C. HOWELL. Long fcap. 8vo, cloth, 2s. 6d.
The Hastings Chess Tournament. Containing the Authorised Account of the 230 Games played Aug.-Sept., 1895. With Annotations by PILLSBURY, LASKER, TARRASCH, STEINITZ, SCHIFFERS, TEICHMANN, BARDELEBEN, BLACKBURNE, GUNSBERG, TINSLEY, MASON, and ALBIN; Biographical Sketches of the Chess Masters, and 22 Portraits. Edited by H. F. CHESHIRE. Cheaper Edition. Crown 8vo, cloth, 5s.

Clare (Austin), Stories by.

For the Love of a Lass. Post 8vo, illustrated boards, 2s.; cloth, 2s. 6d.
By the Rise of the River: Tales and Sketches in South Tynedale. Crown 8vo, cloth, 3s. 6d.

Clive (Mrs. Archer), Novels by. Post 8vo, illust. boards, 2s. each.
Paul Ferroll. | Why Paul Ferroll Killed his Wife.

Clodd (Edward, F.R.A.S.).—Myths and Dreams. Cr. 8vo, 3s. 6d.

Coates (Anne).—Rie's Diary. Crown 8vo, cloth, 3s. 6d.

Cobban (J. Maclaren), Novels by.
The Cure of Souls. Post 8vo, illustrated boards, 2s.
The Red Sultan. Crown 8vo, cloth extra, 3s. 6d.; post 8vo, illustrated boards, 2s.
The Burden of Isabel. Crown 8vo, cloth extra, 3s. 6d.

Coleridge (M. E.).—The Seven Sleepers of Ephesus. Fcap. 8vo,
leatherette, 1s.; cloth, 1s. 6d.

Collins (C. Allston).—The Bar Sinister. Post 8vo, boards, 2s.

Collins (John Churton, M.A.), Books by.
Illustrations of Tennyson. Crown 8vo, cloth extra, 6s.
Jonathan Swift. A Biographical and Critical Study. Crown 8vo, cloth extra, 8s.

Collins (Mortimer and Frances), Novels by.
Crown 8vo, cloth extra, 3s. 6d. each; post 8vo, illustrated boards, 2s. each.

From Midnight to Midnight.	Blacksmith and Scholar.
You Play me False.	The Village Comedy.

Post 8vo, illustrated boards, 2s. each.

Transmigration.	Sweet Anne Page.	Frances.
A Fight with Fortune.	Sweet and Twenty.	

Collins (Wilkie), Novels by.
Crown 8vo, cloth extra, many Illustrated, 3s. 6d. each; post 8vo, picture boards, 2s. each; cloth limp, 2s. 6d. each.

*Antonina.	My Miscellanies.	Jezebel's Daughter.
*Basil.	Armadale.	The Black Robe.
*Hide and Seek.	Poor Miss Finch.	Heart and Science.
*The Woman in White.	Miss or Mrs.?	'I Say No.'
*The Moonstone.	The New Magdalen.	A Rogue's Life.
*Man and Wife.	The Frozen Deep.	The Evil Genius.
*The Dead Secret.	The Law and the Lady.	Little Novels.
After Dark.	The Two Destinies.	The Legacy of Cain.
The Queen of Hearts.	The Haunted Hotel.	Blind Love.
No Name.	The Fallen Leaves.	

₄ Marked * have been reset in new type, in uniform style.

POPULAR EDITIONS. Medium 8vo, 6d. each; cloth, 1s. each.

The Moonstone.	Antonina.	The Dead Secret.

Medium 8vo, 6d. each.

The Woman in White.	The New Magdalen.

Colman's (George) Humorous Works: 'Broad Grins,' 'My Night-gown and Slippers,' &c. With Life and Frontispiece. Crown 8vo, cloth extra, 3s. 6d.

Colquhoun (M. J.).—Every Inch a Soldier. Crown 8vo, cloth, 3s. 6d.; post 8vo, illustrated boards, 2s.

Colt-breaking, Hints on. By W. M. HUTCHISON. Cr. 8vo, cl., 3s. 6d.

Compton (Herbert).—The Inimitable Mrs. Massingham: a Romance of Botany Bay. Crown 8vo, cloth, gilt top, 6s.

Convalescent Cookery. By CATHERINE RYAN. Cr. 8vo, 1s.; cl., 1s. 6d.

Cooper (Edward H.).—Geoffory Hamilton. Cr. 8vo, cloth, 3s. 6d.

Cornish (J. F.).—Sour Grapes: A Novel. Cr. 8vo, cloth, gilt top, 6s.

Cornwall.—Popular Romances of the West of England; or, The Drolls, Traditions, and Superstitions of Old Cornwall. Collected by ROBERT HUNT, F.R.S. With two Steel Plates by GEORGE CRUIKSHANK. Crown 8vo, cloth, 7s. 6d.

Cotes (V. Cecil).—Two Girls on a Barge. With 44 Illustrations by F. H. TOWNSEND. Crown 8vo, cloth extra, 3s. 6d.; post 8vo, cloth, 2s. 6d.

Craddock (C. Egbert), Stories by.
The Prophet of the Great Smoky Mountains. Crown 8vo, cloth, 3s. 6d.; post 8vo, illustrated boards, 2s.
His Vanished Star. Crown 8vo, cloth, 3s. 6d.

Cram (Ralph Adams).—Black Spirits and White. Fcap. 8vo, cloth, 1s. 6d.

Crellin (H. N.), Books by.
Romances of the Old Seraglio. With 28 Illustrations by S. L. WOOD. Crown 8vo, cloth, 3s. 6d
Tales of the Caliph. Crown 8vo, cloth, 2s.
The Nazarenes: A Drama. Crown 8vo, 1s.

Crim (Matt.).—Adventures of a Fair Rebel. Crown 8vo, cloth
extra, with a Frontispiece by DAN. BEARD. 3s. 6d.; post 8vo, illustrated boards, 2s.

Crockett (S. R.) and others. —Tales of Our Coast. By S. R.
CROCKETT, GILBERT PARKER, HAROLD FREDERIC, 'Q.,' and W. CLARK RUSSELL. With 2 Illustrations by FRANK BRANGWYN. Crown 8vo, cloth, 3s. 6d.

Croker (Mrs. B. M.), Novels by. Crown 8vo, cloth extra, 3s. 6d.
each; post 8vo, illustrated boards, 2s. each; cloth limp, 2s. 6d. each.

Pretty Miss Neville.	Interference.	Village Tales & Jungle
Proper Pride.	A Family Likeness.	Tragedies.
A Bird of Passage.	A Third Person.	The Real Lady Hilda.
Diana Barrington.	Mr. Jervis.	Married or Single ?
Two Masters.		

Crown 8vo, cloth extra, 3s. 6d. each.

| Some One Else. | Miss Balmaine's Past. | Beyond the Pale. |
| In the Kingdom of Kerry. | Jason, &c. | Infatuation. |

'To Let,' &c. Post 8vo, picture boards, 2s.; cloth limp, 2s. 6d.
Terence. With 6 Illustrations by SIDNEY PAGET. Crown 8vo, cloth, gilt top, 6s.

Cruikshank's Comic Almanack. Complete in Two SERIES: The
FIRST, from 1835 to 1843; the SECOND, from 1844 to 1853. A Gathering of the Best Humour of THACKERAY, HOOD, MAYHEW, ALBERT SMITH, A'BECKETT, ROBERT BROUGH, &c. With numerous Steel Engravings and Woodcuts by GEORGE CRUIKSHANK, HINE, LANDELLS, &c. Two Vols., crown 8vo, cloth gilt, 7s. 6d. each.
The Life of George Cruikshank. By BLANCHARD JERROLD. With 84 Illustrations and a Bibliography. Crown 8vo, cloth extra, 3s. 6d.

Cumming (C. F. Gordon), Works by. Large cr. 8vo, cloth, 6s. each.
In the Hebrides. With an Autotype Frontispiece and 23 Illustrations.
In the Himalayas and on the Indian Plains. With 42 Illustrations.
Two Happy Years in Ceylon. With 28 Illustrations.
Via Cornwall to Egypt. With a Photogravure Frontispiece.

Cussans (John E.).—A Handbook of Heraldry; with Instructions
for Tracing Pedigrees and Deciphering Ancient MSS, &c. Fourth Edition, revised, with 408 Woodcuts and 2 Coloured Plates. Crown 8vo, cloth extra, 6s.

Cyples (William).—Hearts of Gold. Crown 8vo, cloth, 3s. 6d.

Daudet (Alphonse).—The Evangelist; or, Port Salvation. Crown
8vo, cloth extra, 3s. 6d.; post 8vo, illustrated boards, 2s.

Davenant (Francis, M.A.).—Hints for Parents on the Choice of
a Profession for their Sons when Starting in Life. Crown 8vo, cloth, 1s. 6d.

Davidson (Hugh Coleman).—Mr. Sadler's Daughters. With a
Frontispiece by STANLEY WOOD. Crown 8vo, cloth extra, 3s. 6d.

Davies (Dr. N. E. Yorke-), Works by. Cr. 8vo, 1s. ea.; cl., 1s. 6d. ea.
One Thousand Medical Maxims and Surgical Hints.
Nursery Hints: A Mother's Guide in Health and Disease.
Foods for the Fat: The Dietetic Cure of Corpulency and of Gout.
Aids to Long Life. Crown 8vo, 2s.; cloth limp, 2s. 6d.

Davies' (Sir John) Complete Poetical Works. Collected and Edited
with Introduction and Notes, by Rev. A. B. GROSART, D.D. Two Vols., crown 8vo, cloth, 3s. 6d. each.

Dawson (Erasmus, M.B.).—The Fountain of Youth. Crown 8vo,
cloth extra, with Two Illustrations by HUME NISBET, 3s. 6d.

De Guerin (Maurice), The Journal of. Edited by G. S. TREBUTIEN.
With a Memoir by SAINTE-BEUVE. Translated from the 20th French Edition by JESSIE P. FROTH-INGHAM. Fcap. 8vo, half-bound, 2s. 6d.

De Maistre (Xavier).—A Journey Round my Room. Translated
by HENRY ATTWELL. Post 8vo, cloth limp, 2s. 6d.

De Mille (James).—A Castle in Spain. Crown 8vo, cloth extra, with
a Frontispiece, 3s. 6d.

Derby (The) : The Blue Ribbon of the Turf. With Brief Accounts
of THE OAKS. By LOUIS HENRY CURZON. Crown 8vo, cloth limp, 2s. 6d.

Derwent (Leith), Novels by. Crown 8vo, cloth, 3s. 6d. each.
Our Lady of Tears. | **Circe's Lovers.**

Dewar (T. R.).—A Ramble Round the Globe. With 220 Illustra-
tions. Crown 8vo, cloth extra, 7s. 6d.

De Windt (Harry), Books by.
Through the Gold-Fields of Alaska to Bering Straits. With Map and 33 full-page Illustrations. Cheaper Issue. Demy 8vo, cloth, 6s.
True Tales of Travel and Adventure. Crown 8vo, cloth, 3s. 6d.

Dickens (Charles), About England with. By ALFRED RIMMER. With 57 Illustrations by C. A. VANDERHOOF and the AUTHOR. Square 8vo, cloth, 3s. 6d.

Dictionaries.
The Reader's Handbook of Famous Names in Fiction, Allusions, References, Proverbs, Plots, Stories, and Poems. Together with an ENGLISH AND AMERICAN BIBLIOGRAPHY, and a LIST OF THE AUTHORS AND DATES OF DRAMAS AND OPERAS. By Rev. E. C. BREWER, LL.D. A New Edition, Revised and Enlarged. Crown 8vo, cloth, 7s. 6d.
A Dictionary of Miracles: Imitative, Realistic, and Dogmatic. By the Rev. E. C. BREWER, LL.D. Crown 8vo, cloth, 3s. 6d.
The Wise Short Sayings of Great Men. With Historical and Explanatory Notes by SAMUEL Words, Facts:... Crown 8vo, cloth extra, 7s. 6d.
ELIEZER EDWARDS: Etymological, Historical, and Anecdotal. Crown 8vo, cloth, 6s. 6d.
A Dictionary of Curious, Quaint, and Out-of-the-Way Matters. By Crown 8vo, buckram, 3s. 6d. extra, 3s. 6d.

Dilke (Rt. Hon. Sir Charles D.).—The British Empire.
Crown 8vo, buckram, 3s. 6d.

Dobson (Austin), Works by.
Thomas Bewick and his Pupils. With 95 Illustrations. Square 8vo,
Four Frenchwomen. With Four Portraits. Crown 8vo, buckram, gilt top, 6s.
Eighteenth Century Vignettes. IN THREE SERIES. Crown 8vo, buckram, 6s.
A Paladin of Philanthropy, and other Papers. With 2 Illusts. Cr. 8vo, buckram, 6s.

Dobson (W. T.).—Poetical Ingenuities and Eccentricities. Post 8vo, cloth limp, 2s. 6d.

Donovan (Dick), Detective Stories by.
Post 8vo, illustrated boards, 2s. each; cloth limp, 2s. 6d. each.

The Man-Hunter.	Wanted!	A Detective's Triumphs.
Caught at Last.	Tracked to Doom.	In the Grip of the Law.
Tracked and Taken.		From Information Received.
Who Poisoned Hetty Duncan?		Link by Link. | Dark Deeds
Suspicion Aroused.		Riddles Read.

Crown 8vo, cloth extra, 3s. 6d. each; post 8vo, illustrated boards, 2s. each; cloth, 2s. 6d. each.
The Man from Manchester. With 23 Illustrations.
The Mystery of Jamaica Terrace. | The Chronicles of Michael Danevitch.
Crown 8vo, cloth, 3s. 6d. each.
The Records of Vincent Trill, of the Detective Service. | Tales of Terror.
The Adventures of Tyler Tatlock, Private Detective.
Deacon Brodie; or, Behind the Mask. [Shortly.

Dowling (Richard).—Old Corcoran's Money. Crown 8vo, cl., 3s. 6d.

Doyle (A. Conan).—The Firm of Girdlestone. Cr. 8vo, cl., 3s. 6d.

Dramatists, The Old. Cr. 8vo, cl. ex., with Portraits, 3s. 6d. per Vol.
Ben Jonson's Works. With Notes, Critical and Explanatory, and a Biographical Memoir by WILLIAM GIFFORD. Edited by Colonel CUNNINGHAM. Three Vols.
Chapman's Works. Three Vols. Vol. I. contains the Plays complete; Vol. II., Poems and Minor Translations, with an Essay by A. C. SWINBURNE; Vol. III., Translations of the Iliad and Odyssey.
Marlowe's Works. Edited, with Notes, by Colonel CUNNINGHAM. One Vol.
Massinger's Plays. From GIFFORD'S Text. Edited by Colonel CUNNINGHAM. One Vol.

Dudgeon (R. E., M.D.).—The Prolongation of Life. Crown 8vo, buckram, 3s. 6d.

Duncan (Sara Jeannette: Mrs. EVERARD COTES), Works by.
Crown 8vo, cloth extra, 7s. 6d. each.
A Social Departure. With 111 Illustrations by F. H. TOWNSEND.
An American Girl in London. With 80 Illustrations by F. H. TOWNSEND.
The Simple Adventures of a Memsahib. With 37 Illustrations by F. H. TOWNSEND.
Crown 8vo, cloth extra, 3s. 6d. each.
A Daughter of To-Day. | Vernon's Aunt. With 47 Illustrations by HAL HURST.

Dutt (Romesh C.).—England and India: A Record of Progress during One Hundred Years. Crown 8vo, cloth, 2s.

Early English Poets. Edited, with Introductions and Annotations, by Rev. A. B. GROSART, D.D. Crown 8vo, cloth boards, 3s. 6d. per Volume.
Fletcher's (Giles) Complete Poems. One Vol.
Davies' (Sir John) Complete Poetical Works. Two Vols.
Herrick's (Robert) Complete Collected Poems. Three Vols.
Sidney's (Sir Philip) Complete Poetical Works. Three Vols.

Edgcumbe (Sir E. R. Pearce).— Zephyrus: A Holiday in Brazil and on the River Plate. With 41 Illustrations. Crown 8vo, cloth extra, 5s.

Edwardes (Mrs. Annie), Novels by. Post 8vo, illust. bds., 2s. each.
Archie Lovell. | A Point of Honour.
A Plaster Saint. Crown 8vo, cloth, 3s. 6d.

Edwards (Eliezer).—Words, Facts, and Phrases: A Dictionary of Curious, Quaint, and Out-of-the-Way Matters. Cheaper Edition. Crown 8vo, cloth, 3s. 6d.

Egan (Pierce).—Life in London. With an Introduction by JOHN CAMDEN HOTTEN, and a Coloured Frontispiece. Small demy 8vo, cloth, 3s. 6d.

Egerton (Rev. J. C., M.A.). — Sussex Folk and Sussex Ways. With Introduction by Rev. Dr. H. WACE, and Four Illustrations. Crown 8vo, cloth extra, 5s.

Eggleston (Edward).—Roxy: A Novel. Post 8vo, illust. boards, 2s.

Englishman (An) in Paris. Notes and Recollections during the Reign of Louis Philippe and the Empire. Crown 8vo, cloth, 3s. 6d.

Englishman's House, The: A Practical Guide for Selecting or Building a House. By C. J. RICHARDSON. Coloured Frontispiece and 534 Illusts. Cr. 8vo, cloth

Ewald (Alex. Charles, F.S.A.), Works by.
The Life and Times of Prince Charles Stuart, Counterpiece. Crown 8vo, cloth, 6s.
DER), With a Portrait. Crown 8vo, cloth extra
Stories from the State Papers. With Ill. By JOHN BROWNING. Cr. 8vo, 1s.

Eyes, Our: How to Use of Great Men. By SAMUEL ARTHUR BENT, Revised and Enlarged. Crown 8vo, cloth extra, 7s. 6d.

Faraday (Michael), Works by. Post 8vo, cloth extra, 4s. 6d. each.
The Chemical History of a Candle: Lectures delivered before a Juvenile Audience. Edited by WILLIAM CROOKES, F.C.S. With numerous Illustrations.
On the Various Forces of Nature, and their Relations to each other. Edited by WILLIAM CROOKES, F.C.S. With Illustrations.

Farrer (J. Anson).—War: Three Essays. Crown 8vo, cloth, 1s. 6d.

Fenn (G. Manville), Novels by.
Crown 8vo, cloth extra, 3s. 6d. each ; post 8vo, illustrated boards, 2s. each.
The New Mistress. | Witness to the Deed. | The Tiger Lily. | The White Virgin.

Crown 8vo, cloth 3s. 6d. each.

A Woman Worth Winning.	Double Cunning.	The Story of Antony Grace.
Cursed by a Fortune.	A Fluttered Dovecote.	The Man with a Shadow.
The Case of Ailsa Gray.	King of the Castle.	One Maid's Mischief.
Commodore Junk.	The Master of the Cere-	This Man's Wife.
Black Blood.	monies.	In Jeopardy.

Crown 8vo, cloth, gilt top, 6s. each.
The Bag of Diamonds, and Three Bits of Paste.
A Crimson Crime. | **Running Amok.**

Feuerheerd (H.).—The Gentleman's Cellar ; or, The Butler and Cellarman's Guide. Fcap. 8vo, cloth, 1s.

Fiction, A Catalogue of, with Descriptive Notices and Reviews of over NINE HUNDRED NOVELS, will be sent free by Messrs. CHATTO & WINDUS upon application.

Fin-Bec.—The Cupboard Papers: Observations on the Art of Living and Dining. Post 8vo, cloth limp, 2s. 6d.

Firework-Making, The Complete Art of ; or, The Pyrotechnist's Treasury. By THOMAS KENTISH. With 267 Illustrations. Crown 8vo, cloth, 3s. 6d.

First Book, My. By WALTER BESANT, JAMES PAYN, W. CLARK RUS-SELL, GRANT ALLEN, HALL CAINE, GEORGE R. SIMS, RUDYARD KIPLING, A. CONAN DOYLE, M. E. BRADDON, F. W. ROBINSON, H. RIDER HAGGARD, R. M. BALLANTYNE, I. ZANGWILL, MORLEY ROBERTS, D. CHRISTIE MURRAY, MARY CORELLI, J. K. JEROME, JOHN STRANGE WINTER, BRET HARTE, 'Q.,' ROBERT BUCHANAN, and R. L. STEVENSON. With a Prefatory Story by JEROME K. JEROME, and 185 Illustrations. A New Edition. Small demy 8vo, art linen, 3s. 6d.

Fitzgerald (Percy), Works by.
Little Essays: Passages from the Letters of CHARLES LAMB. Post 8vo, cloth, 2s. 6d.
Fatal Zero. Crown 8vo, cloth extra, 3s. 6d. ; post 8vo, illustrated boards, 2s.

Post 8vo, illustrated boards, 2s. each.

Bella Donna.	The Lady of Brantome.	The Second Mrs. Tillotson.
Polly.	Never Forgotten.	Seventy-five Brooke Street.

Sir Henry Irving: Twenty Years at the Lyceum. With Portrait. Crown 8vo, cloth, 1s. 6d.

Flammarion (Camille), Works by.
Popular Astronomy: A General Description of the Heavens. Translated by J. ELLARD GORE, F.R.A.S. With Three Plates and 288 Illustrations. Medium 8vo, cloth, 10s. 6d.
Urania: A Romance. With 87 Illustrations. Crown 8vo, cloth extra, 5s.

Fletcher's (Giles, B.D.) Complete Poems: Christ's Victorie in Heaven, Christ's Victorie on Earth, Christ's Triumph over Death, and Minor Poems. With Notes by Rev. A. B. GROSART, D.D. Crown 8vo, cloth boards, 3s. 6d.

Forbes (Archibald).—The Life of Napoleon III. With Photogravure Frontispiece and Thirty-six full-page Illustrations. Cheaper Issue. Demy 8vo, cloth, 6s.

Francillon (R. E.), Novels by.
Crown 8vo, cloth extra, 3s. 6d. each; post 8vo, illustrated boards, 2s. each.
One by One. | A Real Queen. | A Dog and his Shadow.
Ropes of Sand. Illustrated.

Post 8vo, illustrated boards, 2s. each.
Queen Cophetua. | Olympia. | Romances of the Law. | King or Knave?
Jack Doyle's Daughter. Crown 8vo, cloth, 3s. 6d.

Frederic (Harold), Novels by. Post 8vo, cloth extra, 3s. 6d. each;
illustrated boards, 2s. each.
Seth's Brother's Wife. | The Lawton Girl.

French Literature, A History of. By HENRY VAN LAUN. Three
Vols., demy 8vo, cloth boards, 22s. 6d.

Fry's (Herbert) Royal Guide to the London Charities, 1900-1.
Edited by JOHN LANE. Published Annually. Crown 8vo, cloth, 1s. 6d.

Gardening Books. Post 8vo, 1s. each; cloth limp. 1s. 6d. each.
A Year's Work in Garden and Greenhouse. By GEORGE GLENNY.
Household Horticulture. By TOM and JANE JERROLD. Illustrated.
The Garden that Paid the Rent. By TOM JERROLD.

Gardner (Mrs. Alan).—Rifle and Spear with the Rajpoots: Being
the Narrative of a Winter's Travel and Sport in Northern India. With numerous Illustrations by the
Author and F. H. TOWNSEND. Demy 4to, half-bound, 21s.

Gaulot (Paul).—The Red Shirts: A Tale of "The Terror." Translated by JOHN DE VILLIERS. With a Frontispiece by STANLEY WOOD. Crown 8vo, cloth, 3s. 6d.

Gentleman's Magazine, The. 1s. Monthly. Contains Stories,
Articles upon Literature, Science, Biography, and Art, and 'Table Talk' by SYLVANUS URBAN.
⁎ Bound Volumes for recent years kept in stock, 8s. 6d. each. Cases for binding, 2s. each.

Gentleman's Annual, The. Published Annually in November. 1s.

German Popular Stories. Collected by the Brothers GRIMM and
Translated by EDGAR TAYLOR. With Introduction by JOHN RUSKIN, and 22 Steel Plates after
GEORGE CRUIKSHANK. Square 8vo, cloth, 6s. 6d.; gilt edges, 7s. 6d.

Gibbon (Chas.), Novels by. Cr. 8vo, cl., 3s. 6d. ea.; post 8vo, bds., 2s. ea.
Robin Gray. With Frontispiece. | Loving a Dream. | The Braes of Yarrow.
The Golden Shaft. With Frontispiece. | Of High Degree.

Post 8vo, illustrated boards, 2s. each.
The Flower of the Forest. | A Hard Knot. | By Mead and Stream.
The Dead Heart. | Queen of the Meadow. | Fancy Free.
For Lack of Gold. | In Pastures Green. | In Honour Bound.
What Will the World Say? | In Love and War. | Heart's Delight.
For the King. | A Heart's Problem. | Blood-Money.

Gibney (Somerville).—Sentenced! Crown 8vo, cloth, 1s. 6d.

Gilbert (W. S.), Original Plays by. In Three Series, 2s. 6d. each.
The FIRST SERIES contains: The Wicked World—Pygmalion and Galatea—Charity—The Princess—
The Palace of Truth—Trial by Jury.
The SECOND SERIES: Broken Hearts—Engaged—Sweethearts—Gretchen—Dan'l Druce—Tom Cobb
—H.M.S. 'Pinafore'—The Sorcerer—The Pirates of Penzance.
The THIRD SERIES: Comedy and Tragedy—Foggerty's Fairy—Rosencrantz and Guildenstern—
Patience—Princess Ida—The Mikado—Ruddigore—The Yeomen of the Guard—The Gondoliers—
The Mountebanks—Utopia.

Eight Original Comic Operas written by W. S. GILBERT. In Two Series. Demy 8vo, cloth,
2s. 6d. each. The FIRST containing: The Sorcerer—H.M.S. 'Pinafore'—The Pirates of Penzance—
Iolanthe—Patience—Princess Ida—The Mikado—Trial by Jury.
The SECOND containing: The Gondoliers—The Grand Duke—The Yeomen of the Guard—
His Excellency—Utopia, Limited—Ruddigore—The Mountebanks—Haste to the Wedding.
The Gilbert and Sullivan Birthday Book: Quotations for Every Day in the Year, selected
from Plays by W. S. GILBERT set to Music by Sir A. SULLIVAN. Compiled by ALEX. WATSON.
Royal 16mo, Japanese leather, 2s. 6d.

Gilbert (William). — **James Duke, Costermonger.** Post 8vo,
illustrated boards, 2s.

Gissing (Algernon).—A Secret of the North Sea. Crown 8vo,
cloth, gilt top, 6s.

Glanville (Ernest), Novels by.
Crown 8vo, cloth extra, 3s. 6d. each ; post 8vo, illustrated boards, 2s. each.
The Lost Heiress: A Tale of Love, Battle, and Adventure. With Two Illustrations by H. NISBET.
The Fossicker: A Romance of Mashonaland. With Two Illustrations by HUME NISBET.
A Fair Colonist. With a Frontispiece by STANLEY WOOD.

The Golden Rock. With a Frontispiece by STANLEY WOOD. Crown 8vo, cloth extra, 3s. 6d.
Kloof Yarns. Crown 8vo cloth, 1s. 6d.
Tales from the Veld. With Twelve Illustrations by M. NISBET. Crown 8vo, cloth, 3s. 6d.
Max Thornton. With 8 Illustrations by J. S. CROMPTON, R.I. Large crown 8vo, cloth, gilt
top, 6s.

Glenny (George).—A Year's Work in Garden and Greenhouse:
Practical Advice as to the Management of the Flower, Fruit, and Frame Garden. Post 8vo, 1s. ; cloth, 1s. 6d.

Godwin (William).—Lives of the Necromancers. Post 8vo, cl., 2s.

Golden Treasury of Thought, The: A Dictionary of Quotations
from the Best Authors. By THEODORE TAYLOR. Crown 8vo, cloth, 3s. 6d.

Goodman (E. J.).—The Fate of Herbert Wayne. Cr. 8vo, 3s. 6d.

Greeks and Romans, The Life of the, described from Antique
Monuments. By ERNST GUHL and W. KONER. Edited by Dr. F. HUEFFER. With 545 Illustrations. Large crown 8vo, cloth extra, 7s. 6d.

Grey (Sir George).—The Romance of a Proconsul: Being the
Personal Life and Memoirs of Sir GEORGE GREY, K.C.B. By JAMES MILNE. With Portrait. SECOND
EDITION. Crown 8vo, buckram, 6s.

Griffith (Cecil).—Corinthia Marazion: A Novel. Crown 8vo, cloth
extra, 3s. 6d.

Gunter (A. Clavering, Author of ' Mr. Barnes of New York ').—
A Florida Enchantment. Crown 8vo, cloth, 3s. 6d.

Habberton (John, Author of ' Helen's Babies '), **Novels by.**
Post 8vo, cloth limp, 2s. 6d. each.
Brueton's Bayou. | **Country Luck.**

Hair, The: Its Treatment in Health, Weakness, and Disease. Translated from the German of Dr. J. PINCUS. Crown 8vo, 1s. ; cloth, 1s. 6d.

Hake (Dr. Thomas Gordon), Poems by. Cr. 8vo, cl. ex., 6s. each.
New Symbols. | **Legends of the Morrow.** | **The Serpent Play.**

Maiden Ecstasy. Small 4to, cloth extra, 8s.

Halifax (C.).—Dr. Rumsey's Patient. By Mrs. L. T. MEADE and
CLIFFORD HALIFAX, M.D. Crown 8vo, cloth, 3s. 6d.

Hall (Mrs. S. C.).—Sketches of Irish Character. With numerous
Illustrations on Steel and Wood by MACLISE, GILBERT, HARVEY, and GEORGE CRUIKSHANK.
Small demy 8vo, cloth extra, 7s. 6d.

Hall (Owen), Novels by. Crown 8vo, cloth, 3s. 6d. each.
The Track of a Storm. | **Jetsam.**

Eureka. Crown 8vo, cloth, gilt top, 6s.

Halliday (Andrew).—Every-day Papers. Post 8vo, boards, 2s.

Hamilton (Cosmo).—Stories by. Crown 8vo, cloth gilt, 3s. 6d. each.
The Glamour of the Impossible. | **Through a Keyhole.**

Handwriting, The Philosophy of. With over 100 Facsimiles and
Explanatory Text. By DON FELIX DE SALAMANCA. Post 8vo, half-cloth, 2s. 6d.

Hanky-Panky: Easy and Difficult Tricks, White Magic, Sleight of
Hand, &c. Edited by W. H. CREMER. With 200 Illustrations. Crown 8vo, cloth extra, 4s. 6d.

Hardy (Iza Duffus).—The Lesser Evil. Crown 8vo, cloth, gt. top, 6s.

Hardy (Thomas).—Under the Greenwood Tree. Post 8vo, cloth
extra, 3s. 6d. ; illustrated boards, 2s. ; cloth limp, 2s. 6d.

Harte's (Bret) Collected Works. Revised by the Author. LIBRARY
EDITION, in Ten Volumes, crown 8vo, cloth extra, 6s. each.

Vol. I. COMPLETE POETICAL AND DRAMATIC WORKS. With Steel-plate Portrait.
 „ II. THE LUCK OF ROARING CAMP—BOHEMIAN PAPERS—AMERICAN LEGEND.
 „ III. TALES OF THE ARGONAUTS—EASTERN SKETCHES.
 „ IV. GABRIEL CONROY. | Vol. V. STORIES—CONDENSED NOVELS, &c.
 „ VI. TALES OF THE PACIFIC SLOPE.
 „ VII. TALES OF THE PACIFIC SLOPE—II. With Portrait by JOHN PETTIE, R.A.
 „ VIII. TALES OF THE PINE AND THE CYPRESS.
 „ IX. BUCKEYE AND CHAPPAREL.
 „ X. TALES OF TRAIL AND TOWN, &c.

Bret Harte's Choice Works, in Prose and Verse. With Portrait of the Author and 40 Illustrations. Crown 8vo, cloth, 3s. 6d.
Bret Harte's Poetical Works. Printed on hand-made paper. Crown 8vo, buckram, 4s. 6d.
Some Later Verses. Crown 8vo, linen gilt, 5s.

Crown 8vo, cloth extra, 3s. 6d. each; post 8vo, picture boards, 2s. each.
Gabriel Conroy.
A Waif of the Plains. With 60 Illustrations by STANLEY L. WOOD.
A Ward of the Golden Gate. With 59 Illustrations by STANLEY L. WOOD.

Crown 8vo, cloth extra, 3s. 6d. each.
A Sappho of Green Springs, &c. With Two Illustrations by HUME NISBET.
Colonel Starbottle's Client, and Some Other People. With a Frontispiece.
Susy: A Novel. With Frontispiece and Vignette by J. A. CHRISTIE.
Sally Dows, &c. With 47 Illustrations by W. D. ALMOND and others.
A Protegee of Jack Hamlin's, &c. With 26 Illustrations by W. SMALL and others.
The Bell-Ringer of Angel's,&c. With 39 Illustrations by DUDLEY HARDY and others
Clarence: A Story of the American War. With Eight Illustrations by A. JULE GOODMAN.
Barker's Luck, &c. With 39 Illustrations by A. FORESTIER, PAUL HARDY, &c.
Devil's Ford, &c. With a Frontispiece by W. H. OVEREND.
The Crusade of the "Excelsior." With a Frontispiece by J. BERNARD PARTRIDGE.
Three Partners; or, The Big Strike on Heavy Tree Hill. With 8 Illustrations by J. GULICH.
Tales of Trail and Town. With Frontispiece by G. P. JACOMB-HOOD.

Post 8vo, illustrated boards, 2s. each.
An Heiress of Red Dog, &c. | **The Luck of Roaring Camp,** &c.
Californian Stories.

Post 8vo, illustrated boards, 2s. each; cloth, 2s. 6d. each.
Flip. | **Maruja.** | **A Phyllis of the Sierras.**

Haweis (Mrs. H. R.), Books by.
The Art of Beauty. With Coloured Frontispiece and 91 Illustrations. Square 8vo, cloth bds., 6s.
The Art of Decoration. With Coloured Frontispiece and 74 Illustrations. Sq. 8vo, cloth bds., 6s.
The Art of Dress. With 32 Illustrations. Post 8vo, 1s.; cloth, 1s. 6d.
Chaucer for Schools. With the Story of his Times and his Work. A New Edition, revised.
With a Frontispiece. Demy 8vo, cloth, 2s. 6d.
Chaucer for Children. With 38 Illustrations (8 Coloured). Crown 4to, cloth extra, 3s. 6d.

Haweis (Rev. H. R., M.A.).—American Humorists: WASHINGTON
IRVING, OLIVER WENDELL HOLMES, JAMES RUSSELL LOWELL, ARTEMUS WARD, MARK
TWAIN, and BRET HARTE. Crown 8vo, cloth, 6s.

Hawthorne (Julian), Novels by.
Crown 8vo, cloth extra, 3s. 6d. each; post 8vo, illustrated boards, 2s. each.
Garth. | **Ellice Quentin.** | **Beatrix Randolph.** With Four Illusts.
Sebastian Strome.   **David Poindexter's Disappearance.**
Fortune's Fool. | **Dust.** Four Illusts.   **The Spectre of the Camera.**

Post 8vo, illustrated boards, 2s. each.
Miss Cadogna. | **Love—or a Name.**

Heckethorn (C. W.), Books by.
London Souvenirs. | **London Memories: Social, Historical, and Topographical.**

Helps (Sir Arthur), Books by. Post 8vo, cloth limp, 2s. 6d. each.
Animals and their Masters. | **Social Pressure.**

Ivan de Biron: A Novel. Crown 8vo, cloth extra, 3s. 6d.; post 8vo, illustrated boards, 2s.

Henderson (Isaac).—Agatha Page: A Novel.   Cr. 8vo, cl., 3s. 6d.

Henty (G. A.), Novels by.
Rujub, the Juggler. With Eight Illustrations by STANLEY L. WOOD. Small demy 8vo, cloth, gilt
edges, 5s.; post 8vo, illustrated boards, 2s.
Colonel Thorndyke's Secret. With a Frontispiece by STANLEY L. WOOD. Small demy 8vo,
cloth, gilt edges, 5s.

Crown 8vo, cloth, 3s. 6d. each.
The Queen's Cup. | **Dorothy's Double.**

Herman (Henry).—A Leading Lady. Post 8vo, cloth, 2s. 6d.

Herrick's (Robert) Hesperides, Noble Numbers, and Complete
Collected Poems. With Memorial-Introduction and Notes by the Rev. A. B. GROSART, D.D.,
Steel Portrait, &c. Three Vols., crown 8vo, cloth boards, 3s. 6d. each.

Hertzka (Dr. Theodor).—Freeland: A Social Anticipation. Translated by ARTHUR RANSOM. Crown 8vo, cloth extra, 6s.

Hesse-Wartegg (Chevalier Ernst von).— Tunis: The Land and the People. With 22 Illustrations. Crown 8vo, cloth extra, 3s. 6d.

Hill (Headon).—Zambra the Detective. Crown 8vo, cloth, 3s. 6d.; post 8vo, picture boards, 2s.

Hill (John), Works by.
Treason-Felony. Post 8vo, boards, 2s. | The Common Ancestor. Cr. 8vo, cloth, 3s. 6d.

Hoey (Mrs. Cashel).—The Lover's Creed. Post 8vo, boards, 2s.

Holiday, Where to go for a. By E. P. SHOLL, Sir H. MAXWELL, Bart., M.P., JOHN WATSON, JANE BARLOW, MARY LOVETT CAMERON, JUSTIN H. McCARTHY, PAUL LANGE, J. W. GRAHAM, J. H. SALTER, PHŒBE ALLEN, S. J. BECKETT, L. RIVERS VINE, and C. F. GORDON CUMMING. Crown 8vo, cloth, 1s. 6d.

Hollingshead (John).—According to My Lights. With a Portrait. Crown 8vo, cloth, gilt top, 6s.

Holmes (Oliver Wendell), Works by.
The Autocrat of the Breakfast-Table. Illustrated by J. GORDON THOMSON. Post 8vo, cloth limp, 2s. 6d. Another Edition, post 8vo, cloth, 2s.
The Autocrat of the Breakfast-Table and The Professor at the Breakfast-Table. In One Vol. Post 8vo, half-bound, 2s.

Hood's (Thomas) Choice Works in Prose and Verse. With Life of the Author, Portrait, and 200 Illustrations. Crown 8vo, cloth, 3s. 6d.
Hood's Whims and Oddities. With 85 Illustrations. Post 8vo, half-bound, 2s.

Hook's (Theodore) Choice Humorous Works: including his Ludicrous Adventures, Bons Mots, Puns, and Hoaxes. With Life of the Author, Portraits, Facsimiles and Illustrations. Crown 8vo, cloth extra, 7s. 6d.

Hooper (Mrs. Geo.).—The House of Raby. Post 8vo, boards, 2s.

Hopkins (Tighe), Novels by. Crown 8vo, cloth, 6s. each.
Nell Haffenden. With 8 Illustrations by C. GREGORY. | For Freedom.

Crown 8vo, cloth, 3s. 6d. each.
'Twixt Love and Duty. With a Frontispiece. | The Incomplete Adventurer.
The Nugents of Carriconna.

Horne (R. Hengist).— Orion: An Epic Poem. With Photograph Portrait by SUMMERS. Tenth Edition. Crown 8vo, cloth extra, 7s.

Hugo (Victor).—The Outlaw of Iceland (Han d'Islande). Translated by Sir GILBERT CAMPBELL. Crown 8vo, cloth, 3s. 6d.

Hume (Fergus).—The Lady from Nowhere. Crown 8vo, cloth, 3s. 6d.

Hungerford (Mrs., Author of 'Molly Bawn'), Novels by.
Post 8vo, illustrated boards, 2s. each; cloth limp, 2s. 6d. each.
Marvel. | A Modern Circe. | Lady Patty.
In Durance Vile. | An Unsatisfactory Lover.

Crown 8vo, cloth extra, 3s. 6d. each; post 8vo, illustrated boards, 2s. each; cloth limp, 2s. 6d. each.
A Maiden All Forlorn. | Lady Verner's Flight. | The Three Graces.
April's Lady. | The Red-House Mystery. | Nora Creina.
Peter's Wife. | The Professor's Experiment. | A Mental Struggle.

Crown 8vo, cloth extra, 3s. 6d. each.
An Anxious Moment. | A Point of Conscience.
The Coming of Chloe. | Lovice.

Hunt's (Leigh) Essays: A Tale for a Chimney Corner, &c. Edited by EDMUND OLLIER. Post 8vo, half-bound, 2s.

Hunt (Mrs. Alfred), Novels by.
Crown 8vo, cloth extra, 3s. 6d. each; post 8vo, illustrated boards, 2s. each.
The Leaden Casket. | Self-Condemned. | That Other Person.
Mrs. Juliet. Crown 8vo, cloth extra, 3s. 6d.

Hutchison (W. M.).—Hints on Colt-breaking. With 25 Illustrations. Crown 8vo, cloth extra, 3s. 6d.

Hydrophobia: An Account of M. PASTEUR's System ; The Technique of his Method, and Statistics. By RENAUD SUZOR, M.B. Crown 8vo, cloth extra, 6s.

Hyne (C. J. Cutcliffe).— Honour of Thieves. Cr. 8vo, cloth, 3s. 6d.

Impressions (The) of Aureole. Post 8vo, blush-rose paper and cloth, 2s. 6d.

Indoor Paupers. By ONE OF THEM. Crown 8vo, 1s. ; cloth, 1s. 6d.

Innkeeper's Handbook (The) and Licensed Victualler's Manual. By J. TREVOR-DAVIES. A New Edition. Crown 8vo, cloth, 2s.

Irish Wit and Humour, Songs of. Collected and Edited by A. PERCEVAL GRAVES. Post 8vo, cloth limp, 2s. 6d.

Irving (Sir Henry) : A Record of over Twenty Years at the Lyceum. By PERCY FITZGERALD. With Portrait. Crown 8vo, cloth, 1s. 6d.

James (C. T. C.). — A Romance of the Queen's Hounds. Post 8vo, cloth limp, 1s. 6d.

Jameson (William).—My Dead Self. Post 8vo, cloth, 2s. 6d.

Japp (Alex. H., LL.D.).—Dramatic Pictures, &c. Cr. 8vo, cloth, 5s.

Jefferies (Richard), Books by. Post 8vo, cloth limp, 2s. 6d. each.
Nature near London. | The Life of the Fields. | The Open Air.
*** Also the HAND-MADE PAPER EDITION, crown 8vo, buckram, gilt top, 6s. each.

The Eulogy of Richard Jefferies. By Sir WALTER BESANT. With a Photograph Portrait. Crown 8vo, cloth extra, 6s.

Jennings (Henry J.), Works by.
Curiosities of Criticism. Post 8vo, cloth limp, 2s. 6d.
Lord Tennyson : A Biographical Sketch. With Portrait. Post 8vo, cloth, 1s. 6d.

Jerome (Jerome K.), Books by.
Stageland. With 64 Illustrations by J. BERNARD PARTRIDGE. Fcap. 4to, picture cover, 1s.
John Ingerfield, &c. With 9 Illusts. by A. S. BOYD and JOHN GULICH. Fcap. 8vo, pic. cov. 1s. 6d.
The Prude's Progress : A Comedy by J. K. JEROME and EDEN PHILLPOTTS. Cr. 8vo, 1s. 6d.

Jerrold (Douglas).—The Barber's Chair; and The Hedgehog Letters. Post 8vo, printed on laid paper and half-bound, 2s.

Jerrold (Tom), Works by. Post 8vo, 1s. ea. ; cloth limp, 1s. 6d. each.
The Garden that Paid the Rent.
Household Horticulture : A Gossip about Flowers. Illustrated.

Jesse (Edward).—Scenes and Occupations of a Country Life. Post 8vo, cloth limp, 2s.

Jones (William, F.S.A.), Works by. Cr. 8vo, cl. extra, 3s. 6d. each.
Finger-Ring Lore : Historical, Legendary, and Anecdotal. With Hundreds of Illustrations.
Credulities, Past and Present. Including the Sea and Seamen, Miners, Talismans, Word and Letter Divination, Exorcising and Blessing of Animals, Birds, Eggs, Luck, &c. With Frontispiece.
Crowns and Coronations : A History of Regalia. With 91 Illustrations.

Jonson's (Ben) Works. With Notes Critical and Explanatory, and a Biographical Memoir by WILLIAM GIFFORD. Edited by Colonel CUNNINGHAM. Three Vols. crown 8vo, cloth extra, 3s. 6d. each.

Josephus, The Complete Works of. Translated by WHISTON. Containing 'The Antiquities of the Jews' and 'The Wars of the Jews.' With 52 Illustrations and Maps. Two Vols., demy 8vo, half-cloth, 12s. 6d.

Kempt (Robert).—Pencil and Palette: Chapters on Art and Artists. Post 8vo, cloth limp, 2s. 6d.

Kershaw (Mark). — Colonial Facts and Fictions : Humorous Sketches. Post 8vo, illustrated boards, 2s. ; cloth, 2s. 6d.

King (R. Ashe), Novels by.
Post 8vo, illustrated boards, 2s. each.
'The Wearing of the Green.' | Passion's Slave. | Bell Barry.

A Drawn Game. Crown 8vo, cloth, 3s. 6d. ; post 8vo, illustrated boards, 2s.

Kipling Primer (A). Including Biographical and Critical Chapters, an Index to Mr. Kipling's principal Writings, and Bibliographies. By F. L. KNOWLES, Editor of 'The Golden Treasury of American Lyrics.' With Two Portraits. Crown 8vo, cloth, 3s. 6d.

Knight (William, M.R.C.S., and Edward, L.R.C.P.). — The Patient's Vade Mecum : How to Get Most Benefit from Medical Advice. Cr. 8vo, cloth, 1s. 6d.

Knights (The) of the Lion : A Romance of the Thirteenth Century. Edited, with an Introduction, by the MARQUESS OF LORNE, K.T. Crown 8vo, cloth extra, 6s.

Lamb's (Charles) Complete Works in Prose and Verse, including 'Poetry for Children' and 'Prince Dorus.' Edited, with Notes and Introduction, by R. H. SHEP-HERD. With Two Portraits and Facsimile of the 'Essay on Roast Pig.' Crown 8vo, cloth, 3s. 6d.
The **Essays of Elia**. Post 8vo, printed on laid paper and half-bound, 2s.
Little Essays: Sketches and Characters by CHARLES LAMB, selected from his Letters by PERCY FITZGERALD. Post 8vo, cloth limp, 2s. 6d.
The **Dramatic Essays of Charles Lamb**. With Introduction and Notes by BRANDER MAT-THEWS, and Steel-plate Portrait. Fcap. 8vo, half-bound, 2s. 6d.

Lambert (George).—The President of Boravia. Crown 8vo, cl., 3s. 6d.

Landor (Walter Savage).—Citation and Examination of William Shakspeare, &c. before Sir Thomas Lucy, touching Deer-stealing, 19th September, 1582. To which is added, **A Conference of Master Edmund Spenser** with the Earl of Essex, touching the State of Ireland, 1595. Fcap. 8vo, half-Roxburghe, 2s. 6d.

Lane (Edward William).—The Thousand and One Nights, commonly called in England **The Arabian Nights' Entertainments.** Translated from the Arabic, with Notes. Illustrated with many hundred Engravings from Designs by HARVEY. Edited by EDWARD STANLEY POOLE. With Preface by STANLEY LANE-POOLE. Three Vols., demy 8vo, cloth, 7s. 6d. ea.

Larwood (Jacob), Works by.
Anecdotes of the Clergy. Post 8vo, laid paper, half-bound, 2s.

Post 8vo, cloth limp, 2s. 6d. each.
Forensic Anecdotes. | **Theatrical Anecdotes.**

Lehmann (R. C.), Works by. Post 8vo, cloth, 1s. 6d. each.
Harry Fludyer at Cambridge.
Conversational Hints for Young Shooters: A Guide to Polite Talk.

Leigh (Henry S.).—Carols of Cockayne. Printed on hand-made paper, bound in buckram, 5s.

Leland (C. Godfrey). — A Manual of Mending and Repairing. With Diagrams. Crown 8vo, cloth, 5s.

Lepelletier (Edmond). — Madame Sans-Gène. Translated from the French by JOHN DE VILLIERS. Post 8vo, cloth, 3s. 6d.; picture boards, 2s.

Leys (John).—The Lindsays: A Romance. Post 8vo, illust. bds., 2s.

Lilburn (Adam).—A Tragedy in Marble. Crown 8vo, cloth, 3s. 6d.

Lindsay (Harry, Author of 'Methodist Idylls'), Novels by.
Crown 8vo, cloth, 3s. 6d. each.
Rhoda Roberts.
The Jacobite: A Romance of the Conspiracy of 'The Forty.'

Linton (E. Lynn), Works by.
An Octave of Friends. Crown 8vo, cloth, 3s. 6d.

Crown 8vo, cloth extra, 3s. 6d. each; post 8vo, illustrated boards, 2s. each.
Patricia Kemball.	**Ione.**	**Under which Lord?** With 12 Illustrations.
The Atonement of Leam Dundas.	**'My Love!'**	**Sowing the Wind.**
The World Well Lost. With 12 Illusts.	**Paston Carew,** Millionaire and Miser.
The One Too Many.	**Dulcie Everton.**	**With a Silken Thread.**

The Rebel of the Family.
Post 8vo, cloth limp, 2s. 6d. each.
Witch Stories. | **Ourselves:** Essays on Women.
Freeshooting: Extracts from the Works of Mrs. LYNN LINTON.

Lowe (Charles, M.A.).—Our Greatest Living Soldiers. With 8 Portraits. Crown 8vo, cloth, 3s. 6d.

Lucy (Henry W.).—Gideon Fleyce: A Novel. Crown 8vo, cloth extra, 3s. 6d.; post 8vo, illustrated boards, 2s.

Macalpine (Avery), Novels by.
Teresa Itasca. Crown 8vo, cloth extra, 1s.
Broken Wings. With Six Illustrations by W. J. HENNESSY. Crown 8vo, cloth extra, 6s.

MacColl (Hugh), Novels by.
Mr. Stranger's Sealed Packet. Post 8vo, Illustrated boards, 2s.
Ednor Whitlock. Crown 8vo, cloth extra, 6s.

Macdonell (Agnes).—Quaker Cousins. Post 8vo, boards, 2s.

MacGregor (Robert).—Pastimes and Players: Notes on Popular Games. Post 8vo, cloth limp, 2s. 6d.

Mackay (Charles, LL.D.). — Interludes and Undertones; or, Music at Twilight. Crown 8vo, cloth extra, 6s.

Mackenna (Stephen J.) and J. Augustus O'Shea.—Brave Men in Action: Thrilling Stories of the British Flag. With 8 Illustrations by STANLEY L. WOOD. Small demy 8vo, cloth, gilt edges, 5s.

McCarthy (Justin), Works by.

A History of Our Own Times, from the Accession of Queen Victoria to the General Election of 1880. LIBRARY EDITION, Four Vols., demy 8vo, cloth extra, 12s. each.—Also a POPULAR EDITION, in Four Vols., crown 8vo, cloth extra, 6s. each.—And the JUBILEE EDITION, with an Appendix of Events to the end of 1886, in Two Vols., large crown 8vo, cloth extra, 7s. 6d. each.

A History of Our Own Times, from 1880 to the Diamond Jubilee. Demy 8vo, cloth extra, 12s.; or crown 8vo, cloth, 6s.

A Short History of Our Own Times. One Vol., crown 8vo, cloth extra, 6s.—Also a CHEAP POPULAR EDITION, post 8vo, cloth limp, 2s. 6d.

A History of the Four Georges and of William the Fourth. By JUSTIN McCARTHY and JUSTIN HUNTLY McCARTHY. Four Vols., demy 8vo, cloth extra, 12s. each.

Reminiscences. With a Portrait. Two Vols., demy 8vo, cloth, 24s. [Vols. III. & IV. shortly.

Crown 8vo, cloth extra, 3s. 6d. each; post 8vo, illustrated boards, 2s. each; cloth limp, 2s. 6d. each.

The Waterdale Neighbours. | **Donna Quixote.** With 12 Illustrations.
My Enemy's Daughter. | **The Comet of a Season.**
A Fair Saxon. | **Linley Rochford.** | **Maid of Athens.** With 12 Illustrations.
Dear Lady Disdain. | **The Dictator.** | **Camiola:** A Girl with a Fortune.
Miss Misanthrope. With 12 Illustrations. | **Red Diamonds.** | **The Riddle Ring.**

The Three Disgraces, and other Stories. Crown 8vo, cloth, 3s. 6d.

Mononia: A Love Story of "Forty-eight." Crown 8vo, cloth, gilt top, 6s.

'The Right Honourable.' By JUSTIN McCARTHY and Mrs. CAMPBELL PRAED. Crown 8vo, cloth extra, 6s.

McCarthy (Justin Huntly), Works by.

The French Revolution. (Constituent Assembly, 1789-91). Four Vols., demy 8vo, cloth, 12s. each.

An Outline of the History of Ireland. Crown 8vo, 1s.; cloth, 1s. 6d.

Ireland Since the Union: Sketches of Irish History, 1798-1886. Crown 8vo, cloth, 6s.

Hafiz in London: Poems. Small 8vo, gold cloth, 3s. 6d.

Our Sensation Novel. Crown 8vo, picture cover, 1s.; cloth limp, 1s. 6d.

Doom: An Atlantic Episode. Crown 8vo, picture cover, 1s.

Dolly: A Sketch. Crown 8vo, picture cover, 1s.; cloth limp, 1s. 6d.

Lily Lass: A Romance. Crown 8vo, picture cover, 1s.; cloth limp, 1s. 6d.

A London Legend. Crown 8vo, cloth, 3s. 6d.

The Royal Christopher. Crown 8vo, cloth, 3s. 6d.

MacDonald (George, LL.D.), Books by.

Works of Fancy and Imagination. Ten Vols., 16mo, cloth, gilt edges, in cloth case, 21s.; or the Volumes may be had separately, in Grolier cloth, at 2s. 6d. each.

Vol. I. WITHIN AND WITHOUT.—THE HIDDEN LIFE.
 „ II. THE DISCIPLE.—THE GOSPEL WOMEN.—BOOK OF SONNETS.—ORGAN SONGS.
 „ III. VIOLIN SONGS.—SONGS OF THE DAYS AND NIGHTS.—A BOOK OF DREAMS.—ROADSIDE POEMS.—POEMS FOR CHILDREN.
 „ IV. PARABLES.—BALLADS.—SCOTCH SONGS.
 „ V. & VI. PHANTASTES: A Faerie Romance. | Vol. VII. THE PORTENT.
 „ VIII. THE LIGHT PRINCESS.—THE GIANT'S HEART.—SHADOWS.
 „ IX. CROSS PURPOSES.—THE GOLDEN KEY.—THE CARASOYN.—LITTLE DAYLIGHT.
 „ X. THE CRUEL PAINTER.—THE WOW O' RIVVEN.—THE CASTLE.—THE BROKEN SWORDS.—THE GRAY WOLF.—UNCLE CORNELIUS.

Poetical Works of George MacDonald. Collected and Arranged by the Author. Two Vols. crown 8vo, buckram, 12s.

A Threefold Cord. Edited by GEORGE MACDONALD. Post 8vo, cloth, 5s.

Phantastes: A Faerie Romance. With 25 Illustrations by J. BELL. Crown 8vo, cloth extra, 3s. 6d.

Heather and Snow: A Novel. Crown 8vo, cloth extra, 3s. 6d.; post 8vo, illustrated boards, 2s.

Lilith: A Romance. SECOND EDITION. Crown 8vo, cloth extra, 6s.

Maclise Portrait Gallery (The) of Illustrious Literary Characters: 85 Portraits by DANIEL MACLISE; with Memoirs—Biographical, Critical, Bibliographical, and Anecdotal—illustrative of the Literature of the former half of the Present Century. by WILLIAM BATES, B.A. Crown 8vo, cloth extra, 3s. 6d.

Macquoid (Mrs.), Works by. Square 8vo, cloth extra, 6s. each.

In the Ardennes. With 50 Illustrations by THOMAS R. MACQUOID.
Pictures and Legends from Normandy and Brittany. 34 Illusts. by T. R. MACQUOID.
Through Normandy. With 92 Illustrations by T. R. MACQUOID, and a Map.
Through Brittany. With 35 Illustrations by T. R. MACQUOID, and a Map.
About Yorkshire. With 67 Illustrations by T. R. MACQUOID.

Magician's Own Book, The: Performances with Eggs, Hats, &c. Edited by W. H. CREMER. With 200 Illustrations. Crown 8vo, cloth extra, 4s. 6d.

Magic Lantern, The, and its Management: Including full Practical Directions. By T. C. HEPWORTH. With 10 Illustrations. Crown 8vo, 1s.; cloth, 1s. 6d.

Magna Charta: An Exact Facsimile of the Original in the British Museum, 3 feet by 2 feet, with Arms and Seals emblazoned in Gold and Colours, 5s.

Mallory (Sir Thomas). — Mort d'Arthur: The Stories of King Arthur and of the Knights of the Round Table. (A Selection.) Edited by B. MONTGOMERIE RANKING. Post 8vo, cloth limp, 2s.

Mallock (W. H.), Works by.

The New Republic. Post 8vo, cloth, 3s. 6d.; picture boards, 2s.
The New Paul and Virginia: Positivism on an Island. Post 8vo, cloth, 2s. 6d.

Poems. Small 4to, parchment, 8s.
Is Life Worth Living? Crown 8vo, cloth extra, 6s.

Margueritte (Paul and Victor).—The Disaster. Translated by
FREDERIC LEES. Crown 8vo, cloth, 3s. 6d.

Marlowe's Works. Including his Translations. Edited, with Notes
and Introductions, by Colonel CUNNINGHAM. Crown 8vo, cloth extra, 3s. 6d.

Massinger's Plays. From the Text of WILLIAM GIFFORD. Edited
by Col. CUNNINGHAM. Crown 8vo, cloth extra, 3s. 6d.

Mathams (Walter, F.R.G.S.). — Comrades All. Fcp. 8vo, cloth
limp, 1s.; cloth gilt, 2s.

Matthews (Brander).—A Secret of the Sea, &c. Post 8vo, illustrated boards, 2s.; cloth limp, 2s. 6d.

Max O'Rell.—Her Royal Highness Woman. Cr. 8vo, cl., 3s. 6d. [May.

Meade (L. T.), Novels by.
A Soldier of Fortune. Crown 8vo, cloth, 3s. 6d.; post 8vo, illustrated boards, 2s.
Crown 8vo, cloth, 3s. 6d. each.
The Voice of the Charmer. With 8 Illustrations.
In an Iron Grip. | On the Brink of a Chasm. | A Son of Ishmael.
The Siren. | The Way of a Woman. | An Adventuress.
Dr. Rumsey's Patient. By L. T. MEADE and CLIFFORD HALIFAX, M.D.
The Blue Diamond. Crown 8vo, cloth, gilt top, 6s.
This Troublesome World. SECOND EDITION. Crown 8vo cloth, gilt top, 6s. [Shortly.

Merivale (Herman).—Bar, Stage, and Platform: Autobiographic
Memories. Demy 8vo, cloth, 12s. [Shortly.

Merrick (Leonard), Novels by.
The Man who was Good. Post 8vo, picture boards, 2s.
Crown 8vo, cloth, 3s. 6d. each.
This Stage of Fools. | Cynthia: A Daughter of the Philistines.

Mexican Mustang (On a), through Texas to the Rio Grande. By
A. E. SWEET and J. ARMOY KNOX. With 265 Illustrations. Crown 8vo, cloth extra, 7s. 6d.

Middlemass (Jean), Novels by. Post 8vo, illust. boards, 2s. each.
Touch and Go. | Mr. Dorillion.

Miller (Mrs. F. Fenwick).—Physiology for the Young; or, The
House of Life. With numerous Illustrations. Post 8vo, cloth limp, 2s. 6d.

Milton (J. L.), Works by. Post 8vo, 1s. each; cloth, 1s. 6d. each.
The Hygiene of the Skin. With Directions for Diet, Soaps, Baths, Wines, &c.
The Bath in Diseases of the Skin.
The Laws of Life, and their Relation to Diseases of the Skin.

Minto (Wm.).—Was She Good or Bad? Crown 8vo, cloth, 1s. 6d.

Mitchell (Edmund).—The Lone Star Rush. With 8 Illustrations
by NORMAN H. HARDY. Crown 8vo, cloth, gilt top, 6s.

Mitford (Bertram), Novels by. Crown 8vo, cloth extra, 3s. 6d. each.
The Gun-Runner: A Romance of Zululand. With a Frontispiece by STANLEY L. WOOD.
The Luck of Gerard Ridgeley. With a Frontispiece by STANLEY L. WOOD.
The King's Assegai. With Six full-page Illustrations by STANLEY L. WOOD.
Renshaw Fanning's Quest. With a Frontispiece by STANLEY L. WOOD.

Molesworth (Mrs.).—Hathercourt Rectory. Post 8vo, illustrated
boards, 2s.

Moncrieff (W. D. Scott-).—The Abdication: An Historical Drama.
With Seven Etchings by JOHN PETTIE, W. Q. ORCHARDSON, J. MACWHIRTER, COLIN HUNTER,
R. MACBETH and TOM GRAHAM. Imperial 4to, buckram, 21s.

Montagu (Irving).—Things I Have Seen in War. With 16 full-
page Illustrations. Crown 8vo, cloth, 6s.

Moore (Thomas), Works by.
The Epicurean; and Alciphron. Post 8vo, half-bound, 2s.
Prose and Verse; including Suppressed Passages from the MEMOIRS OF LORD BYRON. Edited
by R. H. SHEPHERD. With Portrait. Crown 8vo, cloth extra, 7s. 6d.

Morrow (W. C.).—Bohemian Paris of To-Day. With 106 Illustrations by EDOUARD CUCUEL. Small demy 8vo, cloth, gilt top, 6s.

Muddock (J. E.) Stories by.
Crown 8vo, cloth extra, 3s. 6d. each.
Maid Marian and Robin Hood. With 12 Illustrations by STANLEY WOOD.
Basile the Jester. With Frontispiece by STANLEY WOOD.
Young Lochinvar. | The Golden Idol.
Post 8vo, illustrated boards, 2s. each.
The Dead Man's Secret. | From the Bosom of the Deep.
Stories Weird and Wonderful. Post 8vo, illustrated boards, 2s.; cloth, 2s. 6d.

Murray (D. Christie), Novels by.
Crown 8vo, cloth extra, 3s. 6d. each ; post 8vo, illustrated boards, 2s. each.

A Life's Atonement. | A Model Father. | Bob Martin's Little Girl.
Joseph's Coat. 12 Illusts. | Old Blazer's Hero. | Time's Revenges.
Coals of Fire. 3 Illusts. | Cynic Fortune. Frontisp. | A Wasted Crime.
Val Strange. | By the Gate of the Sea. | In Direst Peril.
Hearts. | A Bit of Human Nature. | Mount Despair.
The Way of the World. | First Person Singular. | A Capful o' Nails.

The Making of a Novelist : An Experiment in Autobiography. With a Collotype Portrait Cr. 8vo, buckram. 3s. 6d.
My Contemporaries in Fiction. Crown 8vo, buckram, 3s. 6d.

Crown 8vo, cloth, 3s. 6d. each.

This Little World. | A Race for Millions.
Tales in Prose and Verse. With Frontispiece by ARTHUR HOPKINS.

The Church of Humanity. Crown 8vo, cloth, gilt top, 6s.

Murray (D. Christie) and Henry Herman, Novels by.
Crown 8vo, cloth extra, 3s. 6d. each; post 8vo, illustrated boards, 2s. each.

One Traveller Returns. | The Bishops' Bible.
Paul Jones's Alias, &c. With Illustrations by A. FORESTIER and G. NICOLET.

Murray (Henry), Novels by.
Post 8vo, cloth, 2s. 6d. each.

A Game of Bluff. | A Song of Sixpence.

Newbolt (H.).—Taken from the Enemy. Post 8vo, leatherette, 1s.

Nisbet (Hume), Books by.
'Bail Up.' Crown 8vo, cloth extra, 3s. 6d.; post 8vo, illustrated boards, 2s.
Dr. Bernard St. Vincent. Post 8vo, illustrated boards, 2s.
Lessons in Art. With 21 Illustrations. Crown 8vo, cloth extra, 2s. 6d.

Norris (W. E.), Novels by. Crown 8vo, cloth, 3s. 6d. each ; post 8vo,
picture boards, 2s. each.
Saint Ann's.
Billy Bellew. With a Frontispiece by F. H. TOWNSEND.
Miss Wentworth's Idea. Crown 8vo, cloth, 3s. 6d.

Oakley (John).—A Gentleman in Khaki : A Story of the South
African War. Demy 8vo, picture cover, 1s.

Ohnet (Georges), Novels by. Post 8vo, illustrated boards, 2s. each.
Doctor Rameau. | A Last Love.

A Weird Gift. Crown 8vo cloth, 3s. 6d.; post 8vo, picture boards, 2s.
Love's Depths. Translated by F. ROTHWELL. Crown 8vo, cloth, 3s. 6d.

Oliphant (Mrs.), Novels by. Post 8vo, illustrated boards, 2s. each.
The Primrose Path. | Whiteladies.
The Greatest Heiress in England.

The Sorceress. Crown 8vo, cloth, 3s. 6d.

O'Shaughnessy (Arthur), Poems by :
Fcap. 8vo, cloth extra, 7s. 6d. each.
Music and Moonlight. | Songs of a Worker.

Lays of France. Crown 8vo, cloth extra, 10s. 6d.

Ouida, Novels by. Cr. 8vo, cl., 3s. 6d. ea.; post 8vo, illust. bds., 2s. ea.
Held in Bondage. | A Dog of Flanders. | In Maremma. | Wanda.
Tricotrin. | Pascarel. | Signa. | Bimbi. | Syrlin.
Strathmore. | Chandos. | Two Wooden Shoes. | Frescoes. | Othmar.
Cecil Castlemaine's Gage | In a Winter City. | Princess Napraxine.
Under Two Flags. | Ariadne. | Friendship. | Guilderoy. | Ruffino.
Puck. | Idalia. | A Village Commune. | Two Offenders.
Folle-Farine. | Moths. | Pipistrello. | Santa Barbara.

POPULAR EDITIONS. Medium 8vo, 6d. each ; cloth, 1s. each.
Under Two Flags. | Moths.

Medium 8vo, 6d. each.
Held in Bondage. | Puck.

The Waters of Edera. Crown 8vo, cloth, 3s. 6d.
Wisdom, Wit, and Pathos, selected from the Works of OUIDA by F. SYDNEY MORRIS. Post 8vo, cloth extra, 5s.—CHEAP EDITION, Illustrated boards, 2s.

Page (H. A.).—Thoreau : His Life and Aims. With Portrait. Post
8vo, cloth, 2s. 6d.

Pandurang Hari ; or, Memoirs o[f] a Hindoo. With Preface by Sir
BARTLE FRERE. Post 8vo, Illustrated boards, 2s.

Pascal's Provincial Letters. A New Translation, with Historical
Introduction and Notes by T. M'CRIE, D.D. Post 8vo, half-cloth, 2s.

Paul (Margaret A.).—Gentle and Simple. Crown 8vo, cloth, with
Frontispiece by HELEN PATERSON, 3s. 6d.; post 8vo, illustrated boards, 2s.

Payn (James), Novels by.

Crown 8vo, cloth extra, 3s. 6d. each; post 8vo, illustrated boards, 2s. each.

Lost Sir Massingberd.
Walter's Word. | A County Family.
Less Black than We're Painted.
By Proxy. | For Cash Only.
High Spirits.
A Confidential Agent. With 12 Illusts.
A Grape from a Thorn. With 12 Illusts.

Holiday Tasks.
The Talk of the Town. With 12 Illusts.
The Mystery of Mirbridge.
The Word and the Will.
The Burnt Million.
Sunny Stories. | A Trying Patient.

Post 8vo illustrated boards, 2s. each.

Humorous Stories. | From Exile.
The Foster Brothers.
The Family Scapegrace.
Married Beneath Him.
Bentinck's Tutor.
A Perfect Treasure.
Like Father, Like Son.
A Woman's Vengeance.
Carlyon's Year. | Cecil's Tryst.
Murphy's Master. | At Her Mercy.
The Clyffards of Clyffe.

Found Dead. | Gwendoline's Harvest
Mirk Abbey. | A Marine Residence.
Some Private Views.
The Canon's Ward.
Not Wooed, But Won.
Two Hundred Pounds Reward.
The Best of Husbands.
Halves. | What He Cost Her.
Fallen Fortunes. | Kit: A Memory.
Under One Roof. | Glow-worm Tales.
A Prince of the Blood.

A Modern Dick Whittington; or, A Patron of Letters. With a Portrait of the Author. Crown 8vo, cloth, 3s. 6d.
In Peril and Privation. With 17 Illustrations. Crown 8vo, cloth, 3s. 6d.
Notes from the 'News.' Crown 8vo, cloth, 1s. 6d.
By Proxy. POPULAR EDITION, medium 8vo, 6d. ; cloth, 1s.

Payne (Will).—Jerry the Dreamer. Crown 8vo, cloth, 3s. 6d.

Pennell (H. Cholmondeley), Works by. Post 8vo, cloth, 2s. 6d. ea.

Puck on Pegasus. With Illustrations.
Pegasus Re-Saddled. With Ten full-page Illustrations by G. DU MAURIER.
The Muses of Mayfair: Vers de Société. Selected by H. C. PENNELL.

Phelps (E. Stuart), Works by. Post 8vo, cloth, 1s. 6d. each.

An Old Maid's Paradise. | Burglars in Paradise.

Beyond the Gates. Post 8vo, picture cover, 1s. ; cloth, 1s. 6d.
Jack the Fisherman. Illustrated by C. W. REED. Crown 8vo, cloth, 1s. 6d.

Phil May's Sketch-Book. Containing 54 Humorous Cartoons. Crown folio, cloth, 2s. 6d.

Phipson (Dr. T. L.), Books by. Crown 8vo, art canvas, gilt top, 5s. ea.

Famous Violinists and Fine Violins.
Voice and Violin: Sketches, Anecdotes, and Reminiscences.

Planche (J. R.), Works by.

The Pursuivant of Arms. With Six Plates and 209 Illustrations. Crown 8vo, cloth, 7s. 6d.
Songs and Poems, 1819-1879. With Introduction by Mrs. MACKARNESS. Crown 8vo, cloth, 6s.

Plutarch's Lives of Illustrious Men. With Notes and a Life of Plutarch by JOHN and WM. LANGHORNE, and Portraits. Two Vols., demy 8vo, half-cloth 10s. 6d.

Poe's (Edgar Allan) Choice Works: Poems, Stories, Essays. With an Introduction by CHARLES BAUDELAIRE. Crown 8vo, cloth, 3s. 6d.

Pollock (W. H.).—The Charm, and other Drawing-room Plays. By Sir WALTER BESANT and WALTER H. POLLOCK. With 50 Illustrations. Crown 8vo, cloth gilt, 6s.

Pond (Major J. B.).—Eccentricities of Genius: Memories of Famous Men and Women of the Platform and the Stage. With 91 Portraits. Demy 8vo, cloth, 12s.

Pope's Poetical Works. Post 8vo, cloth limp, 2s.

Porter (John).—Kingsclere. Edited by BYRON WEBBER. With 19 full-page and many smaller Illustrations. Cheaper Edition. Demy 8vo, cloth, 7s. 6d.

Praed (Mrs. Campbell), Novels by. Post 8vo, illust. bds., 2s. each.

The Romance of a Station. | The Soul of Countess Adrian.

Crown 8vo, cloth, 3s. 6d. each; post 8vo, boards, 2s. each.

Outlaw and Lawmaker. | Christina Chard. With Frontispiece by W. PAGET.
Mrs. Tregaskiss. With 8 Illustrations by ROBERT SAUBER.

Crown 8vo, cloth, 3s. 6d. each.

Nulma. | Madame Izan.
'As a Watch in the Night.' Crown 8vo, cloth, gilt top, 6s.

Price (E. C.), Novels by. Crown 8vo, cloth, 3s. 6d. each.

Valentina. | The Foreigners. | Mrs. Lancaster's Rival.

Princess Olga.—Radna: A Novel. Crown 8vo, cloth extra, 6s.

Proctor (Richard A.), Works by.
Flowers of the Sky. With 55 Illustrations. Small crown 8vo, cloth extra, 3s. 6d.
Easy Star Lessons. With Star Maps for every Night in the Year. Crown 8vo, cloth, 6s.
Familiar Science Studies. Crown 8vo, cloth extra, 6s.
Saturn and its System. With 13 Steel Plates. Demy 8vo, cloth extra, 10s. 6d.
Mysteries of Time and Space. With numerous Illustrations. Crown 8vo, cloth extra, 6s.
The Universe of Suns, &c. With numerous Illustrations. Crown 8vo, cloth extra, 6s.
Wages and Wants of Science Workers. Crown 8vo, 1s. 6d.

Pryce (Richard).—Miss Maxwell's Affections. Crown 8vo, cloth,
with Frontispiece by HAL LUDLOW, 3s. 6d.; post 8vo, illustrated boards, 2s.

Rambosson (J.).—Popular Astronomy. Translated by C. B. PITMAN.
With 10 Coloured Plates and 63 Woodcut Illustrations. Crown 8vo, cloth, 3s. 6d.

Randolph (Col. G.).—Aunt Abigail Dykes. Crown 8vo, cloth, 7s. 6d.

Read (General Meredith).—Historic Studies in Vaud, Berne,
and Savoy. With 31 full-page Illustrations. Two Vols., demy 8vo, cloth, 28s.

Reade's (Charles) Novels.
The New Collected LIBRARY EDITION, complete in Seventeen Volumes, set in new long primer type, printed on laid paper, and elegantly bound in cloth, price 3s. 6d. each.

1. **Peg Woffington; and Christie John-stone.**
2. **Hard Cash.**
3. **The Cloister and the Hearth.** With a Preface by Sir WALTER BESANT.
4. **'It is Never Too Late to Mend.'**
5. **The Course of True Love Never Did Run Smooth; and Singleheart and Doubleface.**
6. **The Autobiography of a Thief; Jack of all Trades; A Hero and a Martyr; and The Wandering Heir.**
7. **Love Me Little, Love me Long.**
8. **The Double Marriage.**
9. **Griffith Gaunt.**
10. **Foul Play.**
11. **Put Yourself in His Place.**
12. **A Terrible Temptation.**
13. **A Simpleton.**
14. **A Woman-Hater.**
15. **The Jilt, and other Stories; and Good Stories of Man and other Animals.**
16. **A Perilous Secret.**
17. **Readiana; and Bible Characters.**

In Twenty-one Volumes, post 8vo, illustrated boards, 2s. each.

Peg Woffington. | Christie Johnstone.	Hard Cash. | Griffith Gaunt.
'It is Never Too Late to Mend.'	Foul Play. | Put Yourself in His Place.
The Course of True Love Never Did Run Smooth.	A Terrible Temptation
	A Simpleton. | The Wandering Heir.
The Autobiography of a Thief; Jack of all Trades; and James Lambert.	A Woman-Hater.
Love Me Little, Love Me Long.	Singleheart and Doubleface.
The Double Marriage.	Good Stories of Man and other Animals.
The Cloister and the Hearth.	The Jilt, and other Stories.
	A Perilous Secret. | Readiana.

POPULAR EDITIONS. Medium 8vo, 6d. each ; cloth, 1s. each.
Peg Woffington; and Christie Johnstone. | **Hard Cash.**
Medium 8vo, 6d. each.
'It is Never Too Late to Mend.' | **The Cloister and the Hearth.**

Christie Johnstone. With Frontispiece. Choicely printed in Elzevir style. Fcap. 8vo, half-Roxb. 2s. 6d.
Peg Woffington. Choicely printed in Elzevir style. Fcap. 8vo, half-Roxburghe, 2s. 6d.
The Cloister and the Hearth. In Four Vols., post 8vo, with an Introduction by Sir WALTER BESANT, and a Frontispiece to each Vol., buckram, gilt top, 6s. the set.—Also the LARGE TYPE, FINE PAPER EDITION, pott 8vo, cloth, 2s. net ; leather, 3s. net.
Bible Characters. Fcap. 8vo, leatherette, 1s.

Selections from the Works of Charles Reade. With an Introduction by Mrs. ALEX. IRELAND. Post 8vo, cloth limp, 2s. 6d.

Riddell (Mrs. J. H.), Novels by.
A Rich Man's Daughter. Crown 8vo, cloth, 3s. 6d.
Weird Stories. Crown 8vo, cloth extra, 3s. 6d. ; post 8vo, illustrated boards, 2s.
Post 8vo, illustrated boards, 2s. each.

The Uninhabited House.	Fairy Water.
The Prince of Wales's Garden Party.	Her Mother's Darling.
The Mystery in Palace Gardens.	The Nun's Curse. | Idle Tales.

Rimmer (Alfred), Works by. Large crown 8vo, cloth, 3s. 6d. each.
Rambles Round Eton and Harrow. With 52 Illustrations by the Author.
About England with Dickens. With 58 Illustrations by C. A. VANDERHOOF and A. RIMMER.

Rives (Amelie, Author of 'The Quick or the Dead?'), Stories by.
Crown 8vo, cloth, 3s. 6d. each.
Barbara Dering. | **Meriel: A Love Story.**

Robinson Crusoe. By DANIEL DEFOE. With 37 Illustrations by
GEORGE CRUIKSHANK. Post 8vo, half-cloth, 2s.

Robinson (F. W.), Novels by.
Woman are Strange. Post 8vo, illustrated boards, 2s.
The Hands of Justice. Crown 8vo, cloth extra, 3s. 6d. ; post 8vo illustrated boards, 2s.
The Woman in the Dark. Crown 8vo, cloth, 3s. 6d. ; post 8vo, illustrated boards, 2s.

Robinson (Phil), Works by. Crown 8vo, cloth extra, 6s. each.
The Poets' Birds. | The Poets' Beasts.
The Poets and Nature: Reptiles, Fishes, and Insects.

Roll of Battle Abbey, The: A List of the Principal Warriors who came from Normandy with William the Conqueror, 1066. Printed in Gold and Colours, 5s.

Rosengarten (A.).—A Handbook of Architectural Styles. Translated by W. COLLETT-SANDARS. With 639 Illustrations. Crown 8vo, cloth extra, 7s. 6d.

Ross (Albert).—A Sugar Princess. Crown 8vo, cloth, 3s. 6d.

Rowley (Hon. Hugh), Works by. Post 8vo, cloth, 2s. 6d. each.
Puniana: Riddles and Jokes. With numerous Illustrations.
More Puniana. Profusely Illustrated.

Runciman (James), Stories by. Post 8vo, cloth, 2s. 6d. each.
Grace Balmaign's Sweetheart. | Schools & Scholars.
Skippers and Shellbacks. Crown 8vo, cloth, 3s. 6d.

Russell (Dora), Novels by.
A Country Sweetheart. Post 8vo, picture boards, 2s.
The Drift of Fate. Crown 8vo, cloth, 3s. 6d.

Russell (Herbert).—True Blue; or, 'The Lass that Loved a Sailor.' Crown 8vo, cloth, 3s. 6d.

Russell (W. Clark), Novels, &c., by.
Crown 8vo, cloth extra, 3s. 6d. each ; post 8vo, illustrated boards, 2s. each ; cloth limp, 2s. 6d. each.
Round the Galley-Fire. | An Ocean Tragedy.
In the Middle Watch. | My Shipmate Louise.
On the Fo'k'sle Head. | Alone on a Wide Wide Sea.
A Voyage to the Cape. | The Good Ship 'Mohock.'
A Book for the Hammock. | The Phantom Death.
The Mystery of the 'Ocean Star.' | Is He the Man? | The Convict Ship.
The Romance of Jenny Harlowe. | Heart of Oak. | The Last Entry.
The Tale of the Ten.
Crown 8vo, cloth, 3s. 6d. each,
A Tale of Two Tunnels. | The Death Ship.
The Ship: Her Story. With 50 Illustrations by H. C. SEPPINGS WRIGHT. Small 4to, cloth, 6s.
The "Pretty Polly": A Voyage of Incident. With 12 Illustrations by G. E. ROBERTSON. Large crown 8vo. cloth. gilt edges. 5s.

Saint Aubyn (Alan), Novels by.
Crown 8vo, cloth extra, 3s. 6d. each ; post 8vo, illustrated boards, 2s. each.
A Fellow of Trinity. With a Note by OLIVER WENDELL HOLMES and a Frontispiece.
The Junior Dean. | The Master of St. Benedict's. | To His Own Master.
Orchard Damerel. | In the Face of the World. | The Tremlett Diamonds.
Fcap. 8vo, cloth boards, 1s. 6d. each.
The Old Maid's Sweetheart. | Modest Little Sara.
Crown 8vo, cloth, 3s. 6d. each,
The Wooing of May. | A Tragic Honeymoon. | A Proctor's Wooing.
Fortune's Gate. | Gallantry Bower. | Bonnie Maggie Lauder.
Mary Unwin. With 8 Illustrations by PERCY TARRANT.
Mrs. Dunbar's Secret. Crown 8vo, cloth, gilt top 6s.

Saint John (Bayle).—A Levantine Family. A New Edition. Crown 8vo, cloth, 3s. 6d.

Sala (George A.).—Gaslight and Daylight. Post 8vo, boards. 2s.

Scotland Yard, Past and Present: Experiences of Thirty-seven Years. By Ex-Chief-Inspector CAVANAGH. Post 8vo, illustrated boards, 2s. ; cloth, 2s. 6d.

Secret Out, The: One Thousand Tricks with Cards: with Entertaining Experiments in Drawing-room or 'White' Magic. By W. H. CREMER. With 300 Illustrations. Crown 8vo, cloth extra, 4s. 6d.

Seguin (L. G.), Works by.
The Country of the Passion Play (Oberammergau) and the Highlands of Bavaria. With Map and 37 Illustrations. Crown 8vo, cloth extra, 3s. 6d.
Walks in Algiers. With Two Maps and 16 Illustrations. Crown 8vo, cloth extra, 6s.

Senior (Wm.).—By Stream and Sea. Post 8vo, cloth, 2s. 6d.

Sergeant (Adeline), Novels by. Crown 8vo, cloth, 3s. 6d. each.
Under False Pretences. | Dr. Endicott's Experiment.

Shakespeare for Children: Lamb's Tales from Shakespeare. With Illustrations, coloured and plain, by J. MOYR SMITH. Crown 4to. cloth gilt, 3s. 6d.

Shakespeare the Boy. With Sketches of the Home and School Life, the Games and Sports, the Manners, Customs, and Folk-lore of the Time. By WILLIAM J. ROLFE, Litt.D. A New Edition, with 42 Illustrations, and an INDEX OF PLAYS AND PASSAGES REFERRED TO. Crown 8vo. cloth gilt, 3s. 6d.

Sharp (William).—Children of To-morrow. Crown 8vo, cloth, 6s.

Shelley's (Percy Bysshe) Complete Works in Verse and Prose.
Edited, Prefaced, and Annotated by R. HERNE SHEPHERD. Five Vols., crown 8vo, cloth, 3s. 6d. each.
Poetical Works, in Three Vols.:
Vol. I. Introduction by the Editor; Posthumous Fragments of Margaret Nicholson; Shelley's Corre-
spondence with Stockdale; The Wandering Jew; Queen Mab, with the Notes; Alastor,
and other Poems; Rosalind and Helen; Prometheus Unbound; Adonais, &c.
„ II. Laon and Cythna; The Cenci; Julian and Maddalo; Swellfoot the Tyrant; The Witch of
Atlas; Epipsychidion; Hellas.
„ III. Posthumous Poems; The Masque of Anarchy; and other Pieces.
Prose Works, in Two Vols.:
Vol. I. The Two Romances of Zastrozzi and St. Irvyne; the Dublin and Marlow Pamphlets; A Refu
tation of Deism; Letters to Leigh Hunt, and some Minor Writings and Fragments.
II. The Essays; Letters from Abroad; Translations and Fragments, edited by Mrs. SHELLEY.
With a Biography of Shelley, and an Index of the Prose Works.

Sherard (R. H.).—Rogues: A Novel. Crown 8vo, cloth, 1s. 6d.

Sheridan's (Richard Brinsley) Complete Works, with Life and
Anecdotes. Including his Dramatic Writings, his Works in Prose and Poetry, Translations, Speeches,
and Jokes. Crown 8vo, cloth, 3s. 6d.
The Rivals, The School for Scandal, and other Plays. Post 8vo, half-bound, 2s.
Sheridan's Comedies: The Rivals and **The School for Scandal**. Edited, with an Intro-
duction and Notes to each Play, and a Biographical Sketch, by BRANDER MATTHEWS. With
Illustrations. Demy 8vo, half-parchment, 12s. 6d.

Shiel (M. P.).—The Purple Cloud. By the Author of "The Yellow
Danger." Crown 8vo, cloth, gilt top, 6s.   [Preparing.

Sidney's (Sir Philip) Complete Poetical Works, including all
those in 'Arcadia.' With Portrait, Memorial-Introduction, Notes, &c., by the Rev. A. B. GROSART,
D.D. Three Vols., crown 8vo, cloth boards, 3s. 6d. each.

Signboards: Their History, including Anecdotes of Famous Taverns and
Remarkable Characters. By JACOB LARWOOD and JOHN CAMDEN HOTTEN. With Coloured Frontispiece and 94 Illustrations. Crown 8vo, cloth extra, 3s. 6d.

Sims (George R.), Works by.
Post 8vo, illustrated boards, 2s. each; cloth limp, 2s. 6d. each.

The Ring o' Bells.	**Dramas of Life.** With 60 Illustrations.
Mary Jane's Memoirs.	**Memoirs of a Landlady.**
Tinkletop's Crime.	**My Two Wives.**
Zeph: A Circus Story, &c.	**Scenes from the Show.**
Tales of To-day.	**The Ten Commandments:** Stories.

Crown 8vo, picture cover, 1s. each; cloth, 1s. 6d. each.
The Dagonet Reciter and Reader: Being Readings and Recitations in Prose and Verse
selected from his own Works by GEORGE R. SIMS.

The Case of George Candlemas.	**Dagonet Ditties.** (From The Referee.)

How the Poor Live; and **Horrible London.** With a Frontispiece by F. BARNARD.
Crown 8vo, leatherette, 1s.
Dagonet Dramas of the Day. Crown 8vo, 1s.

Crown 8vo, cloth, 3s. 6d. each; post 8vo, picture boards, 2s. each; cloth limp, 2s. 6d. each.

Mary Jane Married.	**Rogues and Vagabonds.**	**Dagonet Abroad.**

Crown 8vo, cloth, 3s. 6d. each.
Once upon a Christmas Time. With 8 Illustrations by CHARLES GREEN, R.I.
In London's Heart: A Story of To-day.
Without the Limelight: Theatrical Life as it is.
The Small-part Lady, &c.

Sister Dora: A Biography. By MARGARET LONSDALE. With Four
Illustrations. Demy 8vo, picture cover, 4d.; cloth, 6d.

Sketchley (Arthur).—A Match in the Dark. Post 8vo, boards, 2s.

Slang Dictionary (The): Etymological, Historical, and Anecdotal.
Crown 8vo, cloth extra, 6s. 6d.

Smart (Hawley), Novels by.
Crown 8vo, cloth 3s. 6d. each; post 8vo, picture boards, 2s. each.

Beatrice and Benedick.	**Long Odds.**
Without Love or Licence.	**The Master of Rathkelly.**

Crown 8vo, cloth, 3s. 6d. each.

The Outsider.	**A Racing Rubber.**

The Plunger. Post 8vo, picture boards, 2s.

Smith (J. Moyr), Works by.
The Prince of Argolis. With 130 Illustrations. Post 8vo, cloth extra, 3s. 6d.
The Wooing of the Water Witch. With numerous Illustrations. Post 8vo, cloth, 6s.

Snazelleparilla. Decanted by G. S. EDWARDS. With Portrait of
G. H. SNAZELLE, and 65 Illustrations by C. LYALL. Crown 8vo, cloth, 3s. 6d.

Society in London. Crown 8vo, 1s.; cloth, 1s. 6d.

Somerset (Lord Henry).—Songs of Adieu. Small 4to, Jap. vel., 6s.

Spalding (T. A., LL.B.).—Elizabethan Demonology: An Essay on the Belief in the Existence of Devils. Crown 8vo, cloth extra, 5s.

Speight (T. W.), Novels by.
Post 8vo, illustrated boards, 2s. each.
The Mysteries of Heron Dyke. | The Loudwater Tragedy.
By Devious Ways, &c. | Burgo's Romance.
Hoodwinked; & Sandycroft Mystery. | Quittance in Full.
The Golden Hoop. | A Husband from the Sea.
Back to Life.

Post 8vo, cloth limp, 1s. 6d. each.
A Barren Title. | Wife or No Wife?

Crown 8vo, cloth extra, 3s. 6d. each.
A Secret of the Sea. | The Grey Monk. | The Master of Trenance.
A Minion of the Moon. | A Romance of the King's Highway.
The Secret of Wyvern Towers.
The Doom of Siva. | The Web of Fate.
The Strange Experiences of Mr. Verschoyle.

Spenser for Children. By M. H. TOWRY. With Coloured Illustrations by WALTER J. MORGAN. Crown 4to, cloth extra, 3s. 6d.

Spettigue (H. H.).—The Heritage of Eve. Crown 8vo, cloth, 6s.

Stafford (John), Novels by.
Doris and I. Crown 8vo, cloth, 3s. 6d.
Carlton Priors. Crown 8vo, cloth, gilt top, 6s.

Starry Heavens (The): A POETICAL BIRTHDAY BOOK. Royal 16mo, cloth extra, 2s. 6d.

Stedman (E. C.).—Victorian Poets. Crown 8vo, cloth extra, 9s.

Stephens (Riccardo, M.B.).—The Cruciform Mark: The Strange Story of RICHARD TREGENNA, Bachelor of Medicine (Univ. Edinb.) Crown 8vo, cloth, 3s. 6d.

Stephens (Robert Neilson).—Philip Winwood: A Sketch of the Domestic History of an American Captain in the War of Independence; embracing events that occurred between and during the years 1763 and 1786, in New York and London; written by His Enemy in War, HERBERT RUSSELL, Lieutenant in the Loyalist Forces. With Six Illustrations by E. W. D. HAMILTON. Crown 8vo, cloth, gilt top, 6s.

Sterndale (R. Armitage).—The Afghan Knife: A Novel. Post 8vo, cloth, 3s. 6d.; illustrated boards, 2s.

Stevenson (R. Louis), Works by.
Crown 8vo, buckram, gilt top, 6s. each.
Travels with a Donkey. With a Frontispiece by WALTER CRANE.
An Inland Voyage. With a Frontispiece by WALTER CRANE.
Familiar Studies of Men and Books.
The Silverado Squatters. With Frontispiece by J. D. STRONG.
The Merry Men. | Underwoods: Poems.
Memories and Portraits.
Virginibus Puerisque, and other Papers. | Ballads. | Prince Otto.
Across the Plains, with other Memories and Essays.
Weir of Hermiston. | In the South Seas.

A Lowden Sabbath Morn. With 27 Illustrations by A. S. BOYD. Fcap. 8vo, cloth, 6s.
Songs of Travel. Crown 8vo, buckram, 5s.
New Arabian Nights. Crown 8vo, buckram, gilt top, 6s.; post 8vo, illustrated boards, 2s.
—POPULAR EDITION, medium 8vo, 6d. [Shortly.
The Suicide Club; and The Rajah's Diamond. (From NEW ARABIAN NIGHTS.) With Eight Illustrations by W. J. HENNESSY. Crown 8vo, cloth, 3s. 6d.
The Stevenson Reader: Selections from the Writings of ROBERT LOUIS STEVENSON. Edited by LLOYD OSBOURNE. Post 8vo, cloth, 2s. 6d.; buckram, gilt top, 3s. 6d.
Robert Louis Stevenson: A Life Study in Criticism. By H. BELLYSE BAILDON. With 2 Portraits. Crown 8vo, buckram, gilt top, 6s.

Stockton (Frank R.).—The Young Master of Hyson Hall. With numerous Illustrations by VIRGINIA H. DAVISSON and C. H. STEPHENS. Crown 8vo, cloth, 3s. 6d.

Storey (G. A., A.R.A.).—Sketches from Memory. With 93 Illustrations by the Author. Demy 8vo, cloth, gilt top, 12s. 6d.

Stories from Foreign Novelists. With Notices by HELEN and ALICE ZIMMERN. Crown 8vo, cloth extra 3s. 6d.

Strange Manuscript (A) Found in a Copper Cylinder. Crown 8vo, cloth extra, with 19 Illustrations by GILBERT GAUL, 3s. 6d.; post 8vo, illustrated boards, 2s.

Strange Secrets. Told by PERCY FITZGERALD, CONAN DOYLE, FLORENCE MARRYAT, &c. Post 8vo, illustrated boards, 2s.

Strutt (Joseph). — The Sports and Pastimes of the People of England: including the Rural and Domestic Recreations, May Games, Mummeries, Shows, &c., from the Earliest Period to the Present Time. Edited by WILLIAM HONE. With 140 Illustrations. Crown 8vo, cloth extra, 3s. 6d.

Sundowner.—Told by the Taffrail. Cr. 8vo, cloth, 3s. 6d. [*Shortly*.

Surtees (Robert).—Handley Cross; or, Mr. Jorrocks's Hunt.
With 79 Illustrations by JOHN LEECH. A New Edition. Post 8vo, cloth, 2s.

Swift's (Dean) Choice Works, in Prose and Verse. With Memoir,
Portrait, and Facsimiles of the Maps in 'Gulliver's Travels.' Crown 8vo, cloth, 3s. 6d.
Gulliver's Travels, and **A Tale of a Tub.** Post 8vo, half-bound, 2s.
Jonathan Swift: A Study. By J. CHURTON COLLINS. Crown 8vo, cloth extra, 8s.

Swinburne (Algernon C.), Works by.

Selections from the Poetical Works of A. C. Swinburne. Fcap. 8vo 6s.
Atalanta in Calydon. Crown 8vo, 6s.
Chastelard: A Tragedy. Crown 8vo, 7s.
Poems and Ballads. FIRST SERIES. Crown 8vo, or fcap. 8vo, 9s.
Poems and Ballads. SECOND SER. Cr. 8vo, 9s.
Poems & Ballads. THIRD SERIES. Cr. 8vo, 7s.
Songs before Sunrise. Crown 8vo, 10s. 6d.
Bothwell: A Tragedy. Crown 8vo, 12s. 6d.
Songs of Two Nations. Crown 8vo, 6s.
George Chapman. (*See* Vol. II. of G. CHAPMAN'S Works.) Crown 8vo, 3s. 6d.
Essays and Studies. Crown 8vo, 12s.
Erechtheus: A Tragedy. Crown 8vo, 6s.
A Note on Charlotte Bronte. Cr. 8vo, 6s.
A Study of Shakespeare. Crown 8vo, 8s.
Songs of the Springtides. Crown 8vo, 6s.

Studies in Song. Crown 8vo, 7s.
Mary Stuart: A Tragedy. Crown 8vo, 8s.
Tristram of Lyonesse. Crown 8vo, 9s.
A Century of Roundels. Small 4to, 8s.
A Midsummer Holiday. Crown 8vo, 7s.
Marino Faliero: A Tragedy. Crown 8vo, 6s.
A Study of Victor Hugo. Crown 8vo, 6s.
Miscellanies. Crown 8vo, 12s.
Locrine: A Tragedy. Crown 8vo, 6s.
A Study of Ben Jonson. Crown 8vo, 7s.
The Sisters: A Tragedy. Crown 8vo, 6s.
Astrophel, &c. Crown 8vo, 7s.
Studies in Prose and Poetry. Cr. 8vo, 9s.
The Tale of Balen. Crown 8vo, 7s.
Rosamund, Queen of the Lombards: A Tragedy. SECOND EDITION, with a DEDICATORY POEM. Crown 8vo, 6s.

Syntax's (Dr.) Three Tours: In Search of the Picturesque, in Search
of Consolation, and in Search of a Wife. With ROWLANDSON'S Coloured Illustrations, and Life of the Author by J. C. HOTTEN. Crown 8vo, cloth extra, 7s. 6d.

Taine's History of English Literature. Translated by HENRY VAN
LAUN. Four Vols., small demy 8vo, cloth boards, 30s.—POPULAR EDITION, Two Vols., large crown 8vo, cloth extra, 15s.

Taylor (Bayard). — Diversions of the Echo Club: Burlesques of
Modern Writers. Post 8vo, cloth limp, 2s.

Taylor (Tom).—Historical Dramas: 'JEANNE DARC,' ''TWIXT AXE
AND CROWN,' 'THE FOOL'S REVENGE,' 'ARKWRIGHT'S WIFE,' 'ANNE BOLEYNE,' 'PLOT AND PASSION.' Crown 8vo, 1s. each.

Temple (Sir Richard, G.C.S.I.).—A Bird's-eye View of Pictur-
esque India. With 32 Illustrations by the Author. Crown 8vo, cloth, gilt top, 6s.

Thackerayana: Notes and Anecdotes. With Coloured Frontispiece and
Hundreds of Sketches by WILLIAM MAKEPEACE THACKERAY. Crown 8vo, cloth extra, 3s. 6d.

Thames, A New Pictorial History of the. By A. S. KRAUSSE.
With 340 Illustrations. Post 8vo, cloth, 1s. 6d.

Thomas (Annie), Novels by.
The Siren's Web: A Romance of London Society. Crown 8vo, cloth, 3s. 6d.
Comrades True. Crown 8vo, cloth, gilt top, 6s.

Thomas (Bertha), Novels by.
Crown 8vo, cloth, 3s. 6d. each.
The Violin-Player. | **The House on the Scar.** [*Preparing*.
Crown 8vo, cloth, gilt top, 6s. each.
In a Cathedral City. | **The Son of the House.**

Thomson's Seasons, and The Castle of Indolence. With Introduction by ALLAN CUNNINGHAM, and 48 Illustrations. Post 8vo, half-bound, 2s.

Thornbury (Walter), Books by.
The Life and Correspondence of J. M. W. Turner. With Eight Illustrations in Colours and Two Woodcuts. New and Revised Edition. Crown 8vo, cloth, 3s. 6d.
Tales for the Marines. Post 8vo, illustrated boards, 2s.

Timbs (John), Works by. Crown 8vo, cloth, 3s. 6d. each.
Clubs and Club Life in London: Anecdotes of its Famous Coffee-houses, Hostelries, and Taverns. With 41 Illustrations.
English Eccentrics and Eccentricities: Stories of Delusions, Impostures, Sporting Scenes, Eccentric Artists, Theatrical Folk, &c. With 48 Illustrations.

Trollope (Anthony), Novels by.
Crown 8vo, cloth extra, 3s. 6d. each; post 8vo, illustrated boards, 2s. each.
The Way We Live Now. | **Mr. Scarborough's Family.**
Frau Frohmann. | **Marion Fay.** | **The Land-Leaguers.**
Post 8vo, illustrated boards, 2s. each.
Kept in the Dark. | **The American Senator.**
The Golden Lion of Granpere. |

Trollope (Frances E.), Novels by.
Crown 8vo, cloth extra, 3s. 6d. each; post 8vo, illustrated boards, 2s. each.
Like Ships upon the Sea. | **Mabel's Progress.** | **Anne Furness.**

Trollope (T. A.).—Diamond Cut Diamond. Post 8vo, illust. bds., 2s.

Twain's (Mark) Books.
The Author's Edition de Luxe of the Works of Mark Twain, in 22 Volumes limited to 600 Numbered Copies for sale in Great Britain and its Dependencies), price £13 15s. net the Set; or, 12s. 6d. net per Volume. is now complete, and a detailed Prospectus may be had. The First Volume of the Set is SIGNED BY THE AUTHOR. (Sold only in Sets.)

UNIFORM LIBRARY EDITION OF MARK TWAIN'S WORKS.
Crown 8vo, cloth extra, 3s. 6d. each.
Mark Twain's Library of Humour. With 197 Illustrations by E. W. KEMBLR.
Roughing It; and The Innocents at Home. With 200 Illustrations by F. A. FRASER.
The American Claimant. With 81 Illustrations by HAL HURST and others.
*The Adventures of Tom Sawyer.** With 111 Illustrations.
Tom Sawyer Abroad. With 26 Illustrations by DAN BEARD.
Tom Sawyer, Detective, &c. With Photogravure Portrait of the Author.
Pudd'nhead Wilson. With Portrait and Six Illustrations by LOUIS LOEB.
*A Tramp Abroad.** With 314 Illustrations.
*The Innocents Abroad; or, The New Pilgrim's Progress.** With 234 Illustrations. (The Two Shilling Edition is entitled **Mark Twain's Pleasure Trip.**)
*The Gilded Age.** By MARK TWAIN and C. D. WARNER With 212 Illustrations.
*The Prince and the Pauper.** With 190 Illustrations.
*Life on the Mississippi.** With 300 Illustrations.
*The Adventures of Huckleberry Finn.** With 174 Illustrations by E. W. KEMBLR.
*A Yankee at the Court of King Arthur.** With 220 Illustrations by DAN BEARD.
*The Stolen White Elephant.** | *The £1,000,000 Bank-Note.**
The Choice Works of Mark Twain. Revised and Corrected throughout by the Author. With Life, Portrait, and numerous Illustrations.
*** The books marked * may be had also in post 8vo, picture boards, at 2s. each.

Crown 8vo, cloth, gilt top, 6s. each,
Personal Recollections of Joan of Arc. With Twelve Illustrations by F. V. DU MOND.
More Tramps Abroad.
The Man that Corrupted Hadleyburg, and other Stories and Sketches. With a Frontispiece.
Mark Twain's Sketches. Post 8vo, illustrated boards, 2s.

Tytler (C. C. Fraser-).—Mistress Judith: A Novel. Crown 8vo,
cloth extra, 3s. 6d.; post 8vo, illustrated boards, 2s.

Tytler (Sarah), Novels by.
Crown 8vo, cloth extra, 3s. 6d. each; post 8vo, illustrated boards, 2s. each.
Lady Bell. | **Buried Diamonds.** | **The Blackhall Ghosts.** | **What She Came Through.**

Post 8vo, illustrated boards, 2s. each,
Citoyenne Jacqueline.   **The Huguenot Family.**
The Bride's Pass.   **Noblesse Oblige.** | **Disappeared.**
Saint Mungo's City.   **Beauty and the Beast.**

Crown 8vo, cloth, 3s. 6d. each.
The Macdonald Lass. With Frontispiece. | **Mrs. Carmichael's Goddesses.**
The Witch-Wife. | **Rachel Langton.** | **Sapphira.** | **A Honeymoon's Eclipse.**
A Young Dragon.

Upward (Allen), Novels by.
A Crown of Straw. Crown 8vo, cloth, 6s.

The Queen Against Owen. Crown 8vo, cloth, 3s. 6d.; post 8vo, picture boards, 2s.
The Prince of Balkistan. Post 8vo, picture boards, 2s.

Vandam (Albert D.).—A Court Tragedy. With 6 Illustrations by
J. BARNARD DAVIS. Crown 8vo, cloth, 3s. 6d.

Vashti and Esther. By 'Belle' of The World. Cr. 8vo, cloth, 3s. 6d.

Vizetelly (Ernest A.), Books by. Crown 8vo, cloth, 3s. 6d. each.
The Scorpion: A Romance of Spain. With a Frontispiece.
With Zola in England: A Story of Exile. With 4 Portraits.

A Path of Thorns. Crown 8vo, cloth, gilt top, 6s.

Wagner (Leopold).—How to Get on the Stage, and how to
Succeed there. Crown 8vo, cloth, 2s. 6d.

Walford's County Families of the United Kingdom (1901).
Containing Notices of the Descent, Birth, Marriage, Education, &c., of more than 12,000 Distinguished Heads of Families, their Heirs Apparent or Presumptive, the Offices they hold or have held, their Town and Country Addresses, Clubs, &c. Royal 8vo, cloth gilt, 50s.

Waller (S. E.).—Sebastiani's Secret. With 9 Illusts. Cr. 8vo, cl.,6s.

Walton and Cotton's Complete Angler. With Memoirs and Notes
by Sir HARRIS NICOLAS, and 61 Illustrations. Crown 8vo, cloth antique, 7s. 6d.

Walt Whitman, Poems by. Edited, with Introduction, by WILLIAM
M. ROSSETTI. With Portrait. Crown 8vo, hand-made paper and buckram, 6s.

Warden (Florence).—Joan, the Curate. Crown 8vo, cloth, 3s. 6d.

Warman (Cy).—The Express Messenger, and other Tales of the Rail. Crown 8vo, cloth, 3s. 6d.

Warner (Charles Dudley).—A Roundabout Journey. Crown 8vo, cloth extra, 6s.

Wassermann (Lillias).—The Daffodils. Crown 8vo, cloth, 1s. 6d.

Warrant to Execute Charles I. A Facsimile, with the 59 Signatures and Seals. Printed on paper 22 in. 2s.
Warrant to Execute Mary Queen of Scots. A Facsimile, including Queen Elizabeth's Signature and Seal. 2s.

Weather, How to Foretell the, with the Pocket Spectroscope. By F. W. CORY. With Ten Illustrations. Crown 8vo, 1s.; cloth, 1s. 6d.

Westall (William), Novels by.
Trust Money. Crown 8vo, cloth, 3s. 6d.; post 8vo, illustrated boards, 2s.

Crown 8vo, cloth, 6s. each.

| As a Man Sows. | A Red Bridal. Her Lady hip's Secret. | As Luck would have it. |

Crown 8vo, cloth 3s. 6d. each.

A Woman Tempted Him.	Nigel Fortescue.	The Phantom City.
For Honour and Life.	Ben Clough.	Birch Dene.	Ralph Norbreck's Trust.
Her Two Millions.	The Old Factory.	A Queer Race.
Two Pinches of Snuff.	Sons of Belial.	Red Ryvington.
	With the Red Eagle.	

Roy of Roy's Court. With 6 Illustrations. Crown 8vo, cloth, 3s. 6d.
Strange Crimes. (True Stories.) Crown 8vo, cloth, 3s. 6d.
The Old Factory. POPULAR EDITION. Medium 8vo, 6d.

Westbury (Atha).—The Shadow of Hilton Fernbrook: A Ro-mance of Maoriland. Crown 8vo, cloth, 3s. 6d.

Whishaw (Fred.).—A Forbidden Name : A Story of the Court of Catherine the Great. Crown 8vo, cloth, gilt top 6s. [Shortly.

White (Gilbert).—The Natural History of Selborne. Post 8vo, printed on laid paper and half-bound, 2s.

Wilde (Lady). — The Ancient Legends, Mystic Charms, and Superstitions of Ireland ; with Sketches of the Irish Past. Crown 8vo, cloth, 3s. 6d.

Williams (W. Mattieu, F.R.A.S.), Works by.
Science in Short Chapters. Crown 8vo, cloth extra, 7s. 6d.
A Simple Treatise on Heat. With Illustrations. Crown 8vo, cloth, 2s. 6d.
The Chemistry of Cookery. Crown 8vo, cloth extra, 6s.
A Vindication of Phrenology. With Portrait and 43 Illusts. Demy 8vo, cloth extra, 12s. 6d.

Williamson (Mrs. F. H.).—A Child Widow. Post 8vo, bds., 2s.

Wills (C. J.), Novels by.
An Easy-going Fellow. Crown 8vo, cloth, 3s. 6d. | His Dead Past. Crown 8vo, cloth, 6s.

Wilson (Dr. Andrew, F.R.S.E.), Works by.
Chapters on Evolution. With 259 Illustrations. Crown 8vo, cloth extra, 7s. 6d.
Leaves from a Naturalist's Note-Book. Post 8vo, cloth limp, 2s. 6d.
Leisure-Time Studies. With Illustrations. Crown 8vo, cloth extra, 6s.
Studies in Life and Sense. With 36 Illustrations. Crown 8vo, cloth, 3s. 6d.
Common Accidents: How to Treat Them. With Illustrations. Crown 8vo, 1s.; cloth, 1s. 6d.
Glimpses of Nature. With 35 Illustrations. Crown 8vo, cloth extra, 3s. 6d.

Winter (John Strange), Stories by. Post 8vo, illustrated boards, 2s. each; cloth limp, 2s. 6d. each.

| Cavalry Life. | Regimental Legends. |

Cavalry Life and Regimental Legends. LIBRARY EDITION, set in new type and hand-somely bound. Crown 8vo, cloth, 3s. 6d.
A Soldier's Children. With 34 Illustrations by E. G. THOMSON and E. STUART HARDY. Crown 8vo, cloth extra, 3s. 6d.

Wissmann (Hermann von). — My Second Journey through Equatorial Africa. With 92 Illustrations. Demy 8vo, cloth, 16s.

Wood (H. F.), Detective Stories by. Post 8vo, boards, 2s. each.
The Passenger from Scotland Yard. | The Englishman of the Rue Cain.

Woolley (Celia Parker).—Rachel Armstrong ; or, Love and The-ology. Post 8vo, cloth, 2s. 6d.

Wright (Thomas, F.S.A.), Works by.
Caricature History of the Georges ; or, Annals of the House of Hanover. Compiled from Squibs, Broadsides, Window Pictures, Lampoons, and Pictorial Caricatures of the Time. With over 300 Illustrations. Crown 8vo, cloth, 3s. 6d.
History of Caricature and of the Grotesque in Art, Literature, Sculpture, and Painting. Illustrated by F. W. FAIRHOLT, F.S.A. Crown 8vo, cloth, 7s. 6d.

Wynman (Margaret).—My Flirtations. With 13 Illustrations by J. BERNARD PARTRIDGE. Post 8vo, cloth limp, 2s.

Zola (Emile), Novels by. Crown 8vo, cloth extra, 3s. 6d. each.

The Fortune of the Rougons. Edited by ERNEST A. VIZETELLY.
Abbe Mouret's Transgression. Edited by ERNEST A. VIZETELLY.
The Conquest of Plassans. Edited by ERNEST A. VIZETELLY.
Germinal; or, Master and Man. Edited by ERNEST A. VIZETELLY.
The Honour of the Army, and other Stories. Edited by ERNEST A. VIZETELLY. [Shortly.
His Excellency (Eugene Rougon). With Introduction by ERNEST A. VIZETELLY.
The Dram-Shop (L'Assommoir). With Introduction by ERNEST A. VIZETELLY.
The Fat and the Thin. Translated by ERNEST A. VIZETELLY. VIZETELLY.
Money. Translated by ERNEST A. VIZETELLY.
The Downfall. Translated by E. A. VIZETELLY.
The Dream. Translated by ELIZA CHASE. With Eight Illustrations by JEANNIOT.
Doctor Pascal. Translated by E. A. VIZETELLY. With Portrait of the Author.
Lourdes. Translated by ERNEST A. VIZETELLY.
Rome. Translated by ERNEST A. VIZETELLY.
Paris. Translated by ERNEST A. VIZETELLY.
Fruitfulness (Fécondité). Translated and Edited, with an Introduction, by E. A. VIZETELLY.
Work. Translated by ERNEST A. VIZETELLY. [April.

With Zola in England. By ERNEST A. VIZETELLY. With Four Portraits. Crown 8vo, cloth, 3s. 6d.

'ZZ' (L. Zangwill).—A Nineteenth Century Miracle. Cr. 8vo, 3s. 6d.

SOME BOOKS CLASSIFIED IN SERIES.

₊ For fuller cataloguing, see alphabetical arrangement, pp. 1-26.

The Mayfair Library. Post 8vo, cloth limp, 2s. 6d. per Volume.

Quips and Quiddities. By W. D. ADAMS.
The Agony Column of 'The Times.'
A Journey Round My Room. By X. DE MAISTRE. Translated by HENRY ATTWELL.
Poetical Ingenuities. By W. T. DOBSON.
The Cupboard Papers. By FIN-BEC.
W. S. Gilbert's Plays. Three Series.
Songs of Irish Wit and Humour.
Animals and their Masters. By Sir A HELPS.
Social Pressure. By Sir A. HELPS.
Autocrat of Breakfast-Table. By O. W. HOLMES.
Curiosities of Criticism. By H. J. JENNINGS.
Pencil and Palette. By R. KEMPT.
Little Essays: from LAMB'S LETTERS.
Forensic Anecdotes. By JACOB LARWOOD.
Theatrical Anecdotes. By JACOB LARWOOD.
Ourselves. By E. LYNN LINTON.
Witch Stories. By E. LYNN LINTON.
Pastimes and Players. By R. MACGREGOR.
Now Paul and Virginia. By W. H. MALLOCK.
Muses of Mayfair. Edited by H. C. PENNELL.
Thoreau: His Life and Aims. By H. A. PAGE.
Puck on Pegasus. By H. C. PENNELL.
Pegasus Re-saddled. By H. C. PENNELL.
Puniana. By Hon. HUGH ROWLEY.
More Puniana. By Hon. HUGH ROWLEY.
By Stream and Sea. By WILLIAM SENIOR.
Leaves from a Naturalist's Note-Book. By Dr. ANDREW WILSON.

The Golden Library. Post 8vo, cloth limp, 2s. per Volume.

Songs for Sailors. By W. C. BENNETT.
Lives of the Necromancers. By W. GODWIN.
The Autocrat of the Breakfast Table. By OLIVER WENDELL HOLMES.
Tale for a Chimney Corner. By LEIGH HUNT.
Scenes of Country Life. By EDWARD JESSE.
La Mort d'Arthur: Selections from MALLORY.
The Poetical Works of Alexander Pope.
Diversions of the Echo Club. BAYARD TAYLOR.

Handy Novels. Fcap. 8vo, cloth boards, 1s. 6d. each.

Dr. Palliser's Patient. By GRANT ALLEN.
Monte Carlo Stories. By JOAN BARRETT.
Black Spirits and White. By R. A. CRAM.
Seven Sleepers of Ephesus. M. E. COLERIDGE.
The Old Maid's Sweetheart. By A. ST. AUBYN.
Modest Little Sara. By ALAN ST. AUBYN.

My Library. Printed on laid paper, post 8vo, half-Roxburghe, 2s. 6d. each.

The Journal of Maurice de Guerin.
The Dramatic Essays of Charles Lamb.
Citation and Examination of William Shakspeare. By W. S. LANDOR.
Christie Johnstone. By CHARLES READE.
Peg Woffington. By CHARLES READE.

The Pocket Library. Post 8vo, printed on laid paper and hf.-bd., 2s. each.

Gastronomy. By BRILLAT-SAVARIN.
Robinson Crusoe. Illustrated by G. CRUIKSHANK.
Autocrat of the Breakfast-Table and The Professor at the Breakfast-Table. By O. W. HOLMES.
Provincial Letters of Blaise Pascal.
Whims and Oddities. By THOMAS HOOD.
Leigh Hunt's Essays. Edited by E. OLLIER.
The Barber's Chair. By DOUGLAS JERROLD.
The Essays of Elia. By CHARLES LAMB.
Anecdotes of the Clergy. By JACOB LARWOOD.
The Epicurean, &c. By THOMAS MOORE.
Plays by RICHARD BRINSLEY SHERIDAN.
Gulliver's Travels, &c. By Dean SWIFT.
Thomson's Seasons. Illustrated.
White's Natural History of Selborne.

POPULAR SIXPENNY NOVELS.

New Arabian Nights. By R. L. STEVENSON.
Puck. By OUIDA.
A Son of Hagar. By HALL CAINE.
The Orange Girl. By WALTER BESANT. [May.
All Sorts and Conditions of Men. By WALTER BESANT [and JAMES RICE.
The Golden Butterfly. By WALTER BESANT
The Deemster. By HALL CAINE.
The Shadow of a Crime. By HALL CAINE.
Antonina. By WILKIE COLLINS.
The Moonstone. By WILKIE COLLINS.
The Woman in White. By WILKIE COLLINS.
The Dead Secret. By WILKIE COLLINS.
The New Magdalen. By WILKIE COLLINS.
Held in Bondage. By OUIDA.
Moths. By OUIDA.
Under Two Flags. By OUIDA.
By Proxy. By JAMES PAYN.
Peg Woffington; and Christie Johnstone. By CHARLES READE. [READE.
The Cloister and the Hearth. By CHARLES
Never Too Late to Mend. By CHARLES READE.
Hard Cash. By CHARLES READE.
The Old Factory. By WILLIAM WESTALL.

THE PICCADILLY NOVELS.

LIBRARY EDITIONS OF NOVELS, many Illustrated, crown 8vo, cloth extra, 3s. 6d. each.

By Mrs. ALEXANDER.

Valerie's Fate.	Barbara.
A Life Interest.	A Fight with Fate.
Mona's Choice.	A Golden Autumn.
By Woman's Wit.	Mrs. Crichton's Creditor.
The Cost of Her Pride.	The Step-mother.

By F. M. ALLEN.—Green as Grass.

By GRANT ALLEN.

Philistia.	Babylon.	The Great Taboo.
Strange Stories.	Dumaresq's Daughter.
For Maimie's Sake.	Duchess of Powysland.
In all Shades.	Blood Royal.
The Beckoning Hand.	I. Greet's Masterpiece.
The Devil's Die.	The Scallywag.
This Mortal Coil.	At Market Value.
The Tents of Shem.	Under Sealed Orders.

By M. ANDERSON.—Othello's Occupation.

By EDWIN L. ARNOLD.

Phra the Phœnician. | Constable of St. Nicholas.

By ROBERT BARR.

In a Steamer Chair.	A Woman Intervenes.
From Whose Bourne.	Revenge!

By FRANK BARRETT.

Woman of Iron Bracelets.	Under a Strange Mask.
Fettered for Life.	A Missing Witness.
The Harding Scandal.	Was She Justified?

By 'BELLE.'—Vashti and Esther.

By Sir W. BESANT and J. RICE.

Ready-Money Mortiboy.	By Celia's Arbour.
My Little Girl.	Chaplain of the Fleet.
With Harp and Crown.	The Seamy Side.
This Son of Vulcan.	The Case of Mr. Lucraft.
The Golden Butterfly.	In Trafalgar's Bay.
The Monks of Thelema.	The Ten Years' Tenant.

By Sir WALTER BESANT.

All Sorts & Conditions.	Armorel of Lyonesse.
The Captains' Room.	S. Katherine's by Tower
All in a Garden Fair.	Verbena Camellia, &c.
Dorothy Forster.	The Ivory Gate.
Uncle Jack.	Holy Rose	The Rebel Queen.
World Went Well Then.	Dreams of Avarice.
Children of Gibeon.	In Deacon's Orders.
Herr Paulus.	The Master Craftsman.
For Faith and Freedom.	The City of Refuge.
To Call Her Mine.	A Fountain Sealed.
The Revolt of Man.	The Changeling.
The Bell of St. Paul's.	The Charm.

By AMBROSE BIERCE—In Midst of Life.
By HAROLD BINDLOSS, Ainslie's Ju-Ju.
By M. McD. BODKIN.—Dora Myrl.
By PAUL BOURGET.—A Living Lie.
By J. D. BRAYSHAW.—Slum Silhouettes.

By ROBERT BUCHANAN.

Shadow of the Sword.	The New Abelard.
A Child of Nature.	Matt.	Rachel Dene
God and the Man.	Master of the Mine.
Martyrdom of Madeline	The Heir of Linne.
Love Me for Ever.	Woman and the Man.
Annan Water.	Red and White Heather.
Foxglove Manor.	Lady Kilpatrick.
The Charlatan.	

R. W. CHAMBERS.—The King in Yellow.
By J. M. CHAPPLE.—The Minor Chord.

By HALL CAINE.

Shadow of a Crime. | Deemster. | Son of Hagar.
By AUSTIN CLARE.—By Rise of River.
By ANNE COATES.—Rie's Diary.

By MACLAREN COBBAN.

The Red Sultan.	The Burden of Isabel.

By MORT. & FRANCES COLLINS.

Blacksmith & Scholar.	You Play me False.
The Village Comedy.	Midnight to Midnight.

By WILKIE COLLINS.

Armadale.	After Dark.	The Woman in White.
No Name.	Antonina	The Law and the Lady.
Basil.	Hide and Seek.	The Haunted Hotel.
The Dead Secret.	The Moonstone.
Queen of Hearts.	Man and Wife.
My Miscellanies.	Poor Miss Finch.

By WILKIE COLLINS—*continued.*

Miss or Mrs.?	Jezebel's Daughter.
The New Magdalen.	The Black Robe.
The Frozen Deep.	Heart and Science.
The Two Destinies.	The Evil Genius.
'I Say No.'	The Legacy of Cain.
Little Novels.	A Rogue's Life.
The Fallen Leaves.	Blind Love.

M. J. COLQUHOUN.—Every Inch Soldier.

By E. H. COOPER.—Geoffory Hamilton.

By V. C. COTES.—Two Girls on a Barge.

By C. E. CRADDOCK.

The Prophet o' the Great Smoky Mountains.
His Vanished Star.

By H. N. CRELLIN.

Romances of the Old Seraglio.

By MATT CRIM.

The Adventures of a Fair Rebel.

By S. R. CROCKETT and others.

Tales of Our Coast.

By B. M. CROKER.

Diana Barrington.	The Real Lady Hilda.
Proper Pride.	Married or Single?
A Family Likeness.	Two Masters.
Pretty Miss Neville.	In the Kingdom of Kerry
A Bird of Passage.	Interferences.
Mr. Jervis.	A Third Person.
Village Tales.	Beyond the Pale.
Some One Else.	Jason.	Miss Balmaine's Past.
Infatuation.	

By W. CYPLES.—Hearts of Gold.
By ALPHONSE DAUDET.
The Evangelist : or, Port Salvation.
H. C. DAVIDSON.—Mr. Sadler's Daughters
By E. DAWSON.—The Fountain of Youth.
By J. DE MILLE.—A Castle in Spain.

By J. LEITH DERWENT.

Our Lady of Tears. | Circe's Lovers.

By HARRY DE WINDT.

True Tales of Travel and Adventure.

By DICK DONOVAN.

Man from Manchester.	Tales of Terror.
Records of Vincent Trill	Chronicles of Michael
The Mystery of	Danevitch.	Detective.
Jamaica Terrace.	Tyler Tatlock, Private
	Deacon Brodie.

By RICHARD DOWLING.

Old Corcoran's Money.

By A. CONAN DOYLE.

The Firm of Girdlestone.

By S. JEANNETTE DUNCAN.

A Daughter of To-day. | Vernon's Aunt.

By A. EDWARDES.—A Plaster Saint.

By G. S. EDWARDS.—Snazelleparilla.

By G. MANVILLE FENN

Cursed by a Fortune.	A Fluttered Dovecote.
The Case of Ailsa Gray.	King of the Castle
Commodore Junk.	Master of Ceremonies.
The New Mistress.	Eve at the Wheel, &c.
Witness to the Deed.	The Man with a Shadow
The Tiger Lily.	One Maid's Mischief.
The White Virgin.	Story of Antony Grace.
Black Blood.	This Man's Wife.
Double Cunning.	In Jeopardy. |'n'ng.
Bag of Diamonds, &c.	A Woman Worth Win-

By PERCY FITZGERALD.—Fatal Zero

By R. E. FRANCILLON.

One by One.	Ropes of Sand.
A Dog and his Shadow.	Jack Doyle's Daughter.
A Real Queen.	

By HAROLD FREDERIC.

Seth's Brother's Wife. | The Lawton Girl.

By GILBERT GAUL.

A Strange Manuscript Found in a Copper Cylinder

By PAUL GAULOT.—The Red Shirts.

By CHARLES GIBBON.

Robin Gray.	The Golden Shaft.
Loving a Dream.	The Braes of Yarrow.
Of High Degree	

THE PICCADILLY (3/6) NOVELS—*continued.*

By E. GLANVILLE.
The Lost Heiress. | The Golden Rock.
Fair Colonist | Fossicker | Tales from the Veld.

By E. J. GOODMAN.
The Fate of Herbert Wayne.

By Rev. S. BARING GOULD.
Red Spider. | Eve.
CECIL GRIFFITH.—Corinthia Marazion.

By A. CLAVERING GUNTER.
A Florida Enchantment.

By OWEN HALL.
The Track of a Storm. | Jetsam.

By COSMO HAMILTON
Glamour of Impossible. | Through a Keyhole.

By THOMAS HARDY.
Under the Greenwood Tree.

By BRET HARTE.
A Waif of the Plains. | A Protégée of Jack
A Ward of the Golden | Hamlin's.
Gate. [Springs. | Clarence.
A Sappho of Green | Barker's Luck.
Col. Starbottle's Client. | Devil's Ford. [celsior.'
Susy. | Sally Dows. | The Crusade of the 'Ex-
Bell-Ringer of Angel's. | Three Partners.
Tales of Trail and Town | Gabriel Conroy.

By JULIAN HAWTHORNE.
Garth. | Dust. | Beatrix Randolph.
Ellice Quentin. | David Poindexter's Dis-
Sebastian Strome. | appearance.
Fortune's Fool. | Spectre of Camera.

By Sir A. HELPS.—Ivan de Biron.
By I. HENDERSON.—Agatha Page.

By G. A. HENTY.
Dorothy's Double. | The Queen's Cup.

By HEADON HILL.
Zambra the Detective.

By JOHN HILL. The Common Ancestor.

By TIGHE HOPKINS.
'Twixt Love and Duty. | Nugents of Carriconna.
The Incomplete Adventurer.

VICTOR HUGO.—The Outlaw of Iceland.

FERGUS HUME.—Lady from Nowhere.

By Mrs. HUNGERFORD.
A Mental Struggle. | A Maiden all Forlorn.
Lady Verner's Flight. | The Coming of Chloe.
The Red-House Mystery | Nora Creina.
The Three Graces. | An Anxious Moment.
Professor's Experiment. | April's Lady.
A Point of Conscience. | Peter's Wife. | Lovice.

By Mrs. ALFRED HUNT.
The Leaden Casket. | Self-Condemned.
That Other Person. | Mrs. Juliet.

By C. J. CUTCLIFFE HYNE.
Honour of Thieves.

By R. ASHE KING.—A Drawn Game.

By GEORGE LAMBERT.
The President of Boravia.

By EDMOND LEPELLETIER.
Madame Sans-Gêne.

By ADAM LILBURN. A Tragedy in Marble

By HARRY LINDSAY.
Rhoda Roberts. | The Jacobite.

By HENRY W. LUCY.—Gideon Fleyce.

By E. LYNN LINTON.
Patricia Kemball. | The Atonement of Leam
Under which Lord? | Dundas.
'My Love!' | Ione. | The One Too Many.
Paston Carew. | Dulcie Everton.
Sowing the Wind. | Rebel of the Family.
With a Silken Thread. | An Octave of Friends.
The World Well Lost.

By JUSTIN McCARTHY.
A Fair Saxon. | Donna Quixote.
Linley Rochford. | Maid of Athens.
Dear Lady Disdain. | The Comet of a Season.
Camiola. | The Dictator.
Waterdale Neighbours. | Red Diamonds.
My Enemy's Daughter. | The Riddle Ring.
Miss Misanthrope. | The Three Disgraces.

By JUSTIN H. McCARTHY.
A London Legend. | The Royal Christopher

By GEORGE MACDONALD.
Heather and Snow. | Phantastes. /

W. H. MALLOCK.—The New Republic.

P. & V. MARGUERITTE.—The Disaster.

By L. T. MEADE.
A Soldier of Fortune. | On Brink of a Chasm.
In an Iron Grip. | The Siren.
Dr. Rumsey's Patient. | The Way of a Woman.
The Voice of the Charmer | A Son of Ishmael.
An Adventuress.

By LEONARD MERRICK.
This Stage of Fools. | Cynthia.

By BERTRAM MITFORD.
The Gun-Runner. | The King's Assegai.
Luck of Gerard Ridgeley. | Rensh. Fanning's Quest.

By J. E. MUDDOCK.
Maid Marian and Robin Hood. | Golden Idol.
Basile the Jester. | Young Lochinvar.

By D. CHRISTIE MURRAY.
A Life's Atonement. | The Way of the World.
Joseph's Coat. | Bob Martin's Little Girl
Coals of Fire. | Time's Revenges.
Old Blazer's Hero. | A Wasted Crime.
Val Strange. | Hearts. | In Direst Peril.
A Model Father. | Mount Despair.
By the Gate of the Sea. | A Capful o' Nails
A Bit of Human Nature. | Tales in Prose & Verse
First Person Singular. | A Race for Millions.
Cynic Fortune. | This Little World.

By MURRAY and HERMAN.
The Bishops' Bible. | Paul Jones's Alias.
One Traveller Returns.

By HUME NISBET.—'Bail Up!'

By W. E. NORRIS.
Saint Ann's. | Billy Bellew.
Miss Wentworth's Idea.

By G. OHNET.
A Weird Gift. | Love's Depths.

By Mrs. OLIPHANT.—The Sorceress.

By OUIDA.
Held in Bondage. | In a Winter City.
Strathmore. | Chandos. | Friendship.
Under Two Flags. | Moths. | Rufino.
Idalia. [Gage. | Pipistrello. | Ariadne.
Cecil Castlemaine's | A Village Commune.
Tricotrin. | Puck. | Bimbi. | Wanda.
Folle Farine. | Frescoes. | Othmar.
A Dog of Flanders. | In Maremma.
Pascarel. | Signa. | Syrlin. | Guilderoy.
Princess Napraxine. | Santa Barbara.
Two Wooden Shoes. | Two Offenders.
The Waters of Edera.

By MARGARET A. PAUL.
Gentle and Simple.

By JAMES PAYN.
Lost Sir Massingberd. | The Talk of the Town.
A County Family. | Holiday Tasks.
Less Black than We're | For Cash Only.
Painted. | The Burnt Million.
A Confidential Agent. | The Word and the Will.
A Grape from a Thorn. | Sunny Stories.
In Peril and Privation. | A Trying Patient.
Mystery of Mirbridge. | A Modern Dick Whit-
Walter's Word. | tington.
High Spirits. | By Proxy.

By WILL PAYNE.—Jerry the Dreamer.

By Mrs. CAMPBELL PRAED.
Outlaw and Lawmaker. | Mrs. Tregaskiss.
Christina Chard. | Nulma. | Madame Izan.

By E. C. PRICE.
Valentina. | Foreigners. | Mrs. Lancaster's Rival.

By RICHARD PRYCE.
Miss Maxwell's Affections.

By Mrs. J. H. RIDDELL.
Weird Stories. | A Rich Man's Daughter.

By AMELIE RIVES.
Barbara Dering. | Meriel.

By F. W. ROBINSON.
The Hands of Justice. | Woman in the Dark.

Two-Shilling Novels—*continued.*

BY FRANK BARRETT.

Fettered for Life.
Little Lady Linton.
Between Life & Death.
Sin of Olga Zassoulich.
Folly Morrison.
Lieut. Barnabas.
Honest Davie.
A Prodigal's Progress.

Found Guilty.
A Recoiling Vengeance.
For Love and Honour.
John Ford, &c.
Woman of Iron Brace'ts
The Harding Scandal.
A Missing Witness.

By FREDERICK BOYLE.

Camp Notes.
Savage Life.

Chronicles of No-man's
Land.

By Sir W. BESANT and J. RICE.

Ready-Money Mortiboy
My Little Girl.
With Harp and Crown.
This Son of Vulcan.
The Golden Butterfly.
The Monks of Thelema.

By Celia's Arbour.
Chaplain of the Fleet.
The Seamy Side.
The Case of Mr. Lucraft.
In Trafalgar's Bay.
The Ten Years' Tenant.

By Sir WALTER BESANT.

All Sorts and Condi-
tions of Men.
The Captains' Room.
All in a Garden Fair.
Dorothy Forster.
Uncle Jack.
The World Went Very
Well Then.
Children of Gibeon.
Herr Paulus.
For Faith and Freedom.
To Call Her Mine.
The Master Craftsman.

The Bell of St. Paul's.
The Holy Rose.
Armorel of Lyonesse.
S. Katherine s by Tower
Verbena Camellia Ste-
phanotis.
The Ivory Gate.
The Rebel Queen.
Beyond the Dreams of
Avarice.
The Revolt of Man.
In Deacon's Orders.
The City of Refuge.

By AMBROSE BIERCE.
In the Midst of Life.

BY BRET HARTE.

Californian Stories.
Gabriel Conroy.
Luck of Roaring Camp.
An Heiress of Red Dog.

Flip. | Maruja.
A Phyllis of the Sierras.
A Waif of the Plains.
Ward of Golden Gate.

By ROBERT BUCHANAN.

Shadow of the Sword.
A Child of Nature.
God and the Man.
Love Me for Ever.
Foxglove Manor.
The Master of the Mine.
Annan Water.

The Martyrdom of Ma-
deline.
The New Abelard.
The Heir of Linne.
Woman and the Man.
Rachel Dene. | Matt.
Lady Kilpatrick.

By BUCHANAN and MURRAY.
The Charlatan.

By HALL CAINE.
The Shadow of a Crime. | The Deemster.
A Son of Hagar.

By Commander CAMERON.
The Cruise of the 'Black Prince.'

By HAYDEN CARRUTH.
The Adventures of Jones.

By AUSTIN CLARE.
For the Love of a Lass.

By Mrs. ARCHER CLIVE.
Paul Ferroll.
Why Paul Ferroll Killed his Wife.

By MACLAREN COBBAN.
The Cure of Souls. | The Red Sultan.

By C. ALLSTON COLLINS.
The Bar Sinister.

By MORT. & FRANCES COLLINS.

Sweet Anne Page.
Transmigration.
From Midnight to Mid-
night.
A Fight with Fortune.

Sweet and Twenty.
The Village Comedy.
You Play me False.
Blacksmith and Scholar
Frances.

By WILKIE COLLINS.

Armadale. | After Dark.
No Name.
Antonina.
Basil.
Hide and Seek.
The Dead Secret.
Queen of Hearts.
Miss or Mrs.?
The New Magdalen.
The Frozen Deep.
The Law and the Lady
The Two Destinies.
The Haunted Hotel.
A Rogue's Life.

My Miscellanies.
The Woman in White.
The Moonstone.
Man and Wife.
Poor Miss Finch.
The Fallen Leaves.
Jezebel's Daughter.
The Black Robe.
Heart and Science.
'I Say No!'
The Evil Genius.
Little Novels.
Legacy of Cain.
Blind Love.

By M. J. COLQUHOUN.
Every Inch a Soldier.

By C. EGBERT CRADDOCK.
The Prophet of the Great Smoky Mountains.

By MATT CRIM.
The Adventures of a Fair Rebel.

By B. M. CROKER.

Pretty Miss Neville.
Diana Barrington.
'To Let.'
A Bird of Passage.
Proper Pride.
A Family Likeness.
A Third Person.

Village Tales and Jungle
Tragedies.
Two Masters.
Mr. Jervis.
The Real Lady Hilda.
Married or Single ?
Interference.

By ALPHONSE DAUDET.
The Evangelist; or, Port Salvation.

By DICK DONOVAN.

The Man-Hunter.
Tracked and Taken.
Caught at Last!
Wanted!
Who Poisoned Hetty
Duncan ?
Man from Manchester.
A Detective's Triumphs
The Mystery of Jamaica Terrace.
The Chronicles of Michael Danevitch.

In the Grip of the Law.
From Information Re-
ceived.
Tracked to Doom.
Link by Link
Suspicion Aroused.
Dark Deeds.
Riddles Read.

By Mrs. ANNIE EDWARDES.
A Point of Honour. | Archie Lovell.

By EDWARD EGGLESTON.
Roxy.

By G. MANVILLE FENN.

The New Mistress.
Witness to the Deed.

The Tiger Lily.
The White Virgin.

By PERCY FITZGERALD.

Bella Donna.
Never Forgotten.
Polly.
Fatal Zero.

Second Mrs. Tillotson.
Seventy-five Brooke
Street.
The Lady of Brantome

By P. FITZGERALD and others.
Strange Secrets.

By R. E. FRANCILLON.

Olympia.
One by One.
A Real Queen.
Queen Cophetua.

King or Knave ?
Romances of the Law.
Ropes of Sand.
A Dog and his Shadow.

By HAROLD FREDERIC.
Seth's Brother's Wife. | The Lawton Girl.

Prefaced by Sir BARTLE FRERE.
Pandurang Hari.

By GILBERT GAUL.
A Strange Manuscript.

By CHARLES GIBBON.

Robin Gray.
Fancy Free.
For Lack of Gold.
What will World Say ?
In Love and War.
For the King.
In Pastures Green.
Queen of the Meadow.
A Heart's Problem.
The Dead Heart.

In Honour Bound.
Flower of the Forest.
The Braes of Yarrow.
The Golden Shaft.
Of High Degree.
By Mead and Stream.
Loving a Dream.
A Hard Knot.
Heart's Delight.
Blood-Money.

TWO-SHILLING NOVELS—*continued.*

By WILLIAM GILBERT.
James Duke.

By ERNEST GLANVILLE.
The Lost Heiress. | The Fossicker
A Fair Colonist. |

By Rev. S. BARING GOULD.
Red Spider. | Eve.

By ANDREW HALLIDAY.
Every-day Papers.

By THOMAS HARDY.
Under the Greenwood Tree.

By JULIAN HAWTHORNE.
Garth. | Beatrix Randolph.
Ellice Quentin. | Love—or a Name.
Fortune's Fool. | David Poindexter's Dis-
Miss Cadogna. | appearance.
Sebastian Strome. | The Spectre of the
Dust. | Camera.

By Sir ARTHUR HELPS.
Ivan de Biron.

By G. A. HENTY.
Rujub the Juggler.

By HEADON HILL.
Zambra the Detective.

By JOHN HILL.
Treason Felony.

By Mrs. CASHEL HOEY.
The Lover's Creed.

By Mrs. GEORGE HOOPER.
The House of Raby.

By Mrs. HUNGERFORD.
A Maiden all Forlorn. | Lady Verner's Flight.
In Durance Vile. | The Red-House Mystery
Marvel. | The Three Graces.
A Mental Struggle. | Unsat'sfactory Lover.
A Modern Circe. | Lady Patty.
April's Lady. | Nora Creina.
Peter's Wife. | Professor's Experiment.

By Mrs. ALFRED HUNT.
That Other Person. | The Leaden Casket.
Self-Condemned. |

By MARK KERSHAW.
Colonial Facts and Fictions.

By R. ASHE KING.
A Drawn Game. | Passion's Slave.
'The Wearing of the | Bell Barry.
Green.' |

By EDMOND LEPELLETIER.
Madame Sans-Gene.

By JOHN LEYS.
The Lindsays.

By E. LYNN LINTON.
Patricia Kemball. | The Atonement of Leam
The World Well Lost. | Dundas.
Under which Lord? | Rebel of the Family.
Paston Carew. | Sowing the Wind.
'My Love!' | The One Too Many.
Ione. | Dulcie Everton.
With a Silken Thread. |

By HENRY W. LUCY.
Gideon Fleyce.

By JUSTIN McCARTHY.
Dear Lady Disdain. | Donna Quixote.
Waterdale Neighbours. | Maid of Athens.
My Enemy's Daughter | The Comet of a Season.
A Fair Saxon. | The Dictator.
Linley Rochford. | Red Diamonds.
Miss Misanthrope. | The Riddle Ring.
Camiola

By HUGH MACCOLL.
Mr. Stranger's Sealed Packet.

By GEORGE MACDONALD.
Heather and Snow.

By AGNES MACDONELL.
Quaker Cousins.

By W. H. MALLOCK.
The New Republic.

By BRANDER MATTHEWS.
A Secret of the Sea.

By L. T. MEADE.
A Soldier of Fortune.

By LEONARD MERRICK.
The Man who was Good.

By JEAN MIDDLEMASS.
Touch and Go. | Mr. Dorillion.

By Mrs. MOLESWORTH.
Hathercourt Rectory.

By J. E. MUDDOCK.
Stories Weird and Won- | From the Bosom of the
derful. | Deep.
The Dead Man's Secret. |

By D. CHRISTIE MURRAY.
A Model Father. | A Bit of Human Nature.
Joseph's Coat. | First Person Singular.
Coals of Fire. | Bob Martin's Little Girl.
Val Strange. | Hearts. | Time's Revenges.
Old Blazer's Hero. | A Wasted Crime.
The Way of the World. | In Direst Peril.
Cynic Fortune. | Mount Despair.
A Life's Atonement. | A Capful o' Nails
By the Gate of the Sea. |

By MURRAY and HERMAN.
One Traveller Returns. | The Bishops' Bible.
Paul Jones's Alias. |

By HUME NISBET.
'Bail Up!' | Dr. Bernard St. Vincent.

By W. E. NORRIS.
Saint Ann's. | Billy Bellew.

By GEORGES OHNET.
Dr. Rameau. | A Weird Gift.
A Last Love. |

By Mrs. OLIPHANT.
Whiteladies. | The Greatest Heiress in
The Primrose Path. | England.

By OUIDA.
Held in Bondage. | Two Lit. Wooden Shoes.
Strathmore. | Moths.
Chandos. | Bimbi.
Idalia. | Pipistrello.
Under Two Flags. | A Village Commune.
Cecil Castlemaine's Gage | Wanda.
Tricotrin. | Othmar.
Puck. | Frescoes.
Folle Farine. | In Maremma.
A Dog of Flanders. | Guilderoy.
Pascarel. | Ruffino.
Signa. | Syrlin.
Princess Napraxine. | Santa Barbara.
In a Winter City. | Two Offenders.
Ariadne. | Ouida's Wisdom, Wit,
Friendship. | and Pathos.

By MARGARET AGNES PAUL.
Gentle and Simple.

By Mrs. CAMPBELL PRAED.
The Romance of a Station.
The Soul of Countess Adrian.
Outlaw and Lawmaker. | Mrs. Tregaskiss
Christina Chard. |

TWO-SHILLING NOVELS—*continued.*

By RICHARD PRYCE.
Miss Maxwell's Affections.

By JAMES PAYN.

Bentinck's Tutor.
Murphy's Master.
A County Family.
At Her Mercy.
Cecil's Tryst.
The Clyffards of Clyffe.
The Foster Brothers.
Found Dead.
The Best of Husbands.
Walter's Word.
Halves.
Fallen Fortunes.
Humorous Stories.
£200 Reward.
A Marine Residence.
Mirk Abbey.
By Proxy.
Under One Roof.
High Spirits.
Carlyon's Year.
From Exile.
For Cash Only.
Kit.
The Canon's Ward.

The Talk of the Town.
Holiday Tasks.
A Perfect Treasure.
What He Cost Her.
A Confidential Agent.
Glow-worm Tales.
The Burnt Million.
Sunny Stories.
Lost Sir Massingberd.
A Woman's Vengeance.
The Family Scapegrace.
Gwendoline's Harvest.
Like Father, Like Son.
Married Beneath Him.
Not Wooed, but Won.
Less Black than We're Painted.
Some Private Views.
A Grape from a Thorn.
The Mystery of Mirbridge.
The Word and the Will.
A Prince of the Blood.
A Trying Patient.

By CHARLES READE.

It is Never Too Late to Mend.
Christie Johnstone.
The Double Marriage.
Put Yourself in His Place
Love Me Little, Love Me Long.
The Cloister and the Hearth.
Course of True Love.
The Jilt.
The Autobiography of a Thief.

A Terrible Temptation.
Foul Play.
The Wandering Heir.
Hard Cash.
Singleheart and Doubleface.
Good Stories of Man and other Animals.
Peg Woffington.
Griffith Gaunt.
A Perilous Secret.
A Simpleton.
Readiana.
A Woman-Hater.

By Mrs. J. H. RIDDELL.
Weird Stories.
Fairy Water.
Her Mother's Darling.
The Prince of Wales's Garden Party.

The Uninhabited House.
The Mystery in Palace Gardens.
The Nun's Curse.
Idle Tales.

By F. W. ROBINSON.
Women are Strange.
The Hands of Justice.

The Woman in the Dark.

By W. CLARK RUSSELL.
Round the Galley Fire.
On the Fo'k'sle Head.
In the Middle Watch.
A Voyage to the Cape.
A Book for the Hammock.
The Mystery of the 'Ocean Star.'
The Romance of Jenny Harlowe.

An Ocean Tragedy.
My Shipmate Louise.
Alone on Wide Wide Sea.
Good Ship 'Mohock.'
The Phantom Death.
Is He the Man?
Heart of Oak.
The Convict Ship.
The Tale of the Ten.
The Last Entry.

By DORA RUSSELL.
A Country Sweetheart.

By GEORGE AUGUSTUS SALA.
Gaslight and Daylight.

By GEORGE R. SIMS.
The Ring o' Bells.
Mary Jane's Memoirs.
Mary Jane Married.
Tales of To-day.
Dramas of Life.
Tinkletop's Crime.
My Two Wives.

Zeph.
Memoirs of a Landlady.
Scenes from the Show.
The 10 Commandments.
Dagonet Abroad.
Rogues and Vagabonds.

By ARTHUR SKETCHLEY.
A Match in the Dark.

By HAWLEY SMART.
Without Love or Licence.
Beatrice and Benedick.
The Master of Rathkelly.
The Plunger.
Long Odds.

By T. W. SPEIGHT.
The Mysteries of Heron Dyke.
The Golden Hoop.
Hoodwinked.
By Devious Ways.
Back to Life.
The Loudwater Tragedy.
Burgo's Romance.
Quittance in Full.
A Husband from the Sea.

By ALAN ST. AUBYN.
A Fellow of Trinity.
The Junior Dean.
Master of St. Benedict's.
To His Own Master.
Orchard Damerel.
In the Face of the World.
The Tremlett Diamonds.

By R. A. STERNDALE.
The Afghan Knife.

By R. LOUIS STEVENSON.
New Arabian Nights.

By ROBERT SURTEES.
Handley Cross.

By BERTHA THOMAS.
The Violin-Player.

By WALTER THORNBURY.
Tales for the Marines.

By T. ADOLPHUS TROLLOPE.
Diamond Cut Diamond.

By F. ELEANOR TROLLOPE.
Like Ships upon the Sea.
Anne Furness.
Mabel's Progress.

By ANTHONY TROLLOPE.
Frau Frohmann.
Marion Fay.
Kept in the Dark.
The Way We Live Now.
The Land-Leaguers.
The American Senator.
Mr. Scarborough's Family.
Golden Lion of Granpere.

By MARK TWAIN.
A Pleasure Trip on the Continent.
The Gilded Age.
Huckleberry Finn.
Mark Twain's Sketches.
Tom Sawyer.
A Tramp Abroad.
Stolen White Elephant.
Life on the Mississippi.
The Prince and the Pauper.
A Yankee at the Court of King Arthur.
£1,000,000 Bank-Note.

By C. C. FRASER-TYTLER.
Mistress Judith.

By SARAH TYTLER.
Bride's Pass | Lady Bell
Buried Diamonds.
St. Mungo's City.
Noblesse Oblige.
Disappeared.
The Huguenot Family
The Blackhall Ghosts
What She Came Through
Beauty and the Beast.
Citoyenne Jaqueline.

By ALLEN UPWARD.
The Queen against Owen. | Prince of Balkistan.

By WILLIAM WESTALL.
Trust-Money.

By Mrs. F. H. WILLIAMSON.
A Child Widow.

By J. S. WINTER.
Cavalry Life. | Regimental Legends.

By H. F. WOOD.
The Passenger from Scotland Yard.
The Englishman of the Rue Cain.

UNWIN BROTHERS, Printers, 27, Pilgrim Street, London, E.C.